Greenhorn

City Life

Or, Life in New York and Boston

Greenhorn

City Life

Or, Life in New York and Boston

ISBN/EAN: 9783955630843

Auflage: 1

Erscheinungsjahr: 2013

Erscheinungsort: Bremen, Deutschland

Leseklassiker

Contents

CHAPTER I

*A Young Gentleman of Wealth and Fashion — a noble resolve —
the flatterers — the Midnight Encounter — an Adventure — the
Courtezan — Temptation triumphant — how the Night was
passed.*

'What a happy dog I ought to be!' exclaimed Frank Sydney,
as he reposed his slippered feet upon the fender, and sipped his
third glass of old Madeira, one winter's evening in the year 18 — ,
in the great city of New York.

Frank might well say so; for in addition to being as handsome a fellow as one would be likely to meet in a day's walk, he
possessed an ample fortune, left him by a deceased uncle. He was
an orphan; and at the age of twenty-one, found himself surrounded by all the advantages of wealth, and at the same time,
was perfect master of his own actions. Occupying elegant apartments at a fashionable hotel, he was free from any of those petty
cares and vexations which might have annoyed him, and he kept
an establishment of his own; while at the same time he was enabled to maintain, in his rooms, a private table for the entertainment of himself and friends, who frequently repaired thither, to
partake of his hospitality and champagne suppers. With such
advantages of fortune and position, no wonder he exclaimed, as
at the beginning of our tale — 'What a happy dog I ought to be!'

Pursuing the current of his thought Frank half audibly continued —

'Yes, I have everything to make me truly happy — health,
youth, good looks and wealth; and yet it seems to me that I
should derive a more substantial satisfaction from my riches were
I to apply them to the good of mankind. To benefit one's fellow
creatures is the noblest and most exalted of enjoyments — far
superior to the gratification of sense. The grateful blessings of the
poor widow or orphan, relieved by my bounty, are greater music
to my soul, than the insincere plaudits of my professed friends,
who gather around my hearth to feast upon my hospitality, and
yet who, were I to lose my wealth, and become poor, would soon

cut my acquaintance, and sting me by their ingratitude. To-night I shall have a numerous party of these *friends* to sup with me, and this supper shall be the last one to which I shall ever invite them. Yes! My wealth shall be employed for a nobler object than to pamper these false and hollow-hearted parasites. From this night, I devote my time, my energies and my affluence to the relief of deserving poverty and the welfare of all who need my aid with whom I may come in contact. I will go in person to the squalid abodes of the poor — I will seek them out in the dark alleys and obscure lanes of this mighty metropolis — I will, in the holy mission of charity, venture into the vilest dens of sin and iniquity, fearing no danger, and shrinking not from the duty which I have assumed. — Thus shall my wealth be a blessing to my fellow creatures, and not merely a means of ministering to my own selfishness.'

Noble resolve! All honor to thy good and generous heart, Frank Sydney! Thou hast the true patent of nature's nobility, which elevates and ennobles thee, more than a thousand vain titles or empty honors! Thou wilt keep thy word, and become the poor man's friend — the liberal and enlightened philanthropist — the advocate of deserving poverty, and foe to the oppressor, who sets his heel upon the neck of his brother man.

The friends who were to sup with him, arrived, and they all sat down to a sumptuous entertainment. Frank did the honors with his accustomed affability and care; and flowing bumpers were drunk to his health, while the most flattering eulogiums upon his merits and excellent qualities passed from lip to lip. Frank had sufficient discernment to perceive that all this praise was nothing but the ebullitions of the veriest sycophants; and he resolved at some time to test the sincerity of their protestations of eternal friendship.

'Allow me, gentlemen,' said Mr. Archibald Slinkey, a red-faced, elderly man, with a nose like the beak of a poll-parrot — 'to propose the health of my excellent and highly esteemed friend, Frank Sydney. Gentlemen, I am a plain man, unused to flattery, and may be pardoned for speaking openly before the face of our friend — for I will say it, he is the most noble hearted, enlightened, conscientious, consistent, and superlatively good fellow I ever met in the course of my existence.'

'So he is,' echoed Mr. Narcissus Nobbs, a middle-aged gentleman, with no nose to speak of, but possessing a redundancy of chin and a wonderful capacity of mouth — 'so he is, Slinkey; his position — his earning — his talent — his wealth — '

'Oh, d — — n his wealth,' ejaculated Mr. Solomon Jenks, a young gentleman who affected a charming frankness and abruptness in his speech, but who was in reality the most specious flatterer of the entire party. Mr. Jenks rejoiced in the following personal advantages: red hair, a blue nose, goggle eyes, and jaws of transparent thinness.

'D — — n his wealth!' said Jenks — 'who cares for *that*? Sydney's a good fellow — a capital dog — an excellent, d — — d good sort of a whole-souled devil — but his *wealth* is no merit. If he lost every shilling he has in the world, why curse me if I shouldn't like him all the better for it! I almost wish the rascal would become penniless tomorrow, in order to afford me an opportunity of showing him the disinterestedness of my friendship. I would divide my purse with him, take him by the hand and say — Frank, my boy, I like you for yourself alone, and d — — n me if you are not welcome to all I have in the world — That's how I would do it.'

'I thank you gentlemen, for your kind consideration,' said Frank; 'I trust I may never be necessitated to apply to any of my friends, for aid in a disagreeable emergency — but should such ever unfortunately be the case, be assured that I shall not hesitate to avail myself of your generous assistance.'

'Bravo — capital — excellent!' responded the choir of flatterers, in full chorus, and their glasses were again emptied in honor of their host.

It was midnight ere these worthies took their departure. When at length they were all gone, and Frank found himself alone, he exclaimed — 'Thank heaven, I am at last rid of those miserable and servile fellows, who in my presence load me with the most extravagant praise and adulation, while behind my back they doubtless ridicule my supposed credulity. I have too long tolerated them — henceforth, I discard and cast them off.'

He approached the window, and drawing aside the curtain, looked forth into the streets. The moon was shining brightly; and its rays fell with dazzling lustre upon the snow which covered the ground. It was a most lovely night, altho' excessively cold; and Sydney, feeling not the least inclination to retire to rest, said to himself:

'What is to prevent me from beginning my career of usefulness and charity to-night? The hour is late — but misery sleeps not, and 'tis never too late to alleviate the sufferings of distressed humanity. Yes, I will go forth, even at the midnight hour, and perchance I may encounter some poor fellow-creature worthy of my aid, or visit some abode of poverty where I can minister to the comfort of its wretched inmates.'

He threw on an ample cloak, put on a fur cap and gloves, and taking his sword-cane in his hand, left the hotel, and proceeded at a rapid pace thro' the moon-lit and deserted streets. He entered the Park, and crossed over towards Chatham street, wishing to penetrate into the more obscure portions of the city, where Poverty, too often linked with Crime, finds a miserable dwelling-place. Thus far, he had not encountered a single person; but on approaching the rear of the City Hall, he observed the figure of a man issue from the dark obscurity of the building, and advance directly toward him. Sydney did not seek to avoid him, supposing him to be one of the watchmen stationed in that vicinity, but a nearer view satisfied him that the person was no watchman but a man clothed in rags, whose appearance betokened the extreme of human wretchedness. He was of a large and powerful build, but seemed attenuated by want, or disease — or perhaps, both. As he approached Sydney, his gestures were wild and threatening: he held in his hands a large paving-stone, which he raised, as if to hurl it at the other with all his force.

Sydney, naturally conceiving the man's intentions to be hostile, drew the sword from his cane, and prepared to act on the defensive, at the same time exclaiming:

'Who are you, and what do you wish?'

'Money!' answered the other, in a hollow tone, with the stone still upraised, while his eyes glowed savagely upon the young man.

Sydney, who was brave and dauntless, steadily returned his gaze, and said, calmly:

'You adopt a strange method, friend, of levying contributions upon travellers. If you are in distress and need aid, you should apply for it in a becoming manner — not approach a stranger in this threatening and ruffianly style. Stand off — I am armed, you see — I shall not hesitate to use this weapon if — '

The robber burst into a wild, ferocious laugh:

'Fool!' he cried. 'What can your weak arm or puny weapon do, against the strength of a madman? For look you, I am mad with *hunger*! For three days I have not tasted food — for three cold, wretched nights I have roamed thro' the streets of this Christian city, homeless, friendless, penniless! Give me money, or with this stone will I dash out your brains.'

'Unfortunate man,' said Sydney, in accents of deep pity — 'I feel for you, on my soul I do. Want and wretchedness have made you desperate. Throw down your weapon, and listen to me; he who now addresses you is a man, possessing a heart that beats in sympathy for your misfortunes. I have both the means and the will to relieve your distress.'

The robber cast the stone from him, and burst into tears. 'Pardon me, kind stranger,' he cried, 'I did intend you harm, for my brain is burning, and my vitals consumed by starvation. You have spoken to me the first words of kindness that I have heard for a long, long time. You pity me, and that pity subdues me. I will go and seek some other victim.' 'Stay,' said Sydney, 'for heaven's sake give up this dreadful trade of robbery. Here is money, sufficient to maintain you for weeks — make a good use of it — seek employment — be honest, and should you need further assistance, call at — — Hotel, and ask for Francis Sydney. That is my name, and in me you will ever find a friend, so long as you prove yourself worthy.'

'Noble, generous man!' exclaim the robber, as he received a fifty dollar note from the hands of Frank. 'God will reward you for this. Believe me, I have not always been what I now am — a midnight ruffian, almost an assassin. No — I have had friends, and respectability, and wealth. But I have lost them all — all! We shall meet again — farewell!'

He ran rapidly from the spot, leaving Frank to pursue his way alone, and ponder upon this remarkable encounter.

Leaving the Park, and turning to the left, Frank proceeded up Chatham street towards the Bowery. As he was passing a house of humble but respectable exterior, he observed the street door to open, and a female voice said, in a low tone — 'Young gentleman I wish to speak to you.'

Frank was not much surprised at being thus accosted, for his long residence in New York had made him aware of the fact that courtezans often resorted to that mode of procuring 'patronage' from such midnight pedestrians as might happen to be passing their doors. His first impulse was to walk on without noticing the invitation — but then the thought suggested itself to his mind: 'Might I not possibly be of some use or benefit to that frail one? I will see what she has to say.'

Reasoning thus, he stepped up to the door, when the female who had accosted him took him gently by the hand, and drawing him into the entry, closed the door. A lamp was burning upon a table which stood in the passage, and by its light Frank perceived that the lady was both young and pretty; she was wrapped in a large shawl, so that the outlines of her form were not plainly visible, yet it was easy to be seen that she was of good figure and graceful carriage.

'Madame, or Miss,' said Frank, 'be good enough to tell me why — '

'We cannot converse here in the cold,' interrupted the lady, smiling archly. 'Pray, sir, accompany me up-stairs to my room, and your curiosity shall be satisfied.'

Frank (who had his own reasons) motioned her to lead the way; she took the lamp from the table, and ascended the staircase, followed by the young gentleman. The lady entered a room upon the second floor, in which stood a bed and other conveniences denoting it to be a sleeping chamber; a cheerful fire was glowing in the grate. The apartment was neatly and plainly furnished, containing nothing of a character to indicate that its occupant was other than a perfectly virtuous female. No obscene pictures or immodest images were to be seen — all was unexceptionable in point of propriety.

The lady closed and locked the chamber door; then placing two chairs before the fire, she seated herself in one, and requested Frank to occupy the other. Throwing off her shawl, she displayed a fine form and voluptuous bust — the latter very liberally displayed, as she was arrayed in nothing but a loose dressing gown, which concealed neither her plump shoulders, nor the two fair and ample globes, whiter than alabaster, that gave her form a luxurious fullness.

'You probably have sufficient discrimination, sir, to divine my motive in inviting you into this house and chamber,' began the young lady, not without some embarrassment. 'You will readily infer, from my conduct, that I belong to the unfortunate class — '

'Say no more,' said Frank, interrupting her, 'I can readily guess why you accosted me, and as readily comprehend your true position and character. Madame, I regret to meet you in this situation.'

The lady cast down her eyes, and made no immediate reply, but for some minutes continued to trace imaginary figures upon the carpet, with the point of her delicate slipper. Meanwhile, Frank had ample leisure to examine her narrowly. His eyes wandered over the graceful, undulating outlines of her fine form, and lingered admiringly upon the exposed beauties of her swelling bosom; he glanced at her regular and delicate features which were exceedingly girlish and pretty, for she certainly was not much over sixteen years of age. When it is remembered that Frank was a young man of an ardent and impulsive temperament, the reader will not be surprised that the loveliness of this young creature began to excite within his breast those feelings and desires which are inherent in human nature. In fact, he found himself being gradually overcome by the most tumultuous sensations: his heart palpitated violently, his breath grew hurried and irregular, and he could scarcely restrain himself from clasping her to his breast with licentious violence. His passions were still further excited, when she raised her eyes to his face, and glanced at him with a soft smile, full of tenderness and invitation. Frank Sydney was one of the best fellows in the world, and possessed a heart that beat in unison with every noble, generous and kindly feeling; but he was not an angel. No, he was *human*, and subject to all the frailties and passions of humanity. When, therefore, that enticing young woman raised her eyes, swimming with languishing desire, to his face, and smiled so irresistibly, he did precisely what ninety-nine out of every one hundred young men in existence would have done, in the same circumstances — he encircled her slender waist with his arm, drew her to his throbbing breast, and tasted the nectar of her ripe lips, which so plainly invited the salute. Ah Frank, Frank! thou hast gone too far to retract now! Thy hand plays with those ivory globes — thy lips kiss those rounded shoulders, and that beauteous neck — thy brain becomes dizzy, thy senses reel, and thy amorous soul bathes in a sea of rapturous delight!

*****

Truly, Frank Sydney, thou art a pretty fellow to prate about sallying forth at midnight to do good to thy fellow creatures! — Here we find thee, within an hour after thy departure from thy home, on an 'errand of mercy,' embraced in the soft arms of a pretty wanton, and revelling in the delights of voluptuousness. We might have portrayed thee as a paragon of virtue and chastity; we might have described thee as rejecting with holy horror the advances of that frail but exceedingly fair young lady — we might have made a saint of thee, Frank. But we prefer to depict human nature *as it is* not *as it should be;* — therefore we represent thee to be no better than thou art in reality. Many will pardon thee for thy folly, Frank, and admit that it was natural — very natural. Our hero did not return to his hotel until an hour after daybreak. The interval was passed with the young lady of frailty and beauty. He shared her couch; but neither of them slumbered, for at Frank's request, his fair friend occupied the time in narrating the particulars of her history, which we repeat in the succeeding chapter.

CHAPTER II

The Courtezan's story, showing some of the Sins of Religious Professors — A carnal Preacher, a frail Mother, and a lustful Father — a plan of revenge.

'My parents are persons of respectable standing in society; — they are both members of the Methodist Episcopal church, and remarkably rigid in their observance of the external forms and ceremonies of religion. Family worship was always adhered to by them, as well as grace before and after meals. They have ever been regarded as most exemplary and pious people. I was their only child; and the first ten years of my life were passed in much the same manner as those of other children of my sex and condition. I attended school, and received a good education; and my parents endeavored to instill the most pious precepts into my mind, to the end, they said, that I might become a vessel of holiness to the Lord. When I reached my twelfth year, a circumstance occurred which materially diminished my belief in the sanctity and godliness of one of my parents, and caused me to regard with suspicion and distrust, both religion and its professors.

'It was the custom of the pastor of the church to which my parents belonged, to make a weekly round of visits among the members of his congregation. These visits were generally made in the middle of the forenoon or afternoon, during the absence of the male members of the various families. I observed that 'our minister' invariably paid his visits to our house when my father was absent at his place of business. Upon these occasions, he would hold long and private conferences with my mother, who used to declare that these interviews with that holy man did her more substantial *good* than all his preaching. 'It is so refreshing to my soul,' she would say, 'to pray in secret with that good man — he is *so* full of Christian love — so tender in his exhortations — so fervent in his prayers! O that I could meet him every day, in the sanctity of my closet, to strengthen my faith by the outpourings of his inexhaustible fount of piety and Christian love!'

'The *wrestlings with the Lord* of my maternal parent and her holy pastor, must have been both prolonged and severe, judging from the fact that at the termination of these pious interviews, my mother sometimes made her appearance with disordered apparel and disarranged hair; while the violence of her efforts to strengthen her faith was further manifest from the flushed condition of her countenance, and general peculiarity of aspect.

'One afternoon the Reverend Mr. Flanders — for that was the name of our minister — called to see my mother, and as usual they retired together to a private room, for 'holy communion.' Young as I was, my suspicions had long been excited in regard to the nature of these interviews; I began to think that their true object partook more largely of an earthly and carnal character, than either the pastor or my mother would care to have known. Upon the afternoon in question, I determined to satisfy myself on this point; — and accordingly, as soon as they entered the room and closed the door, (which they always locked,) I stole noiselessly up-stairs, and stationed myself in the passage, on the outside of the room, and listened intently. I had scarcely taken up my position, when my ear caught the sound of *kissing*; and applying my eye to the key-hole, I beheld the Rev. Mr. Flanders bestowing the most fervent embraces upon my mother, which she returned with compound interest. The pious gentleman, clasping her around the waist with one arm, proceeded to take liberties which astonished and disgusted me: and my mother not only permitted the revered scoundrel to do this, but actually seemed to encourage him. Soon they placed themselves upon a sofa, in full view of my gaze; and I was both mortified and enraged to observe the wantonness of my mother, and the lasciviousness of her *pious* friend. After indulging in the most obscene and lecherous preliminaries, the full measure of their iniquity was consummated, I being a witness to the whole disgraceful scene. Horrified, and sick at heart, I left the spot and repaired to my own room, where I shed many bitter tears, for the dishonor of my mother and the hypocrisy of the minister filled me with shame and grief. From that moment, I ceased to love and respect my mother, as formerly; but she failed to perceive any alteration in my conduct towards her, and at that time was far from suspecting that I had witnessed the act of her dishonor and disgrace.

'I had always regarded my father as one of the best and most exemplary of men; and after my mother's crime, I comforted myself with the reflection that *he*, at least, was no hypocrite! but in every sense a good and sincere Christian. Nothing happened to shake this belief, until I had reached my fourteenth year; and then, alas! I became too painfully convinced that all *his* professions of piety and holiness were but a cloak to conceal the real wickedness of his heart. It chanced, about this time, that a young woman was received into our family, as a domestic: this person was far from being handsome or in the slightest degree interesting, in countenance — yet her figure was rather good than otherwise. She was a bold, wanton-looking wench; and soon after she came to live with us, I noticed that my father frequently eyed her with something sensual in his glances. He frequently sought opportunities of being alone with her; and one evening, hearing a noise in the kitchen, I went to the head of the stairs, and listened — there was the sound of a tussle, and I heard Jane (the name of the young woman,) exclaim — 'Have done, sire — take away your hands — how dare you?' And then she laughed, in a manner that indicated her words were not very seriously meant. My father's voice next reached me; what he said I could not clearly distinguish; but he seemed to be remonstrating with the girl, and entreating her to grant him some favor; what that favor was, I could readily guess; and that she *did* grant it to him, without much further coaxing, was soon evident to my mind, by certain unmistakable sounds. But I preferred *seeing* to *hearing;* creeping softly down the kitchen stairs, I peeped in at the door, which was slightly ajar, and beheld my Christian papa engaged in a manner that reflected no credit on his observance of the seventh commandment.

'Thus having satisfied myself as to the nature and extent of *his* sanctity and holiness, I softly ascended the stairs, and resumed my seat in the parlor. In less than ten minutes afterwards, the whole family were summoned together around the family altar, and then my excellent and pious father poured out his pure spirit in prayer, returning thanks for having been 'preserved from temptation,' and supplicating that all the members of his household might flee from fleshy lusts, which war against the soul; to which my chaste and saint-like mother responded in a fervent 'Amen.' From that evening, the kitchen wench with whom my father had defiled himself, assumed an air of bold insolence to every one in the house; she refused to perform any of the menial services devolving upon her, and when my mother spoke of dismissing her, my father would not listen to it; so the girl continued with us. She had evidently obtained entire dominion over my father, and did not scruple to use her power to her own advantage; for she flaunted about in showy ribbons and gay dresses, and I had no difficulty in surmising who furnished her with the means of procuring them.

'I still continued to attend the church of the Rev. Mr. Flanders. He used to preach excellent sermons, so far as composition and style of delivery were concerned; his words were smooth as oil; his manner full of the order of sanctity; his prayers were fervid eloquence. Yet, when I thought what a consummate scoundrel and hypocrite he was at heart, I viewed him with loathing and disgust.

'I soon became sensible that this reverend rogue began to view me with more than an ordinary degree of interest and admiration; for I may say, without vanity, that as I approached my fifteenth year, I was a very pretty girl; my form had begun to develop and ripen, and my maiden graces were not likely to escape the lustful eyes of the elderly roues of our 'flock,' and seemed to be particularly attractive to that aged libertine known as the Rev. Balaam Flanders.

'So far from being flattered by the attentions of our minister (as many of our flock were,) I detested and avoided him. Yet his lecherous glances were constantly upon me, whenever I was thrown into his society; even when he was in the pulpit, he would often annoy me with his lustful gaze.

'A bible class of young ladies was attached to the church, of which I was a member. We assembled at the close of divine service in the evening, for the study and examination of the Scriptures. Mr. Flanders himself had charge of this class, and was regarded by all the young ladies (myself excepted) as a 'dear, good man.' When one of us was particularly apt in answering a question or finding a passage, he would playfully chuck the good scholar under the chin, in token of his commendation; and sometimes, even, he would bestow a fatherly kiss upon the fair student of holy writ.

'These little tokens of his amativeness he often bestowed on me; and I permitted him, as I considered such liberties to be comparatively harmless. He soon however went beyond these 'attentions' to me — he first began by passing his hand over my bust, outside my dress, and, growing emboldened by my suffering him to do this, he would slide his hand into my bosom, and take hold of my budding evidences of approaching womanhood. Once he whispered in my ear — 'My dear, what a delicious bust you have!' I was by no means surprised at his conduct or words, for his *faux pas* with my frail mother convinced me that he was capable of any act of lechery. I also felt assured that he lusted after me with all the ardor of his lascivious passions, and I well know that he waited but for an opportunity to attempt my seduction. — I hated the man, both for his adultery with my mother, and his vile intentions towards myself — and I determined to *punish him* for his lewdness and hypocrisy — yes, punish him through the medium of his own bad passions, and in a manner that would torture him with alternate hope and despair; now inspiring him with rapture by apparently almost yielding to his wishes, and then maddening him by my resistance — at the same time resolving not to submit to his desires in any case. This was my plan for punishing the hoary libertine, and you shall see how well I carried it out.

'I did not discourage my reverend admirer in his amorous advances, but on the contrary received them in such a manner as might induce him to suppose that they were rather pleasing to me than otherwise. This I did in order to ensure the success of my scheme — I observed with secret satisfaction that he grew bolder and bolder in the liberties which he took with my person. He frequently accompanied me home in the evening after prayer meeting; and he always took care to traverse the most obscure and deserted streets with me, so as to have a better opportunity to indulge in his licentious freedoms with me, unobserved. Not content with thrusting his hand into my bosom, he would often attempt to pursue his investigations elsewhere: but this I always refused to permit him to do. He was continually embracing and kissing me — and in the latter indulgence, he often disgusted me beyond measure, by the excessive libidinousness which he exhibited — I merely mention these things to show the vile and beastly nature of this man, whom the world regarded as a pure and holy minister of the gospel. Though old enough to be my grandfather, the most hot blooded boy in existence could not have been more wanton or eccentric in the manifestations of his lustful yearnings. In fact, he wearied me almost to death by his unceasing persecution of me; yet I bore it with patience, so as to accomplish the object I had in view.

'I have often, upon the Sabbath, looked at that man as he stood in the pulpit; how pious he appeared, with his high, serene forehead, his carefully arranged gray hair, his mild and saint-like features, his snow-white cravat, and plain yet rich suit of glossy black! How calm and musical were the tones of his voice! — How beautifully he portrayed the happiness of religion, and how eloquently he prayed for the repentance and salvation of poor sinners! Yet how black was his heart with hypocrisy, and how polluted his soul with lust!

'One New Year's evening — I remember it well — my parents went to pay a visit to a relative a short distance out of the city, leaving me in charge of the house; the servants had all gone to visit their friends, and I was entirely alone. I had good reason to suppose that the Rev. Mr. Flanders would call on me that evening, as he knew that my parents would be absent. I determined to improve the opportunity, and commence my system of torture. Going to my chamber, I dressed myself in the most fascinating manner, for my wardrobe was extensive; and glancing in the mirror, I was satisfied of my ability to fan the flame of his passions into fury. I then seated myself in the parlor, where a fine fire was burning: and in a few minutes a hurried knock at the door announced the arrival of my intended victim. I ran down stairs and admitted him, and he followed me into the parlor, where he deliberately took off his overcoat, and then wheeling the sofa in front of the fire, desired me to sit by him. This I did, with apparent hesitation, telling him there was nobody in the house, and I wasn't quite sure it was right for me to stay alone in his company. This information, conveyed with a well assumed maiden bashfulness, seemed to afford the old rascal the most intense delight; he threw his arm around me, and kissed me repeatedly, then his hand began the exploration to which I have alluded. I suffered him to proceed just far enough to set his passions in a blaze; and then, breaking from his embrace, I took my seat at the further end of the sofa, assuring him if he approached me without my permission, I should scream out. This was agony to him; I saw with delight that he was beginning to suffer. He begged, entreated, supplicated me to let him come near me; and at last I consented; upon condition that he should attempt to take no further liberties. To this he agreed, and seating himself at my side, but without touching me, he devoured me with lustful eyes. For some minutes neither of us spoke, but at length he took my hand, and again passed his arm around my waist. I did not oppose him, but remained passive and silent. 'Dear girl,' he whispered, pressing me close to him — 'why need you be so cruel as to deny me the pleasure of love? Consider, I am your minister, and cannot sin: it will therefore be no sin for you to favor me.'

'Oh, sir,' I answered, 'I wish you were a young man — then I could almost — '

'Angelic creature!' he cried passionately — 'true, I am not young, but Love never grows old — no, no, no! Consent to be mine, sweet delicious girl, and — '

'Ah, sir!' I murmured — 'you tempt me sorely — I am but a weak giddy young creature; do not ask me to do wrong, for I fear that I may yield, and how very, very wicked that would be!'

'The reverend gentleman covered my cheeks and lips with hot kisses, as he said — 'Wicked — no! Heaven has given us passions, and we must gratify them. Look at David — look at Solomon — both good men; — they enjoyed the delights of love, and are now saints in Heaven, and why may not we do the same?

Why, my dear, it is the special privilege of the ministry to — '

'Ruin us young girls, sir?' I rejoined, smiling archly. 'Ah, you have set my heart in a strange flutter! I feel almost inclined — if you are sure it is not wicked — very sure — then I — '

'You are mine!' he exclaimed in a hoarse whisper, with frenzied triumph gleaming in his eyes. I never saw anybody look so fearful as he did then; his form quivered with intense excitement — his features appeared as if convulsed — his eyes, almost starting from their sockets, were blood shot and fiery. I trembled, lest in the madness of his passions, he might forcibly overcome me. He anticipated no resistance, imagining that he had an easy prey; but, at that very instant when he thought he was about to intoxicate his vile soul with the delicious draught of sensual delight, I spurned him from me as I would have spurned the most loathsome reptile that crawls amid the foetid horrors of a dungeon vault. — That was the moment of my triumph; I had led him step by step, until he felt assured of his ultimate success: I had permitted him to obtain, as it were, glimpses of a Paradise he was never to enjoy; and at the very moment he thought to have crossed the golden threshold, to enter into the blissful and flowery precincts of that Paradise, he was hurled from the pinnacle of his hopes, and doomed to endure the bitter pangs of disappointment, and the gnawings of a raging desire, never to be appeased!

'Thus repulsed, my reverend admirer did not resume his attempt, for my indignation was aroused, and he saw fierce anger flashing from my eyes. I solemnly declared, that had he attempted forcibly to accomplish his purpose, I would have dashed out his brains with the first weapon I could have laid my hand to!

'Humbled and abashed, he retired to a corner of the room, where he seated himself with an air of mortified disappointment. Yet still he kept his eyes upon me; and as I knew that his desires were raging as violently within him as ever (tho' he dare not approach me,) I devised the following method of augmenting his passions, and inflicting further torture upon him: — In my struggle with him, my dress had become somewhat disarranged and torn; and standing before a large mirror which was placed over the mantle-piece, I loosened my garments, and while pretending to examine the injury which had been done to them, I took especial pains to remove all covering from my neck, shoulders and bosom, which were uncommonly soft and white, as you, my dear, can testify. The sight of my naked charms instantly produced the desired effect upon the minister, who watched my slightest movement with eager scrutiny: he ceased almost to breathe, but panted — yes, absolutely *panted* — with the intensity of his passions. — Oh, how my heart swelled with delight at the agony he was thus forced to endure! Affecting to be unconscious of his presence, I assumed the most graceful and voluptuous attitudes I could think of — and he could endure it no longer; for — would you believe it? — he actually fell upon his knees before me, and groveled at my feet, entreating me, in a hoarse whisper, to kill him at once and end his torments, or else yield myself to him!

'My revenge was now accomplished, and I desired no more. I requested him to arise from his abject posture, and listen to me. Then I told him all I knew of his hypocrisy and wickedness — how I had become aware of his criminal intercourse with my mother, which, combined with his vile conduct and intentions in regard to myself, had induced me to punish him in the manner I had done, by exciting his passions almost to madness, and then repulsing him with disdain. I added, maliciously, that my own passions were warm and ardent, and that my young blood sometimes coursed thro' my veins with all the heat of sensual desire — and that were a man, young and handsome, to solicit my favors, I *might possibly yield*, in a thoughtless moment: but as for *him*, (the minister) sooner than submit to *his* embraces, I would permit the vilest negro in existence, to take me in his arms, and do with me as he pleased.

'All this I told the Rev. Mr. Flanders, and much more; and after listening in evident misery to my remarks, he took himself from the house. After this occurrence, I discontinued my attendance at his church and bible class. When my parents asked me the reason of my nonattendance, I refused to answer them; and at length they became enraged at what they termed my obstinacy, and insisted that I should not fail to attend church on the following Sabbath. — When the Sabbath came, I made no preparation for going to church; which mother perceiving, she began to apply the most reproachful and severe language to me. This irritated me; and without a moment's reflection, I said to her angrily:

'I can well conceive, madam, the reason of your great partiality to the Rev. Mr. Flanders; your many *private interviews* with him have wonderfully impressed you in his favor!'

'Wretch, what do you mean?' stammered my mother in great confusion, and turning pale and red alternately.

'You know very well what I mean, vile woman!' I cried, enraged beyond all power of restraining my speech, and perfectly reckless of the consequences of what I was saying. 'I was a witness of your infamous adultery with the hypocritical parson, and — '

'As I uttered these words, my mother gave a piercing scream, and flew at me with the fury of a tigress. She beat me cruelly, tore my hair and clothes, and being a large and powerful woman, I verily believe she would have killed me, had not my father, hearing the noise, rushed into the room, and rescued me from her grasp. He demanded an explanation of this extraordinary scene, and, in spite of the threatening looks and fierce denial of my mother, I told him all. He staggered and almost fell to the floor, when I thus boldly accused her of the crime of adultery; clinging to a chair for support, he faintly ejaculated — 'My God, can this be true?'

'It is false — I call Heaven to witness, it is false!' exclaimed my wretched and guilty mother — then, overcome by the terrors of the situation, she sank insensible upon the carpet. My father summoned a servant to her assistance; and then bade me follow him into another room. Carefully closing the doors, he turned to me with a stern aspect, and said, with much severity of tone and manner:

'Girl, you have made a serious charge against your mother; you have impugned her chastity and her honor. Adultery is the most flagrant crime that can stain the holy institution of marriage.

If I believed your mother guilty of it, I would cast her off forever!'

'I laughed scornfully as he said this, whereupon he angrily demanded the cause of my ill-timed mirth; and as I detested his hypocrisy, I boldly told him that it ill became *him* to preach on the enormity of the crime of adultery, after having been guilty of that very offence with his kitchen wench! He turned deadly pale at this unexpected retort, and stammered out — 'Then you know all — denial is useless.' I told him how I had witnessed the affair in the kitchen, and reproached him bitterly for the infamous conduct. He admitted the justness of my rebuke, and when I informed him that Mr. Flanders had attempted to debauch me, he foamed with rage, and loaded the reverend libertine with epithets which were decidedly uncomplimentary. Still, he doubted the story of my mother's crime — he could not believe *her* to be guilty of such baseness; but he assured me that he should satisfy himself of her innocence or guilt, then left me, after having made me promise not to expose him in reference to his affair with the servant girl in the kitchen.

'Upon leaving me, my father immediately sought an interview with my mother, who by this time had recovered from her swoon. She was in her chamber; but as I was naturally anxious to know what might pass between my parents, under such unusual circumstances, I stationed myself at the door of the room, as soon as my father had entered, and heard distinctly all that was said.'

CHAPTER III

*Domestic Troubles — A Scene, and a Compromise — an Escape
— various matters amative, explanatory and miscellaneous, in
the Tale of the Courtezan.*

'Well, madam,' said my father, in a cold, severe tone — 'this is truly a strange and serious accusation which our daughter has brought against you. The crime of adultery, and with a Christian minister!'

'Surely,' rejoined my mother, sobbing — 'you will not believe the assertions of that young hussy. I am innocent — indeed, indeed I am.'

'I am inclined to believe that you *are* innocent, and yet I never shall rest perfectly satisfied until you *prove* yourself guiltless in this matter,' rejoined my father, speaking in a kinder tone. 'Now listen to me,' he continued. 'I have thought of a plan by which to put your virtue, and the purity of our pastor, to the test. I shall invite the reverend gentleman to dinner this afternoon, after divine service; and when we have dined, you shall retire with him to this room, for private prayer. You shall go first, and in a few minutes he shall follow you; and I shall take care that no secret communication is held between you, in the way of whispering or warnings of any kind, whether by word or sign. I will contrive means to watch you narrowly, when you are with him in the chamber; and I caution you to beware of giving him the slightest hint to be on his guard, for that would be a conclusive evidence of your guilt. He will of course conduct himself as usual, not knowing that he is watched. If you are innocent, he will pray or converse with you in a Christian and proper manner; but if you ever *have* had criminal intercourse with him, he will, in all human probability, indicate the same in his language and actions. This is most plain; and I trust that the result will clear you of all suspicion.'

'My mother knew it would be useless to remonstrate, for my father was unchangeable, when once he had made up his mind to anything. She therefore was obliged to submit. Accordingly, Mr.

Flanders dined with us that day: once, during the meal, happening to look into his face, I saw that he was gazing at me intently, and I was startled by the expression of his countenance: for that expression was one of the deadliest hate. It was but for an instant, and then he turned away his eyes; yet I still remember that look of bitter hatred. As soon as dinner was over, my mother withdrew, and a few minutes afterwards my father said to the minister:

'Brother Flanders, I am going out for a short walk, to call upon a friend; meantime, I doubt not that Mrs. — — will be happy to hold sisterly and Christian communion with you. You will find her in her chamber.'

'It is very pleasant, my brother,' responded the other — 'to hold private and holy communion with our fellow seekers after divine truth. These family visits I regard as the priceless privilege of the pastor; by them the bond of love which unites him to his flock, is more strongly cemented. I will go to my sister and we will pray and converse together.'

'Saying this, Mr. Flanders arose and left the room; he had scarcely time to ascend the stairs and enter my mother's chamber, when my father quickly and noiselessly followed him, and entered an apartment adjoining. He had previously made a small hole in the wall, and to this hole he applied his eye. So rapid had been his movements, that the minister had just closed the door, when he was at his post of observation; so that it was rendered utterly impossible for my mother to whisper a word or make a sign, to caution her paramour against committing both her and himself. I lost no time in taking up my position at the chamber door, and availed myself of the keyhole as a convenient channel for both seeing and hearing. I saw that my mother was very pale and seemed ill at ease, and I did not wonder at it, for her position was an extremely painful and embarrassing one. She well knew that my father's eye was upon her, watching her slightest movement; she knew, also, that the minister was utterly unaware of my father's *espionage*, and she had good reason to fear that the reverend libertine would, as usual, begin the interview by amorous demonstrations. Oh, how she must have longed to put him on his guard, and thereby save both her honor and her reputation! — But she dare not.

'The minister seated himself near my unhappy mother, and opened the conversation as follows:

'Well, my dear Mrs. — — , I am sorry to inform you that I have tidings of an unpleasant nature to communicate to you. *We are discovered!'*

'These fatal words were uttered in a low whisper; but yet I doubt not that my father had heard them. I could see that my mother trembled violently — yet she spoke not a syllable.

'Yes,' continued the minister, all unconscious of the disclosure he was making to my father — 'Your daughter knows all. She suspected, it seems, the real object of our last interview, when, you recollect, we indulged in a little amative dalliance. — On New Year's evening, during your absence, I called here and saw your daughter, when she reproached me for having debauched you, stating in what manner she had seen the whole affair. Since then, I have had no opportunity of informing you that she knew our intimacy.'

'Still my mother uttered not a single word!'

'This girl,' continued the minister,'must be made to hold her tongue, somehow or other: it would be dreadful to have it reach your husband's ears. But why are you so taciturn to-day, my dear? Come, let us enjoy the present, and dismiss all fear for the future. But first we must make sure that there are no listeners *this* time,' and he approached the door.

'I retreated precipitately, and slipped into another room, while he opened the chamber; seeing no-one on the outside, he closed it again, and locked it. I instantly resumed my station; and I saw the minister approach my mother, (who appeared spellbound,) and clasp her in his arms. He was about to proceed to the usual extreme of his criminality when my father uttered an expression of rage; I instantly ran into the room which had before served me as a hiding place, and in a moment more my father was at the door of my mother's chamber, demanding admission.

After a short delay, the door was opened; and then a scene ensued which defies my powers of description.

"Tis needless to dwell upon the particulars of what followed. My father raved, the pastor entreated, and my mother wept. But after an hour or so, the tempest subsided; the parties arriving at the reasonable conclusion, that what was done could not be undone. Finally it was arranged that Mr. Flanders should pay my father a considerable sum of money, upon condition that the affair be hushed up. — My mother was promised forgiveness for her fault — and as I was the only person likely to divulge the matter, it was agreed that I should be placed under restraint, and not suffered to leave the house, until such time as I should solemnly swear never to reveal the secret of the adultery. — Accordingly, for one month I remained a close prisoner in the house, and at the end of that period, not feeling inclined to give the required pledge of secrecy, I determined to effect my escape, and leave my parents forever. — The thought of parting from them failed to produce the least impression of sadness upon my mind, for from the moment I had discovered the secret of their guilty intrigues, all love and respect for them had ceased. I knew it would be no easy matter for me to depart from the house unperceived, for the servant wench, Janet, was a spy upon my actions; but one evening I contrived to elude her observation, and slipping out of the door, walked rapidly away. What was to become of me, I knew not, nor cared, in my joy at having escaped from such an abode of hypocrisy as my parents' house — for of all the vices which can disgrace humanity, I regard *hypocrisy* as the most detestable.

'Fortunately, I had several dollars in my possession; and I had no difficulty in procuring a boarding house. And now as my story must be getting tedious by its length, I will bring it to a close in as few words as possible. I supported myself for some time by the labor of my needle; but as this occupation afforded me only a slight maintenance, and proved to be injurious to my health, I abandoned it, and sought some other employment. It was about that time that I became acquainted with a young man named Frederick Archer, whose manners and appearance interested me exceedingly, and I observed with pleasure that he regarded me with admiration. Our acquaintance soon ripened into intimacy; we often went to places of amusement together, and he was very liberal in his expenditures for my entertainment. He was always perfectly respectful in his conduct towards me, never venturing upon any undue familiarity, and quite correct in his language. One evening I accompanied him to the Bowery Theatre, and after the play he proposed that we should repair to a neighboring 'Ladies Oyster Saloon,' and partake of refreshments. We accordingly entered a very fashionable place, and seated ourselves in a small room, just large enough to contain a table and sofa. — The oysters were brought, and also a bottle of champagne; and then I noticed that my companion very carefully locked the door of the room. This done, he threw his arms around me, and kissed me. Surprised at this liberty, which he had never attempted before, I scolded him a little for his rudeness; and he promised not to offend again. We then ate our oysters, and he persuaded me to drink some of the wine. Whether it contained a stimulant powder, or because I had never drank any before, I know not; but no sooner had I swallowed a glass of the sparkling liquid, than a strange dizzy sensation pervaded me — not a disagreeable feeling, by any means, but rather a delightful one. It seemed to heat my blood, and to a most extraordinary degree. Rising, I complained of being slightly unwell, and requested Frederick to conduct me out of the place immediately. Alas, sir, why need I dwell upon what followed? Frederick's conquest was an honest one; I suffered him to do with me as he pleased, and he soon initiated me into the voluptuous mysteries of Venus. I confess, I rather sought than avoided this consummation — for my passions were in a tumult, which could only be appeased by full unrestrained gratification.

'From that night my secret frailties with Frederick became frequent. I granted him all the favors he asked; yet I earnestly entreated him to marry me. This he consented to do, and we were accordingly united in the bonds of wedlock. My husband immediately hired these furnished apartments, which I at present occupy; and then he developed a trait in his character, which proved him a villain of the deepest dye. How he made a livelihood, had always to me been a profound mystery; and as he avoided the subject, I never questioned him. But how he intended to live, after our marriage, I soon became painfully aware. *He resolved that I should support him in idleness, by becoming a common prostitute.* When he made this debasing and inhuman proposition to me, I rejected it with the indignation it merited; whereupon he very coolly informed me, that unless I complied, he should abandon me to my fate, and proclaim to the world that I was a harlot before he married me. Finding me still obstinate, he drew a bowie knife, and swore a terrible oath, that unless I would do as he wished, he would kill me! Terrified for my life, I gave the required promise; but he made me swear upon the Bible to do as he wished. He set a woman in the house to watch me during the day, and prevent my escaping, and in the evening he returned, accompanied by an old gentleman of respectable appearance, whom he introduced to me as Mr. Rogers. This person surveyed me with an impertinent stare, and complimented me on my beauty; in a few minutes, Frederick arose and said to me — 'Maria, I am going out for a little while, and in the meantime you must do your best to entertain Mr. Rogers.' He then whispered in my ear — 'Let him do as he will with you, for he has paid me a good price; now don't refuse him, or be in the least degree prudish, or by G — — it shall be worse for you!' Scarcely had he taken his departure, when the old wretch, who had *purchased* me, clasped me in his palsied arms, and prepared to debauch me; in reply to my entreaties to desist, and my appeals to his generosity, he only shook his head, and said — 'No, no, young lady, I have given fifty dollars for you, and you are mine!' The old brute had neither shame, nor pity, nor honor in his breast; he forced me to comply with his base wishes, and a life of prostitution was for the first time opened to me.

'After this event, I attempted no further opposition to my husband's infamous scheme of prostituting myself for his support. Almost nightly, he brought home with him some *friend* of his, who had previously paid him for the use of my person. The money he gains in this way he expends in gambling and dissipation; allowing me scarcely anything for the common necessaries of life, and I am in consequence obliged to solicit private aid from such gentlemen as are disposed to enjoy my favors. My husband rarely sleeps at home, and I see but very little of him; this is a source of no regret to me, for I have ceased to feel the slightest regard for him.

'And now, sir, you have heard the particulars of my history. You will do me the justice to believe that I have been reduced to my present unfortunate position, more through the influence of circumstances, than on account of any natural depravity. — True, I am now what is termed a woman of the town — but still I am not entirely destitute of delicacy or refinement of feeling. I am an admirer of it in others. My parents I have never seen, since the day I quitted their house; but I have heard that my mother has since given birth to a fine boy, the very image of the minister; and also that Jane, my father's paramour, has become the mother of a child bearing an astonishing resemblance to the old gentleman himself!

'If you ask me why I do not escape from my husband, and abandon my present course of living, I would remind you that, as society is constituted, I never can regain a respectable standing in the eyes of the world. No, my course is marked out, and I must adhere to it. I am not happy, neither am I completely miserable; for sometimes I have my moments of enjoyment. When I meet a gentlemanly and intelligent companion, like yourself, disposed to sympathize with the misfortunes of a poor and friendless girl, I am enabled to bear up under my hard lot with something like cheerfulness and hope.'

Thus ended the Courtezan's Tale; and as it was now daylight, Frank Sydney arose and prepared for his departure, assuring her that he would endeavor to benefit her in some way, and generously presenting her with a liberal sum of money, for which she seemed truly grateful. He then bade her farewell, promising to call and see her again ere long.

CHAPTER IV

*A Fashionable Lady — the Lovers — the Negro Paramour —
astounding developments of Crime in High Life — the Accouchement — Infanticide — the Marriage — a dark suspicion.*

The scene changes to that superb avenue of fashion, Broadway; the time, eleven o'clock in the morning, and the place, one of
the noblest mansions which adorn that aristocratic section of the
city.

Miss Julia Fairfield was seated in a luxurious apartment,
lounging over a late breakfast, and listlessly glancing over the
morning newspapers.

This young lady was about eighteen years of age, a beauty,
an heiress, and, per consequence, a *belle*. She was a brunette; her
beauty was of a warm, majestic, voluptuous character; her eyes
beamed with the fire of passion, and her features were full of
expression and sentiment. Her attire was elegant, tasteful, and
unique, consisting of a loose, flowing robe of white satin,
trimmed with costliest lace; her hair was beautifully arranged in
the best Parisian style; and her tiny feet were encased in gold-
embroidered slippers. The peculiarity of her dress concealed the
outlines of her form; yet the garment being made very low in the
shoulders, the upper portions of a magnificently full bust were
visible.

For some time she continued to sip her chocolate and read in
silence; but soon she exclaimed, in a rich, melodious voice —

'Very well, indeed! — and so those odious editors have given
the full particulars of the great ball last night, and have complimented me highly on my grace and beauty! Ah, I never could
have ventured there in any other costume than the one I wore.
These loose dresses are capital things — but my situation becomes more and more embarrassing every day.'

At this moment a domestic announced Mr. Francis Sydney,
and the announcement was followed by the entrance of that gentleman.

'My dear Julia,' said Frank, seating himself — 'you will pardon my intrusion at this unfashionable hour, but I was anxious to learn the state of your health, after the fatigues of last night's assembly.'

'No apology is necessary, my dear Frank,' replied the lady, with a bewitching smile, at the same time giving him her hand, which he tenderly raised to his lips. 'I am in excellent health this morning, although dreadfully bored with *ennui*, which I trust will be dispelled by the enlivening influence of your presence.'

'What happiness do I derive from the reflection, my sweet girl,' said Frank, drawing his chair closer to hers, 'that, in one short month, I shall call you mine! Yes, we shall then stand before the bridal altar, and I shall have the felicity of wedding the loveliest, most accomplished, and purest of her sex!'

'Ah, Francis,' sighed the lady — 'how joyfully will I then bestow upon you the gift of this hand! — my heart you have already.'

These words were said with so much tenderness, and with such a charming air of affectionate modesty, that the young man caught her to his breast and covered her lips with kisses. Struggling from his ardent embrace, Julia said to him, in a tone of reproach, —

'Francis, this is the first time you ever forgot the respect due to me as a lady; but do not repeat the offense, or you will diminish my friendship for you — perhaps, my love also. — When we are *married*,' she added, blushing — 'my person will be wholly yours — but not till then.'

'Pardon me, dear Julia,' entreated Frank, in a tone of contrition — 'I will not offend again.'

The lady held out her hand, and smiled her forgiveness.

'Now that we are good friends again,' said she — 'I will order some refreshments.' She rang a silver bell, and gave the necessary order to a servant, and in a few minutes, cake and wine were brought in by a black waiter, clad in rich livery. The complexion of this man was intensely dark, yet his features were good and regular and his figure tall and well-formed. In his demeanor towards his mistress and her guest, he was respectful in the extreme, seldom raising his eyes from the carpet, and when addressed, speaking in the most servile and humble tone.

After having partaken of the refreshments, and enjoyed half an hour's conversation, Frank arose and took his leave.

As soon as he had gone, an extraordinary scene took place in that parlor.

The black waiter, having turned the key within the lock of the door, approached Miss Fairfield, deliberately threw his arms around her, and kissed her repeatedly! And how acted the lady — she who had reproved her affianced husband for a similar liberty — how acted she when thus rudely and grossly embraced by that black and miscreant menial? Did she not repulse him with indignant disgust, — did she not scream for assistance, and have him punished for the insolent outrage?

No; she abandoned her person to his embraces, and returned them! She, the well-born, the beautiful, the wealthy, the accomplished lady — the betrothed bride of a young gentleman of honor — the daughter of an aristocrat — the star of a constellation of fashion — yielding herself to the arms of a negro servant!

Oh, woman! how like an angel art thou in thy virtue and goodliness! how like a devil, when thou art fallen from thy high estate!

Yes, that black fellow covers her exquisite neck and shoulders with lustful kisses! His hands revel amid the glories of her divine and voluptuous bosom; and his lips wander from her rosy mouth, to the luxurious beauties of her finely developed bust.

'My beautiful mistress!' said the black, 'how kind in you to grant me these favors! What can I do to testify my gratitude?'

'Oh Nero,' murmured the lady 'what if our intimacy should be discovered? yet you are discreet and trustworthy; for from the night I first hinted my desires to you, and admitted you into my chamber, you have behaved with prudence and caution. Yet you are aware of my situation; you know that I am *enciente* by you; all our precautions have failed to prevent that result of our amours. I dress myself in such a way as to keep my condition from observation; no one suspects it. In a month, you know, I am to be married to Mr. Sydney; but I hope to give birth to the child in less than a week from the present time, so that, with good care and nursing, assisted by my naturally robust constitution, I shall recover my health and strength in sufficient time to enable my marriage to pass on without suspicion. I will endeavor to adopt such artifices and precautions as will completely deceive my husband, and he will never know that I am otherwise than he now supposes me. After my marriage, we can continue our intrigues as before, provided we are extremely cautious. Ah, my handsome African, how dearly I love you.'

The guilty and depraved woman sank back upon a sofa, and her paramour clasped her in his arms.

Let no one say that our narrative is becoming too improbable for belief, that the scenes which we depict find no parallel in real life. Those who are disposed to be skeptical with reference to such scenes as the foregoing had better throw this volume aside; for crimes of a much deeper dye, than any yet described, will be brought forward in this tale: crimes that are daily perpetrated, but which are seldom discovered or suspected. We have undertaken a difficult and painful task, and we shall accomplish it; unrestrained by a false delicacy, we shall drag forth from the dark and mysterious labyrinths of great cities, the hidden iniquities which taint the moral atmosphere, and assimilate human nature to the brute creation.

Five days after the occurrences just described, in the middle of the afternoon, Miss Julia Fairfield rode out in her carriage alone, driven by the black, Nero. The vehicle stopped before a house of respectable exterior, in Washington street, and the young lady was assisted to alight; entering the house, she was received by an elderly female, who immediately conducted her to a private room, which contained a bed and furniture of a neat but unostentatious description. The carriage drove away, and Julia remained several hours in the house. At about nine o'clock in the evening, the carriage returned, and she was assisted to enter, being apparently in a very feeble and unwell condition. She reached her own dwelling, and for over a week remained in her chamber, under plea of severe indisposition. When at length she made her appearance, she looked extremely pale, and somewhat emaciated; yet, for the first time in several months, she wore a tight-fitting dress, and her father, unconscious of her crimes, good-naturedly expressed his joy at seeing her 'once more dressed like a Christian lady, and not in the loose and slatternly robes she had so long persisted in wearing.'

The next morning after her visits to the house on Washington Street, the newspapers contained a notice of the discovery of the body of a newborn mulatto child, in the water off the Bowery. That child was the offspring of Miss Julia and the black; it had been strangled, and its body thrown into the water.

About three weeks after her secret accouchement, Julia became the wife of Frank Sydney. An elegant establishment had been prepared for the young couple, in Broadway. Here they repaired after the performance of the marriage ceremony; and now being for the first time alone with his beautiful bride, Frank embraced her with passionate ardor, and was not repulsed.

Ah, happy bridegroom, how little thou knowest the truth! Thou dost not suspect that the lovely woman at thy side, dressed in spotless white, and radiant with smiles — thou dost little think that she, whom thou hast taken to be thy wedded wife, comes to thy arms and nuptial bed, not a pure and stainless virgin, but a wretch whose soul is polluted and whose body is unchaste, by vile intimacy with a negro menial!

The hour waxes late, and the impatient husband conducts his fair bride to the nuptial chamber — Love's hallowed sanctuary.

Two hours afterwards, that husband was pacing a parlor back and forth, with uneven strides, his whole appearance indicative of mental agony. — Pausing, he exclaimed —

'My God, what terrible suspicions cross my mind! I imagined Julia to be an angel of purity and virtue yet now I doubt her! Oh, horrible, horrible! But may not my doubts be facts without any foundation? I will tomorrow consult a physician on the subject. Pray heaven my suspicions may prove to be utterly groundless!'

He was startled by the sound of an approaching foot-step; the door opened, and his wife entered, bearing a light. How seductive she looked, in her white night-dress! how tenderly she caressed him, as with affectionate concern she inquired if he were unwell.

'Dearest Frank,' she said, 'I had fallen into the most delicious slumber I have ever enjoyed; — doubly delicious, because my dreams were of you. Awaking suddenly, I missed you from my arms, and hastened hither to find you. What is the matter, love?'

'Nothing, Julia,' answered the husband; 'I had a slight headache, but it is over now. Return to your chamber, and I will follow you in a few moments.'

She obeyed, and Frank was alone. 'Either that woman is as chaste as Diana,' he said to himself, 'or she is a consummate wretch and hypocrite. But let her not be too hastily condemned. My friend, Dr. Palmer, shall give me his opinion, and if he thinks that she could have been *as she was*, and still be chaste, then I will discard my suspicions; but if, on the contrary, the doctor deems such a condition to be incompatible with chastity, then will I cast her off forever. I cannot endure this fearful state of suspense, would that it were morning!'

Morning came at last, and Sydney sought the residence of Dr. Palmer, with whom he held a long and private consultation. The result of this interview was not very satisfactory to the husband, for the doctor's concluding remarks were as follows: —

'My dear sir, it is impossible for any physician, however great may be his professional knowledge and experience, to decide with positive certainty upon such a matter. Nature has many freaks; the condition of your lady *might* be natural — yet pardon me if, in my own private opinion, I doubt its being so! I have heard of such cases, where the chastity of the lady was un-doubted; yet such cases are exceedingly rare. Your position, Mr. Sydney, is a peculiarly embarrassing and delicate one. I cannot counsel you as a physician; yet, as *a friend*, permit me to advise you to refrain from acting hastily in this matter. Your wife may be innocent; you should consider her so, until you have ocular or other positive evidence of her guilt. Meanwhile, let her not know your suspicions, but watch her narrowly; if she were frail before marriage, she needs but the opportunity to be inconstant after-wards. I have attended upon the lady several times, during slight illness, in my capacity as a physician, and I have had the oppor-tunity to observe that she is of an uncommonly ardent and volup-tuous temperament. Phrenology confirms this; for her amative developments are singularly prominent. — Candidly, her physi-cal conformation strongly impresses me with the belief, that moral principle will scarcely restrain her from unlawful indul-gence, when prompted by inclination.'

'The devil!' muttered Frank, as he retraced his steps home — 'I am about as wise as ever! A pretty opinion Dr. Palmer ex-presses of her, truly! Well, she shall have the benefit of a doubt, and I shall try to look upon her as an innocent woman, until I detect her in an act of guilt. Meanwhile, she shall be watched narrowly and constantly.'

Frank's suspicions with reference to his newly-made wife, did not prevent his carrying out the plan of benevolence which he formed in the first chapter of this narrative. Adopting various disguises, he would penetrate into the most obscure and danger-ous quarters of the city, at all hours of the day and night. The details of many of these secret adventures will be hereafter re-lated.

CHAPTER V

A Thieves' Crib on the Five Points — Bloody Mike — Ragged Pete — the Young Thief, and the stolen Letters — The Stranger — a general Turn-out-Peeling a Lodger — the 'Forty-Foot Cave.'

It was a dreary winter's night, cold, dark, and stormy. The hour was midnight; and the place, the *'Five Points.'*

The narrow and crooked streets which twine serpent-like around that dreaded plague spot of the city were deserted; but from many a dirty window, and through many a red, dingy curtain, streamed forth into the darkness rages of ruddy light, while the sounds of the violin, and the noise of Bacchanalian orgies, betokened that the squalid and vicious population of that vile region were still awake.

In the low and dirty tap-room of a thieves' *crib* in Cross street, are assembled about a dozen persons. The apartment is twenty feet square, and is warmed by a small stove, which is red-hot; a roughly constructed bar, two or three benches, and a table constitute all the furniture. Behind the bar stands the landlord, a great, bull-necked Irishman, with red hair, and ferocious countenance, the proprietor of the elegant appropriate appellation of 'Bloody Mike.' Upon the table are stretched two men, one richly dressed, and the other in rags — both sound asleep. Beneath the table lay a wretched-looking white prostitute, and a filthy-looking negro — also asleep. The remainder of the interesting party are seated around the stove, and sustain the following dialogue:

'Well, blow me tight,' said one, 'if ever I seed such times as these afore! Why, a feller can't steal enough to pay for his rum and tobacco. I haven't made a cent these three days. D — — n me if I ain't half a mind to knock it off and go to work!'

The speaker was a young man, not over one and twenty years of age; yet he was a most wretched and villainous looking fellow. His hair was wild and uncombed; his features bloated and covered with ulcers; his attire miserable and ragged in the extreme; and sundry sudden twitchings of his limbs, as well as frequent violent scratchings of the same, indicated that he was over-run with vermin. This man, whose indolence had made him a common loafer, had become a petty thief; he would lurk around backyards and steal any article he could lay his hands to — an axe, a shovel, or a garment off a line.

'What you say is true enough, Ragged Pete,' said a boy of about fourteen, quite good looking, and dressed with compara-tive neatness. 'A *Crossman* has to look sharp now-a-days to make a *boodle*. And he often gets deceived when he thinks he has made a raise. Why the other day I cut a rich looking young lady's reti-cule from her arm in Broadway and got clear off with it; but upon examining my prize, I found it contained nothing but a handker-chief and some letters. The *wipe* I kept for my own use; as for the letters, here they are — they are not worth a tinker's d — — n, for they are all about love.'

As he spoke, he carelessly threw upon the table several let-ters, which were taken up and examined by Ragged Pete, who being requested by others to read aloud, complied, and opening one, read as follows: —

'*Dear Mistress*, — Since your marriage, I have not enjoyed any of those delicious private *tete-a-tetes* with you, which for-merly afforded us both so much pleasure. Send me word when I can find you alone, and I will fly to your arms.

'Your ever faithful Nero'

'By Jesus!' exclaimed Bloody Mike — 'it's a mighty quare name me gentleman signs himself, any how. And it's making love to another man's wife he'd be, blackguard! Devil the much I blame him for that same, if the lady's continted!'

'Here,' said Ragged Pete, taking up another letter, 'is one that's sealed and directed, and ain't been broke open yet. Let's see what it says.'

Breaking the seal, he read aloud the contents, thus: —

'*Dear Nero*, — I am dying to see you, but my husband is with me so constantly that 'tis next to impossible. He is kind and attentive to me, but oh! how infinitely I prefer *you to him*! I do not think that he has ever suspected that before my marriage, I * * * *Fortunately for us*, Mr. Sydney has lately been in the habit of absenting himself from home evenings, often staying out very late. Where he goes I care not, tho' I suspect he is engaged in some intrigue of his own; and if so, all the better for us, my dear Nero.

'Thus I arrange matters; when he has gone, and I have reason to think he will not soon return, a light will be placed in my chamber window, which is on the extreme left of the building, in the third story. Without this signal, do not venture into the house. If all is favourable my maid, Susan (who is in our secret,) will admit you by the back gate, when you knock thrice. Trusting that we may meet soon, I remain, dear Nero,

'Your loving and faithful JULIA.'

'Hell and furies!' exclaimed one of the company, starting from his seat, and seizing the letter; he ran his eye hastily over it, and with a groan of anguish, sank back upon the bench.

The person who manifested this violent emotion, was a young man, dressed in a mean and tattered garb, his face begrimed corresponding with that of the motley crew by which he was surrounded. He was a perfect stranger to the others present, and had not participated in their previous conversation, nor been personally addressed by any of them.

Bloody Mike, the landlord, deeming this a fit opportunity for the exercise of his authority, growled out, in a ferocious tone —

'And who the devil may ye be, that makes such a bobbaboo about a letter that a *kinchen* stales from a lady's work bag? Spake, ye blasted scoundrel; or wid my first, (and it's no small one) I'll let daylight thro' yer skull! And be what right do ye snatch the letter from Ragged Pete? Answer me *that* ye devil's pup!'

All present regarded the formidable Irishman with awe, excepting the stranger, who gazed at him in contemptuous silence. This enraged the landlord still more, and he cried out —

'Bad luck to ye, who are ye, at all at all? Ye're a stranger to all of us — ye haven't spint a pinney for the good of the house, for all ye've been toasting yer shins furnist the fire for two hours or more! Who knows but ye're a police spy, an officer in disguise, or — '

'Oh, *slash yer gammon*, Bloody Mike,' exclaimed the stranger, speaking with a coarse, vulgar accent — 'I know you well enough, tho' you don't remember *me*. Police spy, hey? Why, I've just come out of *quod* myself, d'y see — and I've got *tin* enough to stand the rum for the whole party. So call up, fellers — what'll ye all have to drink?'

It is impossible to describe the effect of these words on everybody present. Bloody Mike swore that the stranger was a 'rare gentleman', and asked his pardon; Ragged Pete grasped his hand in a transport of friendship; the young thief declared he was 'one of the b'hoys from home;' the negro and the prostitute crawled from under the table, and thanked him with hoarse and drunken voices; the vagabond and well-dressed man on the table, both rolled off, and 'called on.' And the stranger threw upon the counter a handful of silver, and bade them 'drink it up.'

Such a scene followed! Half pints of 'blue ruin' were dispensed to the thirsty throng, and in a short time all, with two or three exceptions, were extremely drunk. The negro and the prostitute resumed their places under the table; the well-dressed man and his ragged companion stretched themselves upon their former hard couch; and Ragged Pete ensconced himself in the fireplace, with his head buried in the ashes and his heels up the chimney, in which comfortable position he vainly essay'd to sing a sentimental song, wherein he [*illegible word*] to deplore the loss of his 'own true love.' (The only sober persons were the stranger, the young thief and the Irish landlord.) The two former of these, seated in one corner, conversed together in low whispers.

'See here, young feller,' said the stranger — 'I've taken a fancy to them two letters, and if you'll let me keep 'em, here's a dollar for you.' The boy readily agreed, and the other continued:

'I say, there's a rum set o' coves in this here crib, ain't there? Who is that well-dressed chap on the table?'

'That,' said the boy, 'is a thief who lately made a large haul, since which time he has been cutting a tremendous swell — but he spent the whole thousand dollars in two or three weeks, and his fine clothes is all that remains. In less than a week he will look as bad as Ragged Pete.'

'And what kind of a cove is the landlord, Bloody Mike?' asked the stranger.

'He is the best friend a fellow has in the world, as long as his money lasts,' replied the boy. 'The moment that is gone, he don't know you. Now you'll see in a few moments how he'll clear everybody out of the house except such as he thinks has money. And, 'twixt you and me, he is the d — — dst scoundrel out of jail, and would as lief kill a man as not.'

At this moment, Bloody Mike came from behind the counter and took a general survey of the whole party. At length his eye settled upon the form of Ragged Pete, in the fireplace; muttering something about 'pinnyless loafers,' he seized that individual by the heels, and dragging him to the door, opened it, and thrust the poor wretch forth into the deep snow and pelting storm! All the rest with the exception of the stranger, the boy thief, and the well dressed man, shared the same fate. But Mike was not done yet; he swore that the well dressed personage should pay for his lodgings, and deliberately he stripped the man of his coat, vest and boots, after which summary proceeding he ejected him from the house, as he had the others.

'Suppose we take up our quarters in some other 'crib',' whispered the boy to the stranger; the latter assented, and they both arose to depart. The landlord invited them to remain and partake of 'something hot,' but they declined this hospitality, and sallied forth into the street.

It was now about two o'clock, and snowing heavily. The stranger, placing himself under the guidance of the boy, followed him around into Orange street. Pausing before a steep cellar, exceedingly narrow, dark and deep, the young thief whispered —

'This is the *forty-foot cave* — the entrance into the *dark vaults*.

[1] You have been down, I suppose?'

The stranger answered in the negative.

'Then come on, if you are not afraid,' said the boy — and followed by his companion, he cautiously began to descend into the dark and dreary chasm.

FOOTNOTES:

[1] It is a fact by no means generally known that there was, beneath the section of New York called the 'Five Points,' a vast subterranean cavern, known as the *dark vaults*. There mysterious passages run in many directions, for a great distance, far beneath the foundations of the houses. Some have supposed that the place was excavated in time of war, for the secretion of ammunition or stores, while others think it was formerly a deep sewer of the city. In these dark labyrinths *daylight* never *shone*: an eternal night prevailed. Yet it swarmed with human beings, who passed their lives amid its unwholesome damps and gloomy horrors. It served as a refuge for monstrous crimes and loathsome wretchedness. The Police rarely ventured to explore its secret mysteries — for Death lurked in its dark passages and hidden recesses. The horrors of this awful place have never heretofore been thoroughly revealed; and now the author of this work will, for the first time, drag forth the ghastly inmates of this charnel-house into the clear light of day.

CHAPTER VI

The Dark Vaults — Scenes of Appalling Horror — The Dead Man — The Catechism — arrangements for a Burglary.

Down, down, they went, far into the bowels of the earth; groping their way in darkness, and often hazarding their necks by stumbling upon the steep and slippery steps. At length the bottom of the 'forty-foot cave' was reached; and the boy grasping the hand of his follower, conducted him thro' a long and circuitous passage. Intense darkness and profound silence reigned; but after traversing this passage for a considerable distance, lights began to illumine the dreary path, and that indistinct hum which proceeds from numerous inhabitants, became audible. Soon the two explorers emerged into a large open space, having the appearance of a vast vault, arched overhead with rough black masonry, which was supported by huge pillars of brick and stone. Encircling this mighty *tomb*, as it might be properly called, were numerous small hovels, or rather *caves*, dug into the earth; and these holes were swarming with human beings.

Here was a *subterranean village*! Myriads of men and women dwelt in this awful place, where the sun never shone; here they festered with corruption, and died of starvation and wretchedness — those who were poor; and here also the fugitive murderer, the branded outlaw, the hunted thief, and the successful robber, laden with his booty, found a safe asylum, where justice *dare not* follow them — here they gloried in the remembrance of past crimes, and anticipated future enormities. Men had no secrets here; — for no treachery could place them within the grasp of the law, and every one spoke openly and boldly of his long-hidden deeds of villainy and outrage.

'Come', said the boy to the stranger — 'let us go the rounds and see what's going on.'

They drew nigh a large, shelving aperture in the earth, on one side of the vault, and looking in saw a man, nearly naked; seated upon a heap of excrement and filthy straw. A fragment of a penny candle was burning dimly near him, which showed him to be literally daubed from head to foot with the vilest filth. Before him lay the carcase of some animal which had died from disease — it was swollen and green with putrefaction; and oh, horrible! we sicken as we record the loathsome fact — the starved wretch was ravenously devouring the carrion! Yes, with his finger nails, long as vultures' claws, he tore out the reeking entrails, and ate them with the ferocity of the grave-robbing hyena! One of the spectators spoke to him, but he only growled savagely, and continued his revolting meal.

'Oh, God!' said the stranger, shuddering — 'this is horrible!'

'Pooh!' rejoined the boy — '*that's* nothing at all to what you will see if you have the courage and inclination to follow me wherever I shall lead you, in these vaults.'

In another cavern an awful scene presented itself. It was an Irish *wake* — a dead body lay upon the table, and the relations and friends of the deceased were howling their lamentations over it. An awful stench emanating from the corpse, indicated that the process of decomposition had already commenced. In one corner, several half-crazed, drunken, naked wretches were fighting with the ferocity of tigers, and the mourners soon joining in the fray, a general combat ensued, in the fury of which, the table on which lay the body was overturned, and the corpse was crushed beneath the feet of the combatants.

Leaving this appalling scene, the boy and the stranger passed on, until they stood before a cave which was literally crammed with human beings. Men and women, boys and girls, young children, negroes, and *hogs* were laying indiscriminately upon the ground, in a compact mass. Some were cursing each other with fierce oaths; and horrible to relate! negroes were lying with young white girls, and several, unmindful of the presence of others, were perpetrating the most dreadful enormities. These beings were vile and loathsome in appearance, beyond all human conception; every one of them was a mass of rags, filth, disease, and corruption. As the stranger surveyed the loathsome group, he said to his guide, with a refinement of speech he had not before assumed —

'Had any one, two hours ago, assured me that such a place as this, containing such horrible inmates, existed in the very heart of the city, I would have given him the lie direct! But I see it for myself, and am forced to believe it.'

'These wretches,' said the boy — 'are many of them related to each other. There are husbands and wives there; mothers and children; brothers and sisters. Yet they all herd together, you see, without regard to nature or decency. Why the crime of *incest* is as common among them as dirt! I have known a mother and her son — a father and his daughter — a brother and sister — to be guilty of criminal intimacy! Those wretched children are many of them the offspring of such unnatural and beastly connections. In my opinion, those hogs have as good a claim to humanity, as those brutes in human form!'

'And how came those hogs to form part of the inhabitants of this infernal place?' asked the stranger.

'You must know,' replied the boy,'that these vaults communicate with the common street *sewers* of the city; well, those animals get into the sewers, to devour the vegetable matter, filth and offal that accumulate there; and, being unable to get out, they eventually find their way to these vaults. Here they are killed and eaten by the starving wretches. And would you believe it? — these people derive almost all their food from these sewers. They take out the decayed vegetables and other filth, which they actually eat; and the floating sticks and timber serve them for fuel. You remember the man we saw devouring the dead animal; well, he took that carcase from the sewer.'

'And what effect does such loathsome diet produce upon them?' asked the other.

'Oh,' was the reply — 'it makes them insane in a short time; eventually they lose the faculty of speech, and howl like wild animals. Their bodies become diseased, their limbs rot, and finally they putrify and die.'

'And how do they dispose of the dead bodies?' asked the stranger.

'*They throw them into the sewer,*' answered the boy, with indifference. His listener shuddered.

'Come,' said the young guide — 'you have only seen the wretched portion of the Dark Vaults. You are sick of such miseries, and well you may be — but we will now pay a visit to a quarter where there are no sickening sights. We will go to the *Infernal Regions!*'

Saying this, he led the way thro' a long, narrow passage, which was partially illumined by a bright light at the further end. As they advanced loud bursts of laughter greeted their ears; and finally they emerged into a large cavern, brilliantly illuminated by a multitude of candles, and furnished with a huge round table. Seated around this were about twenty men, whose appearance denoted them to be the most desperate and villainous characters which can infest a city. Not any of them were positively ragged or dirty; on the contrary, some of them were dressed richly and expensively; but there was no mistaking their true characters, for villain was written in their faces as plainly as though the word was branded on their faces with a hot iron.

Seated upon a stool in the centre of the table was a man of frightful appearance: his long, tangled hair hung over two eyes that gleamed with savage ferocity; his face was the most awful that can be imagined — long, lean, cadaverous and livid, it resembled that of a corpse. No stranger could view it without a shudder; it caused the spectator to recoil with horror. His form was tall and bony, and he was gifted with prodigious strength. This man, on account of his corpse-like appearance was known as 'the Dead Man.' He never went by any other title; and his real name was unknown.

The stupendous villainy and depravity of this man's character will appear hereafter. Upon the occasion of his first introduction in this narrative, he was acting as president of the carousals; he was the first one to notice the entrance of the boy and the stranger; and addressing the former, he said —

'How now, *Kinchen* — who have you brought with you? Is the cove *cross* or *square* — and what does he want in our *ken*?'

'He is a *cross cove*,' answered the boy — 'he is just from *quay*; and wishes to make the acquaintance of the knights of the Round Table.'

'That being the case,' rejoined the Dead Man, 'he is welcome, provided he has the blunt to pay for the *lush* all round.'

The stranger, understanding the import of these words, threw upon the table a handful of money; this generosity instantly raised him high in the estimation of all present. He was provided with a seat at the table, and a bumper of brandy was handed him, which he merely tasted, without drinking.

The boy seated himself at the side of the stranger, and the Dead Man, addressing a person by the name of the 'Doctor,' requested him to resume the narration of his story, in which he had been interrupted by the two newcomers.

The 'Doctor,' a large, dark man, very showily dressed, complied, and spoke as follows: —

'As I was saying, gentlemen, I had become awfully reduced — not a cent in my possession, not a friend in the world, and clothed in rags. One night, half-crazed with hunger, I stationed myself at the Park, having armed myself with a paving stone, determined to rob the first person that came along, even if I should be obliged to dash out his brains. — After a while, a young gentleman approached my lurking place; I advanced towards him with my missile raised, and he drew a sword from his cane, prepared to act on the defensive — but when I mentioned that three days had elapsed since I had taken food, the generous young man, who might easily have overcome me, weak and reduced as I was — took from his pocket a fifty dollar bill, and gave it to me. This generous gift set me on my legs again, and now here am I, a Knight of the Round Table, with a pocket full of rocks, and good prospects in anticipation. Now, the only wish of my heart is to do that generous benefactor of mine a service; and if ever I can do a good action to him, to prove my gratitude, I shall be a happy fellow indeed.'

'Posh!' said the Dead Man, contemptuously — 'don't talk to

me of gratitude — if a man does *me* a service I hate him for it ever afterwards. I never rest till I repay him by some act of treachery or vengeance.'

As the hideous man gave utterance to this abominable sentiment, several females entered the apartment, one of whom led by the hand a small boy of five years of age. This woman was the wife of the Dead Man, and the child was his son.

The little fellow scrambled upon the table, and his father took him upon his knee, saying to the company —

'Pals, you know the blessed Bible tells us to 'train up a child in the way he should go;' very good — now you will see how well I have obeyed the command with this little *kid*. Attend to your catechism, my son. What is your name?'

'Jack the Prig,' answered the boy without hesitation.

'Who gave you that name?'

'The Jolly Knights of the Round Table.'

'Who made you?' asked the father.

'His Majesty, old Beelzebub!' said the child.

'For what purpose did he make you?'

'To be a bold thief all my life, and die like a man upon the gallows!'

Immense applause followed this answer.

'What is the whole duty of man?'

'To drink, lie, rob, and murder when necessary.'

'What do you think of the Bible?'

'It's all a cursed humbug!'

'What do you think of me — now speak up like a man!'

'You're the d — — dest scoundrel that ever went unhung,' replied the boy, looking up in his father's face and smiling.

The roar of laughter that followed his answer was perfectly

deafening, and was heartily joined in by the Dead Man himself, who had taught the child the very words — and those words were true as gospel. The Dead Man knew he was a villain, and gloried in the title. He gave the boy a glass of brandy to drink, as a reward for his cleverness; and further encouraged him by prophesying that he would one day become a great thief.

Room was now made at the table for the women, several of whom were young and good-looking. They were all depraved creatures, being common prostitutes, or very little better; and they drank, swore, and boasted of their exploits in thieving and other villainy, with as much gusto as their male companions. After an hour of so spent in riotous debauchery, the company, wearied with their excesses, broke up, and most of them went to their sleeping places; the Dead Man, the boy and the stranger, together with a man named Fred, remained at the table; and the former, addressing the stranger, said to him —

'And so, young man, you have just come out of *quod*, hey? Well, as you look rather hard up, and most likely haven't a great deal of blunt on hand, suppose I put you in the way of a little profitable business — eh?'

The stranger nodded approvingly.

'Well, then,' continued the Dead Man — 'you must know that Fred Archer here and myself *spotted* a very pretty *crib* on Broadway, and we have determined to *crack* it. The house is occupied by a young gentleman named Sydney, and his wife — they have been married but a short time. We shall have no difficulty in getting into the crib, for Mr. Sydney's butler, a fellow named Davis, is bribed by me to admit us into the house, at a given signal. What say you — will you join us?'

'Yes — and devilish glad of the chance,' replied the stranger, gazing at Fred Archer with much interest. Fred was a good looking young man, genteelly dressed, but with a dissipated, rakish air.

'Very well — that matter is settled,' said the Dead Man. 'Three of us will be enough to do the job, and therefore we shan't want your assistance, *Kinchen*,' he added, addressing the boy. 'It must now be about six o'clock in the morning — we will meet here to-night at eleven precisely. Do not fail, for money is to be made in this affair.'

The stranger promised to be punctual at the appointed hour; and bidding him good night (for it was always night in that place), Fred and the Dead Man retired, leaving the *Kinchen* and the stranger alone together.

'Well,' said the *Kinchen* — 'so it seems that you have got into business already. Well and good — but I must caution you to beware of that Dead Man, for he is treacherous as a rattlesnake. He will betray you, if anything is to be gained by it — and even when no advantage could be gained, he will play the traitor out of sheer malice. He is well aware that I, knowing his real character, would not join him in the business, and therefore he affected to think that my assistance was unnecessary.'

'I will look out for him,' rejoined the stranger — and then added, 'I will now thank you to conduct me out of this place, as I have matters to attend to elsewhere.'

The *Kinchen* complied, and in ten minutes they emerged into the street above, by the same way they had entered.

Here they parted, the stranger having first presented the boy with a liberal remuneration for his services as guide, and made an appointment to meet him on a future occasion.

CHAPTER VII

*The false wife, and the dishonest servant — scene in the Police
Court — capture of the Burglars, and threat of vengeance.*

Mr. Francis Sydney and his lady were seated at dinner, in the
sumptuously furnished dining parlor of their elegant Broadway
mansion. The gentleman looked somewhat pale and ill at ease,
but the lady had never looked more superbly beautiful.

The table was waited upon by Davis, the butler, a respectable looking man of middle age, and Mr. Sydney, from time to
time, glanced furtively from his wife to this man, with a very
peculiar expression of countenance.

'My love,' said Mrs. Sydney, after a pause of several minutes
— 'I have a little favor to ask.'

'You have but to name it, Julia, to ensure it being granted,'
was the reply.

'It is this,' said the lady; — 'our present footman is a stupid
Irishman, clumsy and awkward; and I really wish him to be discharged. And, my dear, I should be delighted to have the place
filled by my father's black footman, who is called Nero. He is civil
and attentive, and has been in my father's family many years. Let
us receive him into our household.'

'Well Julia,' said the husband, 'I will consider on the subject. I
should not like to part with our present footman, Dennis, without
some reluctance — for though uncouth in his manners, he is an
honest fellow, and has served me faithfully for many years. *Honest* servants are exceedingly scarce now-a-days.'

As he uttered these last words, Davis, the butler, cast a sudden and suspicious look upon his master, who appeared to be
busily engaged with the contents of his plate, but who in reality
was steadfastly regarding him from the corner of his eyes.

As soon as dinner was over, the lady retired to her *boudoir;*
Davis removed the cloth and Mr. Sydney was left alone. After
taking two or three turns up and down the room, he paused be-

fore the fireplace and soliloquized thus:

'Curses on my unhappy situation! My wife is an adulteress, and my servants in league with villains to rob me! These two letters confirm the first — and my last night's adventure in the Dark Vaults convinced me of the second. And then the woman just now had the damnable effrontery to request me to take her rascally paramour into my service, in place of my faithful Dennis! She wishes to carry on her amours under my very nose! And that scoundrel Davis — how demure, how innocently he looks — and yet how suspiciously he glanced at me, when I emphasized *honest* servants! He is a cursed villain, and yet not one-tenth part so guilty as this woman, whom I espoused in honorable marriage, supposing her to be pure and untainted and yet who was, previous to our marriage, defiled by co-habitation with a vile negro — and now *after* our marriage, is still desirous of continuing her beastly intrigues. Davis is nothing but a low-born menial, without education or position, but Julia is by birth a lady, the daughter of a man of reputation and honor, moving in a brilliant sphere, possessing education and talent, admired as much for her beauty as for her accomplishments and wit — and for her to surrender her person to the lewd embraces of *any man* — much more a negro menial — is horrible! And then to allow herself to be led to the altar, enhanced her guilt tenfold; but what caps the climax of her crimes, is this last movement of hers, to continue her adulterous intercourse! Heavens! — what a devil in the form of a lovely woman! But patience, patience! I must set about my plan of vengeance with patience.'

The reader of course need not be told, that the stranger of the Dark Vaults, and Frank Sydney, were one and the same person. The adventure had furnished him with the evidences of his wife's criminality and his servant's dishonesty and perfidy.

That same afternoon, the young gentleman sallied forth from his mansion, and took his way to the police office. On his way he mused thus:

'By capturing these two villains, the Dead Man and Fred Archer, I shall render an important service to the community. It is evident that the first of these men is a most diabolical wretch, capable of any crime; and the other, I am convinced, is the same Frederick Archer who is the husband of the unfortunate girl with whom I passed the night not long since, at which time she related to me her whole history. He must be a most infernal scoundrel to make his wife prostitute herself for his support; and he is a *burglar* too, it seems. Society will be benefited by the imprisonment of two such wretches — and this very night shall they both lodge in the Tombs.'

When Frank arrived at the police office, he found a large crowd assembled; a young thief had just been brought in, charged with having abstracted a gentleman's pocket-book from his coat pocket, in Chatham Street. What was Frank's surprise at recognizing in the prisoner, the same boy who had been his companion in the Dark Vaults, on the proceeding night! The lad did not know Frank, for there was no similarity between the ragged, vagabond looking fellow of the night before, and the elegantly dressed young gentleman who now surveyed him with pity and interest depicted in his handsome countenance.

It was a clear case — the young offender was seen in the act, and the pocket-book was found in his possession. The magistrate was about to make out his commitment, when Frank stepped forward, and required what amount of bail would be taken on the premises?

'I shall require surety to the amount of five hundred dollars, as the theft amounts to grand larceny,' replied the magistrate.

'I will bail him, then,' said Frank.

'Very well, Mr. Sydney,' observed the magistrate, who knew the young gentleman perfectly well, and highly respected him.

'You will wait here in the office for me, until I have transacted some business, and then accompany me to my residence,' said Frank — 'I feel interested in you, and, if you are worthy of my confidence hereafter, your future welfare shall be promoted by me.'

Frank had a long private interview with the magistrate. After having made arrangements for the capture of the two burglars, the young man urged the police functionary to take immediate measures for the breaking up of the band of desperate villains who lurked in the Dark Vaults, and the relief of the miserable wretches who found a loathsome refuge in that terrible place. The magistrate listened with attention and then said —

'I have long been aware of the existence of the secret, subterranean Vaults of which you allude, and so have the officers of the police; yet the fact is known to very, very few of the citizens generally. Now you propose that an efficient and armed force of the police and watch, make a sudden descent into the den, with the view of capturing the villains who inhabit it. Ridiculous! — why, sir, the thing is impossible: they have a mysterious passage, unknown to any but themselves, by which they can escape and defy pursuit. The thing has been attempted twenty times, and as often failed. So much for the *villains* of the den; — now in regard to the wretched beings whom you have described, if we took them from that hole, what in the world should we do with them? Put them in the prisons and almshouse, you say. That would soon breed contagion throughout the establishments where they might be placed, and thus many lives would be sacrificed thro' a misdirected philanthropy. No, no — believe me, Mr. Sydney, that those who take up their abode in the Vaults, and become diseased, and rot, and die there, had much better be suffered to remain there, far removed from the community, than to come into contact with that community, and impart their disease and pollution to those who are now healthy and pure. Those vaults may be regarded as the moral sewers of the city — the scum and filth of our vast population accumulate in them. With reference to the desperadoes who congregate there, their living is made by robbery and outrage throughout the city; and all, sooner or later, are liable to be arrested and imprisoned for their offences.'

'I admit the force of your reasoning,' said Frank — 'yet I cannot but deeply deplore the existence of such a den of horrors.'

'A den of horrors indeed!' rejoined the magistrate. 'Why, sir, there are at this moment no less than six murderers in the Vaults — one of whom escaped from his cell the night previous to the day on which he was to be hung. The gallows was erected in the prison yard — but when the sheriff went to bring the convict forth to pay the penalty of his crime, his cell was empty; and upon the wall was written with charcoal, — *'Seek me in the Dark Vaults!'* The police authorities once blocked up every known avenue to the caverns, with the design of starving out the inmates; but they might have waited till doomsday for the accomplishment of that object, as the secret outlet which I have mentioned enabled the villains to procure stores of provisions, and to pass in and out at pleasure. I am glad that your scheme, Mr. Sydney, will tonight place in the grip of the law, two of these miscreants, one of whom, the Dead Man, has long been known as the blackest villain that ever breathed. He is a fugitive from justice, having a year ago escaped from the State Prison, where he had been sentenced for life, for an atrocious murder; he had been reprieved from the gallows, thro' the mistaken clemency of the Executive. He will now be returned to his old quarters, to fulfil his original sentence, and pass the remainder of his accursed life in imprisonment and exclusion from the world, in which he is not fit to dwell.'

Frank now took leave of the magistrate, and, accompanied by the young pickpocket, returned to his own residence. It was now about five o'clock, and growing quite dark; a drizzly rain was falling intermingled with snow. Frank conducted the boy to his library, and having carefully closed and locked the door, said to him —

'Kinchen, don't you know me?'

The boy started, and gazed earnestly at him for a few moments, and then shook his head.

'Wait here a short time, and I will return,' said Frank, and he stepped into a closet adjoining the library, and shut the door.

Ten minutes elapsed; the closet door opened, and a ragged, dirty looking individual entered the library. The boy jumped to his feet in astonishment, and exclaimed —

'Why, old fellow, how the devil came *you* here?'

'Hush,' said Frank — 'I am the man who accompanied you thro' the Vaults last night, and I am also the gentleman who bailed you to-day. Now listen; you can do me a service. You know that the Dead Man, Fred Archer and myself are to enter this house to-night; the two burglars little think that I am the master of the house. It is my intention to entrap those two villains. Take this pistol; conceal yourself in that closet, and remain quiet until you hear the noise of a struggle; then rush to the scene of the conflict, and aid me and the officers in capturing the two miscreants. Rather than either of them should escape, shoot him thro' the head. I am inclined to think that you will prove faithful to me; be honest, and in me you have secured a friend. But I must enlist another person in our cause.'

He rang a bell, and Dennis, the Irish footman, made his appearance. This individual was not surprised to see his master arrayed in that strange garb, for he had often assisted him in similar disguises. Dennis was a large, raw-looking Hibernian, yet possessing an honest open countenance. — Frank explained to him in a few words the state of the case, and the nature of the service required of him; and honest Dennis was delighted with the opportunity of displaying his personal prowess, and fidelity to his master.

'Och, be the powers!' he exclaimed — 'it's nather a sword nor a pistol I want at all, but only a nate little bit of shillalab in my fist, to bate the thieves of the worruld, and scatter them like the praste scatters the divil wid holy water.'

'Very well,' said Frank — 'now, *Kinchen*, you will take your station in the closet, for fear you should be seen by the servants, and you, Dennis, will bring him up some refreshments, and then attend to your ordinary duties as usual. Say not a word to anybody in regard to this affair, and give the other servants to understand that I have gone out, and will not return until tomorrow morning. I shall now leave the house, and at about midnight you may expect me, accompanied by the burglars.'

Saying this, Frank quitted the mansion by a private staircase. Turning into Canal street, he walked towards the Bowery, and not far from where that broad thoroughfare joins Chatham street, he ascended the steps of a dwelling-house, and knocked gently at the door; it was soon opened by the young courtezan with whom Frank had passed the night at the commencement of this tale. She did not recognize the visitor in his altered garb, until he had whispered a few words in her ear, and then uttering an exclamation of pleasure, she requested him to follow her up-stairs.

Frank complied, and after seating himself in the well-remembered chamber, related to the young woman, as briefly as possible, the circumstances under which he had met her husband, Fred Archer, and the share he was to take in the burglary. He concluded by saying —

'I am sure, Mrs. Archer, that you will rejoice in the prospect of getting rid of such a husband. Once convicted and sent to the State Prison, he has no further claim upon you. You will be as effectually separated from him as though you were divorced.'

'I shall be most happy,' said Mrs. Archer — 'to escape from the tyrannical power of that bad man. He has used me brutally of late, and I have often suffered for the common necessaries of life. Oh, how gladly would I abandon the dreadful trade of prostitu-tion and live a life of virtue!'

'And so you shall, by Heavens!' cried Frank, in the warmth of his generous nature. 'Take courage, madam, and after the af-fairs of tonight are settled, your welfare shall be my special care. I will endeavor to procure you a comfortable home in some re-spectable family, where — '

At this moment the street door was opened, and some one was heard ascending the stairs.

'It is my husband!' whispered Mrs. Archer, and pointing to the bed, she requested Frank to conceal himself behind the cur-tains; he did so, and in a moment more, Fred Archer entered the room, and threw himself into a chair.

'Well, by G — — !' he exclaimed — 'it seems impossible for a man to make a living these times! Here I am, without a cursed cent in my pocket. Maria, what money have you in the house?'

'I have no money, Frederick,' replied his wife.

'No money — you lie, cursed strumpet! What do you do with the gains of your prostitution?'

'As God is my witness,' replied the wretched woman, bursting into tears — 'I have not received a cent for the past week; I have even suffered for food; and the lady threatens to turn me out of doors this very night, if the rent is not paid. I know not what to do.'

'Do! — why, d — — n you, do as other w — — s do; go and parade Broadway, until you pick up a flat — ha, ha, ha!' and the ruffian laughed brutally. After a pause, he added —

'Well, I've got an appointment tonight, at eleven o'clock; a little job is to be done, that will fill my pocket with shiners. But don't you expect to get a farthing of the money — no, d — — n you, you must earn your living as other prostitutes earn it. Good bye — I'm off.'

He departed, and Frank emerged from his hiding place. 'What a beastly scoundrel that fellow is!' he thought, as he gazed with pity at the weeping and wretched wife. He was about to address her with some words of comfort, when a loud knocking was heard on the chamber door. Mrs. Archer started, and whispered to Frank that it was the landlady, come to demand her rent — she then in a louder tone, requested the person to walk in.

A stout, vulgar looking woman entered the room and having violently shut the door and placed her back to it, said —

'I've come, Missus, or Miss, or whatever you are, to see if so be you can pay me my rent, as has now been due better nor four weeks, and you can't deny it, either.'

'I am sorry to say, madam,' replied Mrs. Archer,'that I am still unable to pay you. My husband has left me no money, and — '

'Then you will please to bundle out of this house as soon as possible,' retorted the woman, fiercely. 'What am I to let my furnished rooms to a lazy, good-for-nothing hussy like you, as is too proud to work and too good to go out and look for company in the streets, and can't pay me, an honest, hard-working woman, her rent! Am I to put up with — '

'Silence, woman!' interrupted Frank — 'do not abuse this unfortunate female in this manner! Have you no sympathy — no pity?'

'And who are *you*, sir?' demanded the virago, dreadfully enraged — 'how dare *you* interfere, you dirty, ragged, vagabond? Come, tramp out of this, both of you, this very instant, or I shall call in them as will make you!'

Frank made no reply, but very composedly drew from his pocket a handful of silver and gold; at the sight of the money, the landlady's eyes and mouth opened in astonishment — and her manner, from being most insufferably insolent, changed to the most abject servility.

'Oh, sir,' she said, simpering and curtsying — 'I am sure I always had the greatest respect for Mrs. Archer, and I hope that neither you nor her will think hard of me for what I said — I only meant — '

'That will do,' cried Frank, contemptuously — and having inquired the amount due, paid her, and then desired her to withdraw, which she did, with many servile apologies for her insolent rudeness.

The young gentleman then prevailed upon Mrs. Archer to accept of a sum of money sufficient to place her beyond immediate want, and promised to call upon her again in a few days and see what could be done for her future subsistence. She thanked him for his kindness with tears in her eyes; and bidding her farewell, he left the house, and proceeded towards the Five Points.

He had no difficulty in finding the 'forty-foot cave,' the entrance of the Dark Vaults; but, previous to descending, curiosity prompted him to step into the *crib* of Bloody Mike, to see what was going on. He found the place crowded with a motley collection of vagrants, prostitutes, negroes and petty thieves; Ragged Pete was engaged in singing a shocking obscene song, the others joined in the chorus. Clothed in filthy rags, and stupidly drunk, was the man whom Frank had seen the night before so handsomely dressed; Bloody Mike, who had 'peeled' his coat, had since become the possessor of all his other genteel raiment, giving the poor wretch in exchange as much 'blue ruin' as he could drink, and the cast-off garments of a chimney-sweep!

Bloody Mike welcomed Frank with enthusiasm, and introduced him to the company as the 'gintleman that had thrated all hands last night.' At this announcement, the dingy throng gave a loud shout of applause, and crowded about him to shake his hand and assure him how glad they were to see him. These demonstrations of regard were anything but pleasing to our hero, who threw a dollar upon the counter, inviting them all to drink; and, while they were crowding around the bar to receive their liquor, he made his escape from the *crib*, and sought the entrance to the Dark Vaults. Having reached the bottom of the 'forty-foot cave' in safety, he proceeded cautiously along the dark passage which he had before traversed, and passing thro' the first Vault, soon emerged into the cavern of the desperadoes. Here he was met by Fred Archer and the Dead Man, who had been waiting for him.

'Ah, old fellow,' said the latter worthy — 'here you are; it's somewhat before the appointed time, but so much the better. Put it down and drink a bumper of brandy to the success of our enterprise.'

The three seated themselves at the table, and remained over an hour drinking, smoking and conversing. Frank partook very sparingly of the liquor, but the others drank freely. At last the Dead Man arose, and announced that it was time to go. He then began to make his preparations.

Retiring for a short time to an inner cavern, he returned with his arms full of various articles. First, there were three large horse pistols, two of which he gave to his companions, retaining one for himself; then he produced three cloaks to be worn by them, the better to conceal any booty which they might carry off. There was also a dark lantern, and various implements used by burglars. The Dead Man then proceeded to adjust a mask over his hideous face, which so completely disguised him, that not one of his most intimate acquaintances would have known him. The mask was formed of certain flexible materials, and being colored with singular truthfulness to nature, bore a most wonderful resemblance to a human face. The Dead Man, who, without it, carried in his countenance the loathsome appearance of a putrefying corpse, with it was transformed into a person of comely looks. All the preparations being now complete, the party took up their line of march, under the directions of the Dead Man. To Frank's surprise, that worthy did not lead the way out of the cavern by means of the 'forty-foot cave,' but proceeded in a different course, along a passage, dark and damp, its obscurity but partially dispelled by the dim rays of the dark lantern, which was carried by the leader. After traversing this passage for a considerable distance, the Dead Man suddenly paused, and said to Frank —

'You are not acquainted with the Secret Outlet to these Vaults — and as you are not yet a Knight of the Round Table, I dare not trust you, a stranger, with the knowledge of it, until you join us, and prove yourself to be trustworthy. Therefore, we must blindfold you, until we reach the streets above. This is a precaution we use by every stranger who goes out this way.'

'But why do you not leave the Vaults by the 'forty-foot cave' thro' which I entered?' demanded Frank, who was fearful of some treachery.

'Because,' answered the Dead Man — 'there are police officers in disguise constantly lurking around the entrance of that cave, ready to arrest the first suspicious character who may come forth. You were not arrested last night, because you were unknown to the police — but I, or Fred here, would be taken in a jiffy.'

'How would they know *you* in the disguise of that mask?' asked Frank.

'They might recognise me by my form — my gait — my air

— my speech — damn it, they would almost know me by my smell! At all events, I prefer not to risk myself, while there is a safe outlet here. But, if you hesitate, you can return the way you came, and we will abandon the undertaking.'

'No,' said Frank — 'I will proceed.'

The Dead Man bound a handkerchief tightly over Frank's eyes, and led him forward some distance; at length he was desired to step up about a foot, which he did, and found himself standing upon what appeared to be a wooden platform. The other two took their places beside him, and then he heard a noise similar to that produced by the turning of an iron crank; at the same time he became sensible that they were slowly ascending. Soon a dull, sluggish sound was heard, like the trickling of muddy water; and a foetid odor entered the nostrils, similar to the loathsome exhalations of a stagnant pool. Up, up they went, until Frank began to think that they must have attained a vast height from the place whence they had started; but at last the noise of the crank ceased, the platform stood still, and the Dead Man, after conversing for a short time in whispers with some person, took hold of Frank's arm, and led him forward thro' what appeared to be an entry. A door was opened, they passed out, and Frank, feeling the keen air, and snow beneath his feet, knew that they were in the open streets of the city. After walking some distance, and turning several corners the bandage was removed from his eyes, and he found himself in Pearl street, the Dead Man walking by his side, and Fred following on behind.

They soon turned into Broadway, and in less than ten minutes had reached the mansion of Mr. Sydney. The streets were silent and deserted for the hour was late; and the Dead Man whispered to his companions —

'We can now enter the house unobserved. In case of surprise, we must not hesitate to *kill*, sooner than be taken. I will now give the signal.'

He gave a low and peculiar whistle, and after the lapse of a few moments, repeated it. Instantly, the hall door was noiselessly opened by a person whom Frank recognized as Davis, the butler.

The Dead Man beckoned the two others to follow him into the hall, which they did, and the door was closed.

Five minutes after they had entered the house two men who had been concealed behind a pile of bricks and rubbish on the opposite side of the street, crossed over, and passing around to the rear of the house, obtained access to the garden thro' the back gate which had been purposely left unfastened for them. These two men were police officers, who had been for some time on the watch for the burglars. They entered the house thro' the kitchen window, and stationed themselves upon the stairs, in readiness to rush to the assistance of Frank, as soon as he should give the appointed signal.

Meantime, the Dead Man had raised the slide of his dark lantern, and by its light he led the way into the back parlor, followed by the others. Davis had not the remotest suspicion that one of the men, whom he supposed to be a burglar, and whose appearance was that of a ruffian, was his master! No — he looked him full in the face without recognizing him in the slightest degree.

The Dead Man, approaching a side-board, poured out a bumper of wine and tossed it off, after which he drew from his pocket a small iron bar, (called by thieves a *jimmy,*) and applying it to a desk, broke it open in an instant. But it contained nothing of value; — and the burglar, addressing the others, said:

'We must disperse ourselves over the house, in order to do anything. I will rummage the first story: you, Fred, will explore the second, and our new friend here can try his luck in the third. As for you, Davis, you must descend into the kitchen, and collect what silver ware and plate you can find. So now to work.'

At this instant Frank threw himself upon the Dead Man, and exclaimed, in a loud voice:

'Yield, villain!'

'Damnation, we are betrayed!' muttered the ruffian, as with a mighty effort he threw Frank from him, and drew his horse pistol; — levelling it at the young man with a deadly aim, he was about to draw the fatal trigger, when Dennis, the Irish footman, who had been concealed beneath a large dining table, sprang nimbly behind him, and felled him to the carpet with a tremendous blow of his thick cudgel, crying:

'Lie there, ye spalpeen, and rest asy.'

Fred Archer and Davis instantly made for the door, with the intention of escaping — but they were seized by the two policemen, who now rushed to the scene of uproar; the butler and burglar, however, struggled desperately, and one of the policemen was stunned by a heavy blow on his head, with the butt of a pistol, dealt by the hand of Archer, who, thus freed from the grasp of his antagonist, dashed thro' the hall and effected his escape from the house. Davis, however, was quickly overpowered by the other officer, who slipped hand-cuffs upon his wrists, and thus secured him.

All these occurrences took place within the space of two minutes; and the *Kinchen*, who had been secreted in the library upstairs, arrived, pistol in hand, at the scene of action, just as the conflict had terminated.

The Dead Man lay motionless upon the carpet, and Frank began to fear that he was killed; but upon approaching and examining him, he discovered that he still breathed, though faintly. The blow from Dennis' cudgel had apparently rendered him insensible, and blood was flowing from a severe but not serious wound in his head.

The policeman who had been stunned was speedily brought to, by proper treatment; — and it was found that he had sustained but a trifling injury. Frank now approached Davis, and regarding him sternly, said —

'So, sir, you have leagued yourself with burglars, it seems. What induced you to act in this treacherous manner?'

'The promise of a liberal reward,' replied the man, sulkily.

'Your reward will now consist of a residence of several years in the State Prison,' observed his master as he walked away from him.

The noise of the conflict had aroused the inmates of the house from their slumbers, and much alarm prevailed among them, particularly the females, whose screams resounded throughout the building. To quiet them, Dennis was despatched as a messenger, with assurances that the robbers were in safe custody, and no cause for alarm existed. On passing the chamber of his mistress, that lady called to him, desiring to know the cause of the uproar; and when she had learned the details of the affair, she expressed her gratification at the result.

Frank ordered refreshments to be brought up, and while the whole party gathered around the table to partake of a substantial collation, he congratulated the two officers on having secured so desperate and dangerous a villain as the Dead Man. The form of that miscreant was still stretched upon the carpet directly behind Frank, who stood at the table; and as he was supposed to be insensible, from the effect of the heavy blow which he had received, no one deemed it necessary to bestow any attention upon him. But while the officers and others were eating and conversing, the *Kinchen* suddenly uttered an exclamation of alarm, and seizing a wine bottle which stood upon the table, dashed it at the head of the Dead Man, who had arisen upon his knees, and held in his hand a sharp, murderous-looking knife, which he was just on the point of plunging into the side of the unsuspecting Frank! The bottle was broken into shivers against the ruffian's head, and ere he could recover himself, he was disarmed and handcuffed by the officers, one of whom tore the mask from his face; and the spectators shrunk in horror at the ghastly and awful appearance of that corpse-like countenance! Turning his glaring eye upon Frank, he said, in tones of deepest hate —

'Sydney, look at me — *me*, the *Dead Man* — dead in heart, dead in pity, dead in everything save *vengeance*! You have won the game; but oh! think not your triumph will be a lasting one. No, by G — — ! there are no prison walls in the universe strong enough to keep me from wreaking upon you a terrible revenge! I will be your evil genius; I swear to follow you thro' life, and cling to you in death; yes — I will torture you in hell! Look for me at midnight, when you deem yourself most secure; I shall be in your chamber. Think of me in the halls of mirth and pleasure, for I shall be at your elbow. In the lonely forest, on the boundless sea, in far distant lands, I shall be ever near you, to tempt, to torture, and to drive you mad! From this hour you are blasted by my eternal curse!'

***

Half an hour afterwards, the Dead Man and Davis the butler were inmates of the 'Egyptian Tombs.'

CHAPTER VIII

*The Subterranean Cellar — Capture and Imprisonment of the
Black — the Outcast Wife — The Villain Husband — the Murder
and Arrest.*

The next day after the occurrence of the events detailed in
the last chapter, Frank Sydney caused to be conveyed to the negro
footman, Nero, the letter which his wife had addressed to him —
which letter it will be recollected, had been stolen from the lady,
in her reticule, by the young thief, who had sold it and another
epistle from the black, to Frank, at the *crib* of Bloody Mike.

The plan adopted by the much injured husband for the punishment of his guilty wife and her negro paramour, will be developed in the course of the present chapter.

The black, upon receiving the letter, imagined that it came
direct from the lady herself; and much rejoiced was he at the contents, resolving that very night to watch for the signal in the
chamber window of the amorous fair one.

Beneath the building in which Frank resided, was a deep
stone cellar, originally designed as a wine vault; it was built in the
most substantial manner, the only entrance being protected by a
massive iron door — the said door having been attached in order
to prevent dishonest or dissolute servants from plundering the
wine. In the course of the day upon which he had sent the letter
to Nero, Frank paid a visit to this cellar, and having examined it
with great care, said to himself — 'This will answer the purpose
admirably.'

He then summoned Dennis and the *Kinchen* — the latter of
whom he retained in his service — and desired them to remove
the few bottles and casks of wine which still remained in the cellar and deposit them elsewhere. — This being done, a quantity of
straw was procured and thrown in one corner, and then the arrangements were complete.

'Now listen,' said Frank, addressing Dennis and the *Kinchen*;
'a certain person has injured me — irretrievably injured me —

and it is my intention to confine him as a prisoner in this cellar. The matter must be kept a profound secret from the world; you must neither of you breathe a syllable in relation to it, to a living soul. My motive for confiding to you the secret, is this: I may at times find it necessary to be absent from home for a day or so, and it will devolve upon you two to supply the prisoner with his food. Be secret — be vigilant, and your faithfulness shall be rewarded.'

Both of his listeners expressed their willingness to serve him in the matter, and Frank dismissed them, with instructions to await his further orders.

Mrs. Sydney, having lost the letter which she had addressed to Nero (never dreaming that it had fallen into the hands of her husband,) that afternoon, while Frank was engaged in the wine cellar, wrote *another letter* to the black, couched in nearly the same language as her former one, and making precisely the same arrangement in reference to an interview with him in her chamber. This letter she gave to her maid, Susan, to convey privately to the black. It so happened that Frank, who had just finished his business in the wine cellar, encountered the girl as she was emerging from the rear of the house; she held her mistress' letter in her hand, and, confused at meeting Mr. Sydney so unexpectedly, thrust it hastily into her bosom. Frank saw the action, and suspecting the truth, forced the letter from her, broke the seal, and hastily glanced over the contents. It instantly occurred to him that, if he permitted this letter to reach its intended destination, the negro would naturally suspect something wrong, from the fact that he had received that morning a precisely similar letter; and thus Frank's plan might be frustrated. On the other hand, it was necessary for Mrs. Sydney to believe that the letter was safely delivered, in order that she might still suppose her husband to be ignorant of her amour with the black. In view of these considerations, Frank put the letter in his pocket, and then turning to the trembling Susan, said to her, sternly —

'Woman, your agency in this damnable intrigue is known to me, and if you would save yourself from ruin, you will do as I command you. Remain concealed in the house for half an hour, and then go to your mistress and tell her that you have delivered the letter to the black; and say to her that he sends word in reply, that *should the signal be given to-night, he will come to her chamber.* And do you, when you hear him knock thrice upon the gate, admit him, and conduct him to your mistress's chamber. Do this, and you are forgiven for the part you have taken in the business; but if you refuse, by the living God you shall die by my hand!'

'Oh, sir,' sobbed the girl, frightened at the threat, 'I will do all you wish me to.'

'Then you have nothing to fear — but remember, I am not to be trifled with.'

Half an hour afterwards, Susan went up to the chamber of her mistress, and said —

'Well, ma'am, I gave the letter to Nero.'

'And did he send any message?' asked the lady.

'Yes, ma'am,' replied the girl, in obedience to the instructions of Frank — 'he said that if the signal is given to-night, he will come to your chamber.'

'Very well, Susan — you are a good girl, and here is a dollar for you,' said the lady, and then added — 'you will be sure to admit him when he knocks?'

'Oh, yes, ma'am,' replied the maid; and thanking her mistress, she withdrew.

Left alone, the guilty, adulterous woman fell into a voluptuous reverie, in which she pictured to herself the delights which she anticipated from her approaching interview with her sable lover. The possibility of her husband's remaining at home that evening, thereby preventing that interview, did not once obtrude itself upon her mind — so regularly had he absented himself from home every night during the preceding two or three weeks; and as he had never returned before midnight, she apprehended no difficulty in getting her paramour out of the house undiscovered by him.

The conduct of this woman will doubtless appear very extraordinary and unaccountable to those who have not studied human nature very deeply; while the eccentricity of her passion, and the singular object of her desires, will excite disgust. But to the shrewd and intelligent observer of the female heart and its many impulses, the preferences of this frail lady are devoid of mystery. They are readily accounted for — pampered with luxury, and surrounded by all the appliances of a voluptuous leisure, a morbid craving for *unusual indulgences* had commingled with her passions — a raging desire, and mad appetite for a *monstrous* or *unnatural* intrigue — and hence her disgraceful *liaison* with the black.

Were we disposed, what astounding disclosures we could make, of beastly amours among the sons and daughters of the aristocracy! We have known many instances of unnatural births, unquestionably produced by unnatural cohabitations! We once visited the private cabinet of an eminent medical practitioner, whose collection comprised over a hundred half-human monstrosities, preserved; — and we were assured that many were the results of the most outrageous crimes conceivable. — But why dwell upon such a subject, so degrading to humanity? We will pursue the loathsome theme no longer.

Evening came, and after supper Mrs. Sydney retired to her chamber. To her surprise, her husband joined her there; but her surprise increased, and her annoyance was extreme, when he announced his intention of remaining with her that evening, at home!

Disguising her real feelings, and affecting a joy which was a stranger to her heart at the moment, she only smiled as if in approval of his determination. But in her heart she was most painfully disappointed.

'At all events,' she said to herself, 'I will not place a light in my window, which was the signal I arranged with Nero — so I am safe, at least.'

What was her astonishment and dismay, when her husband deliberately took the lamp from the table, and placed it in the window!

Amazed and trembling, she sat for some minutes in silence, while Frank, having lighted a cigar, began smoking with the utmost coolness. At length the conscience-stricken lady ventured to say —

'My dear, why do you place the light in the window?'

'Because it is my whim to do so,' replied Frank.

'It is a singular whim,' remarked his wife.

'Not so singular as the whim of a white lady of my acquaintance, who amalgamates with a negro,' said her husband.

'What do you mean?' demanded the guilty woman, ready to faint with terror and apprehension.

'I mean this, woman — that you are a vile adulteress!' exclaimed Frank, now thoroughly enraged — 'I mean that your abominable conduct is known to me — your true character is discovered. Before your marriage you were defiled by that negro footman, Nero — and since our marriage you have sought the opportunity to renew the loathsome intimacy.'

'What proof have you of this?' murmured the wretched woman, ready to die with shame and terror.

'These letters — this one, addressed to you by the black, and this, which you wrote to him this very afternoon; but it did not reach its destination, for I intercepted it. The one which you wrote a few days ago, and which was stolen from you in your reticule, came into my possession in a manner almost providential — that letter I sent to the place this morning, and he, supposing it came from you, will come to-night to keep the appointment. He will observe the signal agreed upon, and will be admitted into the house, and conducted to this chamber, little imagining who is waiting for him. So you see, madam, both you and your *friend* are in my power.'

It is impossible to describe the expression of despair and misery which overspread the countenance of Mrs. Sydney during the utterance of these words. She attempted to speak, but could not articulate a single syllable — and in another moment had fallen insensible upon the carpet.

Frank raised her and placed her upon the bed; he had scarcely done so, when he heard some one stealthily ascending the stairs, and in another moment the door softly opened, and Nero, the African footman, entered.

Great was his astonishment and alarm on beholding the husband of the lady whom he had come to debauch. His first impulse was to retreat from the room and endeavor to make his escape from the house; but his design was frustrated by Frank, who rushed forward and seized him by the throat, exclaiming, in a tone of furious rage —

'Eternal curses on you, black ruffian, how dare you enter this house?'

The African, recovering somewhat his presence of mind, struggled to release himself from the fierce grasp of Frank, and would probably have succeeded, had not the *Kinchen* entered, and, seizing a chair, dealt him a blow with it which knocked him down. He then drew from his pocket a stout cord, and, with Frank's assistance, bound the negro's arms securely with it.

Nero, though a black, was both educated and intelligent; he knew that he was now in the power of the man who had been so foully wronged, and he conceived that there was but one way to extricate himself from the difficulty — namely, by promises and entreaties.

'Mr. Sydney,' said he, in an humble, submissive tone — 'it is evident that you have discovered my intimacy with that lady, by what means I know not. You have just cause to be indignant and enraged; but I throw myself upon your mercy — and consider, sir, the lady made the first advances, and was I so much to blame for acceding to the wishes of such a lovely woman? Now, sir, if you will suffer me to depart, I promise to leave the city of New York forever, and never will I breathe to another ear the secret of my intimacy with your wife.'

'Think not, accursed miscreant, thus to escape my vengeance,' replied Frank. 'That you are less guilty than that adulterous woman who lies there,' he added, pointing to the bed, 'I admit, and her punishment shall be greater than yours, for she shall endure the pangs of infamy and disgrace, while you only suffer the physical inconvenience of a lengthened imprisonment. I cannot suffer you to go at large after this outrage on my honor as a husband and a man. Attempt no further parley — it is useless, for your fate is sealed.'

Frank took from a bureau drawer a brace of pistols, and commanded the negro to follow him, threatening to shoot him through the head if he made the least noise or resistance. — Nero obeyed, trembling with apprehension and dread. Descending the stairs, Frank conducted him to the cellar, and unlocking the massive iron door, bade him enter; the poor wretch began to supplicate for mercy, but his inexorable captor sternly ordered him to hold his peace, and having unbound his arms, forced him into the dark and gloomy vault, closed the door, and locked it. He then gave the key to the *Kinchen*, requesting him to use the utmost vigilance to prevent the escape of the prisoner, and to supply him every day with sufficient food and water.

'You perceive, my boy,' said Frank, 'that I am disposed to place the utmost confidence in your integrity and faithfulness. From the moment I first saw you, I have been impressed with the belief that you possess a good heart, and some principles of honor. Destitution and bad company have led you astray — but I trust that your future conduct will prove your sincere repentance. I will see the gentleman from whom you attempted to take the pocket-book, and I will compromise the matter with him, so that it shall never come to trial. Be honest — be faithful — be true — and in my house you shall ever have a home, and in me you shall ever have a steadfast friend.'

'Oh, sir,' said the *Kinchen*, his eyes filling with tears — 'your kindness and generosity have made me a different being from what I was. I now view my former life with abhorrence, and sooner would I die than return to it. Ah, it is delightful to lead an honest life, to have a comfortable home, and a kind friend like you, sir. My faithful devotion to your interests will prove my gratitude. I should like, sometime, to tell you my history, Mr. Sydney; and when you have heard it, I am sure that you will say that I deserve some pity, as well as blame.'

'I shall be pleased to hear your story,' replied Frank. 'As you are now regularly in my service, you shall be no longer designated as *Kinchen*, [2] for that name is associated with crime. What is your own proper name?'

'Clinton Romaine,' replied the boy.

'Well, Clinton, you shall hereafter be called by that name. To-morrow I will give you an order on my tailor for a new and complete wardrobe. You had better now retire to bed; as for myself,' he added, gloomily — 'I shall probably enjoy but little rest or sleep to-night.'

Clinton bade his patron good night, and retired; Frank ascended to the chamber of his wife, and found that she had recovered from her swoon, though she was still pale from apprehension and shame. Averting her eyes from her husband's gaze, she sat in moody silence; after a pause of several minutes, Frank said —

'Julia, it is not my intention to waste my breath in upbraiding you — neither will I allude to your monstrous conduct further than to state it has determined me to cast you off forever. You are my wife no longer; you will leave this house to-night, and never again cross its threshold. Take with you your maid Susan, your wardrobe, your jewels — in short, all that belongs to you; you must relinquish the name of Sydney — cease to regard me as your husband, and never, never, let me see your face again.'

These words, uttered calmly and solemnly, produced an extraordinary effect upon the lady; so far from subduing or humiliating her, they aroused within her all the pride of her nature, notwithstanding her recent overwhelming shame. A rich color dyed her cheeks, her eyes sparkled, and her bosom heaved, as she arose, and boldly confronting Frank, said, in passionate tones —

'You cast me off forever! — I thank you for those words; they release me from a painful thralldom. Now am I mistress of my own actions — free to indulge to my heart's content in delightful amours! — I will not return to my father's house — no, for you will doubtless proclaim there the story of my shame, and my father would repulse me with loathing; and even if 'twere not so, I prefer liberty to follow my own inclinations, to the restraint of my parent's house.'

'Wretched woman,' exclaimed Franks — 'are you indeed so lost — so depraved?'

'Fool!' returned the frail lady — 'you cannot understand the fiery and insatiate cravings of my passions. I tell you that I consume with desire — but not for enjoyment with such as *you*, but for delicious amours which are *recherche* and unique! Ah, I would give more for one hour with my superb African, than for a year's dalliance with one like you, so ordinary, so excessively commonplace! Now that the mask is torn from my face, reserve is needless. Know then that I have been a wanton since early girlhood. What strange star I was born under, I know not; but my nature is impregnated with desires and longings which you would pronounce absurd, unnatural, and criminal. Be it so: I care not what you or the world may say or think — my cravings must be satisfied at all hazards. As for relinquishing the name of Sydney, I do so with pleasure — that name has no pleasure for me; I never loved you, and at this moment I hate and despise you. Do you ask me wherefore? — Because you had wit enough to detect me in my intrigues. I shall leave your house tonight, and we meet no more. My future career is plainly marked out: I shall become an abandoned and licentious woman, yielding myself up unreservedly to the voluptuous promptings of my ardent soul. I part from you without regret, and without sorrow do I now bid you farewell forever.'

'Stay a moment,' said Frank, as she was about to leave the room — 'I would not have you to be entirely destitute: I will fill you out a check for a sum of money sufficient to keep you from immediate want.'

He wrote out and signed a check for one thousand dollars,

which he gave her, and then left her without saying another word. She received the donation with evident satisfaction, and immediately began to make her preparations for departure. Her maid, Susan, assisted her; and also informed her in what manner Frank had compelled her to assist in entrapping Nero into the house. Susan, herself being unobserved, had seen the African conveyed to the cellar, and locked in; this fact she also communicated to her mistress, who heard it with much pleasure, as she had anticipated that her paramour would meet with a worse fate than mere confinement. — She determined to effect his release, if possible, although she knew that some time must necessarily elapse before she could hope to accomplish that object.

When all was ready, Julia and her maid seated themselves in a hackney coach which had been procured, and were rapidly driven from that princely mansion, of which the guilty woman had so recently been the proud mistress, but from which she was now an outcast forever.

That night, Frank, in the solitude of his chamber, shed many bitter tears. He mourned over the fallen condition of that beautiful woman, whom, had she been worthy, he would have cherished as his wife, but who had proved herself not only undeserving of his affection, but depraved and wicked to an astonishing degree. Until the fatal moment when he was led to suspect her chastity, he had loved her devotedly and sincerely. How cruelly had he been deceived!

And that night, in the solitude and darkness of his cold and gloomy dungeon, Nero, the African, swore a terrible oath of vengeance upon the white man who had shut him up in that subterranean cell.

Within a week after the capture of the Dead Man and David the butler, those two villains were inmates of the State Prison at Sing Sing — the former to fulfil his original sentence of imprisonment for life, and the latter to undergo an imprisonment for five years, for his participation in the attempted robbery of Mr. Sydney.

Fred Archer, on escaping from the officer in the manner

which we have described, made his way to the Dark Vaults, where he remained concealed for several days, not venturing to appear abroad. At the end of a week he began to grow impatient of the restraint, and, conceiving that no great danger would be incurred if he left his place of refuge in the darkness of night, he resolved to do so; moreover, he was destitute of money, and entertained some hope of being able to extort a sum from his unfortunate wife, whom he had driven to prostitution. Accordingly, at about eight o'clock in the evening, he left the Vaults by means of the secret outlet before alluded to and gaining the street, proceeded at a rapid pace towards the Bowery. In the breast of his coat he carried a huge Bowie knife, with which to defend himself in case any attempt should be made to arrest him.

That very day, Frank Sydney, mindful of his promise, had succeeded in obtaining a situation for Mrs. Archer, in the family of an old lady, an aunt of his, who required the attendance of a young woman as a companion and nurse, she being an invalid. In the afternoon, Mrs. Archer received a visit from the boy, Clinton, who came to announce to her the joyful intelligence of a good home having been secured for her; he then placed the following brief note from Frank in her hands: —

'Mrs. Archer, — Madame: I shall this evening call upon you, to confirm the words of my messenger. The unfortunate career which you have followed, is now nearly ended. Extortion and oppression shall triumph no longer. F.S.'

It was about eight o'clock in the evening when Frank knocked at the door of the house in which Mrs. Archer resided, and he was admitted by the mercenary landlady who figured not very creditably upon a former occasion. She immediately recognized the young gentleman, who was dressed in the garments of a laborer; and very civilly informing him that the young lady was at home, requested him to walk upstairs to her room.

Our hero assumed a disguise upon that occasion, for this reason: he did not know but that the house was publicly regarded as a brothel; and he therefore did not wish to hazard his reputation by being recognized either while entering or leaving the place.

He ascended the stairs and knocked gently at the chamber, which was immediately opened by Mrs. Archer, who pressed his hand with all the warmth of a grateful heart, and placed a chair for him near the fire. — Glancing around the room, Frank saw that she had made every arrangement for her departure: band-boxes and trunks were in readiness for removal, and all her little effects were heaped together in one corner. She herself was dressed with considerable elegance and taste; a close fitting dress of rich silk displayed the fine proportions of her symmetrical form to advantage.

'I know not how to thank you, Mr. Sydney,' she said, seating herself — 'for your generous interest in my welfare; but oh! believe me, I am grateful for your kindness.'

Frank assured her that he had derived much satisfaction from what services it had been in his power to render, tending to her benefit. He then related to her all that had occurred on the night of the attempted robbery at his house — how her husband had made his escape, and was probably lurking in the Dark Vaults.

'Then he is still at large,' said Mrs. Archer, shuddering — 'and I am not yet safe.'

'Fear nothing,' said her benefactor — 'he dare not intrude into the respectable and quiet asylum where you are to be placed. No harm can reach you there.'

'God grant it may be so!' fervently ejaculated the young lady; and at that instant some one was heard stealthily ascending the stairs. 'It is Frederick!' she whispered — 'you had better conceal yourself, to avoid useless altercation.' Frank quickly secreted himself behind the curtains of the bed, his former hiding place: and in another moment Fred Archer entered the room, and closed the door with extreme caution. 'Maria,' he said, roughly — 'I must have money from you to-night; the affair which I spoke to you about, when I was last here, failed most infernally. One of the very fellows who were to assist me in the job, proved to be the owner of the house which we were going to plunder. He had a trap prepared for us, and two of my pals were taken, while I escaped just by a miracle. I dare not go abroad in daylight, for fear of being arrested; and I need money — give it to me!'

'Frederick,' said his wife, mildly — 'I have but a few dollars, and you are welcome to them. I leave this house to-night; I am going to live hereafter a life of honesty and virtue.'

'Indeed!' exclaimed Archer, now observing for the first time the preparations for removal — 'and may I ask where the devil you're going?'

'I do not wish to tell you, Frederick,' replied the lady — 'I shall have a good and comfortable home; let that suffice. I will always pray for your welfare; but we must part forever.'

'Ha! is it so?' he hissed from between his clenched teeth, while the hot blood of anger mantled on his face, and his eyes were lit up with the fires of demoniac passions — 'do you think to desert me and cast me off forever?' — As he spoke, his right hand was thrust into the breast of his coat.

'We must part; my resolution is fixed,' she replied firmly. 'Your treatment of me — '

She paused in affright, for her husband had seized her violently by the arm; then he plucked the gleaming Bowie knife from its sheath, and ere she could scream out, the murderous blade was buried in her heart!

From his place of concealment behind the curtains of the bed, Frank saw the atrocious deed perpetrated. The villain had struck the fatal blow ere he could rush forth and stay his murderous arm. The poor victim sank upon the floor, the lifeblood streaming from her heart. — Ere the horrified witness of the crime could seize the murderer, he had fled from the house with a celerity which defied pursuit.

Frank, overwhelmed with grief at the tragic fate of that erring but unfortunate woman, raised her body in his arms and placed it upon a sofa. He then drew from her bosom the reeking blade of the assassin, and as he did so, the warm blood spouted afresh from the gaping wound, staining his hands and garments with gore.

He bent over the corpse, and contemplated the pallid features with profound sorrow. As he thus gazed mournfully at the face of the dead, holding in his hand the blood-stained knife, the chamber door opened, and the landlady entered the room.

On beholding the awful scene — the bleeding, lifeless form stretched upon the sofa, and the young man standing with a gory knife grasped in his hand — the landlady made the house resound with her shrieks and cries of 'Murder!'

The street door below was forced open and men with hurried footsteps ascended the stairs — in a moment more the chamber was filled with watchmen and citizens.

'Seize the murderer!' exclaimed the landlady, pointing towards Frank. Two watchmen instantly grasped him by the arms, and took from him the bloody knife.

Frank turned deadly pale — he was speechless — his tongue refused its office, for then the dreadful conviction forced itself upon him, that he was regarded as the murderer of that young woman. And how could he prove his innocence? The weight of circumstantial evidence against him was tremendous and might produce his conviction and condemnation to an ignominious death!

Several persons present recognized him as the rich and (until then) respectable Mr. Sydney; and then they whispered among themselves, with significant looks, that he was *disguised!* — clad in the mean garb of a common laborer!

Now it happened that among the gentlemen who knew him, were two of the flatterers who supped with him in the first chapter of this narrative — namely, Messrs. Narcissus Nobbs and Solomon Jenks: the former of whom it will be recollected, was enthusiastic in his praises of Frank, upon that occasion, while the latter boisterously professed for him the strongest attachment and friendship. The sincerity of these worthies will be manifested by the following brief conversation which took place between them, in whispers —

'A precious ugly scrape your friend has got himself into,' said Mr. Nobbs.

'*My* friend, indeed!' responded Mr. Jenks, indignantly — 'curse the fellow, he's no friend of mine! I always suspected that he was a d — — d scoundrel at heart!'

'I always *knew* so,' rejoiced Mr. Nobbs.

Oh, hollow-hearted Jenks and false-souled Nobbs! Ye fitly represent the great world, in its adulation of prosperous patrons — its forgetfulness of unfortunate friends!

Frank Sydney was handcuffed, placed in a coach and driven to the Tombs. Here he was immured in the strong cell which had long borne the title of the 'murderer's room.'

Fred Archer was safely concealed in the secret recesses of the Dark Vaults.

FOOTNOTES:

[2] The term *Kinchen,* in the flash language of the thieves, signifies a boy thief.

CHAPTER IX

The Masquerade Ball — the Curtain raised, and the Crimes of the Aristocracy exposed.

Mrs. Lucretia Franklin was a wealthy widow lady, who resided in an elegant mansion in Washington Place. In her younger days she had been a celebrated beauty; and though she was nearly forty at the period at which we write, she still continued to be an exceedingly attractive woman. Her features were handsome and expressive, and she possessed a figure remarkable for its voluptuous fullness.

Mrs. Franklin had two daughters: Josephine and Sophia. The former was eighteen years of age, and the latter sixteen. They were both beautiful girls, but vastly different in their style of beauty; Josephine being a superb brunette, with eyes and hair dark as night, while Sophia was a lovely blonde, with hair like a shower of sunbeams, and eyes of the azure hue of a summer sky.

In many other respects did the two beautiful sisters differ. The figure of Josephine was tall and majestic; her walk and gestures were imperative and commanding. Sophia's form was slight and sylph-like; her every movement was characterized by exquisite modesty and grace, and her voice had all the liquid melody of the Aeolean harp.

In mind and disposition they were as dissimilar as in their personal qualities. Josephine was passionate, fiery and haughty to an eminent degree; Sophia, on the contrary, possessed an angelic placidity of temper, and a sweetness of disposition which, like a fragrant flower, shed its grateful perfume upon the lowly and humble, as upon the wealthy and proud.

Mrs. Franklin's husband had died two years previous to the date of this narrative; he had been an enterprising and successful merchant, and at his death left a large fortune to his wife. Upon that fortune the lady and her two daughters lived in the enjoyment of every fashionable luxury which the metropolis could afford; and they moved in a sphere of society the most aristocratic and select.

Mr. Edgar Franklin, the lady's deceased husband, was a most excellent and exemplary man, a true philanthropist and a sincere Christian. He was scrupulously strict in his moral and religious notions — and resolutely set his face against the least departure from exact propriety, either in matters divine or temporal. The austerity of his opinions and habits was somewhat distasteful to his wife and eldest daughter, both of whom had a decided predilection for gay and fashionable amusements. Previous to his death, they were obliged to conform to his views and wishes; but after that event, they unreservedly participated in all the aristocratic pleasures of the 'upper ten': and their evenings were very frequently devoted to attendance at balls, parties, theatres, the opera, and other entertainments of the gay and wealthy inhabitants of the 'empire city.'

Mr. Franklin's death had occurred in a sudden and rather remarkable manner. He had retired to bed in his usual good health, and in the morning was found dead by the servant who went to call him.

The body was reclining upon one side in a natural position, and there was nothing in its appearance to indicate either a violent or painful death. Disease of the heart was ascribed as the cause of his sudden demise; and his remains were deposited in the family tomb in St. Paul's churchyard. Many were the tears shed at the funeral of that good man; — for his unaffected piety and universal benevolence had endeared him to a large circle of friends.

The grief of the bereaved widow and eldest daughter was manifested by loud lamentations and passionate floods of tears; but the sorrow of the gentle Sophia, though less violent, was none the less heart-felt and sincere.

There was little sympathy between the haughty, imperious Josephine and her mild, unobtrusive sister. Their natures were too dissimilar to admit of it; and yet Sophia loved the other, and at the same time feared her — she was so cold, so distant, so formal, so reserved. Josephine, on her part, viewed her sister as a mere child — not absolutely as an inferior, but as one unfitted by nature and disposition to be her companion and friend. Her treatment of Sophia was therefore marked by an air and tone of patronizing condescension, rather than by a tender, sisterly affection.

Mrs. Franklin loved both her daughters, but her preference manifestly inclined to Josephine, whose tastes were in exact accordance with her own. Sophia had little or no inclination for the excitement and tumult of fashionable pleasures; and therefore she was left much to herself, alone and dependent upon her own resources to beguile her time, while her mother and sister were abroad in the giddy whirl of patrician dissipation.

But upon the Sabbath, no family were more regular in their attendance at church than the Franklins. Punctually every Sunday morning, the mother and daughter would alight from their splendid carriage opposite St. Paul's church, and seating themselves in their luxuriously cushioned and furnished pew, listen to the brilliant eloquence of Dr. Sinclair, with profound attention. Then, when the pealing organ and the swelling anthem filled the vast dome with majestic harmony, the superb voice of Josephine Franklin would soar far above the rolling flood of melody, and her magnificent charms would become the cynosure of all eyes. Few noticed the fair young creature at her side, her golden hair parted simply over her pure brow, and her mild blue eyes cast modestly upon the page of the hymn-book before her.

Having now introduced Mrs. Lucretia Franklin and her two daughters to the reader, we shall proceed at once to bring them forward as active participants in the events of our history.

It was about three o'clock in the afternoon; in a sumptuous chamber of Franklin House (for by that high-sounding title was the residence of the wealthy widow known,) two ladies were engaged in the absorbing mysteries of a singular toilet.

One of these ladies was just issuing from a bath. Although not young, she was very handsome; and her partially denuded form exhibited all the matured fullness of a ripened womanhood. This lady was Mrs. Lucretia Franklin.

Her companion was her daughter Josephine. This beautiful creature was standing behind her mother; she had just drawn on a pair of broadcloth pants, and was in an attitude of graceful and charming perplexity, unaccustomed as she was to that article of dress. The undergarment she wore had slipped down from her shoulders, revealing voluptuous beauties which the envious fashion of ladies' ordinary attire, usually conceals.

Upon the carpet were a pair of elegant French boots and a cap, evidently designed for Miss Josephine. Various articles of decoration and costume were scattered about: upon a dressing-table (whereon stood a superb mirror,) were the usual luxurious trifles which appertain to a fashionable toilet — perfumes, cosmetics, &c. — and in one corner stood a magnificent bed.

This was the chamber of Josephine; that young lady and her mother were arraying themselves for a grand fancy and masquerade ball to be given that night, at the princely mansion of a millionaire.

By listening to their conversation, we shall probably obtain a good insight into their true characters.

'I am thinking, mamma,' said Josephine — 'that I might have selected a better costume for this occasion, than these boys' clothes. I shall secure no admirers.'

'Silly girl,' responded her mother — 'don't you know that the men will all run distracted after a pretty woman in male attire? Besides, such a costume will display your shape so admirably.'

'Ah, that is true,' remarked the beautiful girl, smiling so as to display her brilliant teeth; and removing her feminine garment, she stood before the mirror to admire her own distracting and voluptuous loveliness.

'And this costume of an Oriental Queen — do you think it will become me, my love,' asked her mother.

'Admirably,' replied Josephine — 'it is exactly suitable to your figure. Ah, mamma, your days of conquest are not over yet.'

'And yours have just begun, my dear. Yours is a glorious

destiny, Josephine; beautiful and rich, you can select a husband
from among the handsomest and most desirable young gentlemen in the city. But you must profit by my experience: do not be
in haste to unite yourself in marriage to a man who, when he
becomes your husband, will restrict you in the enjoyment of those
voluptuous pleasures in which you now take such delight. I 'married in haste and repented at leisure;' after my union with your
father, I found him to be a cold formalist and canting religionist,
continually boring me with his lectures on the sins and folly of
'fashionable dissipation,' as he termed the elegant amusements
suitable to our wealth and rank and discoursing upon the pleasures of the domestic circle, and such humbugs. All this was exceedingly irksome to me, accustomed as I was to one unvarying
round of excitement; but your father was as firm as he was puritanical — and obstinately interposed his authority as a husband,
to prevent my indulging in my favorite entertainments. This state
of affairs continued, my dear, until you attained the age of sixteen, when you began to feel a distaste for the insipidity of a domestic life, and longed for a change. — Our positions were then
precisely similar: we both were debarred from the delights of gay
society, for which we so ardently longed. One obstacle, and one
only, lay in our way; that obstacle was your father — my husband. We were both sensible that we never could enjoy ourselves
in our own way, while he lived; his death alone would release us
from the condition of thralldom in which we were placed — but
as his constitution was robust and his health invariably good, the
agreeable prospect of his death was very remote — and we might
have continued all our lives under the despotic rules of his stern
morality, had we not rid ourselves of him by — '

'For Heaven's sake, mother,' said Josephine, hastily — 'don't
allude to that!'

'And why not,' asked the mother, calmly. 'You surely do not
regret the act which removed our inexorable jailer, and opened
to us such flowery avenues of pleasure? Ah, Josephine, the
deed was admirably planned and skillfully executed. No one
suspects — '

'Once more, mother, I entreat you to make no further allusion to that subject; it is disagreeable — painful to me,' interrupted the daughter, impatiently. 'Besides, sometimes the walls have ears.'

'Well, well, child — I will say no more about it. Let us now dress.'

Josephine, having arranged her clustering hair in a style as masculine as possible, proceeded to invest herself in the boyish habiliments which she had provided. First, she drew on over her luscious charms, a delicately embroidered shirt, of snowy whiteness, and then put on a splendid cravat, in the tasteful fold of which glittered a magnificent diamond. A superb Parisian waistcoat of figured satin was then closely laced over her rounded and swelling bust; a jacket of fine broadcloth, decorated with gold naval buttons and a little cap, similarly adorned, completed her costume. The character she was supposed to represent was that of 'the Royal Middy;' and her appearance was singularly captivating in that unique and splendid dress.

Mrs. Franklin, when attired as the Sultana or Oriental Queen, looked truly regal — the rich and glittering Eastern robes well became her voluptuous style of beauty.

The labor of the toilet being completed, the ladies found that it still lacked an hour or so of the time appointed for them to set out; and while they partook of a slight but elegant repast, they amused themselves and beguiled the time by lively and entertaining chat.

'These masquerade balls are delightful affairs; one can enjoy an intrigue with so much safety, beneath the concealing mask,' remarked Mrs. Franklin.

'And yet last Sabbath, you recollect, Dr. Sinclair denounced masquerades as one of Satan's most dangerous devices for the destruction of souls,' said Josephine.

'True — so he did,' assented her mother — 'but he need never know that we attend them.'

'The Doctor is very strict — yet he is very fascinating,' rejoined her daughter; — 'do you know, mamma, that I am desperately enamored of him? I would give the world could I entice him into an intrigue with me.' And as she spoke, her bosom heaved with voluptuous sensations.

'Naughty girl,' said Mrs. Franklin, smiling complacently — 'I cannot blame you for conceiving a passion for our handsome young pastor. To confess the truth, I myself view him with high admiration, not only as a talented preacher, but also as one who would make a most delightful lover.'

'Delightful indeed!' sighed Josephine — 'but then he is so pure, so strict, so truly and devotedly religious, that it would be useless to try to tempt him by any advances; I should only compromise myself thereby.'

'Well, my dear,' remarked Mrs. Franklin, 'there are other handsome young men in the world, besides our pastor — many who would grovel at your feet to enjoy your favors. By the way, who is your favored one at present?'

'Oh, a young fellow to whom I took a fancy the other day,' replied Josephine, 'he is a clerk, or something of the kind — respectable and educated, but poor. I encountered him in the street — liked his fresh, robust appearance — dropped my glove — smiled when he picked it up and handed it to me — encouraged him to walk me home — invited him in, and made him, as well as myself, extremely happy by my kindness. I permitted him to call frequently, but of course I soon grew tired of him — the affair lacked zeal, romance, piquancy; so, this morning when he visited me, I suffered him to take a last kiss, and dismissed him forever, with a twenty-dollar bill and an intimation that we were in future entire strangers. Poor fellow! he shed tears — but I only laughed, and rang the bell for the servant to show him out. Now, mamma, you must be equally communicative with me, and tell me who has the good fortune to be the recipient of your favors at present.'

'My dear Josey,' said Mrs. Franklin — 'I must really decline according you the required information; you will only laugh at my folly.'

'By no means, mamma,' rejoined the young lady — 'we have both at times been strangely eccentric in our tastes, and must not ridicule each other's preferences, however singular.'

'Well then, you must know that my lover is a very pretty youth of about fifteen, who reciprocates my passion with boyish ardor. You will acknowledge that to a woman of my age, such an amour must be delicious and unique. For a few days past I have not seen the youthful Adonis, who, by the bye, bears the very romantic name of Clinton Romaine. I first met him under very unusual and singular circumstances.'

'Pray, how was that, mamma?' asked Josephine.

'You shall hear,' replied her mother. 'The occurrence which I am about to relate took place a month ago. I was awakened one night from a sound sleep by a noise in my chamber, and starting up in affright, I beheld by the light of a lamp which was burning near the bed, a boy in the act of forcing open my escritoire, with a small instrument which caused the noise. I was about to scream for assistance, when the young rogue, perceiving that he was discovered, advanced to the bed, and quieted me by the assurance that he intended me no personal harm, and implored me to suffer him to depart without molestation, promising never to repeat his nocturnal visit. He then placed upon the table my watch, purse, a casket of jewels, which he had secured about his person — and, in answer to my inquiry as to how he had obtained an entrance into my chamber he informed me that he had climbed into the window by means of a ladder which he had found in the garden. While he was speaking, I regarded him attentively, and was struck with his boyish beauty; for the excitement of the adventure and the danger of his position had caused a flush upon his cheeks and a sparkle in his eyes, which captivated me. I found it impossible to resist the voluptuous feelings which began to steal over me — and I smiled tenderly upon the handsome youth; he, merely supposing this smile to be an indication of my having forgiven him, thanked me and was about to depart in the same manner in which he came, when I intimated to him my willingness to extend a much greater kindness than my pardon. In short, his offence was punished only by sweet impris-

onment in my arms; and delighted with his precocity, I blessed
the lucky chance which had so unexpectedly furnished me with a
youthful and handsome lover. Ere daylight he departed; and has
since then frequently visited me, always gaining access to my
chamber by means of the gardener's ladder. To my regret he has
of late discontinued his visits, and I know not what has become of
my youthful gallant. And now my dear, you have heard the
whole story.'

'Very interesting and romantic,' remarked Josephine, and
consulting her gold watch, she announced that the hour was
come for them to go to the masquerade.

The mother and daughter enveloped themselves in ample
cloaks, and descending the stairs, took their seats in the carriage
which was in readiness at the door. A quarter of an hour's drive
brought them to the superb mansion wherein the entertainment
was to be given. Alighting from the carriage, they were conducted by an obsequious attendant to a small ante-room, where
they deposited their cloaks, and adjusted over their faces the sort
of half-mask used on such occasions. A beautiful boy, dressed as
a page, then led the way up a broad marble stair case, and throwing open a door, they were ushered into a scene of such magnificence, that for a moment they stood bewildered and amazed, tho'
perfectly accustomed to all the splendors of fashionable life.

A fine-looking elderly man, without a mask and in plain
clothes, advanced towards the mother and daughter; this gentleman was Mr. Philip Livingston, the host — a bachelor of fifty,
reputed to be worth two millions of dollars. The page who had
waited upon the two ladies, whispered their names in Mr. Livingston's ear; and after the usual compliments, he bowed, and
they mingled with the glittering crowds which thronged the
rooms.

We feel almost inadequate to the task of describing the won-
ders of that gorgeous festival; yet will make the attempt, for
without it, our work would be incomplete.

Livingston House was an edifice of vast dimensions, built in
the sombre but grand Gothic style of architecture. Extensive

apartments communicated with each other by means of massive folding doors, which were now thrown open, and the eye wandered through a long vista of brilliantly lighted rooms, the extent of which seemed increased ten-fold by the multitude of immense mirrors placed on every side. Art, science and taste had combined to produce an effect the most grand and imposing; rare and costly paintings, exquisite statuary, gorgeous gildings, were there, in rich profusion. But the most magnificent feature of Livingston House was its conservatory, which was probably the finest in the country, second only in beauty to the famous conservatory of the Duke of Devonshire in England. A brief description of this gem of Livingston House may prove interesting to the reader.

Leaving the hall through an arch tastefully decorated with flowers and evergreens, the visitor descended a flight of marble steps, and entered the conservatory, which occupied an extensive area of ground, and was entirely roofed with glass. Though the season was winter and the weather intensely cold, a delightful warmth pervaded the place, produced by invisible pipes of heated water. The atmosphere was as mild and genial as a summer's eve; and the illusion was rendered still more complete by a large lamp, suspended high above, and shaped like a full moon; this lamp, being provided with a peculiar kind of glass, shed a mild, subdued lustre around, producing the beautiful effect of a moonlit eve! On every side rare exotics and choice plants exhaled a delicious perfume; tropic fruits grew from the carefully nurtured soil; — orange, pomegranate, citron, &c. Gravelled walks led through rich shrubbery, darkened by overhanging foliage. Mossy paths, of charming intricacy, invited the wanderer to explore their mysterious windings. At every turn a marble statue, life-sized, met the eye: here the sylvan god Pan, with rustic pipes in hand — here the huntress Diana, with drawn bow — here the amorous god Cupid, upon a beautiful pedestal on which was sculptured these lines, said to have been once written by Voltaire under a statue of the heathen divinity:

'Whoe'er thou art, thy master see; —
He was, or is, or is to be.'

In the centre of this miniature Paradise was an artificial cascade, which fell over a large rock into a lake o'er whose glassy waters several swans with snow white plumage were gliding; and on the brink of this crystal expanse, romantic grottos and classic temples formed convenient retreats for the weary dancers from the crowded halls. In short, this magnificent conservatory was furnished with every beautiful rarity which the proprietor's immense wealth could procure, and every classic and graceful adornment which his refined and superior taste could suggest.

Mrs. Franklin and her daughter, who had come on purpose to engage in amorous intrigues, agreed to separate, and accordingly they parted, the mother remaining in the ball room, while Josephine resolved to seek for adventures amid the mysterious shades of the conservatory.

Over five hundred persons had now assembled in the halls appropriated to dancing; and these were arrayed in every variety of fancy and picturesque costume possible to be conceived. The grave Turk, the stately Spanish cavalier, the Italian bandit and the Grecian corsair, mingled together without reserve; — and the fairer portion of creation was represented by fairies, nuns, queens, peasant girls and goddesses.

Mrs. Franklin soon observed that she was followed by a person in the dress of a Savoyard; he was closely masked, and his figure was slight and youthful. Determined to give him an opportunity to address her, the lady strolled to a remote corner of the hall, whither she was followed by the young Savoyard, who after some apparent hesitation, said to her —

'Fair Sultana, pardon my presumption, but methinks I have seen that queenly form before.'

'Ah, that voice!' exclaimed the delighted lady — 'thou art my little lover, Clinton Romaine.'

'It is indeed so,' said the boy, gallantly kissing her hand. The lady surveyed him with wanton eye.

'Naughty truant!' she murmured, drawing him towards her — 'why have you absented yourself from me so long? Do you no longer desire my favors?'

'Dear madam,' replied Clinton — 'I am never so happy as when in your arms; but I have recently entered the service of a good, kind gentleman, who has been my benefactor; and my time is devoted to him.'

'Come with me,' said the lady, 'to a private room, for I wish to converse with you without being observed.'

She led the way to a small anteroom, and having carefully fastened the door to prevent intrusion, clasped the young Savoyard in her arms.

***

Half an hour afterwards, the boy and his aristocratic mistress issued from the ante-room, and parted. Clinton wandered thro' the halls, and descending into the conservatory, entered a temple which stood upon the margin of the little lake, threw himself upon a luxurious ottoman, and abandoned himself to his reflections.

'How ungrateful I am,' he said half aloud — 'to engage in an intrigue with that wicked, licentious woman, while my poor master, Mr. Sydney, is languishing in a prison cell, charged with the dreadful crime of murder! And yet I know he is innocent. I remember carrying his note to Mrs. Archer on the fatal day; I knew not its contents, but I recollect the words which he instructed me to say to her — they were words of friendship, conveying to her an assurance that he had procured for her a situation with his aunt. Surely, after sending such a message, he would not go and murder her! And his aunt can testify that such an arrangement was made, in reference to Mrs. Archer. Oh, that I could obtain admission to the cell of my poor master, to try to comfort him, to whom I owe so much! But alas! the keepers will not admit me; they remember that I was once a thief, and drive me from the prison door with curses.

'I am persuaded in my own mind,' continued Clinton, following the course of his reflections — 'that Fred Archer is the murderer of that woman. I know he secretes himself in the Dark Vaults, but I dare not venture there to seek him, for my agency in the arrest of the Dead Man is known to the 'Knights of the Round Table,' and were I to fall in their power, they would assuredly kill me. Now, what has brought me here to-night? — Not a desire for pleasure; but a faint hope of encountering amid the masked visitors, the villain Archer; for I know that he, as well as the other desperadoes in the Vaults, frequently attends masquerade balls, in disguise, on account of the facilities afforded for robbery and other crimes. Oh that I might meet him here to-night — I would boldly accuse him of the murder, and have him taken into custody, trusting to chance for the proofs of his guilt, and the innocence of my master.'

It may be well here to observe that it was comparatively easy for such characters as Archer and his companions to gain admission to such a masquerade ball as we are describing. In the bustle and confusion of receiving such a large company, they found but little difficulty in slipping in, unnoticed and unsuspected.

'And that horrible Dead Man,' continued Clinton — 'thank God, he is now safe within the strong walls of the State Prison, there to pass the remainder of his earthly existence. How awfully he glared upon me, on the night of his capture! Oh, if he were at large, my life would be in continued danger; I should not sleep at night, for terror; I should tremble lest his corpse-like face should appear at my bedside, and his bony fingers grapple me by the throat! Yes, thank God — he is deprived of the power to injure me; I am safe from his fiend-like malice.'

At this moment, Clinton heard foot-steps approaching, and presently some one said —

'Let us enter this little temple, where we can talk without being overheard.'

The blood rushed swiftly through Clinton's veins, and his heart beat violently; for these words were spoken in the well-known voice of Fred Archer! With great presence of mind he instantly crept beneath the ottoman on which he had been lying; and the next moment two persons entered the temple, and seated themselves directly above him.

'It was, as you say,' remarked Archer to his companion in a low tone — 'a most extraordinary piece of good luck for me that Sydney was taken for that murder which I committed; suspicions are diverted from me, and he will swing for it, that's certain. I'm safe in regard to that business.'

'And yet, I almost regret, Fred,' said the other, speaking in an almost inaudible whisper — 'that Sydney is in the grip of the Philistines; my vengeance upon him would have been more terrible than a thousand deaths by hanging. Well, since it is so, let him swing, and be d — — d to him!'

A long conversation here followed, but the two men spoke in such a low tone, that Clinton could only hear a word now and then. He was, however, certain as to the identity of Fred Archer; and he determined not to lose sight of that ruffian without endeavoring to have him taken into custody.

At length the two men arose and quitted the temple, followed at a safe distance by the boy.

At the bottom of the marble steps which led to the halls above, Fred Archer and his companion paused for a few moments, and conversed in whispers; then the two parted, the former ascending the steps, while the latter turned and advanced slowly towards Clinton.

The boy instantly started in pursuit of Archer; but as he was about to pass the person who had just quitted the company of that villain, his progress was arrested by a strong arm, and a voice whispered in his ear — 'Ah, Kinchen, well met! — come with me!'

Clinton attempted to shake off the stranger's grasp — but he was no match for his adversary, who dragged him back into the little temple before mentioned, and regarded him with a terrible look.

'Who are you — and what means this treatment of me?' demanded the boy, trembling with affright.

The mysterious unknown replied not by words — but

slowly raised the mask from his face. Clinton's blood ran cold with horror; for, by the dim and uncertain light, he beheld the ghastly, awful features of THE DEAD MAN!

'Said I not truly that no prison could hold me? — vain are all stone walls and iron chains, for I can burst them asunder at will! I had hoped to avenge myself on that accursed Sydney, in a terrible appalling manner; but the law has become the avenger — he will die upon the gallows, and I am content. Ha, ha, ha! how he will writhe, and choke while I shall be at liberty, to read the account of his execution in the papers, and gloat over the description of his dying agonies! But I have an account to settle with you, Kinchen; you recollect how you hurled the wine-bottle at my head, as I was about to stab Sydney on the night of my capture — thereby preventing me from securing a speedy and deadly revenge at that time? Now, what punishment do you deserve for that damnable piece of treachery to an old comrade?'

Thus spoke the terrible Dead Man, as he glared menacingly upon the affrighted and trembling Clinton, whose fears deprived him of all power of utterance.

'Sydney will hang like a dog,' continued the hideous miscreant, the words hissing from between his clenched teeth — 'My revenge in that quarter shall be consummated, while you, d — — d young villain that you are, shall — '

'Sydney shall not suffer such a fate, monster!' exclaimed Clinton, his indignation getting the better of his fears, as he looked the villain boldly in the face — 'there are two witnesses, whose testimony can and will prove his innocence.'

'And who may those two witnesses be?' demanded the Dead Man scornfully.

'I am one — and Sydney's aunt, Mrs. Stevens, who resides at No. — — Grand Street, is the other,' replied Clinton.

'And what can you testify to in Sydney's favor?' asked the other in a milder tone.

'I can swear that Mr. Sydney sent me with a note to the lady who was murdered, and desired me to inform her that he had procured a good situation for her with his aunt — thus plainly showing the friendly nature of his feelings and intentions towards her,' replied Clinton.

'And this aunt — what will be the nature of her testimony?' inquired the Dead Man, with assumed indifference.

'Mrs. Stevens can testify that the nephew Mr. Sydney strongly recommended her to receive the poor unfortunate lady into her service — and that arrangements were made to that effect,' answered the boy, unsuspiciously.

The Dead Man seemed for a moment lost in deep thought. 'So it appears that there are two witnesses whose testimony might tend to the acquittal of Sydney,' he thought to himself. 'Those two witnesses must be put out of the way; one of them is now in my power — he is done for; I am acquainted with the name and residence of the other, and by G — — d, she shall be done for, too! — Kinchen,' he said aloud, turning savagely to the boy — 'You must accompany me to the Dark Vaults.'

'Never,' exclaimed Clinton, resolutely — 'rather will I die here. If you attempt to carry me forcibly with you, I will struggle and resist — I will proclaim to the guests in the ball room your dread character and name; the mask will be torn from your face, and you will be dragged back to prison, from whence you escaped.'

For the second time did the Dead Man pause, and reflect profoundly. He thought somewhat in this wise: — 'There is no possible means of egress from this place, except thro' the ball room, which is crowded with guests. True, I might bind and gag the Kinchen, but his struggles would be sure to attract attention — and my discovery and capture would be the result. It is evident, therefore, that I cannot carry him forcibly hence, with safety to myself. Shall I murder him? No, damn it, 'tis hardly worth my while to do that — and somehow or other, these murders almost invariably lead to detection. The devil himself couldn't save my neck if I were to be hauled up on another murder — yet, by hell, I must risk it in reference to that Mrs. Stevens, whose testimony would be apt to save her accursed nephew, Sydney, from the gallows. Yes, I must slit the old lady's windpipe; but the Kinchen — what the devil shall I do to keep him from blabbing, since I can't make up my mind to kill him?'

Suddenly, a horrible thought flashed through the villain's mind.

'Kinchen,' he whispered, with a fiend-like laugh — 'I have thought of a plan by which to silence your tongue forever.'

He drew a huge clasp-knife from his pocket. Ere Clinton could cry out for assistance, the monster grasped him by the throat with his vice-like fingers — the poor boy's tongue protruded from his mouth — and oh, horrible! the incarnate devil, suddenly loosening his hold on the throat, quick as lightning caught hold of the tongue, and forcibly drew it out to its utmost tension — then, with one rapid stroke of his sharp knife, he cut it off, and threw it from him with a howl of savage satisfaction. 'Now, d — — n you,' exclaimed the Dead Man — 'see if you can testify in court!'

The victim sank upon the floor, weltering in his blood, while the barbarian who had perpetrated the monstrous outrage, fled from the conservatory, passed through the ball room and proceeded with rapid strides towards the residence of Mrs. Stevens, Sydney's aunt, in Grand Street, having first put on the mask which he wore to conceal the repulsive aspect of his countenance. He found the house without difficulty, for he remembered the number which poor Clinton had given him; and ascending the steps, he knocked boldly at the door.

The summons was speedily answered by a servant who ushered the Dead Man into a parlor, saying that her mistress would be down directly. In a few moments the door opened and Mrs. Stevens entered the room.

This lady was a widow, somewhat advanced in years, and in affluent circumstances. Her countenance was the index of a benevolent and excellent heart; and in truth she was a most estimable woman.

'Madam,' said the Dead Man — 'I have called upon you at the request of your unfortunate nephew, Francis Sydney.'

'Oh, sir,' exclaimed the old lady, shedding tears — 'how is the poor young man — and how does he bear his cruel and unjust punishment? — for unjust it is, as he is innocent of the dreadful crime imputed to him. Alas! the very day the poor lady was murdered, he called and entreated me to take her into my service, to which I readily consented. Oh, he is innocent, I am sure.'

'Mrs. Stevens,' said the villain — 'I have something of a most important nature to communicate, relative to your nephew; are we certain of no interruption here? — for my intelligence must be delivered in strict privacy.'

'We are alone in this house,' replied the unsuspecting lady. 'The servant who admitted you has gone out on a short errand, and you need fear no interruption.'

'Then, madam, I have to inform you that — '

While uttering these words, the Dead Man advanced towards Mrs. Stevens, who stood in the centre of the apartment; he assumed an air of profound mystery, and she, supposing that he was about to whisper in her ear, inclined her head toward him. That movement was her last on earth; in another instant she was prostrate upon the carpet, her throat encircled by the fingers of the ghastly monster; her countenance became suffused with a dark purple — blood gushed from her mouth, eyes and nostrils — and in a few minutes all was over!

The murderer arose from his appalling work, and his loathsome face assumed, beneath his mask, an expression of demoniac satisfaction.

''Tis done!' he muttered — 'damn the old fool, she thought I was a friend of her accursed nephew's. But I must leave the corpse in such a situation that it may be supposed the old woman committed suicide.'

He tore off the large shawl which the poor lady had worn, and fastened it about her neck; then he hung the body upon the

parlor door, and placed an overturned chair near its feet, to lead
to the supposition that she had stood upon the chair while adjust-
ing the shawl about her neck and then overturned it in giving the
fatal spring. This arrangement the Dead Man effected with the
utmost rapidity and then forcing open a bureau which stood in
the parlor, he took from the drawer various articles of value, jewelry, &c., and a pocket-book containing a considerable sum of
money — forgetting, in his blind stupidity, that the circumstances
of a robbery having taken place, would destroy the impression
that the unfortunate old lady had come to her death voluntarily
by her own hands.

The murderer then fled from the house and that night he and
Archer, in the mysterious depths of the Dark Vaults, celebrated
their bloody exploits by mad orgies, horrid blasphemy, and demoniac laughter.

We left Clinton weltering in his blood upon the floor of the
temple in the conservatory. The poor mangled youth was discovered in that deplorable situation shortly after the perpetration of
the abominable outrage which had deprived him of the blessed
gift of speech forever. He was conveyed to the residence of Dr.
Schultz, a medical gentleman of eminent skill, who stopped the
effusion of blood, and pronounced his eventual recovery certain.
But oh! who can imagine the feelings of the unfortunate boy,
when returning consciousness brought with it the appalling conviction that the faculty of expressing his thoughts in words was
gone forever, and henceforward he was hopelessly dumb! By
great exertion he scrawled upon a piece of paper his name and
residence; a carriage was procured, and he was soon beneath the
roof of his master, Mr. Sydney, under the kind care of honest
Dennis and the benevolent housekeeper.

And Sydney — alas for him! Immured in that awful sepul-
chre of crime, the Tombs — charged with the deed of murder,
and adjudged guilty by public opinion — deserted by those
whom he had regarded as his friends, suffering from confinement
in a noisome cell, and dreading the ignominy of a trial and the
horrors of a public execution — his fair fame blasted forever by
the taint of crime — what wonder that he, so young, so rich, so

gifted with every qualification to enjoy life, should begin to doubt the justice of divine dispensation, and, loathing existence, pray for death to terminate his state of suspense and misery!

But we must not lose sight of Josephine Franklin; her adventures at the masquerade hall were of too amorous and exciting a nature to be passed lightly over, in this mirror of the fashions, follies and crimes of city life. — Our next chapter will duly record the particulars of the fair lady's romantic intrigues on that brilliant and memorable occasion.

CHAPTER X

*The Amours of Josephine — The Spanish Ambassador, and the
Ecclesiastical Lover.*

Josephine, dressed as the 'Royal Middy,' entered the conservatory, and strolled leisurely along a gravelled walk which led to a little grotto composed of rare minerals and shells. Entering this picturesque retreat, she placed herself upon a seat exquisitely sculptured from marble, and listened to the beautiful strains of music which proceeded from the ball room.

While thus abandoning herself to the voluptuous feelings of the moment, she observed that a tall, finely formed person in the costume of a Spanish cavalier, passed the grotto several times, each time gazing at her with evident admiration. He was masked, but Josephine had removed her mask, and her superb countenance was fully revealed. The cavalier had followed her from the ball-room, but she did not perceive him until he passed the grotto.

'I have secured an admirer already,' she said to herself, as a smile of satisfaction parted her rosy lips. 'I must encourage him, and perhaps he may prove to be a desirable conquest.'

The cavalier saw her smile and, encouraged by that token of her complaisance, paused before the grotto, and addressed her in a slightly foreign accent: —

'Fair lady, will you suffer me to repose myself for a while in this fairy-like retreat?'

'I shall play off a little prank upon this stranger,' thought Josephine to herself — 'it will serve to amuse me.' And then she burst into a merry laugh, as she replied —

'I have no objection in the world, sir, to your sharing this grotto with me; but really, you make a great mistake — you suppose me to be a lady; but I'm no more a lady than you are, don't you see that I'm a *boy*?'

'Indeed! — a *boy*!' Exclaimed the stranger, surveying Jose-

phine with great interest. 'By heaven, I took you for a female; and
though you are a boy, I will say that you are an extremely pretty
one.'

He entered into the grotto, and seated himself at her side.
Taking her hand, he said —

'This hand is wonderfully fair and soft for a boy's. Confess,
now — are you not deceiving me?'

'Why should I deceive you?' asked Josephine — 'if my hand
is fair and soft, it is because I have been brought up as a gentleman, and it has never become soiled or hardened by labor.'

'And yet,' rejoined the stranger, passing his hand over the
swelling outlines of her bosom, which no disguise could entirely
conceal — 'there seems to me to be something feminine in these
pretty proportions.'

'You doubtless think so,' replied Josephine, removing his
hand — 'but you greatly err. The fact is, my appearance is naturally very effeminate, and sometimes it is my whim to encourage
the belief that I am a female. I came here to-night, resolved to
produce that impression; and you see with what a successful
result — you yourself imagined me to be a lady dressed in male
attire, but again I assure you that you never were more mistaken
in your life. The fullness of my bosom is accounted for, when I
inform you that my vest is very skillfully *padded*. So now I hope
you will be no longer skeptical in regard to my true sex.'

'I no longer doubt you, my dear boy,' said the stranger, gazing at Josephine with increased admiration. 'Were you a lady, you
would be beautiful, but as a boy you are doubly charming. Be not
surprised when I assure you that you please me ten times — aye,
ten thousand times more, as a boy, than as a woman. By heaven, I
must kiss those ripe lips!'

'Kiss *me*!' responded Josephine, laughing — 'come, sire, this
is too good — you must be joking.'

'No, beautiful boy, I am serious,' exclaimed the stranger, ve-
hemently — 'you may pronounce my passion strange, unac-

countable, and absurd, if you will — but 'tis none the less violent
or sincere. I am a native of Spain, a country whose ardent souls
confine not their affections to the fairest portion of the human
race alone, but — '

'What mean you?' demanded Josephine, in astonishment.
The stranger whispered a few words in her ear, and she drew
back in horror and disgust.

'Nay, hear me,' exclaimed the Spaniard, passionately — 'it is
no low-born or vulgar person who solicits this favor; for know,'
he continued, removing his mask — 'that I am Don Jose Velasquez, ambassador to this country from the court of Spain; and
however high my rank, I kneel at your feet and — '

'Say no more, sir,' said Josephine, interrupting him, and rising as she spoke — 'it is time that you should know that your first
supposition in reference to me was correct. I am a woman. I did
but pretend, in accordance with a suddenly conceived notion, to
deceive you for a while, but that deception has developed an iniquity in the human character, the existence of which I have heard
before, but never fully believed till today. Your unnatural iniquity
inspires me with abhorrence; leave me instantly and attempt not
to follow me, or I shall expose you to the guests, in which case *His
Excellency* Don Jose Velasquez, ambassador to this country from
the court of Spain, would become an object of derision and contempt.'

The Spaniard muttered a threat of vengeance and strode
hastily away. Josephine put on her mask, and leaving the grotto,
was about to return to the ball-room, when a gentleman, plainly
but richly attired in black velvet, and closely masked, thus accosted her in a respectful tone —

'Lady — for your graceful figure and gait betray you, notwithstanding your boyish disguise — suffer me to depart so far
from the formality of fashionable etiquette as to entreat your ac-
ceptance of me as your *chaperon* through this beautiful place.'

This gentleman's speech was distinguished by a voice uncommonly melodious, and an accent peculiarly refined; he was

evidently a person of education and respectable social position. The tones of his voice struck Josephine as being familiar to her; yet she could not divine who he was, and concluded that there only existed an accidental resemblance between his voice and that of some one of her friends. His manner being so frank, and at the same time so gentleman-like and courteous, that she replied without hesitation —

'I thank you, sir — I will avail myself of your kindness.' She took his proffered arm, and they began slowly to promenade the principal avenue of the conservatory, engaged at first in that polite and desultory discourse which might be supposed to arise between a lady and gentleman who meet under such circumstances.

At length, becoming fatigued, they entered a pretty little arbor quite remote from observation, and seated themselves upon a moss-covered trunk. After a few commonplace observations, the gentleman suddenly addressed Josephine in a start of ardent passion.

'Lady,' he exclaimed, taking her hand and pressing it tenderly, 'pardon my rudeness; but I am overcome by feelings which I never before experienced. Although your face is concealed by your mask, I know you are beautiful — the rich luxuriance of your raven hair, and the exquisite proportions of this fair hand, are proofs of the angelic loveliness of your countenance. Am I presumptuous and bold — does my language give you offence? — if so, I will tear myself from your side, though it will rend my heart with anguish to do so. You do not speak — you are offended with me; farewell, then — '

'Stay,' murmured Josephine — 'I am not offended, sire — far from it; you are courteous and gallant, and why should I be displeased?' The gentleman kissed her hand with rapture.

'Oh,' said he, in a low tone — 'I am entranced by your kindness. You will be surprised when I assure you that I am but a novice in the way of love; and yet I most solemnly declare that never before have I pressed woman's hand with passion — never before has my heart beat with the tumult of amorous inclination

— never before have I clasped woman's lovely form as I now clasp yours.' And he encircled the yielding form of Josephine with his arms.

'Why have you been such a novice in the delights of love?' she asked, permitting him to clasp her passionately to his breast.

'Dear lady,' he replied — 'my position in life is one that precludes me in a great measure from the enjoyment of sensual indulgences; and I have heretofore imagined myself impervious to the attacks of Venus; but ah! you have conquered me. My leisure moments have been devoted to study and contemplation; I ventured here to-night to be a spectator of the joys of others, not designing to participate in those joys myself. The graceful voluptuousness of your form, developed by this boyish costume, fired my soul with new and strange sensations, which, so help me heaven! I never experienced before. Ah, I would give half of my existence to be allowed to kiss those luscious lips!'

'You can have your wish at a far less expense,' murmured the lady, her bosom heaving with passionate emotions.

'But first remove that mask,' said the gentleman, enraptured at the success of the first intrigue of his life.

'I have no objection to uncover my countenance, provided you bestow upon me a similar favor,' replied Josephine.

'I am most anxious to preserve my *incognito*,' said the gentleman, in a tone of hesitation. 'My standing and peculiar occupation in life are entirely incompatible with such a festival as this, and my reputation would be dangerously compromised, if not utterly ruined. Nay, then, since you insist upon it, fair creature, I will unmask, trusting to your honor as a lady to keep my secret.'

He uncovered his face, and Josephine was thunderstruck when she recognized in the amorous stranger, no less a personage than Dr. Sinclair, the pious and eloquent rector of St. Paul's.

Yes — that learned and talented divine, who had so often denounced the sins and follies of the fashionable world, and declaimed particularly against the demoralizing influences of mas-

querade balls — that young and handsome preacher, whose exalted reputation for sanctity and holiness had induced the amorous Josephine and her licentious mother to suppose him inacces-
sible to their lustful glances, and far removed from the power of
temptation — that model of purity and virtue was now present at
this scene of profligate dissipation, gazing into the wanton eyes of
a beautiful siren, his face flushed with excitement, and his heart
palpitating with eager desire!

For a few moments Josephine sat overcome by astonishment,
and could not utter a single syllable.

'You seem surprised, dear lady,' said Dr. Sinclair — 'may I
ask if you have ever seen me before?'

'You can read in my countenance an answer to your question,' replied Josephine, taking off her mask.

'Heavens, Miss Franklin!' exclaimed the divine. It was now
his turn to be astonished.

'We meet under extraordinary circumstances,' said Dr. Sinclair after a short and somewhat embarrassing pause. 'Had I
known that you are one who every Sabbath sits under my minis-
tration, no earthly consideration would have induced me to dis-
close myself — not even the certainty of enjoying your favors.
However, you know me now, and 'tis impossible to recall the
past; therefore, beautiful Miss Franklin, do not withhold from the
preacher that kindness which you would have granted to the
private gentleman. — Let us religiously preserve our secret from
the knowledge of the world: when we meet in company, let it be
with the cold formality which exists between persons who are
almost strangers; but now let us revel in the joys of love.'

The superb but profligate Josephine needed no urgent persuasion to induce her to become a guilty participator in a criminal
liaison with the handsome young rector whom she had so long
regarded with the eyes of desire; — *hers* was the conquest, that
unprincipled lady of fashion; and *he* was the victim, that recreant
fallen minister of the gospel.

Humbled and conscience-stricken, Dr. Sinclair left Livingston House and returned to his own luxurious but solitary home; while Josephine was driven in her carriage to Franklin House, the flush of triumph on her cheeks and her proud, guilty heart reeling with exultation.

CHAPTER XI

*The Condemnation to Death — the Burglar's Confession and
Awful Fate in the Iron Coffin.*

The arrest of Frank Sydney for the murder of Maria Archer created an immense excitement throughout the whole community. — His wealth, standing in society, and former respectability caused many to believe him innocent of the dreadful crime imputed to him; but public opinion generally pronounced him guilty. The following article, extracted from a newspaper published at that period, will throw some light upon the views held in reference to the unhappy young man, and show how the circumstances under which he was arrested operated prejudicially to him: —

'ATROCIOUS MURDER. Last night, about nine o'clock, cries of murder were heard proceeding from the house No. — Bowery. The door was forced open by several citizens and watchmen, who, on entering a room on the second story, found the body of a young woman named Maria Archer stretched upon a sofa, her throat cut in a horrible manner, and standing over the corpse a young gentleman named Francis Sydney, holding in his hand a large Bowie knife, covered with blood. The landlady, Mrs. Flint, stated that Maria had that afternoon announced her intention to remove from the house in the evening; at about eight o'clock, Mr. Sydney called, *disguised*, and went up into the room of the deceased; — after a while, she (the landlady), being surprised that Maria did not begin to remove, went up to her room, and on opening the door, saw the young woman lying upon the sofa, her throat cut, and Mr. Sydney standing over her with the knife in his hand. On seeing this she screamed for assistance, and her cries had brought the watchman and citizens into the house, as we have stated.

'Mr. Sydney is a very wealthy young man, and has heretofore been highly respected. There can be no doubt of his guilt. He had probably formed a criminal connection with Mrs. Archer, whose character for chastity did not stand very high; it is supposed that it was in consequence of this intimacy that Mrs. Sydney recently separated from her husband. It is also presumed that a quarrel arose between Sydney and his paramour in consequence of his refusal to supply her with what money she demanded. This belief is predicated upon the following note, in the handwriting of Sydney, which was found upon the person of his murdered victim: —

'Mrs. Archer. — Madam: I shall this evening call upon you to confirm the words of my messenger. The unfortunate career which you have followed, is now nearly ended. Extortion and oppression shall triumph no longer. F.S.'

'This note, it will be perceived, accuses her of extortion and contains a threat, &c. Alarmed at this, the poor young woman determined to leave the house that night — but was prevented by her paramour who barbarously slew her.

'The prisoner, whose appearance and behavior after his arrest proved his guilt, was conveyed to the Tombs, to await his trial for one of the most atrocious murders that has stained our criminal courts for many years.'

Thus it will be seen that poor, innocent Frank was regarded as the murderer.

It is needless for us to enter into the particulars of his trial: suffice it to say, he was convicted of the murder and sentenced to death. The evidence, though entirely circumstantial, was deemed positive against him. Mrs. Flint testifying that he was the only person who had entered the house that evening, and the situation in which she had discovered him, the murderous weapon in his hand, and his clothes stained with blood, admitted not a doubt of his guilt in the minds of the jury, who did not hesitate to bring in their fatal verdict, conscientiously believing it to be a just one.

A few days previous to his trial, the public were astounded by the intelligence that Mrs. Stevens, the prisoner's aunt, had committed suicide by hanging; and her nephew's disgrace and peril were supposed to have been the cause of the rash act. But when it came to be discovered that a robbery had been committed in the house, and it was stated by the servant that a strange man had sought and obtained an interview with the unfortunate old lady that evening, the public opinion took a different turn, and the belief became general that she had been murdered by some unknown miscreant, whose object was to plunder the house. No one suspected that she had been slain to prevent her from giving favorable testimony at the trial of her nephew Francis Sydney.

The diabolical outrage perpetrated upon the boy Clinton at the masquerade ball soon became noised abroad, and gave rise to many surmises, and much indignation; tho' no one as yet imagined that any connection existed between that horrible affair and the brutal murder of Mrs. Stevens.

After his conviction and condemnation to death, Sydney was placed in irons, and treated with but little indulgence by the petty officials who have charge of the Tombs. An application on his behalf was made to the Governor, in the hope of either obtaining a pardon, or a commutation of his sentence to imprisonment, but the executive functionary refused to interfere, and Frank prepared for death.

The day before that fixed upon for his execution, a lady applied for admission to the prisoner's cell, her request was granted, and Frank was astonished by the entrance of Julia, his guilty and discarded wife!

Did she come to entreat his forgiveness for her crime, and to endeavor to administer consolation and comfort to him in this his last extremity?

No, the remorseless and vindictive woman had come to exult over his misfortunes, and triumph over his downfall!

'So, miserable wretch,' she said, in a tone of contempt — 'You are at last placed in a situation in which I can rejoice over your degradation and shame! A convicted, chained murderer, to die to-morrow — ha, ha, ha!' and she laughed with hellish glee.

'Accursed woman,' cried Frank, with indignation — 'why have you come to mock my misery? Have you the heart to rejoice over my awful and undeserved fate?' and the poor young man, folding his arms, wept bitterly, for his noble and manly nature was for the time overcome by the horror of his situation.

'Yes, I have come to gloat upon your misery,' replied the vile, unfeeling woman. 'To-morrow you will die upon the gallows, and your memory will be hated and condemned by those who believe you to be guilty. I am convinced in my own mind that you are innocent of the murder; yet I rejoice none the less in your fate. Your death will free me from all restraint; I can adopt an assumed name, and removing to some distant city, entrap some rich fool into a marriage with me, whose wealth will administer to my extravagance, while I secretly abandon myself to licentious pleasures. Sydney, I never loved you — and when you discovered my intimacy with my dear African, I hated you — oh, how bitterly! When you cast me off, I vowed revenge upon you; but my vengeance will be satisfied to-morrow, when you pay the forfeit of another's crime. And now in the hour of your disgrace and death, I spit upon and despise you!'

'Begone, vile strumpet that you are,' exclaimed Frank, starting to his feet — 'taunt me no more, or you will drive me to commit an actual murder, and send your blackened soul into the presence of your offended Creator!'

'Farewell, forever,' said Julia, in a tone of indifference, and she left her poor, wronged husband to his own bitter reflections. Shortly after her departure, a clergyman entered the cell, and remained with the prisoner until long after midnight, preparing him for the awful change he was to undergo on the morrow.

***

That very night Fred Archer issued from the secret outlet of the Dark Vaults, and bent his steps in the direction of Wall street.

This street is the great focus around which all the most extensive financial operations of the great metropolis are carried on. It is occupied exclusively by banks, brokers' and insurance offices, and establishments of the like character.

It was midnight when Archer turned into Wall street from Broadway. The moon was obscured by clouds, and the street was entirely deserted. He paused before a large, massive building in the neighborhood of the Exchange, and glanced around him in every direction to assure himself that he was unobserved. Seeing no one, he ascended the marble steps, drew from his pocket a huge key, and with it unlocked the door; he entered, and closing the door after him, carefully re-locked it.

'So far all is well,' muttered the burglar, as he ignited a match and lighted a piece of wax candle which he had brought with him. 'It's lucky that I obtained an impression of that lock in wax, and from it made this key, or I might have had the devil's trouble in getting in.'

He advanced along the passageway, and opening a large door covered with green baize, entered a commodious apartment, containing a long table covered with papers, a desk, chairs, and other furniture, suitable to a business office. In one corner stood an immense safe, six feet in height and four in depth; this safe, made of massive plates of iron and protected by a door of prodigious strength, contained the books, valuable papers, and cash belonging to the — — Insurance Company. Archer advanced to the safe, and took from his pocket a piece of paper, on which some words were written; this paper he examined with much attention.

'Here,' said he, 'I have the written directions, furnished me by the locksmith who made the lock attached to the safe, by which I can open it. Curse the fellow, a cool hundred dollars was a round sum of money to give him for this little bit of paper, but without it I never could see the interior of his iron closet, tho' I have an exact model of the key belonging to it, made from an impression in wax, which I bribed the clerk to get for me.'

Pursuing the directions contained in the paper, he touched a small spring concealed in the masonry adjoining the safe, and instantly a slide drew back in a panel of the door, revealing a key-hole. In this he inserted a key, and turned it, but found that he could not unlock it; he therefore had recourse to his paper a second time, which communicated the secret of the only method by which to open the door. Following those directions implicitly, he soon had the satisfaction of turning back the massive bolts which secured the door; a spring now only held it fast, but this was easily turned by means of a small brass knob, and the heavy door swung back upon its gigantic hinges, to the intense delight of the burglar, who anticipated securing a rich booty.

Nor was he likely to be disappointed; for upon examination he found that the safe contained money to a large amount. A small tin cash box was full of bank-notes of various denominations; and in a drawer were several thousands of dollars in gold.

'My fortune is made, by G — — d!' exclaimed the burglar, as he stood within the safe, and began hastily to transfer the treasures to his pockets. The light of his candle, which he held in his hand, shed a faint glow upon the walls and ceiling of the apartment.

'The devil!' muttered Archer — 'my success thus far must not destroy my prudence. If that light were to be seen from these windows, suspicion would be excited and I might be disagreeably interrupted.'

Reaching out his arm, he caught hold of the door of the safe, and pulled it violently towards him so that the light of his candle might not betray him. The immense mass of iron swung heavingly upon its hinges, and closed with a sharp *click*; the spring held it fast, and on the inside of the door there was no means of turning back that spring. Like lightning the awful conviction flashed through the burglar's mind that he was *entombed alive*!

Vain, vain were his efforts to burst forth from his iron coffin; as well might he attempt to move the solid rock! He shrieked aloud for assistance — but no sound could penetrate through those iron walls! He called upon God to pity him in that moment of his awful distress — but that God, whom he had so often blasphemed, now interposed not His power to succor the vile wretch, thus so signally punished.

No friendly crevice admitted one mouthful of air into the safe, and Archer soon began to breathe with difficulty; he became sensible that he must die a terrible death by suffocation. Oh, how he longed for someone to arrive and release him from his dreadful situation, even though the remainder of his days were passed within the gloomy walls of a prison! How he cursed the money, to obtain which he had entered that safe, wherein he was now imprisoned as securely as if buried far down in the bowels of the earth! With the howl of a demon he dashed the banknotes and glittering gold beneath his feet, and trampled on them. Then, sinking down upon the floor of the safe, he abandoned himself to despair.

Already had the air of that small, confined place become fetid and noisome; and the burglar began to pant with agony, while the hot blood swelled his veins almost to bursting. A hundred thousand dollars lay within his grasp — he would have given it all for one breath of fresh air, or one draught of cold water.

As the agonies of his body increased, the horrors of his guilty conscience tortured his soul. The remembrance of the many crimes he had committed arose before him; the spirit of his murdered wife hovered over him, ghastly, pale and bloody. Then he recollected that an innocent man was to be hung on the morrow, for that dreadful deed which *he* had perpetrated; and the thought added to the mental tortures which he was enduring.

A thought struck the dying wretch; it was perhaps in his power to make some atonement for his crimes — he might save an innocent man from an ignominious death. No sooner had that thought suggested itself to his mind, than he acted upon it, for he knew that his moments were few; already he felt the cold hand of death upon him. He took a piece of chalk from his pocket, and with a feeble hand traced the following words upon the iron door of the safe: —

'My last hour is come, and I call on God, in whose awful presence I am shortly to appear, to witness the truth of this dying declaration. I do confess myself to be the murderer of Maria Archer. The young man Sydney is innocent of that crime. God have mercy — '

He could write no more; his brain grew dizzy and his senses

fled. It seemed as if his iron coffin was red-hot, and he writhed in all the agony of a death by fire. Terrible shapes crowded around him, and the spirit of his murdered wife beckoned him to follow her to perdition. A mighty and crushing weight oppressed him; blood gushed from the pores of his skin; his eyes almost leaped from their sockets, and his brain seemed swimming in molten lead. At length Death came, and snapped asunder the chord of his existence; the soul of the murderer was in the presence of its Maker.

***

Morning dawned upon the doomed Sydney, in his prison cell; the glad sunbeams penetrated into that gloomy apartment, shedding a glow of ruddy light upon the white walls. That day at the hour of noon, he was to be led forth to die — he, the noble, generous Sydney, whose heart teemed with the most admirable qualities, and who would not wantonly have injured the lowest creature that crawls upon the Creator's footstool — he to die the death of a malefactor, upon the scaffold!

The day wore heavily on; Frank, composed and resigned, was ready to meet his fate like a man. He had heard the deep voice of the Sheriff, in the hall of the prison, commanding his subordinates to put up the scaffold; he had heard them removing that cumbrous engine of death from an unoccupied cell, and his ear had caught the sound of its being erected in the prison yard. Then he knelt down and prayed.

His hour had come. They came and removed his irons; they clothed him in the fearful livery of the grave. His step was firm and his eye undaunted as he passed into the prison yard, and stood beneath the black and frowning gallows.

The last prayer was said; the last farewell spoken; and many a hard-hearted jailer and cruel official turned aside to conceal the tears which would flow, at the thought that in a few moments that fine young man, so handsome, so talented and so noble to look upon, would be strangling and writhing with the tortures of the murderous rope, and soon after cut down, a ghastly and disfigured corpse.

The Sheriff adjusted the rope, and there was an awful pause; a man was tottering on the verge of eternity!

But oh, blessed pause — 'twas ordained by the Almighty, to snatch that innocent man from the jaws of death! At that critical moment, a confused murmur was heard in the interior of the prison; the Sheriff, who had his hand upon the fatal book, which alone intervened between the condemned and eternity, was stopped from the performance of his deadly office, by a loud shout that rent the air, as a crowd of citizens rushed into the prison yard, exclaiming —

'Hold — stay the execution!'

The Mayor of the city, who was present, exchanged a few hurried words with the foremost of the citizens who had thus interrupted the awful ceremony; and instantly, with the concurrence of the Sheriff, ordered Sydney to be taken from the gallows, and conducted back to his cell, there to await the result of certain investigations, which it was believed would procure his entire exoneration from the crime of which he had been deemed guilty, and his consequent release from imprisonment.

It appeared that an officer connected with the — — Insurance Company, on opening the safe that morning at about half-past eleven o'clock, discovered the dead body of the burglar, the money scattered about, and the writing upon the door. The officer, who was an intelligent and energetic man, instantly comprehended the state of affairs, and hastened with a number of other citizens to the Tombs, in order to save an innocent man from death. Had he arrived a few moments later, it might have been too late; but as it was, he had the satisfaction of rescuing poor Sydney from a dreadful fate, and the credit of saving the State from the disgrace of committing a judicial murder.

A dispatch was immediately sent to the Governor, at Albany, apprising him of these facts. The next day a letter was received from His Excellency, in which he stated that he had just perused the evidence which had produced the conviction of Mr.

Sydney, and that evidence, besides being merely circumstantial, was, to his mind, vague and insufficient. The pressure of official business had prevented him from examining the case before, but had he reviewed the testimony, he would assuredly have granted the prisoner a reprieve. The dying confession of the burglar, the husband of the murdered woman, left not the slightest doubt of Mr. Sydney's innocence; and His Excellency concluded by ordering the prisoner's immediate discharge from custody.

Sydney left the prison, and, escorted by a number of friends, entered a carriage and was driven to his residence in Broadway. Here he was received with unbounded joy and hearty congratulations by all his household, including honest Dennis, and poor, dumb Clinton, who could only manifest his satisfaction by expressive signs.

'I will avenge thee, poor boy,' whispered Frank in his ear, as he cordially pressed his hand.

A tall man, wrapped in a cloak, had followed Frank's carriage, and watched him narrowly as he alighted and entered his house. This man's eyes alone were visible, and they glared with a fiend-like malignity upon the young gentleman; turning away, he muttered a deep curse, and a momentary disarrangement of the cloak which hid his face, revealed the horrible lineaments of the DEAD MAN!

CHAPTER XII

*Showing how the Dead Man escaped from the State Prison at
Sing Sing.*

The New York State Prison is situated at Sing Sing, a village
on the banks of the Hudson river, a few miles above the city. Being built in the strongest manner, it is deemed almost an impossi-
bility for a prisoner to effect his escape from its massive walls.
The discipline is strict and severe, and the system one of hard
labor and unbroken silence, with reference to any conversation
among the convicts — though in respect to the last regulation, it
is impossible to enforce it always, where so many men are
brought together in the prison and workshops attached to it.

The Dead Man, (who it will be recollected formerly made his
escape from the prison,) on being returned there, after his capture
by the two officers at Sydney's house, was locked in one of the
cells, and left to his own not very agreeable reflections. He had
been sentenced to imprisonment for life; and as his conduct and
character precluded all hope of his ever being made the object of
executive clemency, he was certain to remain there during the
rest of his days, unless he could again manage to escape; and this
he determined to do, or perish in the attempt.

For three days he was kept locked in his solitary cell, the
only food allowed him being bread and water. On the third day
he was brought out, stripped, and severely flogged with the *cats*,
an instrument of torture similar to that used (to our national disgrace be it said,) on board of the men-of-war in our naval service.
Then, with his back all lacerated and bleeding, the miscreant was
placed at work in the shop where cabinet making was carried on
— that having been his occupation in the prison, previous to his
escape; an occupation which he had learned, while a boy, within
the walls of some penitentiary.

The convict applied himself to his labor with a look which
only bespoke a sullen apathy; but in his heart there raged a hell of
evil passions. That night when he was locked in his cell, he slept
not, but sat till morning endeavoring to devise some plan of es-

cape.

The next day it chanced that he and another convict employed in the cabinet-maker's shop were engaged in packing furniture in large boxes to be conveyed in a sloop to the city of New York. These boxes, as soon as they were filled and nailed up, were carried down to the wharf, and stowed on board the sloop, which was to sail as soon as she was loaded. It instantly occurred to the Dead Man that these operations might afford him a chance to escape; and he determined to attempt it, at all hazards.

Upon an elevated platform in the centre of the shop (which was extensive) was stationed an overseer, whose duty it was to see that the convicts attended strictly to their work, and held no communication with each other. This officer had received special instructions from the Warden of the prison, to watch the Dead Man with all possible vigilance, and by no means to lose sight of him for a single moment, inasmuch as his former escape had been accomplished through the inattention of the overseer who had charge of him. Upon that occasion, he had watched for a favorable moment, slipped out of the shop unperceived, entered the Warden's dwelling house (which is situated within the walls of the prison) and helping himself to a suit of citizen's clothes, dressed himself therein, and deliberately marched out of the front gate, before the eyes of half a dozen keepers and guards, who supposed him to be some gentleman visiting the establishment, his hideous and well-known features being partially concealed by the broad-brimmed hat of a respectable Quaker.

To prevent a repetition of that maneuver, and to detect any other which might be attempted by the bold and desperate ruffian, the overseer kept his eyes almost constantly upon him, being resolved that no second chance should be afforded him to 'take French leave.' The Dead Man soon became conscious that he was watched with extraordinary vigilance; he was sagacious as well as criminal, and he deemed it to be good policy to assume the air of a man who was resigned to his fate, knowing it to be inevitable. He therefore worked with alacrity and endeavored to wear upon his villainous face an expression of contentment almost amounting to cheerfulness.

Near him labored a prisoner whose countenance indicated good-nature and courage; — and to him the Dead Man said, in an almost inaudible whisper, but without raising his eyes from his work, or moving his lips: —

'My friend, there is something in your appearance which assures me that you can be trusted; listen to me with attention, but do not look towards me. I am sentenced here for life: I am anxious to escape, and a plan has suggested itself to my mind, but you must assist me — will you do it?'

'Yes, poor fellow, I will, if it lies in my power, provided you were not sent here for any offence which I disapprove of,' replied the other, in a similar tone. 'I was sentenced here for the term of seven years, for manslaughter; a villain seduced my daughter, and I shot him dead — the honor of my child was worth a million of such accursed lives as his. — I consider myself guilty of no crime; he sacrificed my daughter to his lust, and then abandoned her — I sacrificed him to my vengeance, and never regretted the deed. The term of imprisonment will expire the day after to-morrow, and I shall then be a free man; therefore, I can assist you without running any great risk of myself. But you shall not have my aid if you were sent here for any deliberate villainy or black crime — for, thank God! I have a conscience, and that conscience permits me, though a prisoner, to call myself an honest man.'

'Be assured,' whispered the Dead Man, perceiving the necessity of using a falsehood to accomplish his ends — 'that I am neither a deliberate villain nor hardened criminal; an enemy attacked me, and in *self defense* I slew him, for which I was sentenced here for life.'

'In that case,' rejoined the other — 'I will cheerfully assist you to escape from this earthly hell — for self-defense is Nature's first law. Had you been a willful murderer, a robber, or aught of that kind, I would refuse to aid you — but the case is different. — But what is your plan?'

'I will get into one of these boxes, and you will nail on the cover, and I shall be conveyed on board the sloop, which will sail in less than an hour hence. When the vessel arrives at New York I shall perhaps have an opportunity to get on shore unperceived, and escape into the city, where I know of a place of refuge which the devil himself could not find,' — and the Dead Man chuckled inwardly as he thought of the Dark Vaults.

'The plan is a good one, and worthy of a trial,' said the other. 'But the overseer has his eye constantly upon you — how can you escape his vigilance?'

'There's the only difficulty,' replied the Dead Man — and his subtle brain was beginning to hatch some plan of surmounting that difficulty, when a large party of visitors, among whom were several ladies, entered the shop.

Now the overseer was a young man, and withal a tolerably good-looking one; and among the ladies were two or three whose beauty commended them to his gallant attentions.

He therefore left his station on the platform, and went forward to receive them, and make himself agreeable.

'Now's my time, by G — — d!' whispered the Dead Man to his fellow prisoner; instantly he lay down in one of the boxes, and the other nailed on the cover securely. A few moments afterwards, the box which contained the Dead Man was carried down to the wharf, by two convicts, and placed on board the vessel.

Meanwhile, the overseer had become the oracle of the party of ladies and gentlemen who had visited the shop; surrounded by the group, he occupied half an hour in replying to the many questions put to him, relative to the prison discipline, and other matters connected with it. In answer to a question addressed to him concerning the character of those under his charge, the overseer remarked in a tone of much self-complacency:

'I have now in this shop a convict who is the most diabolical villain that ever was confined in this prison. He is called the Dead Man, from the fact that his countenance resembles that of a dead person. He was sentenced here for life, for a murder, but contrived to escape about a year ago. However, he was arrested on a burglary not long since, sent back here, and placed under my particular care. I flatter myself that he will not escape a second time. Step this way, ladies and gentlemen, and view the hideous criminal.'

With a smirk of satisfaction, the overseer presented his arm to a pretty young lady, whose dark eyes had somewhat smitten him, and led the way to the further end of the shop, followed by the whole party.

The Dead Man was nowhere to be seen!

'Hullo, here! Where the devil is that rascal gone?' cried the overseer, in great alarm, gazing wildly about him. 'Say, you fellows there, where is the Dead Man?'

This inquiry, addressed to the convicts who were at work in that part of the shop, was answered by a general 'don't know, sir.'

With one exception they all spoke the truth; for only the man who had nailed the Dead Man in the box, was cognizant of the affair, and he did not choose to confess his agency in the matter. An instant search was made throughout the premises, but without success — and the officers of the prison were forced to arrive at the disagreeable conclusion that the miscreant had again given them the slip. Not one of them had suspected that he was nailed up in a box on board the sloop which was then on her way to New York. The Warden sent for the luckless overseer who had charge of the escaped convict, and sternly informed him that his services were no longer needed in that establishment; he added to the discomfiture of the poor young man by darkly hinting his suspicions that he (the overseer) had connived at the escape of the prisoner — but, as the reader knows, this charge was unfounded and unjust.

The distance between Sing Sing and the city is not great: wind and tide both being favorable, the vessel soon reached her place of destination, and was attached to one of the numerous wharves which extend around the city. The boxes of furniture on board were immediately placed upon carts, for conveyance to a large warehouse in Pearl street.

The tightness of the box in which the Dead Man was placed, produced no small inconvenience to that worthy, who during the passage was nearly suffocated; however, he consoled himself with the thought that in a short time he would be free. The box was about six feet in length; and two in breadth and depth; and in this narrow compass the villain felt as if he were in a coffin. He was greatly rejoiced when the men who were unloading the vessel raised the box from the deck and carried it towards one of the carts.

But oh, horrible! unconscious that there was a man in the box, they stood it upon one end, and the Dead Man was left *standing upon his head.* The next moment the cart was driven rapidly over the rough pavement, towards the warehouse.

There were but two alternatives left for him — either to endure the torments of that unnatural position until the box was taken from the cart, or to cry out for some one to rescue him, in which case, clothed as he was in the garb of the prison, he would be immediately recognized as an escaped convict, and sent back to his old quarters. This latter alternative was so dreadful to him that he resolved to endure the torture if possible; and he could not help shuddering when he thought that perhaps he might be placed in the same position in the warehouse!

The drive from the wharf to Pearl street occupied scarce five minutes, yet during that brief period of time, the Dead man endured all the torments of the damned. The blood settled in his head, and gushed from his mouth and nostrils; unable to hold out longer, he was about to yell in his agony for aid, when the cart stopped, and in a few moments he was relieved by his box being taken down and carried into the warehouse, where, to his inexpressible joy, it was placed in a position to cause him no further inconvenience. The warehouse being an extensive one, many persons were employed in it; and he deemed it prudent to remain in his box until night, as the clerks and porters were constantly running about, and they would be sure to observe him if he issued from his place of concealment then.

As he lay in his narrow quarters, he heard the voices of two persons conversing near him, one of whom was evidently the proprietor of the establishment.

'We have just heard from Sing Sing,' said the proprietor —
'that the villain they call the Dead Man made his escape this
morning, in what manner nobody knows. I am sorry for it, because such a wretch is dangerous to society; but my regret that he
has escaped arises principally from the fact that he is an excellent
workman, and I, as contractor, enjoyed the advantages of his
labor, paying the State a trifle of thirty cents a day for him, when
he could earn me two dollars and a half. This system of convict
labor is a glorious thing for us master mechanics, though it plays
the devil with the journeymen. Why, I formerly employed fifty
workmen, who earned on an average two dollars a day; but since
I contracted with the State to employ its convicts, the work which
cost me one hundred dollars a day I now get for *fifteen* dollars.'
And he laughed heartily.

'So it seems,' remarked the other,'that you are enriching
yourself at the expense of the State, while honest mechanics are
thrown out of employment.'

'Precisely so,' responded the proprietor — 'and if the *honest
mechanics*, as you call them, wish to work for me, they must
commit a crime and be sent to Sing Sing, where they can enjoy
that satisfaction — ha, ha, ha.'

Just then, a poor woman miserably clad, holding in her hand
a scrap of paper, entered the store, and advanced timidly to
where the wealthy proprietor and his friend were seated.

The former, observing her, said to her in a harsh tone —

'There, woman, turn right around and march out, and don't
come here again with your begging petition, or I'll have you
taken up as a vagrant.'

'If you please, sir,' answered the poor creature, humbly — 'I
haven't come to beg, but to ask if you won't be so kind as to pay
this bill of my husband's. It's only five dollars, sir, and he is lying
sick in bed, and we are in great distress from want of food and
fire-wood. Since you discharged him he has not been able to get
work, and — '

'Oh, get out!' interrupted the wealthy proprietor, brutally —

'don't come bothering *me* with your distress and such humbug. I paid your husband more than he ought to have had — giving two dollars a day to a fellow, when I now get the same work for thirty cents! If you're in distress, go to the Poor House, but don't come here again — d'ye hear?'

The poor woman merely bowed her head in token of assent, and left the store, her pale cheeks moistened with tears. The friend of the wealthy proprietor said nothing, but thought to himself, 'You're a d — — d scoundrel.' And, reader, we think so too, though not in the habit of swearing.

She had not proceeded two dozen steps from the store, when a rough-looking man in coarse overalls touched her arm, and thus addressed her:

'Beg your pardon, ma'am, but I'm a porter in the store of that blasted rascal as wouldn't pay your poor husband's bill for his work, and treated you so insultingly; I overheard what passed betwixt you and him, and I felt mad enough to go at him and *knock blazes* out of him. No matter — every dog has his day, as the saying is; and he may yet be brought to know what poverty is. I'm poor, but you are welcome to all the money I've got in the world — take this, and God bless you.'

The noble fellow passed three or four dollars in silver into her hand, and walked away ere she could thank him.

The recording angel above opened the great Book wherein all human actions are written, and affixed another *black mark* to the name of the wealthy proprietor. There were many black marks attached to that name already.

The angel then sought out another name, and upon it impressed the stamp of a celestial seal. It was the name of the poor laborer.

Oh, laborer! Thou art uncouth to look upon: thy face is unshaven, thy shirt dirty, and lo! thy overalls smell of paint and grease; thy speech is ungrammatical, and thy manners unpolished — but give us the grasp of thy honest hand, and the warm feelings of thy generous heart, fifty, yes a million times sooner

than the mean heart and niggard hand of the selfish cur that calls
itself thy master!

And oh, wealthy proprietor how smooth and smiling is thy
face, how precise thy dress and snow-white thy linen! thy words
(except to the poor,) are well-chosen and marked with strict
grammatical propriety. — The world doffs its hat to thee, and
calls thee 'respectable,' and 'good.' Thou rotten-hearted villain! —
morally thou art not fit to brush the cowhide boots of the MAN
that thou callst thy servant! Out upon ye, base-soul'd wretch!

The countenance of the wealthy proprietor, which had assumed a severe and indignant expression at the woman's audacity, had just recovered its wonted smile of complacency, when a
gentleman of an elderly age and reverend aspect entered the
store. He was attired in a respectable suit of black, and his neck
was enveloped in a white cravat.

'My dear Mr. Flanders,' said the proprietor, shaking him
warmly by the hand, 'I am delighted to see you. Allow me to
make you acquainted with my friend, Mr. Jameson — the Rev.
Balaam Flanders, our worthy and beloved pastor.'

The two gentlemen bowed, and the parson proceeded to unfold the object of his visit.

'Brother Hartless,' said he to the proprietor, 'I have called
upon you in behalf of a most excellent institution, of which I have
the honor to be President; I allude to the 'Society for Supplying
Indigent and Naked Savages in Hindustan with Flannel Shirts.'
The object of the Society, you perceive, is a most philanthropic
and commendable one; every Christian and lover of humanity
should cheerfully contribute his mite towards its promotion —
Your reputation for enlightened views and noble generosity has
induced me to call upon you to head the list of its patrons —
which list,' he added in a significant whisper, 'will be published
in full in the *Missionary Journal and Cannibal's Friend,* that excellent periodical.'

'You do me honor,' replied Mr. Hartless, a flush of pride suf-
fusing his face; then, going to his desk, he wrote in bold charac-

ters, at the top of a sheet of paper —

'Donations in aid of the Society for Supplying Indigent and Naked Savages in Hindustan with Flannel Shirts.

— Paul Hartless. $100.00'

This document he handed to the parson, with a look which clearly said 'What do you think of that?' and then, producing his pocket-book, took from thence a bank-note for one hundred dollars, which he presented to the reverend gentleman, who received the donation with many thanks on behalf of the 'Society for Supplying, &c.' and then left.

All this time the Dead Man lay in his box, impatiently awaiting the arrival of evening, when the store would be closed, and an opportunity afforded him to emerge from the narrow prison in which he was confined. Once, he came very near being discovered; for a person chanced to enter the warehouse accompanied by a dog, and the animal began smelling around the box in a manner that excited some surprise and remark on the part of those who observed it. The dog's acute powers of smell detected the presence of some person in the box: fortunately, however, for the Dead Man, the owner of the four-legged inquisitor, having transacted his business, called the animal away, and left the store.

Mr. Hartless, in the course of some further desultory conversation with Mr. Jameson, casually remarked —

'By the way, my policy of insurance expired yesterday, and I meant to have it renewed today; however, tomorrow will answer just as well. But I must not delay the matter, for this building is crammed from cellar to roof with valuable goods, and were it burnt down tonight, or before I renew my insurance, I should be a beggar!'

The Dead Man heard this, and grinned with satisfaction. The day wore slowly away, and at last the welcome evening came; the hum of business gradually ceased, and finally the last person belonging to the warehouse, who remained, took his departure, having closed the shutters and locked the door; then a profound silence reigned throughout the building.

'Now I may venture to get out of this accursed box,' thought the escaped convict: — and he tried to force off the cover, but to his disappointment and alarm, he found that it resisted all his efforts. It had been too tightly nailed on to admit of its being easily removed.

'Damnation!' exclaimed the Dead Man, a thousand fears crowding into his mind, — 'it's all up with me unless I can burst off this infernal cover.' And, cursing the man who had fastened it on so securely, he redoubled his efforts.

He succeeded at last; the cover flew off, and he arose from his constrained and painful position with feelings of the most intense satisfaction. All was pitch dark, and he began groping around for some door or window which would afford him egress from the place. His hand soon came in contact with a window; he raised the sash, and unfastened the shutters, threw them open, when instantly a flood of moonlight streamed into the store, enabling him to discern objects with tolerable distinctness. The window, which was not over five feet from the ground, overlooked a small yard surrounded by a fence of no great height; and the Dead Man, satisfied with the appearance of things, proceeded to put into execution a plan which he had formed while in the box. The nature of that plan will presently appear.

After breaking open a desk, and rummaging several drawers without finding anything worth carrying off, he took from his pocket a match, and being in a philosophical mood, (for great rascals are generally profound philosophers,) he apostrophized it thus:

'Is it not strange, thou little morsel of wood, scarce worth the fiftieth fraction of a cent, that in thy tiny form doth dwell a Mighty Power, which can destroy thousands of dollars, and pull down the great fabric of a rich man's fortune? Thy power I now invoke, thou little minister of vengeance; for I hate the aristocrat who expressed his regret at my escape, because, forsooth! my services were valuable to him! — and now, as the flames of fire consume his worldly possessions, so may the flames of eternal torment consume his soul hereafter!'

Ah, Mr. Hartless! that was an unfortunate observation you made relative to the expiration of your term of insurance. Your words were overheard by a miscreant, whose close proximity you little suspected. Your abominable treatment of that poor man is about to meet with a terrible retribution.

The Dead Man placed a considerable quantity of paper beneath a large pile of boxes and furniture; he then ignited the match, and having set fire to the paper, made his exit through the window, crossed the yard, scaled the fence, and passing through an alley gained the street, and made the best of his way to the Dark Vaults.

In less than ten minutes after he had issued from that building, fierce and crackling flames were bursting forth from its doors and windows. The streets echoed with the cry of *Fire* — the deep-toned bell of the City Hall filled the air with its notes of solemn warning and the fire engines thundered over the pavement towards the scene of conflagration. But in vain were the efforts of the firemen to subdue the raging flames; higher and higher they rose, until the entire building was on fire, belching forth mingled flame, and smoke, and showers of sparks. At length the interior of the building was entirely consumed, and the tottering walls fell in with a tremendous crash. The extensive warehouse of Mr. Paul Hartless, with its valuable contents, no longer existed, but had given place to a heap of black and smoking ruins!

The reader is now acquainted with the manner of the Dead Man's escape from Sing Sing State Prison, and the circumstances connected with that event.

CHAPTER XIII

The African and his Mistress — the Haunted House — Night of Terror.

Nero, the African, still remained a prisoner in the vault beneath Sydney's house. He was regularly supplied with his food by Dennis, who performed the part of jailer, and was untiring in his vigilance to prevent the escape of the negro under his charge.

One afternoon a boy of apparently fifteen or sixteen years of age called upon Dennis and desired to speak with him in private. He was a handsome lad, of easy, graceful manners, and long, curling hair; his dress was juvenile, and his whole appearance extremely prepossessing.

The interview being granted, the boy made known the object of his call by earnestly desiring to be permitted to visit the imprisoned black.

'Is it the *nager* ye want to see?' exclaimed Dennis — 'and how the devil did ye know we had a nager shut up in the cellar, any how?'

'Oh,' replied the boy, 'a lady of my acquaintance is aware of the fact, and she sent me here to present you with this five dollar gold piece, and to ask your consent to my delivering a short message to the black man.'

'Och, be the powers, and is that it?' muttered Dennis, half aloud, as he surveyed the bright coin which the boy had placed in his hand — 'I begin to smell a rat, faith; this gossoon was sent here by Mr. Sydney's blackguard wife, who has such a hankering after the black divil — not contented with her own lawful husband, and a decent man he is, but she must take up wid that dirty nager, bad luck to her and him! My master gave me no orders to prevint any person from seeing the black spalpeen; and as a goold yankee sovereign can't be picked up every day in the street, faith it's yerself Dennis Macarty, that will take the responsibility, and let this good-looking gossoon in to see black Nero, and bad luck to him!'

Accordingly, the worthy Irishman produced a huge key from his pocket, and led the way to the door of the vault, which he opened, and having admitted the youth, relocked it, after requesting the visitor to knock loudly upon the door when he desired to come out.

'Who is there?' demanded the negro in a hollow voice, from a remote corner of the dungeon.

'Tis I, your Julia!' answered the disguised woman, in a soft whisper — for it was no other than Sydney's guilty wife.

'My good, kind mistress!' exclaimed the black, and the next moment he had caught the graceful form of his paramour in his arms. We shall not offend the reader's good taste by describing the disgusting caresses which followed. Suffice it to say, that the interview was commenced in such a manner as might have been expected under the circumstance.

The first emotions of rapture at their meeting having subsided, they engaged in a long and earnest conversation.

We shall not weary the reader's patience by detailing at length what passed between them; suffice it to say, they did not separate until a plan had been arranged for the escape of Nero from that dungeon vault.

When Julia left the abode of her husband, in the manner described in Chapter VIII, she took apartments for herself and her maid Susan at a respectable boarding house near the Battery. Representing herself to be a widow lady recently from Europe, she was treated with the utmost respect by the inmates of the establishment, who little suspected that she was the cast-off wife of an injured husband, and the mistress of a negro! She assumed the name of Mrs. Belmont; and, to avoid confusion, we shall hereafter designate her by that appellation.

Mrs. Belmont was very well satisfied with her position, but she was well aware that she could not always maintain it, unless she entrapped some wealthy man into an amour or marriage with her; for her pecuniary resources, though temporarily sufficient for all her wants, could not last always. In this view of the case, she deemed it expedient to hire some suitable and genteel dwelling-house, where she could carry on her operations with less restraint than in a boarding-house. She accordingly advertised for such a house; and the same day on which her advertisement appeared in the paper, an old gentleman called upon her, and stated he was the proprietor of just such a tenement as she had expressed a desire to engage.

'This house, madam,' said the old gentleman, 'is a neat three-story brick edifice, situated in Reade street. It is built in the most substantial manner, and furnished with every convenience; moreover, you shall occupy it upon your own terms.'

'As to that,' remarked Mrs. Belmont, 'if the house suits me, you have but to name the rent, and it shall be paid.'

'Why, madam,' replied the old gentleman, with some embarrassment of manner — 'it is my duty to inform you that a silly prejudice exists in the minds of some people in the neighborhood of the house, and that prejudice renders it somewhat difficult for me to procure a tenant. You will smile at the absurdity of the notion, but nevertheless I assure you that a belief generally prevails that the house is *haunted*.'

'Are there any grounds for each a supposition?' inquired the lady, with an incredulous smile, yet feeling an interest in the matter.

'Why,' replied the owner, 'all who have as yet occupied the house have, after remaining one to two nights in it, removed precipitately, declaring that the most dreadful noises were heard during the night, tho' none have positively affirmed that they actually *saw* any supernatural visitant. These tales of terror have so frightened people that the building has been unoccupied for some time; and as it is a fine house, and one that cost me a good sum of money, I am extremely anxious to get a tenant of whom only a very moderate rent would be required. The fact is, I am no believer in this *ghost* business; the people who lived in the house were probably frightened by pranks of mischievous boys, or else their nervous, excited imaginations conjured up fancies and fears which had no reasonable foundation. Now, madam, I have candidly told you all; it remains for you to decide whether you will conform to a foolish prejudice, or, rising above the superstitions of the vulgar and ignorant, become the occupant of my *haunted* house — which, in my belief, is haunted by naught but mice in the cupboards and crickets in the chimneys.'

Mrs. Belmont reflected for a few moments, and then said —

'If the house suits me upon examination, I will become your tenant, notwithstanding the ghostly reputation of the building.'

'I am delighted, my dear madam,' rejoined the old gentleman, with vivacity, 'to find in you a person superior to the absurd terrors of weak-minded people. If you will do me the honor to accompany me to Reade street, I will go over the house with you, and if you are pleased with it, the bargain shall be completed upon the spot.'

This proposal was acceded to by Mrs. Belmont, who, after putting on her cloak and bonnet, took the arm of the old gentleman and proceeded with him up Broadway. A walk of little more than ten minutes brought them to Reade street, into which they turned; and in a few moments more the old gentleman paused before a handsome dwelling-house, standing about twenty feet back from the line of the street. The house did not adjoin any other building, but was located upon the edge of an open lot of considerable extent.

'This is the place,' said the guide as he took a key from his pocket; then, politely desiring the lady to follow him, he ascended the steps, unlocked the front door, and they entered the house. The rooms were of course entirely empty, yet they were clean and in excellent condition. — The parlors, chambers and other apartments were admirably arranged and Mrs. Belmont, after going all over the house, expressed her perfect satisfaction with it, and signified her wish to remove into it the next day. The terms were soon agreed upon; and Mr. Hedge (for that was the name of the landlord,) after delivering the key into her hands, waited upon her to the door of her boarding-house, and then took his leave.

The next morning, at an early hour, Mrs. Belmont began

making preparations to occupy her new abode. From an extensive dealer she hired elegant furniture sufficient to furnish every apartment in the house; and, by noon that day, the rooms which had lately appeared so bare and desolate, presented an aspect of luxury and comfort. The naked walls were covered with fine paintings, in handsome frames; rich curtains were hung in the windows, and upon the floors were laid beautiful carpets. — The mirrors, sofas, chairs and cabinets were of the costliest kind; a magnificent piano was placed in the parlor, and the lady took care that the chamber which she intended to occupy was fitted up with all possible elegance and taste. A voluptuous bed, in which Venus might have revelled, was not the least attractive feature of that luxurious sleeping apartment. Every arrangement being completed, and as it was still early in the afternoon, Mrs. Belmont resolved to carry out a plan which she had formed some days previously — a plan by which she could enjoy an interview with Nero the black. The reader is already aware that she disguised herself in boys' clothes, and accomplished her object without much difficulty.

That evening, Mrs. Belmont was seated in the comfortable parlor of her new abode, before a fine fire which glowed in the ample grate, and diffused a genial warmth throughout the apartment. She had just partaken of a luxurious supper; and the materials of the repast being removed, she was indulging in reflections which were far more pleasing at that moment, than any which had employed her mind since her separation from her husband.

She was attired with tasteful simplicity; for although she expected no company that evening, she had taken her usual pains to dress herself becomingly and well, being a lady who never neglected her toilet, under any circumstances — a trait of refinement which we cannot help admiring, even in one so depraved and abandoned as she was.

As she lounged indolently upon the sofa, complacently regarding her delicate foot, which, encased in a satin slipper, reposed upon the rich hearth-rug, her thoughts ran somewhat in the following channel — :

'Well — I am now not only mistress of my own actions, but also mistress of a splendidly furnished house. Ah, 'twas a fortunate day for me when I separated from that man I once called husband! Yet with what cool contempt he treated me on the night when he commanded me to leave his house forever! How bitterly I hate that man — how I long to be revenged upon him. Not that he has ever injured me — oh, no — 'tis I that have injured him; therefore do I hate him, and thirst for revenge! And poor Nero, whom I visited this afternoon in his dungeon — how emaciated and feeble has he become by close confinement in that gloomy place! His liberation must be effected, at all hazards; for strange as it is, I love the African passionately. Now, as regards my own position and affairs: I am young, beautiful, and accomplished — skilled in human nature and intrigue. Two distinct paths lie before me, which are equally desirable: as a virtuous widow lady, I can win the love and secure the hand of some rich and credulous gentleman, who, satisfied with having obtained a pretty wife, will not be too inquisitive with reference to my past history. In case of marriage, I will remove to Boston with my new husband: for not being divorced from Sydney, (how I hate that name!) I should be rendered liable to the charge of bigamy, if the fact of my second marriage should transpire. — On the other hand, leaving marriage entirely out of the question: As a young and lovely woman, residing alone, and not under the protection of male relatives, I shall attract the attention of wealthy libertines, who will almost throw their fortunes at my feet to enjoy my favors. Selecting the richest of these men, it will be my aim to infatuate him by my arts, to make him my slave, and then to deny him the pleasure for which he pants, until he gives me a large sum of money; this being done, I can either surrender myself to him, or still refuse to afford him the gratification he seeks, as suits my whim. When he becomes wearied of my perverseness and extortion, I will dismiss him, and seek another victim. Those with whom I shall thus have to deal, will be what the world calls respectable men — husbands, fathers — perhaps professedly pious men and clergymen — who would make any sacrifice sooner than have their amours exposed to their wives, families, and society generally. Once having committed themselves with me, I shall have a hold upon them, which they never can shake off; — a hold which will enable me to draw money from their well-filled coffers, whenever my necessities or extravagances require it. I may practice whatever imposition or extortion on them I choose, with perfect impunity; they will never dare to use threats or violence towards me, for the appalling threat of *exposure* will curb their tempers and render them tamely submissive to all my exactions and caprices. Thus will I reap a rich harvest from those wealthy votaries of carnal pleasure whom I may allure to my arms, while at the same time I can for my own gratification unrestrainedly enjoy the embraces of any lover whom I may happen to fancy. Ah, I am delightfully situated at present, and have before me a glorious and happy career!'

We have devoted considerable space to the above reflections of this unprincipled woman, because they will serve to show her views in reference to her present position, and her plans for the future.

The agreeable current of her meditations was interrupted by the entrance of her maid Susan.

'Well, ma'am,' said the abigail, 'I have obeyed all your orders; I have locked all the doors, and fastened all the shutters, so that if the ghost *should* pay us a visit, it will have to get in through the keyhole. But oh! my gracious! how terrible it is for you and I, ma'am, two poor weak women, as a body might say, to be all alone together in a house that is haunted!'

'Sit down, Susan,' said Mrs. Belmont, who was herself not altogether devoid of superstitious fears. 'Are you so foolish as to believe in *ghosts*? Do you think that the spirits of dead people are allowed to re-visit the earth, to frighten us out of our wits? No, no — we have reason to fear the *living*, but not those who are dead and buried.'

'But, if you please, ma'am,' rejoined Susan, in a solemn tone, 'I once seed a ghost with my own eyes, and not only seed it, but *felt* it, too.'

'Indeed — and pray how did that happen?' inquired her mistress.

'I'll tell you all about it, ma'am,' replied Susan, who, by the way, was rather a pretty young woman, though she was, like all ladies' maids, a prodigious talker. 'You see, ma'am, I once went to live in the family of a minister, and a very excellent man he was, as prayed night and morning, and said grace afore meals. Oh, he was a dreadful clever gentleman, 'cause he always used to kiss me when he catch'd me alone, and chuck me under the chin, and tell me I was handsome. Well, Saturday the minister's wife and family went to pay a visit to some relations in New Jersey, and was to stay for two or three days; but the minister himself didn't go with them, 'cause he was obliged to stay and preach on Sunday. — Now comes the dreadful part of my story, ma'am, and it is true as gospel. — That Saturday night, about twelve o'clock, I was awoke by hearing the door of my little attic bed-room softly open; and by the light of the moon I seed a human figger, all dressed in white, come into the room, shut the door, and then walk towards my bed. Oh, I was dreadfully frightened, to be sure; and just as I was going to scream out, the ghost puts his hand upon me and says — *hush!* which skeer'd me so that I almost fainted away. Well, ma'am, what does the ghost do next but take ondecent liberties with me, and I was too much frightened to say, 'have done, now!' And then the awful critter did what no ghost ever did before to me, nor man neither. — Oh, I actually fainted away two or three times; I did indeed. After a while it went away, but I was in such a flutter that I couldn't sleep no more that night. The next morning I up and told the minister how I had seed a ghost, and how it had treated me; and the minister he smiled, and said he guessed I'd get over it, and gave me some money, telling me not to say anything more about it, 'cause it might frighten the folks. Now, ma'am, after that, you needn't wonder that I believe in ghosts.'

Mrs. Belmont was highly amused by this narration of her maid's experience in supernatural visitation; and the hearty laughter in which she indulged at the close of the story, dispelled in a great measure those unpleasant feelings which had begun to gain the ascendancy over her. While under the influence of those feelings, she had intended to request Susan to sleep with her in her chamber; but as such an arrangement would betray *fear* on her part, while she was most anxious to appear bold and courageous, she concluded to occupy her sleeping apartment alone. Susan herself would have been very glad to share the room of her mistress; but as a suggestion to that effect, coming from her, might have seemed presumptuous and impertinent, she said nothing about it. Accordingly, when the hour for retiring arrived, Mrs. Belmont retired to her chamber, where she dismissed her maid, saying that she should not want her services any more that night; and poor Susan was obliged to ascend to her solitary apartment, which she did with many fearful misgivings, and the most dreadful apprehensions in regard to ghosts, coupled with much painful reflection relative to the unpleasantness of sleeping *alone* — in a haunted house.

Mrs. Belmont disrobed herself, yet ere she retired to her couch, she paused before a large mirror to admire her own naked and voluptuous beauty. While she was surveying herself, she gave utterance to her thoughts in words: —

'Ah, these charms of mine will procure me friends and fortune. What man could resist the intoxicating influence of such glorious loveliness of face and person as I possess!'

Scarcely had she uttered these words, when her ear was greeted by a low sound, which bore some resemblance to a laugh. Terrified and trembling, she cast a rapid glance around the room, but could see nobody; she then examined a small closet which adjoined the chamber and looked under the bed, not knowing but that some person might be concealed there — but she could uncover nothing to account for the noise which she had heard. It then occurred to her to open the door of her chamber; but as she was about to do so, an appalling thought flashed thro' her mind.

'What if some terrible being is now standing at the outside of that door?' and she shrank from opening it. She deeply regretted that she had not requested her maid Susan to sleep with her, as she crept into bed, leaving a candle burning on the table.

For about a quarter of an hour she listened intensely, but the sound which had alarmed her was not repeated; and she began to reason with herself upon the absurdity of her fears. Finally she succeeded in persuading herself that she had in reality heard nothing, but had been deceived by her own imagination. Still, she could not entirely dissipate her fears; she recollected that the house had the reputation of being 'haunted' — and, though she was naturally neither timid nor superstitious, a vague and undefinable dread oppressed her, as she lay in that solitary chamber, where reigned a heavy gloom and profound stillness.

It was an hour after midnight when she awoke from an uneasy slumber into which she had fallen; and the first object which met her gaze, was a human figure, enveloped from head to toe in white drapery, standing near her bed!

Yes, there it stood, with the upper part of a ghastly face alone visible, pointing at her with its finger, and freezing her soul with the steady glare of its eyes.

Long, long stood that dreadful apparition; its attitude seemed to be either menacing or warning. The terrified woman, under the influence of a painful fascination, could not avert her gaze from it; and the spectre stood until the candle was entirely consumed, and the room was wrapped in profound darkness. Then the Form glided to the bedside, and laid its cold hand upon her brow. *Thou shalt see me again!* it whispered, and then passed noiselessly from the room.

Mrs. Belmont gave one loud and piercing scream, and then sank into a state of insensibility.

CHAPTER XIV

A Glimpse of the Crimes and Miseries of a Great City.

After his narrow escape from an ignominious death, Frank Sydney resumed his nocturnal wanderings thro' the city, in disguise, in order to do deeds of charity and benevolence to those who needed his aid. One night, dressed in the garb of a sailor, and wearing an immense pair of false whiskers, he strolled towards the Five Points, and entered the 'crib' of Bloody Mike. That respectable establishment was filled as usual with a motley collection of gentlemen of undoubted reputation — thieves, vagabonds, homeless wretches, and others of the same stamp, among whom were some of the most miserable looking objects possible to be conceived.

At the moment of Frank's entrance, Ragged Pete was engaged in relating the particulars of a horrible event which had occurred upon the preceding night on the 'Points.' The incident is a *true* one, and we introduce it here to show what awful misery exists in the very midst of all our boasted civilization and benevolence: —

'You see, fellers,' said Ragged Pete, leisurely sipping a gill of *blue ruin*, which he held in his hand — 'the victim was a woman of the town, as lived upstairs in Pat Mulligan's crib in this street. She had once been a decent woman, but her husband was a drunken vagabond, as beat and starved her to such an extent, that she was obliged to go on the town to keep herself from dying of actual starvation. Well, the husband he was took up and sent to quod for six months, as a common vagrant; and the wife she lived in Mulligan's crib, in a room as hadn't a single article of furniture in it, exceptin' a filthy old bed of straw in one corner. A week ago, the poor cretur was taken ill, and felt herself likely to become a mother, but the brutes in the house wouldn't pay no attention to her in that situation, but left her all to herself. What she must have suffered during that night and the next day, you can imagine; and towards evening Pat Mulligan goes to her room, and finds her almost dead, with her poor child in her arms, wrapped up in an old blanket. Well, what does Pat do but ax her for his rent, which she owed him; and because the poor woman had nothing to pay him, the Irish vagabond (axing your pardon, Bloody Mike,) bundles her neck and crop into the street, weak and sick as she was, with a hinfant scarce a day old, crying in her arms. The weather was precious cold, and it was snowing, and to keep herself and child from freezing to death, as she thought, she crept into a hog-pen which stands in Pat's yard. And this morning she was found in the hog-pen, stone dead, and the hogs were devouring the dead body of the child, which was already half ate up! I'll tell you what, fellers,' exclaimed Ragged Pete, dashing a tear from his eye, and swallowing the remainder of his gin — 'I'm a hard case myself, and have seen some hard things in my time, but d — — n me if the sight of that poor woman's corpse and the mutilated body of her child, didn't set me to thinking that this is a great city, where such a thing takes place in the very midst of it!'

'Three groans for Pat Mulligan!' roared a drunken fellow from beneath the table.

The groans were rendered with due emphasis and effect; and then one of the drunken crowd proposed that they should visit the 'crib' of Mr. Mulligan, and testify their disapprobation of that gentleman's conduct in a more forcible and striking manner.

This proposal was received with a shout of approbation by the drunken crew, and was warmly seconded by Bloody Mike himself, who regarded Mr. Patrick Mulligan as a formidable rival in his line of business, and therefore entertained feelings strongly hostile to his fellow-countryman. Then forth sallied the dingy crowd, headed by Ragged Pete, (who found himself suddenly transformed into a hero,) and followed by Frank Sydney, who was desirous of seeing the issue of this strange affair.

The house occupied by Mulligan was an old, rotten tenement, which would undoubtedly have fallen to the ground, had it not been propped up by the adjoining buildings; and as it was, one end of it had settled down, in consequence of the giving away of the foundation, so that every room in the house was like a steep hill. The lower room was occupied as a groggery and dance-hall, and was several feet below the level of the street.

Into this precious den did the guests of Bloody Mike march, in single file. It had been previously agreed between them, that Ragged Pete would give the signal for battle, by personally attacking no less a person than Mr. Mulligan himself. Frank also entered, and taking up a secure position in one corner, surveyed the scene with interest.

Seated in the corner, upon an inverted wash-tub, was an old negro, whose wool was white as snow, who was arrayed in a dirty, ragged, military coat which had once been red. This sable genius rejoiced in the lofty title of 'the General;' he was playing with frantic violence on an old, cracked violin, during which performance he threw his whole body into the strangest contortions, working his head, jaws, legs and arms in the most ludicrous manner. The 'music' thus produced was responded to, 'on the floor,' by about twenty persons, who were indulging in the 'mazy dance.' The company included old prostitutes, young thieves, negro chimney-sweeps, and many others whom it would be difficult to classify.

The room being small and very close, and heated by an immense stove, the stench was intolerable. — Behind the bar was a villainous looking Irishman, whose countenance expressed as much intellect or humanity as that of a hog. This was Pat Mulligan, and he was busily engaged in dealing out the delectable nectar called 'blue ruin' at the very moderate rate of one penny per gill.

A *very* important man, forsooth, was that Irish 'landlord,' in the estimation of himself and customers. — None dare address him without prefixing a deferential *'Mr.'* to his name; and Frank Sydney was both amused and irritated as he observed the brutal insolence with which the low, ignorant ruffian treated the poor miserable wretches, from whose scanty pence he derived his disgraceful livelihood.

'Mr. Mulligan,' said a pale, emaciated woman, whose hollow cheek and sunken eye eloquently proclaimed her starving condition — 'won't you trust me for a sixpenny loaf of bread until tomorrow? My little girl, poor thing, is dying, and I have eaten nothing this day.' And the poor creature wept.

'Trust ye!' roared the Irishman, glaring ferociously upon her — 'faith, it's not exactly *trust* I'll give ye; but I'll give ye a beating that'll not leave a whole bone in your skin, if ye are not out of this place in less time than it takes a pig to grunt.'

The poor woman turned and left the place, with a heavy heart, and Ragged Pete, deeming this a good opportunity to begin hostilities, advanced to the bar with a swagger, and said to the Irishman, —

'You're too hard upon that woman, Pat.'

'What's that to you, ye dirty spalpeen?' growled Mulligan, savagely.

'This much,' responded Pete, seizing an immense earthen pitcher which stood on the counter, and hurling it with unerring aim at the head of the Irishman. The vessel broke into a hundred pieces, and though it wounded Mulligan dreadfully, he was not disabled; for, grasping an axe which stood within his reach, he rushed from behind the bar, and swinging the formidable weapon aloft, he would have cloven in twain the skull of Ragged Pete, had not that gentleman evaded him with much agility, and closing with him, bore him to the floor, and began to pummel him vigorously.

No sooner did the customers of Pat Mulligan see their dreaded landlord receiving a sound thrashing, then all fear of him vanished; and, as they all hated the Irish bully, and smarted under the remembrance of numerous insults and wrongs sustained at his hands, they with one accord fell upon him, and beat him within an inch of his life. Not content with this mode of retaliation, they tore down the bar, demolished the glasses and decanters, spilled all the liquor, and in short caused the flourishing establishment of Mr. Pat Mulligan to assume a very forlorn appearance.

While this work of destruction was going on, the alarm was given that a body of watchmen had assembled outside the door, and was about to make an advance upon the 'crib.' To exit the house now became the general intent; and several had already beaten a retreat through the rear of the premises, when the watchman burst into the front door, and made captives of all who were present. Frank Sydney was collared by one of the officials, and although our hero protested that he had not mingled in the row, but was merely a spectator, he was carried to the watch-house along with the others.

When the party arrived at the watch-house, (which is situated in a wing of the 'Tombs,') the prisoners were all arrayed in a straight line before the desk of the Captain of the Watch, for that officer's examination. To give the reader an idea of the way in which justice is sometimes administered in New York, we shall detail several of the individual examinations, and their results: —

'What's your name?' cried the Captain, addressing the first of the prisoners. 'Barney McQuig, an' plaze yer honor,' was the reply, in a strong Hibernian accent.

A sort of under-official, who was seated at the desk, whispered in the ear of the Captain of the Watch —

'I know him, he's an infernal scoundrel, but he *votes our ticket*, and you let him slide, by all means.'

'McQuig, you are discharged,' said the Captain to the prisoner.

'Why, sir, that man was one of the worst of the rioters, and he is, besides, one of the greatest villains on the Points,' remarked a watchman, who, having only been recently appointed, was comparatively *green*, and by no means *au fait* in the method of doing business in that 'shop.'

'Silence, sir!' thundered the Captain — 'how dare you dispute my authority? I shall discharge whom I please, damn you; and you will do well if you are not discharged from your post for your interference.'

The indignant Captain demanded the name of the next prisoner, who confessed to the eccentric Scriptural cognomen of 'Numbers Clapp.'

'I know *him*, too,' again whispered the under-official — 'he is a common and notorious thief, but he is useful to us as a *stool pigeon*, [3] and you must let him go.'

'Clapp, you can go,' said the Captain; and Mr. Numbers Clapp lost no time in conveying himself from the dangerous vicinity of justice; though such *justice* as we here record, was not very dangerous to *him*.

'Now, fellow, what's *your* name?' asked the Captain of a shabbily dressed man, whose appearance strongly indicated both abject poverty and extreme ill health.

'Dionysus Wheezlecroft,' answered the man, with a consumptive cough.

'Do you know him?' inquired the Captain, addressing the under-official, in a whisper.

'Perfectly well,' replied the other — 'he is a poor devil, utterly harmless and inoffensive, and is both sick and friendless. He was formerly a political stump orator of some celebrity; he worked hard for his party, and when that party got into power, it kicked him to the devil, and he has been flat on his back ever since.'

'What party did he belong to? — *ours?*' asked the Captain.

'No,' was the reply; and that brief monosyllable of two letters, sealed the doom of Dionysus Wheezlecroft.

'Lock him up,' cried the Captain — 'he will be *sent over* for six months in the morning.' And so he was — not for any crime, but because he did not belong to *our party*.

Several negroes, male and female, who could not possibly belong to any party, were then summarily disposed of; and at last it came to Frank's turn to be examined.

'Say, you sailor fellow,' quoth the Captain, 'what's your name?'

Frank quietly stepped forward, and in as few words as possible made himself known; he explained the motives of his disguise, and the circumstances under which he had been induced to enter the house of Pat Mulligan. — The Captain, though savage and tyrannical to his inferiors, was all smiles and affability to the rich Mr. Sydney.

'Really, my dear sir,' said he, rubbing his hands, and accompanying almost every word with a corresponding bow, 'you have disguised yourself so admirably, that it would puzzle the wits of a lawyer to make out who you are, until you should *speak*, and then your gentlemanly accent would betray you. Allow me to offer you ten thousand apologies, on behalf of my men, for having dared to subject you to the inconvenience of an arrest; and permit me also to assure you that if they had known who you were, they would not have molested you had they found you demolishing all the houses on the Points.'

'I presume I am at liberty to depart?' said Frank; and the Captain returned a polite affirmative. Our hero left the hall of judgment, thoroughly disgusted with the injustice and partiality of this petty minion of the law; for he well knew that had he himself been in reality nothing more than a poor sailor, as his garb indicated, the three words, 'lock him up,' would have decided his fate for that night; and that upon the following morning the three words, 'send him over,' would have decided his fate for the ensuing six months.

When Frank was gone, the Captain said to the under official:

'That is Mr. Sydney, the young gentleman who was convicted of murder a short time ago, and whose innocence of the crime was made manifest in such an extraordinary manner, just in time to save his neck. He is very rich, and of course I could not think of locking *him* up.'

The Captain proceeded to examine other prisoners, and Frank went in quest of other adventures, in which pursuit we shall follow him.

As he turned into Broadway, he encountered a showily dressed courtezan, who, addressing him with that absence of ceremony for which such ladies are remarkable, requested him to accompany her home.

'This may lead to something,' thought Frank; and pretending to be somewhat intoxicated, he proffered her his arm, which she took, at the same time informing him that her residence was in Anthony street. This street was but a short distance from where they had met; a walk of five minutes brought them to it, and the woman conducted Frank back into a dark narrow court, and into an old wooden building which stood at its further extremity.

'Wait here a few moments, until I get a light,' said the woman; and entering a room which opened from the entry, she left our hero standing in the midst of profound darkness. — Hearing a low conversation going on in the room, he applied his ear to the key-hole, and listened, having good reason to suppose that he himself was the object of the discourse.

'What sort of a man does he appear to be?' was asked, in a voice which sent a thrill through every nerve in Frank's body — for it struck him that he had heard it before. It was the voice of a man, and its tones were peculiar.

'He is a sailor,' replied the woman — 'and as he is somewhat drunk now, the powder will soon put him to sleep, and then — '

The remainder of the sentence was inaudible to Frank; he had heard enough, however, to put him on his guard; for he felt convinced that he was in one of those murderous dens of prostitution and crime, where robbery and assassination are perpetrated upon many an unsuspecting victim.

In a few minutes the woman issued from the room, bearing a lighted candle; and requesting Frank to follow, she led the way up a crooked and broken stair-case, and into a small chamber, scantily furnished, containing only a bed, a table, a few chairs, and other articles of furniture, of the commonest kind.

Our hero had now an opportunity to examine the woman narrowly. — Though her eyes were sunken with dissipation, and her cheeks laden with paint, the remains of great beauty were still discernible in her features, and a vague idea obtruded itself, like a dim shadow, upon Frank's mind, that this was not the *first* time he had seen her.

'Why do you watch me so closely?' demanded the woman, fixing her piercing eyes upon his countenance.

'Ax yer pardon, old gal, but aren't you going to fetch on some grog?' said our hero, assuming a thick, drunken tone, and drawing from his pocket a handful of gold and silver coin.

'Give me some money, and I will get you some liquor,' rejoined the woman, her eyes sparkling with delight, as she saw that her intended victim was well supplied with funds. Frank gave her a half dollar, and she went down stairs, promising to be back in less than ten minutes.

During her absence, and while our hero was debating whether to make a hasty retreat from the house, or remain and see what discoveries he could make tending to throw light on the character and practices of the inmates, the chamber door opened, and to his surprise a small boy of about five years of age entered, and gazed at him with childish curiosity.

'Surely I have seen that little lad before,' thought Frank; and then he said, aloud —

'What is your name, my boy?'

'*Jack the Prig,*' replied the little fellow.

Frank started; memory carried him back to the Dark Vaults, where he had heard the Dead Man *catechise* his little son, and he recollected that the urchin had, on that occasion, made the same reply to a similar question. By referring to the sixth chapter of this work, the reader will find the questions and answers of that singular catechism.

Resolving to test the matter further, our hero asked the boy the next question which he remembered the Dead Man had addressed to his son, on that eventful night: —

'Who gave you that name?'

'*The Jolly Knights of the Round Table,*' replied the boy, mechanically.

'By heavens, 'tis as I suspected!' thought Frank — 'the child's answers to my questions prove him to be the son of the Dead Man; the voice which I heard while listening in the passage, and which seemed familiar to me, was the voice of that infernal miscreant himself: and the woman whom I accompanied hither, and whom I half fancied I had seen before — that woman is his wife.'

The boy, probably fearing a return of his mother, left the room; and Frank continued his meditations in the following strain: —

'The mystery begins to clear up. This house is probably the one that communicates with the *secret outlet* of the Dark Vaults, through which I passed, blindfolded, accompanied by those two villains, Fred Archer, and the Dead Man. The woman, no doubt, entices unsuspecting men into this devil's trap, and after *drugging* them into a state of insensibility, hands them over to the tender mercies of her hideous husband, who, after robbing them, casts them, perhaps, into some infernal pit beneath this house, there to die and rot! — Good God, what terrible iniquities are perpetrated in the very heart of this great city — iniquities which are unsuspected and unknown! And yet the perpetrators of them often escape their merited punishment, while I, an innocent man, came within a hair's breadth of perishing upon the scaffold for another's crime! But I will not question the divine justice of the Almighty; the guilty may elude the punishment due their crimes, in this world, but vengeance will overtake them in the next. It shall, however, henceforth be the great object of my life, to bring one stupendous miscreant to the bar of human justice — the Dead Man whose escape from the State Prison was followed by his outrage upon Clinton Romaine, by which the poor boy was forever deprived of the faculty of speech; and 'tis my firm belief that 'twas by his accursed hand my aunt was murdered; she was too elevated in character, and too good a Christian, to commit suicide, and *he* is the only man in existence who could slay such an excellent and honorable woman! Yes — something tells me that the Dead Man is the murderer of my beloved relative, and never will I rest till he is in my power, that I may wreak upon him my deadly vengeance!'

Hearing a footstep on the stairs, he assumed an attitude and expression of countenance indicative of drowsiness and stupidity. A moment afterwards, the woman entered, and placed upon the table a small pitcher containing liquor. Taking from a shelf two tumblers, she turned her back towards Frank, and drew from her bosom a small box, from which she rapidly transferred a few grains of fine white powder into one of the tumblers; then going to a cupboard in one corner, she put a teaspoonful of loaf sugar into each of the tumblers, and placing them upon the table, requested our hero to 'help himself.'

Frank poured some liquor into the tumbler nearest him, and looking askance at the woman as he did so, he saw that her features wore a smile of satisfaction; she then supplied her own glass, and was about to raise it to her lips, when our hero said, in a gruff, sleepy tone —

'I say, old woman, you haven't half sweetened this grog of mine. Don't be so d — d stingy of your sugar, for I've money enough to pay for it.'

The woman turned and went to the closet to get another spoonful of the article in question; when Frank, with the rapidity of lightning, *changed the tumblers*, placing the deadly dose designed for him, in the same spot where the woman's tumbler had stood. This movement was accomplished with so much dexterity, that when she advanced to the table with the sugar, she failed to notice the alteration.

'Well, old gal — here's to the wind that blows, the ship that goes, and the lass that loves a sailor!' And delivering himself of this hackneyed nautical toast, the pretended seaman drank off the contents of his glass, an example which was followed by the female miscreant, who responded to Frank's toast by uttering aloud the significant wish —

'May your sleep to-night be sound!'

'Ay, ay, I hope so, and yours, too,' grumbled our hero, placing an enormous quid of tobacco in his cheek, in order to remove the unpleasant taste of the vile liquor which he had just drank.

There was a pause of a few minutes; when suddenly the woman grasped Frank convulsively by the arm, and gazed into his countenance with wildly gleaming eyes.

'Tell me,' she gasped, like one in the agonies of strangulation — 'tell me the truth, for God's sake — *did you change those tumblers?*'

'I did,' was the answer.

'Then I am lost!' she almost shrieked — 'lost, lost! The liquor which I drank contained a powder which will within half an hour sink me into a condition of insensibility, from which I shall only awake a raging maniac! I am rightly served — for I designed that to be *your* fate!'

'Wretched woman, I pity you,' said Frank, in a tone of commiseration.

'I deserve not your pity,' she cried, writhing as if in great bodily torment — 'my soul is stained with the guilt of a thousand crimes — and the only reparation I can make you, to atone for the wrong I intended, is to warn you to fly from this house as from a pestilence! This is the abode of murder — it is a charnel-house of iniquity; fly from hence, as you value your life — for an hour after midnight my husband, the terrible Dead Man, will return, and although you frustrated me, you cannot escape his vengeance, should he find you here. Ah, my God! my brain burns — the deadly potion is at work!'

And thus the miserable woman continued to rave, until the powerful drug which she had taken fully accomplished its work, and she sank upon the floor in a state of death-like insensibility.

'Thou art rightly served,' thought Frank, as he contemplated her prostrate form — 'now to penetrate into some of the mysteries of this infernal den!' Taking the candle from the table, he began his exploration in that fearful house.

In the apartment which adjoined the chamber he discovered little 'Jack the Prig,' fast asleep in bed. In the restlessness of slumber, the boy had partially thrown off the bed-clothes, and he exhibited upon his naked breast the picture of a gallows, and a man hanging! This appalling scene had been drawn with India ink, and pricked into the flesh with needles, so that it never could be effaced. It was the work of the boy's hideous father, who, not contented with training up his son to a life of crime, was anxious that he should also carry upon his person, through life, that fearful representation of a criminal's doom.

'Would it not be a deed of mercy,' thought our hero — 'to take the poor boy from his unnatural parents, and train him up to a life of honesty and virtue? If I ever get the father in my power, I will look after the welfare of this unfortunate lad.'

Frank left the room, and descending the stairs, began to explore the lower apartments of the house. In one, he found a large collection of tools, comprising every implement used by the villains in their depredations. There were dark lanterns, crowbars, augers, London *jimmies*, and skeleton keys, for burglary; also, spades, pickaxes, and shovels, which were probably used in robbing graves, a crime which at that period was very common in New York. A large quantity of clothing of all kinds hung upon the walls, from the broadcloth suit of the gentleman down to the squalid rags of the beggar; these garments Frank conjectured to be *disguises*, a supposition which was confirmed by the masks, false whiskers, wigs and other articles for altering the person, which were scattered about.

In a small closet which communicated with this room, our hero found dies for coining, and a press for printing counterfeit bank-notes; and a table drawer, which he opened containing a quantity of false coin, several bank-note plates, and a package of counterfeit bills, which had not yet been signed.

Having sufficiently examined these interesting objects, Frank passed into the next room, which was of considerable extent. It was almost completely filled with goods of various kinds, evidently the proceeds of robberies. There were overcoats, buffalo robes, ladies' cloaks and furs, silk dresses, shawls, boxes of boots and shoes, cases of dry goods, and a miscellaneous assortment of articles sufficient to furnish out a large store. The goods in that room were worth several thousands of dollars.

'I shall now seek to discover the *secret outlet* of the Dark Vaults,' thought Frank, as he descended into the cellar of the house. Here he gazed about him with much interest; the cellar was damp and gloomy and his entrance with the light disturbed a legion of rats, which went scampering off in every direction, from a corner in which they had collected together; as the young man approached that corner, a fetid, sickening odor saluted his nostrils and a fearful thought flashed across his mind; a moment afterwards, his blood curdled with horror, for before him lay the dead body of a man, entirely naked, and far advanced in state of decomposition; and upon that putrefying corpse had the swarm of rats been making their terrible banquet!

Sick with horror and disgust, Frank precipitately retreated from the loathsome and appalling spectacle, satisfied that he had beheld one of the Dead Man's murdered victims; and he shuddered as he thought that such might have been *his* fate!

In the centre of the cellar an apparatus of singular appearance attracted his notice; and approaching it he instantly became convinced that this was the *secret outlet* for which he sought. Four strong, upright posts supported two ponderous iron crossbars, to which were attached four ropes of great thickness and strength, these ropes were connected with a wooden platform, about six feet square; and beneath the platform was a dark and yawning chasm.

Closely examining this apparatus, our hero saw that by an ingenious contrivance, a person standing on the platform could, by turning a crank, raise or lower himself at will. He cautiously approached the edge of the chasm, and holding down the light, endeavored to penetrate through the darkness; but in vain — he could see nothing, though he could faintly hear a dull, sluggish sound like that produced by the flowing of a vast body of muddy water, and at the same time an awful stench which arose from the black gulf, compelled him to return a short distance.

'The mystery is solved,' he thought — 'that fearful hole leads to the subterranean sewers of the city, and also to the Dark Vaults beyond them. By means of that platform, the villains of the *Infernal Regions* below, can pass to and from their den with facility and safety.'

At this moment he heard the vast bell of the City Hall proclaiming the hour of midnight; and he remembered that the woman had told him that her husband, the Dead Man, would return in an hour from that time. At first it occurred to him to await the miscreant's coming, and endeavor to capture him — but then he reflected that the Dead Man might return accompanied by other villains, in which case the plan would not only be impracticable, but his own life would be endangered.

'And even were the villain to come back alone,' thought Frank, 'were I to spring upon him, he might give some signal which would bring to his aid his band of desperadoes from the Vaults below. No — I must not needlessly peril my own life; I will depart from the house now, satisfied for the present with the discoveries I have made, and trusting to be enabled at no distant time to come here with a force sufficient to overcome the hideous ruffian and all his band.'

Leaving the cellar, he traversed the entry and attempted to open the front door; but to his surprise it was securely locked, nor could all his efforts push back the massive bolts which held it fast. He re-entered the room, and examining the windows, found them furnished with thick iron bars like the windows of a prison, so that to pass through them was impossible; and further investigation resulted in the unpleasant conviction that he was a prisoner in that dreadful house, with no immediate means of escape.

He again descended into the cellar, and began seriously to reflect upon the realities of his situation. He was a young man of determination and courage: yet he could not entirely subdue those feelings of uneasiness and alarm which were natural under the circumstances. He was alone, at midnight, in that abode of crime and murder; near him lay the corpse of an unfortunate fellow creature, who had without a doubt fallen by the hand of an assassin; he was momentarily expecting the return of that archmiscreant, who would show him no mercy; a deep, unbroken silence, and an air of fearful mystery, reigned in that gloomy cellar and throughout that awful house — and before him, dark and yawning as the gate of hell, was that black and infernal pit which led to the subterranean caverns of the Dark Vaults, far below.

'I will sell my life dearly, at all events,' thought our hero, as he drew a bowie knife from his breast, and felt its keen, glittering edge; then impelled by a sudden thought, he advanced to the mouth of the pit, and cut the four ropes, which sustained the wooden platform, so nearly asunder, that they would be almost sure to break with a slight additional weight.

He had scarcely accomplished this task, when a strange, unnatural cry resounded throughout the cellar — a cry so indescribably fearful that it chilled his blood with horror. It was almost instantly followed by a low and melancholy wail, so intense, so solemn, so profoundly expressive of human misery, that Frank was convinced that some unfortunate being was near him, plunged in deepest anguish and distress.

In a few moments the sound entirely ceased, and silence resumed its reign; then Frank, actuated by the noble feelings of his generous nature, said, in a loud voice —

'If there is any unhappy creature who now hears me, and who needs my charitable aid, let him or her speak, that I may know where to direct my search.'

No answer was returned to this request; all was profoundly silent. Frank, however, was determined to fathom the mystery; accordingly, he began a careful search throughout the cellar, and finally discovered in an obscure corner an iron door, which was secured on the outside by a bolt — to draw back this bolt and throw open this door, was but the work of a moment; and our hero was about to enter the cell thus revealed, when a hideous being started from the further end of the dungeon, and with an awful yell rushed out into the cellar, and hid itself in a deep embrasure of the wall.

Whether this creature were human or not, the rapidity of its flight prevented Frank from ascertaining, he cautiously advanced to the place where it had concealed itself, and by the dim light of the lamp which he carried, he saw, crouching down upon the cold, damp earth, a *living object* which appalled him; it was a human creature, but so horribly and unnaturally deformed, that it was a far more dreadful object to behold than the most loathsome of the brute creation.

It was of pygmy size, its shrunk limbs distorted and fleshless, and its lank body covered with filthy rags; its head, of enormous size, was entirely devoid of hair; and the unnatural shape as well as the prodigious dimensions of that bald cranium, betokened beastly idiocy. Its features, ghastly and terrible to look upon, bore a strange resemblance to those of the *Dead Man*! and its snake-like eyes were fixed upon Frank with the ferocity of a poisonous reptile about to spring upon its prey.

'Who art thou?' demanded our hero, as he surveyed the hideous object with horror and disgust.

It answered not, but again set up its low and melancholy wail. Then with extraordinary agility, it sprang from its retreat, and bounding towards the dungeon, entered, and crouched down in one corner, making the cellar resound with its awful shrieks.

''Tis more beast than human,' thought Frank — 'I will fasten it in its den, or it may attack me;' and closing the door, he secured it with the bolt. As he did so, he heard the deep-toned bell peal forth the hour of — *one*!

'It is the hour appointed for the return of the Dead Man!' said our hero to himself, with a shudder; and instantly it occurred to him that he might have descended to the Dark Vaults and escaped that way, had he not cut the ropes which supported the platform. But then he reflected that on reaching the Vaults he would be almost certain to fall into the power of the villains assembled there; and he ceased to regret having cut the ropes.

His attention was suddenly arrested by observing the platform descend into the abyss, moved by an unseen agency; for the apparatus was so contrived, that a person in the Vaults below could lower or raise the platform at will, by means of a rope connected with it.

Frank had anticipated that the Dead Man would enter the house through the front door; but he now felt convinced that the miscreant was about to ascend on the platform from the Vaults; and he said to himself —

"Tis well — these almost severed ropes will not sustain the villain's weight, and if he attains to any considerable height, and then falls, his instant death is certain.'

The platform reached the bottom of the abyss — a short pause ensued, and then it began slowly to ascend; higher, higher it mounted, until our hero, fearing that the rope might not break, was about to cut it again, when a yell of agony reached his ear from the depths of the pit, and at the same moment the slackened condition of the rope convinced him that the platform had fallen. He listened, and heard a sound like the plunging of a body into water; then all was silent as the grave.

'The villain has met with a just doom,' thought Frank; and no longer apprehensive of the return of his mortal enemy, he left the cellar, and entering the room above, in which the stolen goods were deposited, threw himself upon a heap of clothes and garments, and fell into a deep slumber.

It was broad daylight when he awoke; and starting up, his eyes rested upon an object which caused him to recoil with horror. The woman whom he had left insensible from the effects of the powerful drug which she had taken, was standing near him, her eyes rolling with insanity, her hair dishevelled, her clothes torn to rags and her face scratched and bleeding, she having in her own madness inflicted the wounds with her own nails.

'Ha!' she exclaimed — 'had'st thou not awakened, I would have killed thee! Thy heart would have made me a brave breakfast, and I would have banqueted on thy life-blood! Go hence — go hence! thou shalt not unfold the awful mysteries of this charnel-house! — Ye must not behold the murdered man who lies rotting in the cellar, nor open the dark dungeon of the deformed child of crime! — 'tis the hideous offspring of hideous parents — my child and the Dead Man's! 'Twas a judgement from Heaven, that monstrous being; we dare not kill it, so we shut it up from the light of day. Go hence — go hence, or I will fly at thee and tear thine eyes out!'

Frank left the room, and ascended to the chamber, hoping to find a key which would enable him to unlock the front door; and in a table drawer he discovered one, which he doubted not would release him from his imprisonment. Before departing, he wrote the following words on a scrap of paper: —

'If the villain known as the *Dead Man* still lives, he is informed that he is indebted to *me* for his unexpected fall last night. Let the miscreant tremble — for I have penetrated the mysteries of this infernal den, and my vengeance, if not ordinary justice, will speedily overtake him!

SYDNEY.'

Leaving the note upon the table, Frank descended the stairs, unlocked the door, and departed from that abode of crime and horror.

FOOTNOTES:

[3] A *stool pigeon* is a person who associates with thieves, in order to betray their secrets to the police officers, in reference to any robbery which has been committed, or which may be in contemplation. As a reward for furnishing such information, the *stool pigeon* is allowed to steal and rob, *on his own account,* with almost perfect impunity.

CHAPTER XV

*Showing the pranks played in the Haunted House by the two
Skeletons.*

When Mrs. Belmont awoke from the swoon into which she
had fallen, at sight of the terrible apparition which had visited
her, daylight was shining through the windows of her chamber.
She immediately recalled to mind the events of the preceding
night, and resolved to remove without delay from a house which
was troubled with such fearful visitants.

Her maid Susan soon entered, to assist her in dressing; and
she learned that the girl had neither seen nor heard anything of a
mysterious or ghostly nature, during the night. But when the lady
related what *she* had seen, the terror of poor Susan knew no
bounds, and she declared her determination not to sleep alone in
the house another night.

While at breakfast, a visitor was announced, who proved to
be the landlord, Mr. Hedge. The old gentleman entered with
many apologies for his intrusion, and said —

'To confess the truth, my dear madam, I am anxious to learn
how you passed the night. Were you disturbed by any of the gob-
lins or spectres which are supposed to haunt the house?'

Julia related everything which had occurred, and Mr. Hedge
expressed great astonishment and concern.

'It is singular — very singular, and fearful,' said he musingly
— 'a terrible blot seems to rest upon this house; I must abandon
the hope of ever having it occupied, as I presume you now desire
to remove from it, as a matter of course?'

'Such *was* my intention,' replied Julia, 'but you will be surprised when I assure you that within the last hour I have changed
my mind, and am now resolved to remain here. To me there is a
charm in mystery, even when that mystery, as in the present instance, is fraught with terror. I think I need entertain no apprehension of receiving personal injury from these ghostly night-
walkers, for if they wished to harm me, they could have done so

last night. Hereafter, my maid shall sleep in my chamber with me; I shall place a dagger under my pillow, with which to defend myself in case of any attempted injury or outrage — and I shall await the coming of my spectral friend with feelings of mingled dread and pleasure.'

'I am delighted to hear you say so,' rejoined the old gentleman, as he surveyed the animated countenance and fine form of the courageous woman with admiration. In truth, Julia looked very charming that morning; she was dressed in voluptuous *dishabille*, which partially revealed a bust whose luxurious fullness and exquisite symmetry are rarely equalled by the divine creations of the sculptor's art.

'She is very beautiful,' thought the old gentleman; and the sluggish current of his blood began to course thro' his veins with something of the ardor of youth.

Mr. Hedge was a wealthy old bachelor; — and like the majority of individuals, who belong to that class, he adored pretty women, but had always adored them *at a distance*. To him, woman was a divinity; he bowed at her shrine, but dared not presume to taste the nectar of her lips, or inhale the perfume of her sighs. He had always regarded such familiarity as a type of sacrilege. But now, seated *tete-a-tete* with that charming creature, and feasting his eyes upon her voluptuous beauty, his awe of the divinity merged into a burning admiration of the woman.

Julia knew that Mr. Hedge was rich. 'He admires me,' thought she, — 'he is old, but wealthy; I will try to fascinate him, and if he desires me to become either his wife or mistress, I will consent, for a connection with him would be to my pecuniary advantage.'

And she *did* fascinate him, as much by her sparkling wit and graceful discourse, as by her charms of person. She related to him a very pleasing little fiction entirely the offspring of her own fertile imagination, which purported to be a history of her own past life. She stated that she was the widow of an English gentleman; she had recently come to America, and had but few acquaintances, and still fewer friends; she felt the loneliness of her situation, and admitted that she much desired a friend to counsel and protect her; the adroit adventuress concluded her extemporaneous romance by adroitly insinuating that her income was scarcely adequate to her respectable maintenance.

Mr. Hedge listened attentively to this narrative, and religiously believed every word of it. While the lady was speaking, he had drawn his chair close to hers, and taken one of her small, delicate hands in his. We must do him the justice to observe, that though her beauty had inspired him with passion, he nevertheless sincerely sympathised with her on account of her pretended misfortunes — and, supposing her to be strictly virtuous, he entertained not the slightest wish to take advantage of her unprotected situation.

'My dear young lady,' said he — 'although I have known you but a very short time, I have become exceedingly interested in you. I am an old man — old enough to be your father; and as a father I now speak to you. — What I am about to say, might seem impertinent and offensive in a young man, but you will pardon it in me. You have unconscientiously dropped a hint touching the insufficiency of your income to maintain you as a lady should be maintained. I am rich — deign to accept from me as a gift — or as a loan, if you will — this scrap of paper; 'tis valueless to me, for I have more money than I need. The gift — or loan — shall be repeated as often as your necessities require it.'

He squeezed a bank-note into her hand — and when she, with affected earnestness, desired him to take it back, assuring him that she needed no immediate pecuniary aid, he insisted that she should retain it; and shortly afterwards he arose and took his leave, having easily obtained permission to call upon her the next day.

'Egad, she would make me a charming wife — if she would only have me,' thought the old gentleman, as he left the house.

'Five hundred dollars!' exclaimed Julia, as she examined the bank-note which he had given her — 'how liberal! I have fairly entrapped the silly old man; he is too honorable to propose that I should become his mistress, and he will probably offer me his hand in marriage. I will accept him at once — and to avoid detection, I shall remove with my venerable husband to Boston, which I have heard is a charming city, where a woman of fashion and intrigue can lead a glorious and brilliant career.'

That night she retired early to rest, and her maid Susan shared her chamber — an arrangement highly satisfactory to the abigail, who was glad of company in a house where ghosts were in the habit of perambulating during the night.

Neither mistress nor maid closed an eye in slumber — but midnight came, and they had not seen nor heard anything of a ghostly nature. Yet strange events were taking place in the house, — events which will throw light upon the fearful mysteries of the place.

It was about an hour after midnight, when a large stone among those of which the foundation of the house was built, turned slowly upon pivots, revealing an aperture in the wall, and at the same instant the glare of a lantern shone into the cellar.

From the aperture emerged two persons of frightful appearance, one of whom carried the lantern; they were both dressed in tight-fitting garments of black cloth, upon which was daubed in white paint the figure of a skeleton; and each of their faces had been blacked, and then drawn over with the representation of a skull. Seen by an imperfect light, they exactly resembled two skeletons.

'By Jesus!' exclaimed one of them, in a tone which was anything but hollow or sepulchral — 'let's put for the pantry and see what there is to *ate*, for be the powers I'm starved wid hunger!'

'That's the talk, Bloody Mike — - so we will,' responded the other worthy, who was no other than our old friend Ragged Pete, though his nearest relatives would never have recognized him in the disguise he then wore.

Mike and Pete ascended to the pantry, and began a diligent search after provisions.

'Glory to ould Ireland, here's grand illigant ham!' exclaimed the first mentioned individual, as he dragged from a shelf a large dish containing the article he had named.

'And blow me tight if here isn't a cold turkey and a pan of pudding,' rejoined Pete, whose researches had also been crowned with success.

'Faith, it's ourselves, Peter, dear, that'll have a supper fit for the bishop of Cork, an' that's a big word,' remarked Mike, as he triumphantly placed upon a table the savory viands above mentioned, and 'fell to' with surpassing vigor, an example in which he was followed by his comrade.

'This playing the ghost is a good business, by jingo!' said Pete, with his mouth full of ham.

'True for ye!' replied the Irish skeleton, his articulation rendered indistinct by the masses of turkey which were fast travelling down his throat to his capacious stomach.

The repast was not finished until they had devoured every atom of the provisions; and then Pete went in quest of something to 'wash the wittles down with,' as he expressed it.

Upon a sideboard in the adjoining room he found wines and liquors of excellent quality, which he and his companion were soon engaged in discussing, with as much ease and comfort as if they were joint proprietors of the whole concern.

The two gentlemen grew quite cosey and confidential over their wine, and as their conversation mainly referred to matters in which the reader perhaps feels an interest, we shall so far intrude upon their privacy as to report the same.

'I've news to tell you, Mike,' said Pete — 'the Dead Man has somehow or other found out that the lady who moved into this house yesterday, is the wife of Mr. Sydney, the rich chap that he hates so infernally 'cause he had him arrested once. Well, you know that last night some one cut the ropes that hoists the platform from the Vaults, so that the Dead Man fell and came nigh breaking his neck; and as it is, he's so awfully bruised that he won't have the use of his limbs for some time to come — besides, he fell into the sewers, and would have been drowned, if I hadn't heerd him, and dragged him out. The chap wot played him that trick was this same Sydney; for a note was found this morning in Anthony street crib, bragging about it, and signed with his name. Now it seems that his wife that lives in this house, and who we are trying to skeer out of it, as we have done all the others that ever lived here — it seems that *she* hates Sydney like thunder and wants to be revenged on him for something — and that the Dead Man found that out, too. So 'our boss' thinks he'll try and set up a partnership with this Mrs. Belmont, as she calls herself — and with her aid he calculates to get Mr. Sydney into his power. If the lady and him sets up business together, our services as ghosts won't be wanted any longer; and I'm very sorry for it, because we've had glorious times in this house, frightening people, and making them believe the place was haunted.'

As this long harangue rendered Pete thirsty, he extinguished his eloquence for a few moments in a copious draught of choice Burgundy.

'That row at Pat Mulligan's last night was a divilish nate affair,' remarked Mike.

'Yes,' said Pete — 'and we all got bundled off to the watch-house; but the Captain let me go — he always does, because I vote for his party. After I got clear, I came here, wrapped in a great sheet, and went up into Mrs. Belmont's chamber; after frightening the poor woman almost to death, I goes up to the bed, puts my hand on her face, and tells her that she'd see me agin — whereupon she gives a great shriek, and I cut my puck through the hole in the cellar.'

'Be the powers,' remarked Bloody Mike — 'it's a great convenience entirely, to have thim sacret passages from the Vault into intarior of houses; there's two of thim, one under the crib in Anthony street, and the other under this dacent house in *Rade* street.'

'Yes, you're right,' said Pete — 'but come, let's do our business and be off — it's near three o'clock.'

The two worthies mounted the stairs with noiseless steps, and pausing before Mrs. Belmont's chamber, Ragged Pete gave utterance to an awful groan. A stifled shriek from the interior of the room convinced them the inmates were awake and terribly frightened.

Pete's groan was followed by a violent *hiccuping* on the part of Bloody Mike — for, to confess the truth, that convivial gentleman had imbibed so freely that he was, in vulgar parlance, most essentially drunk.

'Stop that infernal noise, and follow me into the room,' whispered Pete, who, having confined himself to wine instead of brandy, was comparatively sober.

'Lade on, I'm after ye!' roared the Irish skeleton. Pete, finding the door locked gave it a tremendous kick, and it burst open with a loud crash.

Julia and her maid screamed with horror and affright, as they beheld two hideous forms resembling skeletons come rushing into the room.

Ragged Pete advanced to the bedside of Mrs. Belmont, and threw himself into an approved pugilistic attitude, as if challenging that lady to take a 'set to' with him; while Bloody Mike stumbled over the prostrate form of the lady's maid, who occupied a temporary bed upon the floor. Forgetting his assumed part, he yelled out for something to drink, and forthwith began to sing in tones of thunder, the pathetic Hibernian ballad commencing with —

'A sayman courted a farmer's daughter,
That lived convenient to the Isle of Man.'

'The devil! — you'll spoil all,' muttered Pete, as he seized Mike, and with difficulty dragged him from the room. 'Ain't you a nice skeleton, to get drunk and sing love songs,' he whispered contemptuously, pulling his inebriated comrade downstairs after him: 'No dacent ghost ever gets as corn'd as you be,' he added, as they entered the 'hole in the wall;' after which the stone was turned into its place, which it fitted so exactly, that the most criti-

164

cal eye could not have discovered anything to indicate that it had ever been moved at all.

Mrs. Belmont was now fully satisfied in her own mind that there was nothing supernatural about the nocturnal intruders, but that they were in reality substantial flesh and blood, and though she could not divine how they had entered the house, she was much relieved and comforted by the assurance that it was with *living* men she had to deal — a conviction which was amply confirmed the next morning, when the havoc done to the eatables and drinkables was announced to her by the indignant Susan.

In the afternoon Mr. Hedge called upon her as appointed, and dined with his interesting and fascinating tenant.

After dinner, Julia caused the sofa to be wheeled in front of the glorious fire which glowed in the grate (for the weather was intensely cold) and seating herself, invited the old gentleman to place himself at her side.

Then she exerted all her fine powers of discourse to increase his admiration, and draw from him a declaration of love, and an offer of marriage.

Wine was brought in, and gradually their spirits became enlivened by the sparkling genii of the grape. The old man felt the fires of youth careering through his veins, and his withered cheek was suffused with a flush of passion.

'Beautiful Julia,' said he — 'I observe that you have a magnificent piano; will you favor me with an air?'

She smiled an assent, and her aged admirer conducted her to the instrument with the most ceremonious politeness. After a brilliant prelude, executed with artistic delicacy and skill, she dashed off into a superb Italian air, which raised her listener (who was passionately devoted to music,) into the seventh heaven of ecstasy.

'Glorious! — grand!' were his exclamations of delight, when she had finished the air and she needed no urgent persuasion to induce her to favor him with another.

Artfully and admirably did she compose an extempore song, adapted to immediate circumstances, beginning — 'I love no vain and fickle youth,' and beautifully depicting the love of a young woman for a man advanced in years. She sung it with a most touching air, and threw into her countenance and style an expression of melting tenderness.

Ere she had terminated, the old gentleman was kneeling at her feet; and pressing her fair hand to his lips.

'Divine creature,' he murmured — 'can you pardon the presumption and foolishness of an old man, who dares to love you? Your beauty and your fascinations have conquered and bewildered me. I know that the proposal coming from me, is madness — I know that you will reject my suit with disdain — yet hear me Julia; I am an old, rich and solitary man — I need some gentle ray of sunshine to gild my few remaining years — I need some beautiful creature, like yourself, to preside over my gloomy household, and cheer me in my loneliness by her delightful society and the music of her voice. Boundless wealth shall be at your command; no restraint shall ever be placed upon the number of your servants, the splendor of your carriages and equipages, the costliness of your jewels; and the magnificence of your amusements. Speak — and seal my destiny.'

And Julia *did* speak, and became the affianced wife of Mr. Hedge. Her operations thus far had been crowned with triumphant success.

It was arranged that their marriage should take as privately as possible in one month, from that day. — Julia suggested that, immediately after their union, they should remove to Boston, and take up their permanent residence in that city, to which proposal the old gentleman gave a cheerful consent.

'And if you have no objection, my dear Julia,' said he, 'we will be united by Dr. Sinclair, the young and excellent rector of St. Paul's, to which church I belong.'

Julia signified her compliance with the arrangement. She had both seen and admired the young rector, and thought him handsome — very handsome.

Previous to Mr. Hedge's departure that evening, he presented her with a large sum of money, to defray, he said, the expenses necessary to be incurred in her preparations for the marriage. Then the enamored old gentleman kissed her hand, and took his leave.

When he was gone, Julia abandoned herself to the pleasing thoughts engendered by her present brilliant prospects. While in the midst of these agreeable meditations, she was interrupted by the sound of a footstep behind her; and turning, she beheld a man of an aspect so hideous and revolting, that she screamed with terror.

'Hush! be silent, madam — I mean you no harm,' said the man, as he closed the door, and seated himself at her side upon the sofa. Julia gazed on him with surprise and dread. His face, which at best was the most loathsome and horrible ever worn by man, was mangled and bruised as if by some severe and terrible injury; he moved with evident pain and difficulty, and carried one of his arms in a sling.

'Our interview shall be brief, and to the point,' said the mysterious visitor. 'I am he who is called the *Dead Man*, and I am not disposed to quarrel with the title, for I like it. — You and your history are known to me; it matters not how I obtained my information; you are styled Mrs. Belmont, a widow — but you are the discarded wife of Francis Sydney, and half an hour ago you engaged yourself in marriage to Mr. Hedge, the owner of this house.'

Julia started with alarm, for she felt that she was in the power of that terrible man.

'What is the object of your visit?' she asked.

'Listen and you shall know. I have a secret subterranean cavern which communicates with the cellar of this building, and 'twas by that means I entered the house to-night. Myself and friends often find it convenient to carry stolen goods through this house into our den; and in order to have the place all to ourselves, we have heretofore frightened away the people who have come here to live; thus the house is reputed to be haunted. 'Twas our design to frighten you away, also; but having discovered *who and what you are*, I've concluded to explain the mystery, and set up a copartnership with you.'

'And in what business can *we* possibly be connected together?' asked Julia, with ill-concealed disgust.

'In the business of *vengeance*!' thundered the Dead Man, foaming with rage. 'Tell me, woman — do you hate Sydney?'

'I do! — and would sell my soul to be revenged upon him,' she replied with flashing eyes.

'Enough!' cried the other, with triumphant joy — 'I knew you would join me in my plan of vengeance. Now, madam, from this moment we are friends — *partners*, rather let me say — and there's my hand upon it.' And he gripped her hand almost fiercely, while she shuddered at the awful contact. It seemed as if she were touching a corpse.

'Hereafter,' continued the miscreant, — 'you shall rest at night securely in this house, undisturbed by pretended ghosts. Do you see these wounds and bruises? — for them I am indebted to Sydney; my wife is a raging maniac, and I am also indebted to him for *that* — and by eternal hell! when I get him in my power, he shall die by inches; he shall suffer every slow torture which my ingenuity can devise; his brain shall burn, and when death shall end his torments, I have sworn to eat his heart; and by G — — , *I'll do it!*'

'But how will you get him into your power?' asked Julia, delighted with the prospect of revenging herself upon poor Frank.

'I will contrive some means of deluding him into this house; and once in here, he shall never again behold the light of day,' replied the Dead Man, as he arose to withdraw.

'Stay a moment,' said Julia, with some embarrassment — 'there is also a colored man in Sydney's house, and — '

'I know it — he shall be liberated,' interrupted the Dead

Man, and added — 'you shall see me again to-morrow — farewell.'

He left the room, descended to the cellar, and passed through the secret passage to the Dark Vaults.

That night at about the hour of twelve, the dark figure of a man crossed the garden in the rear of Frank Sydney's house, and approached the iron door of the wine-vault wherein Nero, the African, was imprisoned. By the aid of skeleton keys he unlocked the door, and bade the prisoner come forth.

The negro obeyed, surprised and delighted at his unexpected deliverance.

'To whom am I indebted for this friendly act?' he asked.

'I have no time to answer questions,' replied the Dead Man, for it was he. 'Hasten to your mistress at No. — Reade street, and remember your motto as well as mine must be — 'Vengeance on Sydney!''

'Yes — vengeance on Sydney,' muttered the black, from between his clenched teeth, as he hurried away in the direction of Reade street.

'He will be another agent to assist me in torturing my enemy,' said the Dead Man to himself, as he bent his rapid footsteps towards the Dark Vaults.

Nero soon reached the residence of Mrs. Belmont, in Reade street. He was admitted into the house by Susan, who informed him that her mistress had not yet retired. The black quickly mounted the stairs, and entering the room, was about to rush forward and clasp the lady in his arms, when she checked him by a movement of disgust, desired him not to approach her, and pointing to a chair in a distant corner, coldly requested him to seat himself there.

Why did that unprincipled and licentious woman thus repulse the former partner of her guilty joys — he who had so long been the recipient of her favors, and the object of her unhallowed love? Was it because he was emaciated, filthy and in rags, the

results of his long imprisonment in a loathsome dungeon? No —
that was not the reason of her repulsing him.

Julia was a woman wildly capricious in her nature; she was a
creature of sudden impulses — her most passionate love would
often instantly change to bitterest hate. In this instance, her love
for the African had entirely and forever ceased, and she now
viewed him with contemptuous disgust, wondering that she
could ever have had such a *penchant* for him.

''Tis strange,' she thought, 'that I ever could descend to an intrigue with that vile negro. Heavens! I loathe the very sight of
him!'

Nero, on his part, was astounded at this unexpected recep-
tion; he had anticipated a night of voluptuous bliss with his former paramour, and he could not divine the cause of her sudden
rejection of him.

'My dear Julia, why this coldness? — what have I done to offend you?' he demanded, after a short pause.

'Presume not to call me *your dear Julia*, fellow,' she replied
scornfully. 'You have done nothing to offend me, but the days of
our familiarity are over. The liberties which I permitted you to
take, and the indulgences which I formerly granted to you, can
never be repeated. I will not condescend to explain myself farther
than to remark, that all my former regard for you has ceased, and
I now view you not only with indifference, but with positive dis-
like. I procured your liberation from that dungeon merely because it was on my account you were placed there. You can, if
you choose, re-enter my service as footman, and your wages shall
be the same as those of any other servant of your class; but remember — henceforth I am the mistress, and you the menial, and
any presumption on your part, or attempt at familiarity, shall be
instantly followed by your discharge. Clean yourself of that filth,
and begin your duties to-morrow, as a respectful, orderly and
obedient servant. You can go now.'

Nero left the room, humbled and crest-fallen, inwardly resolved to revenge himself upon that proud and abandoned

woman, should the opportunity ever present itself.

Gentlest of readers, we now invite thee to accompany us to view other scenes and other characters in our grand drama of human life, and its many crimes.

CHAPTER XVI

Showing the Voluptuous Revellings of the Rector and the Licentious Josephine, and illustrating the Power of Temptation over Piety and Morality.

Alas, for Dr. Sinclair! the masquerade ball, and the triumph of Josephine Franklin, were but the commencement of a career of folly and crime on his part. From that fatal night in after years of remorse and misery, he dated his downfall.

He became a frequent visitor at the Franklin House, and continued his guilty amour, with unabated zeal. Yet neither his own idolizing congregation, nor the admiring world, suspected his frailty; he was regarded as the most exemplary of Christians, and the best of men. When in the pulpit, it was often remarked that he seemed absent-minded, and ill at ease; he did not preach with his usual fluent and fervid eloquence, nor pray with his accustomed earnest devotion. In person, too, he was changed; his eyes were red, as if with weeping; his cheeks were pale and haggard, and the rosy hue of health was gone. His dress was frequently neglected and disordered, and he even sometimes appeared with his hair uncombed, and his face unshaved. These indications of mental and personal irregularity were much noticed and commented upon by his congregation, comprised as it was of people the most aristocratic and particular.

'Our dear pastor is ill,' said they, with looks of concern and sympathy; but in answer to the numerous questions addressed to him in reference to the state of his health, he denied the existence of all bodily ailment.

'Then he must be affected with some mental disquietude,' said they, and forthwith he was beset by a tribe of comforters; one of whom had at last the audacity to affirm that the Doctor's breath smelt unpleasantly of wine!

This insinuation was received with contempt, for the brethren and sisters of the congregation would not believe anything discreditable to the beloved rector, and he continued to enjoy their confidence and esteem, long after they had begun to observe something very singular in his conduct and appearance.

But in truth, Dr. Sinclair had fallen from his high estate, and become a wine bibber and a lover of the flesh. His stern integrity, his sterling piety, and his moral principle, were gone forever; the temptress had triumphed and he was ruined.

Why are ministers of the gospel so prone to licentiousness? is a question often asked, and is often answered thus — Because they are a set of hypocritical libertines. But we say, may not we see the reason in this: the female members of a church are apt to regard their minister with the highest degree of affectionate admiration — as an idol worthy to be worshipped. They load him with presents — they spoil him with flattery — they dazzle him with their glances, and encourage him by their smiles. Living a life of luxurious ease, and enjoying a fat salary, he cannot avoid experiencing those feelings which are natural to all mankind. He is very often thrown into the society of pretty women of his flock, under circumstances which are dangerously fascinating. The 'sister,' instead of maintaining a proper reserve, grows too communicative and too familiar, and the minister, who is but a man, subject to all the weaknesses and frailties of humanity, often in an unguarded moment forgets his sacred calling, and becomes the seducer — though we question if literal *seduction* be involved, where the female so readily *complies* with voluptuous wishes, which perchance, she responds to with as much fervor as the other party entertains them. Therefore, we say that licentiousness on the part of ministers of the gospel is produced in *very many* cases by the encouragements held out to them by too admiring and too affectionate sisters.

One evening, Dr. Sinclair repaired to Franklin House at an early hour, for he had engaged to dine with Josephine. He was admitted by a tall, fresh-looking country lad, who had recently entered the house in the capacity of footman, having been selected for that station by Mrs. Franklin herself, as the lady had conceived a strong admiration of his robust form and well-proportioned limbs.

The Doctor found Josephine in her *boudoir*, voluptuously reclining upon a damask ottoman, and languidly turning over the leaves of a splendid portfolio of engravings.

'Ah, my dear Doc,' she exclaimed, using a familiar abbreviation of Doctor, 'I am devilish glad to see you, for I am bored to death with *ennui*. Heigho!'

'And if I may presume to inquire, Josey,' said the Doctor — 'what have you there to engage your attention?'

'Oh, views from nature,' she laughingly replied, handing him the portfolio for his inspection.

Turning over the leaves, the Doctor found, somewhat to his astonishment, that the engravings were of rather an obscene character, consisting principally of nude male figures; — and upon these specimens of a perverted art had she been feasting her impure imagination. The time had been, when the Doctor would have turned with pain and disgust from such an evidence of depravity; but he had lately become so habituated to vice, that he merely smiled in playful reproach, and leisurely examined the pictures.

'I commend your taste,' said he, at length. 'Our preferences are both strictly classical; you dote upon the Apollo Belvedere, while in you I worship a Venus.'

'Yes — *you* are my Apollo,' she rejoined, with a glance of passion, encircling him with her arms.

***

Dinner was magnificently served in an apartment whose splendor could scarce have been surpassed in a kingly palace.

They dined alone; for Mrs. Franklin was invisible — and so, also, was the comely young footman!

After dinner, came wine — bright, sparkling wine, whose magical influence gilds the dull realities of life with the soft radiance of fairy land! How the foaming champagne glittered in the silver cup, and danced joyously to the ripe, pouting lip of beauty, and the eloquent mouth of divinity! How brilliant became their

174

eyes, and what a glorious roseate hue suffused their cheeks!

Again and again was the goblet drained and replenished, until the maddening spell of intoxication was upon them both. Hurrah! away with religion, and sermonizing, and conscience! Bacchus is the only true divinity, and at his rosy shrine let us worship, and pledge him in brimming cups of the bright nectar, the drink of the gods!

Then came obscene revels and libidinous acts. The depraved Josephine, attired in a superb robe of lace, her splendid bust uncovered, and her cheeks flushed with wine, danced with voluptuous freedom, while the intoxicated rector, reeling and flourishing a goblet, sang a lively opera air, in keeping with her graceful but indelicate movements. Then — but we will not inflict upon the reader the disgusting details of that evening's licentious extravagances.

Midnight came and the doctor, tipsy as he was, saw the necessity of taking his departure; for though urged by Josephine to pass the night with her, he dared not comply, knowing that his absence from home all night would appear strange and suspicious to his housekeeper and domestics, and give rise to unpleasant inquiries and remarks. He therefore sallied forth, and though he staggered occasionally, he got along tolerably well, until he encountered a watchman standing half asleep in a doorway, muffled up in his huge cloak; and then, with that invincible spirit of mischief which characterizes a drunken man, the Doctor determined to have a 'lark' with the night guardian, somewhat after the fashion of the wild, harem-scarem students at the University at which he had graduated — in which pranks he had often participated.

Leaning against a lamp-post support, he began singing, in a loud and boisterous manner —

'Watchman — hic — tell us of the — hic — night.'

Now it happened that the watchman was one of those surly ruffians who never stop to remonstrate with a poor fellow, in whom wine has triumphed over wit. Instead of kindly inquiring his address, and conducting the unfortunate gentleman to his residence, the self-important petty official adopted the very means to irritate him and render him more boisterous. In a savage, brutal manner, he ordered the doctor to 'stop his d — — d noise, and move on, or he'd make him!'

'Nay, friend, thou art insolent,' remarked the young gentleman, who drunk as he was, could not brook the insults of the low, vulgar ruffian.

'Insolent, am I? — take that, and be d — — d to you!' cried the fellow, raising a heavy bludgeon, and dealing the poor Doctor a blow on the head which felled him senseless to the ground, covered with blood.

'That'll teach you genteel chaps not to meddle with us *officers*,' growled the watchman. 'I wonder what he's got about him — perhaps some dangerous weapon — let's see.' Thrusting his hand into the pockets of his victim, he drew forth a valuable gold watch, and a purse containing a considerable sum of money. Why did he so rapidly transfer these articles to this own pockets? Was if for the purpose of restoring them to the owner, on the morrow? We shall see.

'I 'spose I'd better lug him to the watch-house,' said the 'officer' — and he struck his club three times on the pavement, which summoned another 'officer' to his assistance. The two then raising the wounded man between them, conducted him towards the Tombs.

The Doctor, awaking from his unconsciousness, and feeling himself in the grasp of the watchman, instantly comprehended the state of affairs, and shuddered as he thought of his exposure and ruin. The fumes of the wine which he had drunk, had entirely subsided; but he felt himself weak from loss of blood, sick from his recent debauch, while the wound on his head pained him terribly. Oh, how bitterly he deplored his connection with that depraved woman, who had been the cause of his downfall!

The awful dread of exposure prompted him to appeal to the mercy of his captors.

'Watchman,' said he, 'pray conduct me to my home, or suffer me to go there myself, for with shame I confess it, I am a gospel minister, and wish to avoid exposure.'

The two fellows laughed scornfully. 'Don't think to come that gammon over us,' said they. 'A minister indeed! — and picked up blind drunk in the street at midnight!'

'But I have money about me, and will pay you well,' said the Doctor.

The man who had struck him with the club, knowing that he had no money, affected to be indignant at this attempt to 'bribe an officer,' and refused to release him.

Oh, hapless fate! — truly the 'way of transgressors is hard.' The learned and eloquent Dr. Sinclair — the idol of his aristocratic and fashionable congregation — whose words of piety and holiness were listened to with attention by admiring thousands every Sabbath day — was incarcerated in the watch-house! Yes — thrust into a filthy cell, among a swarm of felons, vile negroes, vagabonds and loafers — the scum of the city!

The cell was about twenty feet square; one half of it was occupied by a platform, at a height of four feet from the floor. This platform was called the 'bunk,' and it was covered with the prostate forms of about twenty men, including the ragged beggar, the raving drunkard, and the well-dressed thief — all huddled together, and shivering with the cold, which was intense. The stone floor of the cell was damp and covered with filth; yet upon it, and beneath the *bunk*, several wretched beings were stretched, some cursing each other and themselves, others making the place resound with hideous laughter, while one was singing, in drunken tones, a shockingly obscene song.

Into this den of horrors was Dr. Sinclair rudely thrust; for no one believed his statement that he was a clergyman, and indeed his appearance, when undergoing the examination of the Captain of the Watch, was anything but clerical. His face was covered with blood, his clothes soiled and disordered, his hat crushed, and his manner wild and incoherent. It is more than probable that, had the Captain known who he was, he would have ordered his immediate discharge.

Groping his way along the damp, cold walls of his cell, which was in profound darkness, the Doctor stumbled over a person who was lying upon the floor, writhing in the agonies of *delirium tremens.* In frantic rage, this miserable creature seized the rector's leg, and bit it horribly, causing him to utter a cry of agony, which was responded to by roars of laughter from the hellish crew. Extricating himself with difficulty from the fierce clutch of the maniac, the unhappy gentleman seated himself upon a large iron pipe which ran through the cell, and prayed for death.

Slowly passed the dreadful night away; and the first faint rays of morning, struggling through the narrow aperture in the wall, revealed an appalling sight. Men made hideous and inhuman by vice and wretchedness lay stretched amid the filth and dampness of that dungeon, glaring at each other with savage eyes. And soon the awful discovery was made, that one of their number had, during the night, been frozen to death! Yes — there, beneath the *bunk,* cold and ghastly, lay the rigid corpse of a poor fellow creature, whose only crime had been his poverty! Out upon such justice and such laws, which tolerate such barbarities to one whose misfortunes should be pitied, not visited by the damnable cruelty of the base hirelings of a corrupt misgovernment!

It is not our wish to devote much time to the relation of unimportant particulars; suffice it to say, that Dr. Sinclair was brought before the police for drunkenness, and was also charged with having violently assaulted Watchman Squiggs, who had taken him in custody!

'You see, yer honor, I was going my rounds, when up comes this ere chap and knocks me down, and would have killed me, if I hadn't hit him a light tap on the head with my club. Then I rapped for help, and — '

'That's enough!' growled the magistrate, who had himself been drunk the night before, and was made irritable by a severe headache — 'that's enough — he struck an officer — serious offence — looks guilty — old offender — thief, no doubt — send him up for six months!'

The Doctor whispered a few words in the ear of the magistrate, who rubbed his eyes and regarded him with a look of astonishment, saying —

'Bless my soul, is it possible? Dr. Sinclair — humph! Sentence is revoked — you're discharged; the devil! — about to send you up for six months — a great mistake, upon my word — ha, ha, ha!'

The rector turned to watchman Squiggs, and said to him, sternly —

'Fellow, when I fell into your infernal clutches, I had a watch and money about me; they are now missing; can you give any account of them?'

The watchman solemnly declared he knew nothing about them! The Doctor felt no inclination to bandy words with the scoundrel; he paused a moment to reflect upon the best course to pursue, under the disagreeable circumstances in which he found himself placed. A feasible plan soon suggested itself, and leaving the police office, he stepped into a hackney coach, and requested the driver to convey him with all despatch to Franklin house. Arrived there, he dismissed the vehicle, and ascending to Josephine's chamber, explained to her the whole affair, and threw himself upon a sofa to obtain a few hours' necessary repose.

As soon as he had left the police office, the magistrate whispered to the watchman —

'Squiggs, I know very well that you took that gentleman's watch and money. Don't interrupt me — I say, *I know you did.* Well, you must share the spoils with me.'

'I'll take my oath, yer honor — '

'*Your oath!* — that's a good one!' cried the magistrate, laughing heartily. — 'd'ye think I'd believe you on oath? Why, man, you just now perjured yourself in swearing that Parson Sinclair assaulted you — whereas *you* beat him horribly with your club, with little provocation, and stole his watch and money. I know you, Squiggs; you can't gammon me. Once for all, will you share the booty with me?'

The rascal dared not hesitate any longer; so with great reluctance he drew the plunder from his pocket, and divided it equally with 'his honor,' who reserved the watch for himself, it being a splendid article, of great value.

Is any one disposed to doubt the truth of this little sketch? We assure the reader it is not in the least degree exaggerated. The local magistracy of New York included many functionaries who were dishonest and corrupt. Licentiousness was a prominent feature in the characters of some of these unworthy ministers of justice. Attached to the police office was a room, ostensibly for the private examination of witnesses. When a witness happened to be a female, and pretty, 'his honor' very often passed an hour or so in this room with her, carefully locking the door to prevent intrusion; and there is every reason to suppose that his examination of her was both close and searching.

We remember an incident which occurred several years ago, which is both curious and amusing. A beautiful French girl — a fashionable courtezan — was taken to the police office, charged with stealing a lady's small gold watch. Her accuser was positive that she had the article about her; her pocket, reticule, bonnet, hair, and dress were searched without success. The rude hand of the officer invaded her voluptuous bosom, but still without finding the watch. 'Perhaps she has it in her mouth,' suggested the magistrate; but no, it was not there. 'Where can she have hidden it? I am certain she has it somewhere on her person,' remarked the accuser. 'I will examine her in private,' quoth the magistrate, and he directed the girl to follow him into the adjoining room. His honor locked the door, and said to the fair culprit — 'My dear, where have you concealed the watch?' In the most charming broken English imaginable, Mademoiselle protested her innocence of the charge, with such passionate eloquence, that his honor began to think the accuser must be mistaken. 'At all events,' thought he, 'she is a sweet little gipsy;' and he forthwith honored her with a shower of amorous kisses, which she received with the most bewitching *naivete*; but when he began to make demonstrations of a still more decided nature, she resisted, though unsuccessfully, for his honor was portly and powerful, and somewhat 'used to things.' But lo! to his astonishment, he *discovered the watch* — and in *such* a place! French ingenuity alone could have devised such a! method of concealment, and legal research alone could have discovered it.

We left Dr. Sinclair in the chamber of Josephine, at Franklin House, reposing after the exciting and disagreeable adventures of the preceding night. He awoke at noon, somewhat refreshed, and entered a bath while Josephine sent a servant to purchase a suit of clothes, as those which he had worn were so soiled and torn as to be unfit for further service.

Reclining luxuriously in the perfumed water of the marble bath, the Doctor experienced a feeling of repose and comfort. He had long learned to disregard the 'still, small voice' of his own conscience; and, provided he could reach his home and answer all inquiries without incurring suspicion — provided, also, his having been incarcerated in the watch-house should not be exposed — he was perfectly contented.

His clothes being brought him, he dressed himself, and joining Josephine in the parlor, partook of a refreshing repast; then, bidding farewell to his 'lady-love,' he took his departure, and proceeded to his own residence. In answer to the earnest inquiries of the members of his household, he stated that he had passed the night with a friend in Brooklyn; and entering his study, he applied himself to the task of writing his next Sunday's sermon.

CHAPTER XVII

Illustrating the truth of the proverb that 'Murder will out,' and containing an Appalling Discovery.

Two or three days after the above events, Dr. Sinclair was sent for by a woman lying at the point of death. He found her occupying the garret of an old, crazy tenement in Orange street; she was stretched upon a miserable bed, covered only by a few rags, and her short breathings, sunken cheeks, and lustreless eyes, proclaimed that the hand of death was upon her. Though young in years, her appearance indicated that she had passed through much suffering, destitution and sin.

'Are you the clergyman?' she asked in a faint voice.

'I am; what can I do for you, my good woman?' said the Doctor, seating himself on a rickety stool at the bedside.

'Oh, sir,' cried the invalid, evidently in great mental distress, 'I want you to pray for me. Do you think there is any hope for such a sinner as I have been? I am dying, and my soul is lost — forever!'

In his own heart, the rector felt his unfitness to administer comfort in such a case, considering his own wickedness; yet he strove to quiet the uneasiness of the poor creature, by assuring her that there was hope for the 'chief of sinners.' At her request he prayed with her; and then she addressed him as follows: —

'There is something on my mind which I must make confession of, or I shall not die easy — something that will make you shrink from me, as from a guilty wretch, who deserves no mercy. I am a *murderess!*'

'A murderess!' echoed the Doctor, starting back with horror; after a few moments' pause, he added — 'proceed with your confession.'

'I will, sir. Four years ago, I entered the service of Mrs. Lucretia Franklin, in Washington Place.'

The Doctor started again — this time with surprise; and he

listened with attentive interest to the woman's narrative.

'Mrs. Franklin's husband,' she resumed, 'was a very rich man, and very religious and strict; his daughter Sophia took after him much, and was a very good girl; but his wife and daughter Josephine were exactly contrary to him, for they were very giddy and gay, always going to theatres, and balls, and such like places, keeping late hours, and acting so dissipated like, that at last Mr. Franklin was determined to put a stop to it entirely, and make them stay at home. So he told them that he shouldn't allow them to go on as they had any longer; and having once said the word, he stuck to it. My lady and Miss Josephine were both very much dissatisfied with Mr. Franklin, on account of his being so strict with them; and I could plainly see that they began to hate him. It is now about two years ago, and Josephine was in her sixteenth year (ah, sir, I have good reason to remember the time,) when I found myself in the way to become a mother, having been led astray by a young man, who deceived me under a promise of marriage, and then deserted me. Well, sir, my situation was at last noticed by my lady and her daughter, and one evening they called me up into a chamber, and accused me of being a lewd girl. Falling on my knees, I acknowledged my fault, and implored them to pity and forgive me, and not turn me off without a character. Then Miss Josephine spoke harshly to me, and asked me how I dared do such a thing, and bring disgrace upon their house and family; and her mother threatened to send me to jail, which frightened me so that I promised to do anything in the world if they would forgive me. *'Will you do any thing we command you to do,* if we forgive you?' asked Mrs. Franklin; and I said that I would. *'You must swear it,'* said Miss Josephine; and getting a Bible, they made me swear a dreadful oath to do as they bid me. They then told me that there was one thing I must do, and they would give me as much money as I wanted; they said I must *kill Mr. Franklin!* On hearing such a horrible request, I almost fainted; and told them that I never would do such a dreadful thing. But they reminded me of my oath, and at last threatened and frightened me so, that I consented to do the awful deed. *'It must be done to-night!'* said Miss Josephine, and her eyes seemed to flash fire; then she gave me some brandy to drink, which flew into my brain, and I felt myself able to do anything, no matter how wicked it might be. — They staid with me until midnight, and made me drink brandy until I was almost crazy. You must know, sir, that Mr. Franklin slept in a separate room from my lady, ever since their disagreement; upon that dreadful night he retired to bed at about ten o'clock. Well — but oh, my God! how can I tell the dreadful truth! — yet I must nerve myself to confess the whole matter. At midnight, Mrs. Franklin brought into the room a small copper cup, which contained a small quantity of *lead*; this cup she held over the lamp until the lead was melted as thin as water; and then she handed it to me, and told me to go softly into her husband's room, and *pour the lead into his ear!* I DID IT! Yes, as God is my Judge, I did it! — The poor gentleman was lying on his side, in a sound sleep; with a steady hand I poured the liquid metal into his ear — *it did not awake him!* he merely shuddered once, and died. — The next morning he was found by his servant, stiff and cold. Some people talked of 'disease of the heart,' others, of 'apoplexy,' many, of 'the visitation of God,' while some shrugged their shoulders, and said nothing. But *I* knew the secret of his death! He was buried with great pomp in the family tomb in St. Paul's churchyard. My confession is made. After the funeral, my lady and Josephine gave me plenty of money. 'Go,' said they, 'to some other city, and take up your abode; you will never the mention the manner in which Mr. Franklin came to his death, for such a disclosure would bring your own neck to the halter, without injuring us — *your hand* alone did the deed!' I went to Boston, and gave birth to a stillborn child; my money soon went and I became a common prostitute. — Disease soon overtook me — but why dwell upon the misfortunes and wanderings of a wretch like me? A week ago, I found myself again in New York, the inmate of this garret; to-day I felt myself dying, and sent for a clergyman to hear my dying confession. I am exhausted; I can say no more — God have mercy on me!'

'One word more,' cried the rector; 'by what name were you known to the Franklins?'

'Mary Welch,' she replied, faintly.

The wretched creature soon afterwards breathed her last.

The Doctor left a sufficient sum of money with the inmates of the house to defray the expenses of the woman's funeral, and took his departure from that scene of wretchedness. As he retraced his steps to his own dwelling, his thoughts were of the most painful nature; the woman's confession, implicating Josephine and her mother in the crime of murder, horrified him, and gave rise to the most terrible reflections. In his own heart he could not doubt the truth of the wretched woman's statement, made as it was on her death-bed, and just as she was about to be ushered into the presence of her Maker.

'My God!' thought the rector, entering his study, and throwing himself distractedly into a seat — 'to what a dreadful disclosure have I listened — Josephine the murderess of her father! Mrs. Franklin the murderess of her husband! Can it be possible? — Alas, I cannot doubt it; for why should that woman, at the awful moment of her dissolution, tell a falsehood? I remember now the circumstances of Mr. Franklin's death; it was sudden and unaccountable, and privately spoken of with suspicion, as to its cause; yet those suspicions never assumed any definite shape. — The poor gentleman was buried without any post mortem examination, and the singular circumstances of his death were gradually forgotten. But now the awful mystery is revealed to me; he met his death at the hands of that miserable woman, at the instigation of Josephine and her mother.'

But the Doctor's most painful thoughts arose from the reflection that he had formed a criminal connection with such a vile, guilty creature as Josephine. He had learned to tolerate her licentiousness and her consummate hypocrisy; he had loved her with passionate fervor, while he had only regarded her as a frail, beautiful woman, who, having become enamored of him, had enticed him to her arms. But now she stood before him as a wretch capable of any crime — as the murderess of her own father; and all his love and admiration for her were turned into a loathing hate; and while he had no intention of denouncing her and her mother to the authorities of justice, he determined to have but one more interview with her, and at that interview to reproach her for her crime, and cast her off forever.

'But previous to that interview,' thought he, 'I will make assurance doubly sure; I will find means to enter the vault wherein Mr. Franklin's body was interred; I will examine the remains, and as my knowledge of human anatomy is considerable, I shall have no difficulty in discovering the evidences of foul play, if such evidences exist. Having thus satisfied myself beyond the shadow of a doubt that Mr. Franklin was murdered, I can with confidence accuse Josephine and her mother of the deed; and from that moment, all connection between me and that wicked woman shall cease forever. I have been infatuated and enslaved by her seductive beauty and her fascinating favors; but thank God, I am myself again, and resolved to atone for the past, by leading a life of purity and virtue for the future.'

That night the Doctor was called on to perform the marriage ceremony at the house of a friend, at a distant part of the city; and it was late when he set out to return to his own home.

It was a dismal night, dark and starless; the sky was laden with impending storm, and the rector shuddered as he looked forward into the gloom, and contrasted it with the scene of light and gaiety which he had just left. His heart was oppressed with a heavy weight; for he could not shake off the dreadful thought that Josephine — beautiful and accomplished Josephine — whom he had loved with a fervent though unholy passion — was a *murderess*!

While hurrying on with rapid strides, his mind tortured by such painful reflections, a tall figure suddenly stood before him, and a voice whispered —

'Deliver your money, or die!'

The rector perceived that the robber had his arm raised, and that he held in his hand a large knife, ready to strike in case of resistance or alarm. Dr. Sinclair was no coward; had there been a single chance in his favor, he would have grappled with the robber, rather than yield to his demand; yet he was slender and by no means powerful — he was also unarmed; and besides, the idea flashed through his mind that the desperado might be of use to him, and these considerations prompted him to speak in a conciliatory tone and manner: —

'Friend,' said he, 'unfortunately for you I am but a poor parson, and have only about me a few dollars, which I have just received as my fee for uniting a happy couple in the holy bonds of wedlock. What I have you are welcome to; here is my purse.'

The robber took the purse, and was about to move off, when the rector called to him and said, —

'Stay, friend; you are the very man I want to assist me in a dangerous enterprise — one that requires courage, and strength, and skill; if you engage to aid me, your reward shall be liberal — what say you?'

'You must first tell me what it is you want done,' replied the robber.

'I want to break open a tomb in St. Paul's churchyard, and examine a dead body; and to do this I shall require an assistant,' said the Doctor, in a low tone.

'That is all well enough,' rejoined the robber; 'but how do I know that you are not laying a plan to entrap me into the clutches of the law, for having robbed you?'

'Pshaw!' exclaimed the Doctor, disdainfully, 'why should I seek to entrap you? You have only relieved me of a few dollars, and what care I for that! Draw near, and examine me closely; do I look like a man who would tell a base lie, even to bring a robber to justice? — have I not the appearance of a gentleman? I pledge you my sacred word of honor, that I meditate no treachery against you.'

'Enough — I am satisfied,' said the robber, after having scrutinized the Doctor as closely as the darkness would admit of — 'when is this thing to be done?'

'To-morrow night will probably be stormy, and suitable for the purpose,' replied Dr. Sinclair. 'Meet me precisely as the clock strikes the hour of midnight, at the great gate on the lower extremity of the Park; you must come provided with such tools as will be necessary to effect an entrance into the tomb, which is probably secured by a strong padlock; also bring with you a lantern, and the means of lighting it. My object in thus disturbing the repose of the dead, is of no consequence to you; it will be sufficient for you to understand that you are hired to perform a service, which is to be well paid for when completed — you comprehend me?'

'I do,' said the robber, 'and shall not fail to meet you at the time and place appointed; if you have no more to say to me, I will now bid you good night.'

'Good night,' said the Doctor; 'and pray, my good friend, do not menace any other belated traveller with that ugly knife of yours.'

The robber laughed, and turning on his heel, strode away in the darkness, while the rector continued on his way towards his residence. When he reached his house, and had entered the door, a person emerged from the darkness, and by the light of a street lamp which was near, read the name upon the door-plate. — The Doctor had been followed home by the robber.

'All right,' muttered the latter worthy, as he walked away — 'he lives in that house, and his name is Dr. Sinclair. Men of his class don't generally play the spy or traitor; so I can safely keep the appointment. He is not a physician or surgeon; therefore what in the devil's name should he want to break into a tomb for? No matter; to-morrow night will explain the mystery.' And the robber's form was lost in the darkness.

As the Doctor had predicted, the night which followed the adventure just related, was stormy; the snow fell thick and fast, and the darkness was intense. As the clock struck the hour of midnight, a figure muffled in a cloak slowly emerged from the lower extremity of the Park, and paused at the great gate which forms the Southern angle of that vast enclosure. He had waited there but a few minutes, when he was joined by another person, who asked him —

'Well, Sir Robber, is it you?'

'All right, sir; you see I am punctual,' replied the robber. The other person was of course the rector.

Without any further conversation, the two proceeded down Broadway, until they stood before the magnificent church of St. Paul's. This splendid edifice, of Grecian architecture, was situated on the border of an extensive burying ground, which with the church itself, was surrounded by an iron railing of great height. Finding the front gate secured by a massive lock, the robber applied himself to the task of picking it, with an instrument designed for that purpose. This was soon accomplished, and entering the enclosure, the two passed around the rear of the church, and stood among the many tomb-stones which marked the last resting place of the quiet dead.

The rector, being well acquainted with the arrangements of the ground, had no difficulty in finding the tomb he wished to enter. A plain marble slab, upon which was sculptured the words 'Franklin Family,' denoted the spot. It required the united strength of both the men to raise this slab from the masonry on which it rested. This being done, they stepped into the aperture, descended a short flight of stone steps, and found their further progress arrested by an iron door, secured by an immense padlock.

'It will now be necessary to light my lantern; I can do so with safety,' said the robber. And igniting a match, he lighted a dark lantern which he had brought with him. Dr. Sinclair then, for the first time, distinctly beheld the features of his midnight companion; and he started with horror — for the most diabolically hideous countenance he had ever seen or dreamed of in his life, met his gaze. The robber observed the impression he had made upon his employer, and grinned horribly a ghastly smile.

'You don't like my looks, master,' said he, gruffly.

'I certainly cannot call you handsome,' replied the Doctor, trying to smile — 'but no matter — you will answer my purpose as well as a comelier person. Let us proceed with our work; can you break or pick this padlock?'

The robber made no reply, but drew from his pocket a bunch

of skeleton keys, with which he soon removed the padlock; and the heavy iron door swung upon its rusty hinges with a loud creaking noise.

'D — — n and blast that noise!' growled the robber.

'Silence, fellow!' cried the rector, authoritatively; 'you are standing in the chamber of the dead, and such profanity is out of place here — no more of it.'

This reproof was received with a very ill grace by the robber, who glared savagely upon his reprover, and seemed almost inclined to spring upon him and strangle him on the spot — no difficult thing for him to do, for the Doctor was of slender build, while he himself possessed a frame unusually muscular and powerful.

They entered the vault, and the feeble rays of the lantern shone dimly on the damp green walls, and on the few coffins which were placed upon shelves.

An awful odor pervaded the place, so loathsome, so laden with the effluvia of death and corruption, that the rector hesitated, and was more than half inclined to abandon the undertaking; but after a moment's reflection —

'No,' he said, mentally — 'having gone thus far, it would ill become me to retreat when just on the point of solving the terrible mystery; I will proceed.'

He advanced and examined the coffins, some of which were so much decayed, that their ghastly inmates were visible through the large holes in the crumbling wood. At length he found one, in a tolerable state of preservation, upon which was a gold plate bearing the name of Edgar Franklin. Satisfied that this was the one he was in search of, he desired the robber to come forward and assist in removing the lid, which being done, a fleshless skeleton was revealed to their view.

'Now, fellow,' said the Doctor, 'I am about to make a certain investigation, of which you must not be a witness; therefore, you will retire to the outer entrance of the tomb, and wait there until I call you. Your reward shall be in proportion to your faithful obedience of my orders.'

Casting a look of malignant hate at the young gentleman, the robber withdrew from the vault, shutting the iron door behind him; and as he did so, he muttered a deep and terrible curse.

'Now may Heaven nerve me to the performance of this terrible task!' exclaimed the rector, solemnly; and bending over the coffin, he held the lantern in such a position as enabled him to gaze into the interior of the skull, through the eyeless sockets.

But oh, horrible — within that skull was a mass of live corruption — a myriad of grave worms banquetting upon the brains of the dead!

The Doctor reeled to the iron door of the vault, threw it open, and eagerly breathed the fresh air from above. This somewhat revived him, and he called on his assistant to come down. The robber obeyed, and was thus addressed by his employer —

'Friend, I have overrated my own powers — perhaps your nerves are stronger, your heart bolder than mine. Go to that coffin which we opened, search the interior of the skull, and if you find anything in it singular, or in the least degree unusual, bring it to me. — Here is a pocket-book containing money to a large amount; take it and keep it, but do as I have requested.'

The robber took the pocket-book and went into the vault. Horror could not sicken *him*; the terrors of death itself had no terror for him.

After the lapse of a few moments, he exclaimed — 'I have found something!' and advancing to the door, he handed to the doctor a small object, having first wiped it with an old handkerchief.

Overcoming his repugnance by a powerful effort, the doctor walked back into the vaults towards the lantern, which still remained upon the coffin-lid.

Upon examining the article which had been taken from the skull, he found it to be *a piece of lead*, of an irregular shape and weighing nearly two ounces.

'My belief in the guilt of Josephine and her mother is confirmed,' thought he. 'Shall I deliver them into the hands of justice? that must be decided hereafter; at all events, I will accuse them of the crime, and discontinue all connection with the wretched Josephine forever.'

Having carefully placed the piece of lead in his pocket, he advanced to the door, with the intent of leaving the robber to fasten on the lid of the coffin. To his surprise and horror he discovered that the door was locked! He knocked frantically against it, but was only answered by a low laugh from the outside.

'Wretch — villain!' he exclaimed. 'What mean you by this trick? Open the door instantly, I command you!'

'Fool!' cried the robber, contemptuously. 'I obey your commands no longer. You shall be left in this tomb to rot and die. You spoke to me with scorn, and shall now feel my vengeance. Think not, that I am ignorant of your true object in entering this tomb; — there has been a *murder* committed, and you sought for evidence of the crime. That evidence is now in your possession; but the secret is known to me, and I shall not fail to use it to my advantage. I shall seek out the Franklins, and inform them of the discovery which places them completely in my power. Farewell, parson — ; I leave you to your agreeable meditations, and to the enjoyment of a long, sound sleep!'

The miserable rector heard the sound of the ruffian's departing footsteps; with a wild cry of anguish and despair he threw himself against the iron door, which yielded not to his feeble efforts, and he sank exhausted upon the floor, in the awful conviction that he was buried alive!

Soon the horrors of his situation increased to a ten-fold degree — for he found himself assailed by a legion of rats. These creatures attacked him in such numbers that he was obliged to act on the defensive; and all his exertions were scarce sufficient to keep them from springing upon him, and tearing his flesh with their sharp teeth.

To his dismay he observed that the light of the lantern was growing dim and came near to being exhausted; darkness was about to add to the terrors of the place. Nerved to desperation, though faint and sick with the awful stench of that death vault, he searched about for some weapon with which to end his miserable existence. While thus engaged, he stumbled over a heavy iron crowbar which lay in one corner and seizing it with a cry of joy, applied it with all his force to the door of his loathsome prison.

It yielded — he was free! for the slab had not been replaced over the tomb, owing to the robber's inability to raise it. Falling on his knees, the rector thanked God for his deliverance; and ascending the steps, stood in the burial-ground, just as the lamps in the tomb below had become extinguished.

He was about to make his way out of the grave-yard, when he heard the sound of approaching footsteps, and low voices; and just as he had concealed himself behind a tall tomb-stone, he saw, through the thick darkness, two men approach the uncovered tomb from which he emerged only a few minutes before.

"Twas fortunate I met you, Ragged Pete,' said one; 'for without your aid I never could have lifted this stone into its place; and if it were left in its present position, it would attract attention in the morning, and that cursed parson might be rescued from the tomb. Take hold, and let's raise it on.'

'Werry good — but are you sure that the chap is down there still?' demanded Ragged Pete; 'hadn't we better go down and see if he hasn't took leg bait?'

'Pshaw, you fool!' rejoined the first speaker, angrily; 'how could he escape after I had locked him in? There's an iron door, fastened with a padlock as big as your head; so hold your tongue, and help me raise the stone to its place.'

This was done with considerable difficulty; and the two men sat down to rest after their labor.

'The parson won't live over night; if he is not devoured by the rats, he is sure to be suffocated,' remarked the man who had fastened the doctor in the tomb.

'Somehow or other,' said Ragged Pete, 'whoever offends you is sure to be punished in some dreadful and unheard-of manner. By thunder, I must try and keep in your good graces!'

'You will do well to do so,' rejoined his companion, 'my vengeance is always sure to overtake those who cross my path. Pete, I have led a strange life of crime and wickedness, from my very cradle, I may say, up to the present time. See, the storm is over, and the stars are shining brightly. It lacks several hours of daybreak; and as I feel somewhat sociably inclined, suppose I tell you my story? I have a flask of brandy in my pocket, and while we are moistening our clay, you shall listen to the history of one whose proudest boast is, he never did a good action, but has perpetrated every enormity in the dark catalogue of crimes.'

Ragged Pete expressed his desire to hear the story; and even Dr. Sinclair, in his place of concealment, prepared to listen with attention. Probably the reader has already guessed that the robber was no other than the terrible *Dead Man*; such was indeed the case; it was that same villain, who has occupied so prominent a place in the criminal portions of our narrative. We shall devote a separate chapter to his story.

CHAPTER XVIII

The Dead Man's story; being a tale of many Crimes.

'I never knew who my parents were; they may have been saints — they may have been devils; but in all probability they belonged to the latter class, for when I was three weeks old, they dropped me upon the highway one fine morning near the great city of Boston, to which famous city belongs the honor of my birth! Well, I was picked up by some Samaritans, who wrapped me up in red flannel, and clapped me in the Alms House. Behold me, then, a pauper!

'I throve and grew; my constitution was iron — my sinews were steel, and my heart a lion's. Up to the age of twelve, I was as other children are — I cried when I was whipped, and submitted when oppressed. At twelve, I began to reason and think; I said to myself, — Before me lies the world, created for the use of all its inhabitants. I am an inhabitant and entitled to my share — but other inhabitants, being rogues and sharpers, refuse to let me have my share. The world plunders me — in turn, I will plunder the world!

'At fourteen, I bade adieu to the Alms House, without the knowledge or consent of the overseer. I exchanged my grey pauper suit for a broadcloth of a young nabob, which I accidentally found in one of the chambers of a fashionable hotel, in Court street. Behold me, then, a gentleman! But I had no money; and so took occasion to borrow a trifling sum from an old gentleman, one night, upon one of the bridges which lead from Boston to Charleston. Do you ask how he came to give me credit? Why, I just tapped him on the head with a paving stone tied up in the corner of a handkerchief, after which delicate salutation he made not the slightest objection to my borrowing what he had about him. The next day it was said that a man's body had been found on the bridge, with his skull severely smashed — but what cared I?

'Gay was the life I led; for I was young and handsome. You laugh — but I was handsome then — my features had not the deathlike expression which they now wear. By and by you shall learn how I acquired the hideousness of face which procured for me the title of the *Dead Man*.

'One day I made too free with a gentleman's gold watch on the Common; and they shut me up for five years in the Stone University, where I completed my education at the expense of the State. At twenty I was free again. Behold me, then, a thoroughly educated scoundrel! I resolved to enlarge my modes of operation, and play the villain on a more extensive scale.

'Hiring an office in a dark alley in Boston, I assumed the lofty title of Doctor Sketers. My shelves were well stocked with empty phials and bottles — my windows were furnished with curtains, upon which my assumed name was painted in flaming capitals. The columns of the newspapers teemed with my advertisements, in which I was declared to be the only regular advertising physician — one who had successfully treated twenty-five millions of cases of delicate unmentionable complaints. Certificates of cure were also published by thousands, signed by people who never existed. Having procured an old medical diploma, I inserted my borrowed name, and exhibited it as an evidence of my trustworthiness and skill. The consequence of all this was, I was overrun with patients, none of whom I cured. My private entrance for ladies often gave admission to respectable unmarried females, who came to consult me on the best method of suppressing the natural proofs of their frailty. From these I would extract all the money possible and then send them to consult the skillful agent of Madam R — — . A thriving, profitable business, that of quackery! From it I reaped a golden harvest, and when that became tiresome, I put on a white neckcloth, and became a priest.

'Behold me a deacon, and a brother beloved! Who so pious, so exemplary, so holy as I! I lived in an atmosphere of purity and prayer; prayer seasoned my food before meals, and washed it down afterwards; prayer was my nightcap when I went to bed and my eye opener in the morning. At length I began to pray so fervently with the younger and fairer sisters of the flock, that the old ones, with whom I had no desire to pray, began to murmur — so, growing tired of piety, I kicked it to the devil, and joined the ranks of temperance.

'For over a year I lectured in public, and got drunk in private — glorious times! But at last people began to suspect that I was inspired by the spirit of alcohol, instead of the spirit of reform. A committee was appointed to wait on me and smell my breath — which they had no sooner done than they smelt a rat — and while some were searching my heart, others searched my closet, and not only discovered a bottle of fourth-proof, but uncovered a pile of counterfeit bank notes, there concealed. Reacting like a man of genius, my conduct was both forcible and striking; I knocked three of the brethren down, jumped out of the back window, scaled a fence, rushed through an alley, gained the street and was that afternoon on a steamboat bound for New York.

'On the passage, I observed a gentleman counting a pile of money; he was a country merchant, going to purchase goods. The weather was intensely warm, and many of the passengers slept on deck; among these was the country merchant. He lay at a considerable distance from the others and the night was dark. I stole upon him, and passed my long Spanish knife through his heart. — He died easy — a single gasp and all was over. I took his money, and threw his body over to the fishes. 'Twas my second murder — it never troubled me, for I never had a conscience. I entered New York, for the first time, with a capital of three thousand dollars, got by the murder of the country merchant; and this capital I resolved to increase by future murders and future crimes.

'I will now relate a little incident of my life, which will serve to show the bitterness of my hatred towards all mankind. For several years I had lived in various families, in a menial capacity, my object, of course, being robbery, and other crimes. It chanced that I once went to live in the family of a wealthy gentleman, whose wife was the most beautiful woman I ever saw; and her loveliness inspired me with such passion, that one day, during her husband's absence, I ventured to clasp her in my arms — struggling from my embrace, she repelled me with indignant scorn, and commanded me to leave the house instantly. I obeyed, swearing vengeance against her, and her family; and how well that oath was kept! About a week after my dismissal from the family, being one night at the theatre, I saw Mr. Ross, the husband of the lady whom I had insulted, seated in the boxes. Keeping my eye constantly upon him, I saw him when he left the theatre, and immediately followed him, though at such a distance as to prevent his seeing me. Fortunately his way home lay through a dark and lonely street; in the most obscure part of that street, I quickened my steps until I overtook him — and just as he was about to turn around to see who followed him, I gave him a tremendous blow on his right temple with a heavy slung shot, and he fell to the earth without a groan. I knew that I had killed him and was glad of it — it was my third murder. After dragging his body into a dark alley, so that he might not be found by the watchman, I rifled his pockets of their contents, among which was the night-key of his house, which I regarded as a prize of inestimable value.

'Leaving the corpse of Mr. Ross in the alley, I went straight to his house in Howard street, and admitted myself by means of the night-key which I had found in his pocket. A lamp was burning in the hall; I extinguished it and groped my way up stairs to the chamber of Mrs. Ross with the situation of which I was well acquainted. On opening the chamber door, I found to my intense delight that no light or candle was burning within; all was in darkness. Approaching the bed, I became convinced that the lady was in a sound sleep; this circumstance added greatly to my satisfaction. Well, I deliberately stripped myself and got into bed; still she awoke not. Think you I was troubled with any remorse of conscience, while lying at the side of the wronged woman whose husband had just been slain by my hand? Not a bit of it; I chuckled inwardly at the success of my scheme, and impatiently waited an opportunity to take every advantage of my position. At last she awoke; supposing me, of course, to be her husband, she gently chided me for remaining out so late; I did not dare suffer her to hear the sound of my voice, but replied to her in whispers. She suspected nothing — and I completed my triumph! Yes, the proud, beautiful woman who had treated me with such scorn, was then my slave. I had sacrificed her honor on the altar of my duplicity and lust!

'Morning came, and its first beams revealed to my victim the extent of her degradation — she saw through the deception, and with a wild cry, fell back senseless. Hastily dressing myself, I stepped into an adjoining room where the two children of Mrs. Ross were sleeping; they were twins, a boy and a girl, three years of age, and pretty children they were. I drew my pocket knife, to cut their throats; just then they awoke, and gazed upon me with bright, inquiring eyes — then recognizing me, their rosy cheeks were dimpled with smiles, and they lisped my name. Perhaps you think their innocence and helplessness touched my heart — hah! no such thing; I merely changed my mind, and with the point of my knife cut out their beautiful eyes! having first gagged them both, to prevent their screaming. Delicious fun, wasn't it? Then I bolted down stairs, but was so unfortunate as to encounter several of the servants, who had been aroused by their mistress's shriek. Frightened at my appearance, (for I was covered with the children's blood,) they did not arrest my flight, and I made good my escape from the house. That scrape was my last for some time; for people were maddened by the chapter of outrages committed by me on that family — the murder of the husband, the dishonor of the wife, and the blinding of those two innocent children. I was hunted like a wild beast from city to city; large rewards were offered for my apprehension, and minute descriptions of my entire person flooded every part of the country. But my cunning baffled them all; for two months I lived in the woods, in an obscure part of New Jersey, subsisting upon roots, and wild herbs, and wild berries, and crawling worms, which I dug from the earth. One day in my wanderings, I came across a gang of counterfeiters, who made their rendezvous in a cave; these were congenial spirits for me — I told them my story, and became one of them. The gang included several men of superior education and attainments, among whom was a celebrated chemist.

'This man undertook to procure for me a certain chemical preparation which he said would alter and disfigure my features so that I never could be recognized, even by those who were most intimately acquainted with me. He was as good as his word; he furnished me with a colorless liquid, contained in a small phial, directing me to apply it to my face at night, but cautioning me particularly to avoid getting any of it into my eyes. His directions were followed by me, to the very letter; — during the night, my face seemed on fire, but I heeded not the torture. Morning came — the pain was over; I arose, and rushed to a mirror. Great God! I scarce knew myself, so terribly changed was my countenance. My features, once comely and regular, had assumed the ghastly, horrible and death-like appearance they now wear. Oh, how I hugged myself with joy when I found myself thus impenetrably disguised! Never did the face of beauty have half the charms for me, that my blanched and terrific visage had! 'I will go forth into the great world again — no one will ever recognize me!' thought I; and bidding adieu to my brother counterfeiters, I returned to New York. Ha, ha, ha! how people shrank from me! how children screamed at my approach; how mothers clasped their babes to their breasts as I passed by, as though I were the destroying angel! The universal terror which I inspired was to me a source of mad joy. Having ample means in my possession, I began a career of lavish expenditure and extravagant debauchery, until the eye of the police was fastened upon me with suspicion; and then I deemed it prudent to act with more caution. — About that time I became aware of the existence of the Dark Vaults, and the 'Jolly Knights of the Round Table.' Soon after my meeting with that jovial crew, the law put its iron clutch on me for a murder — a mere trifle; I passed my knife between a gentleman's ribs one night in the street, just to tickle his heart a bit, and put him in a good humor to lend me some money, but the fool died under the operation, having first very impolitely called out *Murder!* which resulted in my being captured on the spot by two of those night prowlers known as watchmen. Well, my ugly face was against me, and I could give no good account of myself — therefore they (the judge and jury) voted me a hempen cravat, to be presented and adjusted one fine morning between the hours of ten and twelve. But his Excellency the Governor, (a particular friend of mine,) objected to such a summary proceeding, as one calculated to deprive society of its brightest ornament; he therefore favored me with a special permit to pass the rest of my useful life within the walls of a place vulgarly termed the State Prison — a very beautiful edifice when viewed from the outside. I did not long remain there, however, to partake of the State's hospitality — to be brief, I ran away, but was carried back again, after being a year at liberty, through the instrumentality of Sydney, whom may the devil confound! But again I escaped — you know in what manner; and you are well acquainted with most of my adventures since — my cutting out the boy *Kinchen's* tongue, my murder of Mrs. Stevens, and other matters not necessary for me to repeat.'

'But,' said Ragged Pete, with some hesitation, 'you haven't told me of your wife, you know.'

'Wife — ha, ha, ha!' and the Dead Man laughed long and loud; there was something in his laugh which chilled the blood, and made the heart beat with a nameless terror.

'True, Pete, I have not yet told you about my wife, as you call her. But you shall hear. What would you say if I told you that Mrs. Ross, the lady whose husband I murdered, whose children I blinded, and whom I so outrageously deceived herself — what would you say if you were told that the woman who passes for my wife, is that same lady?'

'I should say it was a thing impossible,' replied Pete.

'It is true,' rejoined the Dead Man. — 'Listen: — when I left my counterfeiting friends in New Jersey, and returned to New York with my new face, I learned by inquiry that Mrs. Ross was living with her blind twins in a state of poverty, her husband's property, at his death, having been seized upon by his creditors, leaving her entirely destitute. I found her in an obscure part of the city, subsisting upon the charity of neighbors, the occupant of a garret. The woman's misfortunes, through me, had ruined her intellect; — she had grown fierce and reckless, — as wild as a tigress. I sat down and conversed with her; she knew me not. 'You are hideous to look upon,' said she, 'and I like you for it. The world is fair, but it has robbed me of husband, honor and taken away my children's eye-sight. Henceforward, all that is hideous I will love!' I saw that her brain was topsy-turvy, and it rejoiced me. Her children were still pretty, though they were blind; and it almost made me laugh to see them grope their way to their mother's side, and turning their sightless eyes toward her, ask, in childish accents, — 'Mamma, what made the naughty man put out our eyes?' Well, the woman, with a singular perversity of human nature, liked me, and commenced to place herself under my protection. She could be of service to me; but her children were likely to prove a burden — and so I got rid of them.'

'What did you do with them — no harm, I hope?' asked Pete.

'Certainly not — the Dark Vaults were not a fit place of abode for the blind babes, and so I sent them to take up their abode in another place, and that was heaven; to explain, I cut their throats, and threw their bodies into the sewers.'

'Monster — inhuman villain!' was the involuntary exclamation of Dr. Sinclair, in his hiding-place behind the tomb-stone.

'Ha — who spoke?' cried the Dead Man, jumping to his feet, and gazing eagerly about him. 'Pete, did you hear anything?'

'I heerd a noise, that's certain — but perhaps 'twas only the wind a whistling among these old tomb-stones,' answered Pete.

'Most probably it was,' rejoined the other — 'for who the devil could be here to-night, besides ourselves? Well, to resume my story: after I had made away with the children, their mother never asked for them; she seemed to have forgotten that she ever had children at all. She manifested a strange unnatural liking for me; not love, but the fierce attachment of a tigress for her keeper. She obeyed me in everything; and finding her such an easy instrument in my hands, I took pains to instruct her in all the mysteries of city crimes. By parading the streets like a woman of the town, she enticed men to my Anthony street crib (which you know communicates with the Vaults,) and by the aid of the drugging powder our victims were soon made unresisting objects of robbery and murder. You know how she allured Sydney into the house, disguised as a sailor, and how the rascal caused her to swallow the dose intended for him — also how he cut the ropes of the platform the same night, which nearly cost me my life. Ever since the woman took the powder, she has been a raging maniac, and I am deprived of her valuable services. May the devil scorch that Sydney!'

'You have had two children by her,' remarked Pete.

'Yes, the first one, that infernal dwarf, whom I call my Image; we kept him shut up in the cellar, in Anthony street. Our second child, whom I have christened Jack the Prig, takes after his mother, and a smart little fellow he is. Why man, he can pick a pocket in as workmanlike a manner as either of us. He will make a glorious thief, and will shed honor on his father's name. The day when he commits murder will be the happiest day of my life.'

Ragged Pete, having imbibed the greater part of the contents of the brandy flask, now suggested to his companion that they should take their departure. The Dead Man assented and the worthy pair took themselves off, little thinking that every word which had been said, was heard by him whom they supposed to be imprisoned in the tomb below.

The rector emerged from his place of concealment, and went to his home with a heavy heart. Though he had himself become, in a measure, depraved and reckless of his moral and religious obligations, still he was horrified and astounded at the awful evidences of crime which had been revealed to him that night. — The miscreant's tale of murder and outrage, told with such cool indifference, and with an air of sincerity that left no doubt of its perfect truth, appalled him; and the proof he had obtained of the guilt of Josephine and her mother struck his soul with horror. Ere he sought his couch, he prayed long and earnestly for the forgiveness of his past transgressions, and for strength to resist future temptations.

CHAPTER XIX

Showing how Mrs. Belmont was pursued by a hideous ruffian.

The time appointed for the marriage of Mr. Hedge to Mrs. Belmont approached. The enamored old gentleman paid her frequent visits, and supplied her liberally with funds, nor did he neglect to make her most costly presents. Julia's position and prospects, with reference to her contemplated marriage, were certainly very gratifying to her; yet there was one thing which troubled her exceedingly and was a source of constant apprehension and dread.

The uneasiness proceeded from the fact that she was completely in the power of the Dead Man, who knew that she was the cast-off wife of Sydney — cast off for the crime of adultery with a black — and who could at any time, by exposing her true character to Mr. Hedge, ruin her schemes in that quarter forever. She knew too well that the deadly villain was as deceitful as he was criminal; and she knew not at what moment he might betray her to her intended husband.

The Dead Man was disposed to take every advantage in his power over her. The secret passage into the cellar admitted him into the house at all hours of the day and night; and his visits were frequent. At first his treatment of her was more respectful than otherwise; but gradually he grew familiar and insolent, and began to insinuate that as she had formerly granted her favors to a negro, she could not object to treat HIM with equal kindness. This hint she received with disgust; and assuming an indignant tone, bade him relinquish all thought of such a connection, and never recur to the subject again.

But the villain was not to be repulsed; each time he visited her he grew more insulting and audacious, until at last his persecutions became almost unbearable to the proud and beautiful woman, who viewed him with loathing and abhorrence.

One afternoon, about a fortnight previous to the time fixed on for her marriage, she was seated in her chamber, engaged in reflections which partook of the mingled elements of pleasure and pain. The day was dark and gloomy, and the wind sighed mournfully around the house, and through the leafless branches of the trees which fronted it. Suddenly the door of the chamber was opened, and the Dead Man entered. Julia shuddered, for the presence of that terrible man inspired her with a nameless dread. He seated himself familiarly at her side — and on glancing at him, she perceived, to her alarm, that he was much intoxicated. His eyes rolled wildly, and his loathsome features were convulsed and full of dark and awful meaning.

'Well, my bird,' said he in an unsteady voice — 'by Venus and by Cupid, I swear thou art beautiful today! Nay, thou need'st not shrink from me — for I have sworn by Satan to taste thy ripe charms within this very hour!'

He attempted to clasp her in his arms, but she pushed him from her with a look of such disgust, that he became enraged and furious. Drawing a sharp knife from his pocket, he seized her by her arm, and hissed from between his clenched teeth —

'Hark'ee, woman, I have borne with your d — — d nonsense long enough, and now if you resist me I'll cut that fair throat of yours from ear to ear — I will by hell!'

She would have screamed with affright, but he grasped her by the throat, and nearly strangled her.

'Silly wench,' he cried, as he released her and again placed himself at her side — 'why do you provoke me into enmity, when I would fain be your lover and friend? Mine you must be — mine you shall be, if I have to murder you!'

Miserable Julia! thy wickedness has met with a terrible retribution; thou art a slave to the lust and fury of a monster more dreadful than the venomous and deadly cobra di capello of the East!

Ye who revel in guilty joys, and drink deep of the nectar in the gilded cup of unhallowed pleasures — beware! Though the draught be delicious as the wines of Cypress, and though the goblet be crowned with flowers, fragrant as the perfume of love's sighs — a coiled serpent lurks in the dregs of the cup, whose deadly fang will strike deep in the heart and leave there the cankering sores of remorse and dark despair. Ye who bask in the smiles of beauty, and voluptuously repose on the soft couch of licentiousness — beware! That beauty is but external; beneath the fair surface lie corruption, disease, and death!

The ruffian, having accomplished his triumph, developed a new trait in the fiendish malignity of his nature. He would have the wretched lady become his menial — he would have her perform for him the drudgery of a servant. He ordered her to bring him wine, and wait upon him; and enforced the command with a blow, which left a red mark upon her beautiful white shoulder.

'Henceforward,' cried he, with an oath, 'I am your master, and you are my slave. Hesitate to obey me in any thing which I may desire you to do, and I will denounce you to Mr. Hedge as a vile adulteress and impostor, unworthy to become his wife, even if you had no husband living. Dare to refuse my slightest wish, and I will prevent your marriage under pain of being sent to the State Prison for the crime of bigamy.'

By these and other threats did the ruffian compel the unhappy Julia to obey him. She brought him wine and waited upon him; and was obliged to submit to every species of insult and degradation. Nor was this the only refinement of cruelty which only his own infernal ingenuity could have devised; he resolved that Nero, the black, should be a witness of her humiliation; and accordingly he rang the bell, and ordered the negro to be sent up. Nero entered the room, and observing the triumphant chuckle of the Dead Man, and the dejected look of his mistress, with his natural acuteness instantly comprehended the true state of affairs. The contempt with which Julia had treated him was still fresh in his memory, and led him to view that lady with hatred; he therefore determined to add to her chagrin and hatred on the present occasion, by enjoying the scene as much as possible.

'Sit down, Nero,' said the Dead Man, with a sardonic grin — 'this beautiful lady, who formerly showered her favors upon you, has transferred her kindness to me; I have just tasted the joys of heaven in her arms. Is she not a superb creature?'

'Divinely voluptuous,' replied the African, rubbing his hands and showing his white teeth.

'She is so,' said the other — 'but the virtue of obedience is her most prominent and excellent quality. Mark how she will obey me in what I order her to do: Julia, love, my shoes are muddy; take them off my feet, and clean them.'

The high-born lady was about to give utterance to an indignant refusal, when a terrible glance from her tyrant assured her that resistance would be useless. His savage brutality — the blow he had given her — her forced submission to his loathsome embraces — and the consciousness that she was completely in his power, compelled her to obey the degrading command.

Yes — that lovely, educated and accomplished lady actually took off the vile ruffian's dirty shoes, with her delicate hands; then with an elegant pearl handled pen-knife, she scraped off the filth, and afterwards, at the orders of her *master*, washed them with rose-water in a china ewer, and wiped them with a cambric handkerchief — and all in the presence of her negro footman.

This task being completed, the Dead Man requested Nero to retire; and then he inflicted new and nameless indignities upon his poor victim. Once, when she shudderingly refused to obey some horrible request, he struck her violently in the face, and the crimson blood dyed her fair cheek.

To be brief, the stupendous villain, in the diabolical malignity of his nature, derived a fierce pleasure from ill-treating and outraging that frail, but to him inoffensive woman. Her defenceless situation might have excited compassion in the breast of a less brutal ruffian; but when had his stony heart ever known compassion?

Nero entered the room to inform his mistress that Mr. Hedge was below, having called on his accustomed evening visit.

'Wash the blood from your face, then go and receive him,' said the Dead Man. 'I shall station myself in the adjoining room, to see and hear all that passes between you.'

Poor Julia removed from her face the sanguinary stains, and endeavoring to arrange her hair so as to conceal the wound which had been inflicted upon her; all in vain, however, for Mr. Hedge noticed it the first moment she entered the room.

'My own dear Julia,' said he, in a tone of much concern, and taking her hand — 'what has caused that terrible bruise upon your cheek? And my God! you look pale and ill — speak, dearest, and tell me what is the matter.'

She could not reply; but burst into tears; the old gentleman's kindness of manner, contrasted with the savage cruelty of her persecutor, had overcome her. Mr. Hedge strove to comfort her, as a father might comfort a distressed child; and his kindness filled her soul with remorse, in view of the great deceit she was practising upon him. Still, she could not muster sufficient resolution to confess that deceit. Considering herself just on the eve of securing a great prize, she could not bring herself to ruin all by a confession of her true character. In answer to his renewed inquiries, she stated that her wound had been caused by a severe fall; but she assured him that it was nothing serious. The Dead Man grinned with satisfaction, as, with his ear applied to the key-hole, he heard her thus account for the wound inflicted by his own villainous hand.

Mr. Hedge did not remain long that evening: but ere his departure he presented Julia with a magnificent set of diamonds, which had cost him near a thousand dollars.

'Wear these, my dear Julia, for my sake,' said he — 'and though they cannot increase your charms, they may serve to remind you of me when I am absent. A fortnight more, and I shall claim you for my own bride; then, in the beautiful city of Boston, we will be enabled to move in that sphere of society and fashion which your loveliness and accomplishments so eminently qualify you to adorn.'

After Mr. Hedge had taken his leave, the Dead Man entered the room with a smile of satisfaction.

'By Satan,' cried he — 'Mrs. Belmont, as you call yourself,

that old gallant of yours is devilish liberal, and there's no reason why I should not come in for a share of his generosity. These diamonds I shall carry off with me, and you can tell him that you were robbed — and so you are; ha, ha, ha! So you're going to Boston after you're married — hey? Well, I'll go to Boston too; and you must always keep me plentifully supplied with cash to insure my silence with regard to matters that you don't wish to have known. I'll leave you now; but listen: — to-morrow I intend to make a grand effort to get Francis Sydney into my power. Does that intelligence afford you pleasure?'

'Yes,' replied Julia, forgetting in her hatred of Sydney, the cruelty of the Dead Man — 'yes, it does; give me but the opportunity to see him writhe with agony, and I forgive your barbarous treatment of me to-day.'

'That opportunity you shall have,' rejoined the ruffian — 'come, I am half inclined to be sorry for having used you so; but d — — n it, 'tis my nature, and I cannot help it. My heart even now hungers after outrage and human blood — and Sydney — Sydney shall be the victim to appease that hunger!'

Saying this, he quitted the room, leaving Julia to her own reflections, which were of the most painful nature. The only thought which shed a gleam of joy into her heart, was the prospect of soon gratifying her spirit of revenge upon Sydney, whom she unjustly regarded as the author of her troubles.

CHAPTER XX

Frank Sydney in the Power of his Enemies — his incarceration in the Dark Dungeon, with the Dwarf.

The next day after the occurrence just related, Frank Sydney, as was his custom, took a leisurely stroll down the most fashionable promenade of the metropolis — Broadway; this magnificent avenue was thronged with elegantly dressed ladies and gentlemen, who had issued forth to enjoy the genial air of a fine afternoon.

At one of the crossings of the street, our hero observed an old woman, respectfully dressed, but nearly double with age and infirmity, and scarcely able to crawl along, in great danger of being run over by a carriage which was being driven at a furious rate. Frank humanely rushed forward, and dragged the poor creature from the impending danger, just in time to save her from being dashed beneath the wheels of the carriage. She faintly thanked her deliverer, but declared her inability to proceed without assistance. On inquiring where she resided, he learned that it was in Reade street, which was but a short distance from where they then stood; and he generously offered her the support of his arm, saying that he would conduct her home, an offer which was thankfully accepted. They soon reached her place of abode, which was a house of genteel appearance, and at the invitation of the old lady, Frank entered, to rest a few moments after his walk.

He had scarcely seated himself in the back parlor, when he was horrified and astounded at what he saw.

The old woman, throwing off her cloak, bonnet and mask, stood before him, erect and threatening; and our hero saw that he had been made the dupe of the *Dead Man!*

'Welcome, Sydney, welcome!' cried the miscreant, his features lighted up with a demon's triumph — 'at last thou art in my power. Did I not play my part well? Who so likely to excite thy compassion as an old lady in distress; 'twas ably planned and executed. Thou hast fallen into the trap, and shall never escape. But there are others who will be gratified to see thee, Frank. Nero

— Julia — the bird is caught at last!'

These last words were uttered in a loud tone; and were immediately responded to by the entrance of Julia and the black. The woman's eyes flashed fire when she beheld the object of her hate; she advanced towards him and spat in his face, saying —

'May the fires of hell consume thee, heart and soul, detested wretch — thou didst cast me from thee, friendless and unprotected, when a kind reproof might have worked my reformation. Through thee I have become the victim of a ruffian's lust, the object of his cruelty; I have been struck like a dog, (look at this mark upon my cheek,) and I have been compelled to minister to the disgusting and unnatural lechery of a monster — all through thee, thou chicken-hearted knave, who even now doth tremble with unmanly terror!'

'Woman, thou art a liar!' exclaimed our hero, rising and boldly confronting his three enemies — 'I do tremble, but with indignation alone! Dare you charge your misfortune upon me? Did you not dishonor me by adultery with this vile negro? — and then to talk to me of kind reproof! Pshaw, thou double-eyed traitorous w — — e! — I had served thee rightly had I strangled thee on the spot, and thrown thy unclean carcase to the dogs!'

'Silence, curse ye, or I'll cut out your tongue as I did the *Kinchen's*!' roared the Dead Man, drawing his knife. 'Nero, what cause of complaint have you against this man?'

'Cause enough,' replied the black — 'he shut me up in a dark dungeon for having gratified the wishes of his licentious wife.'

'Enough,' cried the Dead Man — 'I will now state my grounds of complaint against him. Firstly — he played the spy upon me, and was the cause of my being returned to the State Prison, from which I had escaped. Secondly — he discovered the secrets of my Anthony street crib, and administered a drug to my wife which has deprived her of reason. And thirdly he is my mortal foe, and I hate him. Is that not enough?'

'It is — it is!' replied Julia and the African. The Dead Man continued:

'Now, Sydney, listen to me: you behold the light of day for the last time. But 'tis not my wish to kill you at once — no, that would not satisfy my vengeance. You shall die a slow, lingering death; each moment of your existence shall be fraught with a hell of torment; you will pray for death in vain; death shall not come to your relief for years. Each day I will rack my ingenuity to devise some new mode of torture. To increase the horrors of your situation, you shall have a companion in your captivity — a being unnatural and loathsome to look upon — a creature fierce as a hyena, malignant as a devil. Ha, you turn pale; you guess my meaning. You are right; you shall be shut up in the same dungeon with my Image! the deformed and monstrous dwarf, whom Heaven (if there is one,) must have sent as a curse and a reproach to me; he shall now become your curse and punishment!'

Poor Frank heard this awful doom pronounced which he could not repress. He could have borne any ordinary physical torture with fortitude; but the thought of being shut up in that noisome dungeon with a being so fearful and loathsome as the Image, made him sick and faint; and when the Dead Man and the negro seized him in their powerful grasp, in order to convey him to the dungeon, he could make no resistance, even if resistance had been of any avail. Julia did not accompany them, but contented herself with a glance of malignant triumph at her husband.

They descended to the cellar, and entered the secret passage, which they traversed in profound darkness. This passage communicated directly with the cellar of the house in Anthony street; a walk of ten minutes brought them to it, and when they had entered it, the Dead Man ignited a match and lit a lamp.

The appearance of the cellar was precisely the same as when Frank had last seen it. — There was the same outlet and the moveable platform; there, in that dim and distant corner, lay the putrefying corpse; and there, too, was the iron door of the dungeon, secured on the outside by the massive bolt.

At that moment the fearful inmate of that dungeon set up its strange, unnatural cry.

'Hark — my Image welcomes you, Sydney,' whispered the

Dead Man, and, assisted by the African, he hurried his victim towards the dungeon door.

'In God's name,' said Frank, imploringly — 'I beseech you to kill me at once, rather than shut me up with that fearful creature — for death is preferable to that!'

But the two ruffians only laughed — and drawing back the bolt, they opened the iron door, and thrust their victim into the dungeon; then closing the door, they pushed the bolt into its place, and left him to an eternal night of darkness and horror.

He heard the sound of their department footsteps; groping his way to a corner of the dungeon, he sat down upon the cold stone floor. Had he been alone he could have reconciled himself to his situation; but the consciousness of being in such fearful company, froze his blood with horror.

Soon his eyes became accustomed to the darkness; and as a very faint glimmer of light stole in over the door of the dungeon, he was enabled to see objects around him, though very indistinctly. With a shudder, he glanced around him; and there, cowering in one corner, like some hideous reptile, its green eyes fixed upon him, sat the Image of the Dead Man — the terrible Dwarf!

Hour after hour did that mis-shapen thing gaze upon our hero, until a strange feeling of fascination came over him — his brain grew dizzy, and he felt as if under the influence of a horrible dream. Then it uttered its strange, unnatural cry, and with the crawling motion of a snake, stole to his side. He felt its breath, like the noisome breath of a charnel-house, upon his cheek; he felt its cold, clammy touch, and could not thrust it from him; it twined its distorted, fleshless arms around him, and repeated its awful yell. Then Sydney fell prostrate upon the floor, insensible.

When he recovered from his swoon, (in which he had lain for many hours) he felt numbed with cold, sick with the foetid atmosphere of the place, and faint with hunger. The dwarf was ferociously devouring some carrion which had been thrown into the dungeon; and the creature made uncouth signs to our hero, as if inviting him to eat. But on examining the food he found it to be

so repulsive, that he turned from it in disgust, and resolved,
sooner than partake of it, to let starvation put an end to his misery.

CHAPTER XXI

Josephine and Mrs. Franklin receive two important Visits.

Josephine Franklin and her mother were languidly partaking of a late breakfast, and indolently discussing the merits of the Italian opera, to which they had both been on the preceding night.

It not being the hour for fashionable calls, both ladies were attired with an extreme negligence which indicated that they anticipated seeing no company. And yet, to the eyes of a true connoisseur in beauty, there was something far more seductive in those voluptuous dishabilles, than there could have been in the most magnificent full dress. The conversation in which they were engaged, was characteristic of them both: —

'I think, mamma,' said Josephine — 'that the most captivating fellow on the stage last night, was the Signor Stopazzi, who played the peasant. Ah, what superb legs! what a fine chest! what graceful motions! I am dying to get him for a lover!'

'What, tired of the handsome Sinclair already?' asked Mrs. Franklin with a smile.

'Indeed, to confess the truth, mamma,' replied Josephine — 'the Doctor is becoming somewhat *de trop* — and then, again, those Italians make such delightful lovers; so full of fire, and passion, and poetry; and music, and charming romance — ah, I adore them!'

'Apropos of Italian lovers,' said her mother. 'I once had one; I was then in my sixteenth year, and superbly beautiful. My Angelo was a divine youth, and he loved me to distraction. Once, in a moment of intoxicating bliss, he swore to do whatever I commanded him, to test the sincerity of his life; and I playfully and thoughtlessly bade him go and kill himself for my sake. The words were forgotten by me, almost as soon as uttered. Angelo supped with me that night, and when he took his leave, he had never seemed gayer or happier. The next day, at noon, I received a beautiful bouquet of flowers, and a perfumed billet-doux; they were from Angelo. On opening the missive, I found that it contained the most eloquent assurance of his sincere love — but, to my horror, in a postscript of two lines he expressed his intention of destroying himself ere his note could reach me, in obedience to my command. Almost distracted, I flew to his hotel; my worst fears were confirmed. Poor Angelo was found with his throat cut, and quite dead, with my miniature pressed to his heart.' [4]

'Delightfully romantic!' exclaimed Josephine — 'how I should like to have a lover kill himself for my sake!'

But the brilliant eyes of her mother were suffused with tears. Just then a servant in livery entered and announced —

'Dr. Sinclair is below, and craves an audience with Mrs. Franklin and Miss Josephine.'

'Let him come up,' said Josephine, with a gesture of some impatience; for, in truth, she was beginning to be tired of the rector, and longed for a new conquest.

Dr. Sinclair entered with a constrained and gloomy air.

'My dear Doc,' cried Josephine, with affected cordiality — 'how opportunely that you called! I was just now wishing that you would come.'

'Ladies,' said the Doctor, solemnly — 'I have recently made a terrible, a most astonishing discovery.'

'Indeed! and pray what is it?' cried both mother and daughter.

'It is that Mr. Edgar Franklin, whose death was so sudden and unaccountable, was basely murdered!'

The mother and daughter turned pale, and losing all power of utterance, gazed at each other with looks of wild alarm.

'Yes,' resumed the Doctor — 'I have in my possession evidence the most conclusive, that he met his death by the hands of a murderess, who was urged to commit the deed by two other devils in female shape.'

'Doctor — explain — what mean you?' gasped Josephine, while her mother seemed as if about to go into hysterics.

'In the first place I will ask you if you ever knew a woman named Mary Welch?' said the Doctor; then after a pause, he added — 'your looks convince me that you have known such a person; that woman recently died in this city, and on her death-bed she made the following confession.'

The rector here produced and read a paper which he had drawn up embodying the statement and confession which the woman Welch had made to him, just before her death. As the reader is acquainted with the particulars of that confession it is unnecessary for us to repeat them.

Having finished the perusal of this document, the rector proceeded to relate an account of his visit to the tomb of Mr. Franklin, and concluded his fearfully interesting narrative by producing the lump of lead which had been taken from the skull of the murdered man.

It is impossible to describe the horror and dismay of the two wretched and guilty women, when they saw that their crime was discovered. Falling on their knees before the rector, they implored him to have mercy on them and not hand them over to justice. — They expressed their sincere repentance of the deed, and declared that sooner than suffer the ignominy of an arrest, they would die by their own hands. Josephine in particular did not fail to remind Dr. Sinclair of the many favors she had granted him and hinted that her exposure would result in his own ruin, as his former connection with her would be disclosed, if herself and mother were arrested and brought to trial.

'Were I inclined to bring you to justice, the dread of my own exposure would not prevent me; for no personal consideration should ever restrain me from doing an act of justice, provided the public good would be prompted thereby. But I do not see the necessity of bringing you to the horrors of a trial and execution; much rather would I see you allowed a chance of repentance. Therefore, you need apprehend no danger from me; the secret of your crime shall not be revealed by me. But I warn you that the secret is known to another, who will probably use his knowledge to his own advantage; the matter lies between you and him. I shall now leave this house, never again to cross its threshold; but ere I depart, let me urge you both before God to repent of your sins. Josephine, I have been very guilty in yielding to your temptations; but the Lord is merciful, and will not refuse forgiveness to the chief of sinners. Farewell — we shall meet no more: for I design shortly to retire from a ministerial life, of which I have proved myself unworthy; and shall take up my abode in some other place, and lead a life of obscurity and humble usefulness.'

With these words the Doctor took his departure, leaving the mother and daughter in a state of mind easier to be imagined than described. Josephine was the first to break the silence which succeeded his exit from the house: —

'So our secret is discovered,' said she. — 'Perdition! who would have thought that our crime could ever be found out in that manner? Mother, what are we to do?'

'I know not what to say,' replied Mrs. Franklin. 'One thing, however, is certain; that whining parson will never betray us. He said that the dread of his own folly would not deter him from denouncing us, but he lies — that dread of being exposed will alone keep his mouth shut. Yet, good Heavens! he assures us that the secret is known to another person, who will not scruple to use the knowledge to his advantage. Who can that person be? And what reward will he require of us, to ensure his silence?'

'Mother,' said Josephine, in a decided tone — 'We must quit this city forever. We can dwell here no longer with safety. Let us go to Boston, and dwell there under an assumed name. I have heard that Boston is a great city, where licentiousness and hypocrisy abound, in secret; where the artful dissimulator can cloak himself with sanctity, and violate with impunity every command of God and man. Yes, Boston is the city for us.'

'I agree with you, my dear,' rejoined her mother — 'it is the greatest lust market of the Union. You will be surprised to learn that several of my old schoolmates are now keeping fashionable boarding houses for courtezans in that city and from the business derive a luxurious maintenance. There is my friend Louisa Atwill, whose history I have often narrated to you and there, too, is Lucy Bartlett, and Rachel Pierce, whose lover is the gay and celebrated Frank Hancock, whom I have often seen — nor must I omit to mention Julia Carr, whose establishment is noted for privacy, and is almost exclusively supported by married men. All these with whom I occasionally correspond testify to the voluptuous temperament of the Bostonians, among whom you will be sure to make many conquests.'

We merely detail this conversation for the purpose of showing the recklessness and depravity of these two women. They had just acknowledged themselves guilty of the crime of murder; and could thus calmly converse on indifferent and sinful topics, immediately after the departure of their accuser, and as soon as their first excitement of fear had subsided.

While thus arranging their plans for the future, the servant in livery again entered, to announce another visitor.

'He is a strange looking man,' said the servant, 'and when I civilly told him that the ladies received no company before dinner, he gave me such a look as I shall never forget, and told me to hold my tongue and lead the way — good Lord, here he comes now!'

The terrified servant vanished from the room, as a tall figure stalked in, wrapped in a cloak. The ladies could scarce repress a shriek, when throwing aside his hat and cloak, the stranger exhibited a face of appalling hideousness; and a fearful misgiving took possession of their minds, that this was the other person who was in the secret of their crime.

'You are the two Franklin ladies I presume — mother and daughter — good!' and the stranger glanced from one to the other with a fierce satisfaction.

'What is your business with us?' demanded Josephine, haughtily.

'Ha! young hussey, you are very saucy,' growled the stranger savagely — 'but your pride will soon be humbled. In the first place, are we alone, and secure from interruption?'

'We are — why do you ask?' said Mrs. Franklin.

'Because your own personal safety demands that our interview be not overheard,' replied the man. 'As you are fashionable people, I will introduce myself. Ladies, I am called the Dead Man, and have the honor to be your most obedient servant. Now to business.'

The Dead Man proceeded to relate those circumstances with which the reader is already acquainted, connected with his visit to the tomb of Mr. Franklin, and the manner in which he had come to the knowledge of that gentleman's murder. He omitted, however, to state that he had shut up the rector in the tomb, for he firmly believed in his own mind that Dr. Sinclair had perished.

'You perceive,' said he, when he had finished these details — 'it is in my power to have you hung up at any time. Now, to come to the point at once — what consideration will you allow me if I keep silent in regard to this affair?'

'Of course you require money,' remarked Josephine, who was disposed to treat the matter in as business-like a manner as possible.

'Why — yes; but not money alone,' replied the Dead Man, with a horrible leer; — 'you are both devilish handsome, and I should prefer to take out a good portion of my reward in your soft embraces. You shudder ladies; yet would not my arms around those fair necks of yours be pleasanter than an ugly rope, adjusted by the hands of the hangman? You will one day admit the force of the argument; at present I will not press the matter, but content myself with a moderate demand on your purse. Oblige me with the loan — ha, ha! — of the small trifle of one thousand dollars.'

After a moment's consultation with her daughter, Mrs. Franklin left the room to get the money from her *escritoire*. The door had scarcely closed upon her, when the Dead Man advanced to Josephine, caught her in his arms, despite her resistance, imprinted numberless foul kisses upon her glowing cheeks, her ripe lips, and alabaster shoulders. It was a rare scene; Beauty struggling in the arms of the Beast!

The lecherous monster did not release her until he heard her mother returning. Mrs. Franklin handed to him a roll of bank-notes, and said —

'There is the amount you asked for and you must grant that you are liberally paid for your silence. I trust that you will consider the reward sufficient, and that we shall see you no more.'

'Bah!' exclaimed the ruffian, as he deposited the money in his pocket — 'do you think I will let you off so cheaply? No, no, my pretty mistress — you may expect to see me often; and at my next visit I must have something besides money — a few little amative favors will then prove acceptable, both from you and your fair daughter, whose lips, by Satan! are as sweet to my taste as human blood. I know very well you will attempt to run away from me, by secretly removing from the city; but hark'ee — though you remove to hell, and assume the hardest name of Beelzebub's family of fourth cousins — I'll find you out! Remember, I have said it. Adieu.'

And bowing with mock politeness, the miscreant took his departure from the house.

'Good heavens!' exclaimed Mrs. Franklin — 'we are completely in the power of that dreadful man. We must leave the city, without delay, for Boston; yet we will spread the report that we are going to Philadelphia, in order to escape from that monster, if possible.'

'A monster indeed!' said Josephine shuddering — 'during your absence from the room, he took the most insolent liberties with me, and besmeared me with his loathsome kisses. How horrible it will be, if he ever finds us out, and compels us to yield our persons to his savage lust!'

'True,' said her mother — 'and yet, for my own part, sooner than pay him another thousand, I would yield to his desires; for the manner in which we have squandered money, during the last two years, has fearfully diminished my fortune, and there is but a very small balance of cash in my favor at the bank. This house must be sold, together with all our furniture, in order to replenish our funds. Now, my dear, we must make preparations for our instant departure for Boston.'

Mrs. Franklin summoned her servants, paid them their wages, and discharged them all, with the exception of her handsome footman, whom she determined to leave in charge of the house, until it was sold, after which he was privately requested to join his mistress in Boston; he was particularly directed to state, in answer to all inquiries, that the family had gone to Philadelphia. Simon, (for this was the footman's name) promised implicit obedience to these orders; and was rewarded for his fidelity by a private *tete-a-tete* with his fair patron, during which many kisses were exchanged, and other little tokens of affection were indulged in; after which she gave him the keys of the house, charging him not to visit the wine-cellar too often, and by all means not to admit a woman into the house, under pain of her eternal displeasure.

That same afternoon, the two ladies took passage in a steamer for Boston. They were received on board by the handsome and gentlemanly Captain, who, being somewhat of a fashionable man, had some slight acquaintance with the aristocratic mother and her beauteous daughter. He courteously insisted that they should occupy his own state-room; and they accordingly took possession of that elegant apartment, where they ordered tea be served; and, at their invitation, the Captain supped with them. The repast over, he apologized to the ladies for his necessary absence; and sent the steward to them with a bottle of very choice wine.

The state-room was divided into two apartments by a curtain of silk; and in each of these apartments was a magnificent bed. The floor was handsomely carpeted, and the walls were adorned with superb mirrors and pictures. The Captain was a man of taste, and his cabin was a gem of luxury and splendor.

As the stately steamer ploughed her way through the turbid waters of the Sound, many were the scenes which took place on board of her, worthy to be delineated by our pen. Though it is our peculiar province to write of city crimes, we nevertheless must not omit to depict some of the transactions which occurred during the passage, and which may be appropriately classed under the head of steamboat crimes.

At the hour for retiring, the ladies' cabin was filled with the feminine portion of the passengers, who began to divest themselves of their garments in order to court the embraces of the drowsy god. There was the simpering boarding-school miss of sixteen; the fat wife of a citizen with a baby in her arms, and another in anticipation; the lady of fashion, attended by her maid; the buxom widow, attended by a lap-dog, musical with silver bells, and there, too, was the elderly dame, attended by a host of grandchildren, to the horror of an old maid, who declares she 'can't BEAR young ones,' which is true enough, literally.

Now it is a fact beyond dispute, that ladies, among themselves, when no males are present, act and converse with more freedom from restraint, than a company of men; and the fact was never more forcibly illustrated than upon this occasion. The boarding-school miss, *en chemise*, romped with the buxom widow, who was herself in similar costume. The citizen's fat wife lent her baby to the old maid, who wanted to know how it seemed; and was rewarded for her kindness by a token of gratitude on the baby's part, which caused the aforesaid old maid to drop the little innocent like a hot potato. The fashionable lady, who dressed for bed as for a ball, was arrayed in a very costly and becoming night-dress, ornamented with a profusion of lace and ruffles; and standing before a mirror, was admiring her own charms; yet she painted, and had false teeth — defects which were atoned for by a fine bust and magnificent ankle. Her maid, a stout, well-looking girl, was toying with a very pretty boy of eight or nine years of age, and when unobserved, embraced and kissed him with an ardor which betokened a good share of amative sensibility on her part.

'The men are such odious creatures, I positively cannot endure them,' remarked the old maid.

'And yet they are very *useful,* and sometimes agreeable,' said the buxom widow, with an arch smile, (she was handsome, if she *was* a widow,) and glancing significantly at the citizen's fat wife.

'Pooh!' exclaimed the old maid, climbing into her berth, and privately taking off her wig, (she was bald,) — 'I can take my pick of ten thousand men, yet I wouldn't have one of them.' (She had been pining for an offer twenty years!)

The buxom widow got into her berth, which she shared with her lapdog; and as the little animal dove under the bed-clothes and became invisible, it is difficult to conjecture in what precise locality he stowed himself! The fashionable lady 'turned in' after the most approved manner; and as the berths were somewhat scarce, her maid generously offered to share her couch with little Charley, an offer which that interesting youth at first declined, saying he was afraid of her, she 'squeezed him so,' but his scruples were overcome by her assurances that the offence should not be repeated, and Charley concluded to accept the offer.

Those scenes did not pass unwitnessed for two men were standing outside, looking thro' one of the windows, from which the curtain had been partially drawn. Both these men were respectably dressed, and both were over sixty years of age; yet they viewed the unconscious and undressed ladies with lecherous delight.

'But, deacon,' said one — 'do look at that one standing before the glass; what breasts — what legs — what a form — what — heavens! I shall go crazy if I look much longer!'

'Now, in my way of thinking,' said the deacon — 'that young thing of sixteen is the most delicious little witch of the entire lot; — what a fair skin — what elastic limbs — what wantonness in every look and movement! There's a youthfulness and freshness about her, which render her doubly attractive.'

'Ah, they are all going to retire, and we shall lose our sport. — By the way, deacon, what kind of a set are they that I'm going to preach to, in Boston?' asked the Rev. John Marrowfat — for it was that noted hero of pulpit oratory, amours and matrimony!

'Oh, they're a set of soft-pated fools,' replied deacon Small, 'preach hell-fire and brimstone to 'em, they'll swallow everything you say, and give you a devilish good salary into the bargain.'

A young man, small and thin, and well dressed, now approached, and grasped the deacon by the hand.

'Why, this is an unexpected pleasure,' said the young man — 'who would have thought of seeing you here?'

'I am happy to meet you, brother,' said the deacon — 'brother Marrowfat, allow me to introduce you to Samuel Cough, a distinguished advocate of temperance.'

'What are you going to do in Boston, Sam?' asked deacon Small.

'Oh, going to astonish the natives a little, that's all,' replied Mr. Cough. 'That was a bad scrape I got into, in Albany; I got infernally drunk, and slept in a brothel, which was all very well, you know, and nothing unusual — but people *found it out*! Well, I got up a cock-and-bull story about drinking drugged soda, and some people believe it and some don't. Now, when I get *corned*, I keep out of sight. — Ah, temperance spouting is a great business! But come, gentlemen — it won't do for us to be seen drinking at the bar; I've got a bottle of fourth-proof brandy in my pocket; let's take a swig all around.'

And producing the article in question, Mr. Cough took a very copious swig, and passed the bottle to the others, who followed his example. We shall now leave this worthy trio, with the remark that they all got very comfortably drunk previous to retiring for the night. Mr. Cough turned into his berth with his boots on and a cigar in his mouth; Mr. Marrowfat sung obscene songs, and fell over a chair; and deacon Small rushed into the gentleman's cabin, and offered to fight any individual present, for a trifling wager. He was finally carried to bed in the custody of the bootblack.

Among the passengers was a very handsome lad, twelve or fourteen years of age, whose prepossessing appearance seemed to attract the attention of a tall gentleman, of distinguished bearing, enveloped in a cloak. — He wore a heavy moustache, and his complexion was very dark. He paid the most incessant attention to the boy, making him liberal presents of cake and fruit, and finally gave him a beautiful gold ring, from his own finger.

This man was a foreigner — one of those beasts in human shape whose perverted appetites prompts them to the commission of a crime against nature. Once before, in the tenth chapter of this narrative, we took occasion to introduce one of those fiends to the notice of the reader; it was at the masquerade ball, where the Spanish ambassador made a diabolical proposal to Josephine Franklin, whom he supposed to be a boy. It is an extremely delicate task for a writer to touch on a subject so revolting; yet the crime actually exists, beyond the shadow of a doubt, and therefore we are compelled to give it place in our list of crimes. We are about to record a startling fact — in New York, there are boys who *prostitute* themselves from motives of gain; and they are liberally patronized by the tribe of genteel foreign vagabonds who infest the city. It was well known that the principal promenade for such cattle was in the Park, where they might be seen nightly; and the circumstance had been more than once commented upon by the newspapers. — Any person who has resided in New York for two or three years, knows that we are speaking the truth. Nor is this all. There was formerly a house of prostitution for that very purpose, kept by a foreigner, and splendidly furnished; here lads were taken as apprentices, and regularly trained for the business; — they were mostly boys who had been taken from the lowest classes of society, and were invariably of comely appearance. They were expensively dressed in a peculiar kind of costume; half masculine and half feminine; and were taught a certain style of speech and behaviour calculated to attract the beastly wretches who patronize them. For a long time the existence of this infernal den was a secret; but it eventually leaked out, and the proprietor and his gang were obliged to beat a hasty retreat from the city, to save themselves from the summary justice of Lynch law.

But to return to the steamboat. The foreigner called the lad aside, and the following conversation ensued: —

'My pretty lad, this cabin is excessively close, and the bed inconvenient. I have a very nice state-room, and should be happy to have you share it with me.'

'Thank you, sir,' answered the boy — 'if it would cause you no inconvenience — '

'None whatever; come with me at once,' said the other, and they ascended to the deck, and entered his state room. It is proper to observe, that the youth was perfectly innocent, and suspected not the design of his new *friend*. Half an hour afterwards he dashed from the state room with every appearance of indignation and affright; seeking one of the officers of the boat he told his story, and the result was that the foreign gentleman and his baggage were set ashore at a place destitute of every thing but rocks, and over ten miles from any house; very inconvenient for a traveller, especially at night, with a storm in prospect. The miserable sodomite should have been more harshly dealt with.

To return to Josephine and her mother, whom we left in the Captain's elegant state room.

We must here remark that Sophia Franklin, the gentle, angelic sister of the depraved Josephine, had gone to spend a month or so with an aunt, (her father's sister,) in Newark, N.J., which circumstance will account for not accompanying her mother and sister in their flight from New York. It may be as well to add that she was in blissful ignorance of her father having been murdered, and of course, knew nothing of the discovery of that fact by Dr. Sinclair.

'Thank heaven,' cried Josephine, raising the wine glass to her vermilion lips — 'we are at last clear of that odious New York! I feel as if just liberated from a prison.'

'The feeling is natural, my dear,' rejoined her mother — 'you are no longer in constant dread of that horrible fellow who is so savagely amorous with regard to both of us. We have fairly given him the slip, and it will be difficult for him to find us.'

'Don't you think, mamma,' asked the young lady — 'that the Captain, who so politely surrendered this beautiful cabin for our accommodation, is a splendid fellow? Really, I am quite smitten with him.'

'So am I,' remarked her mother — 'he is certainly very handsome, and it is hard that he should be turned out of his cabin on our account. Why cannot we all three sleep here? I am sure he needs but a hint to make him joyfully agree to such an arrangement.'

'I understand you mamma,' said Josephine, her eyes sparking with pleasure — 'you will see what a delicate invitation I'll give him; but I won't be selfish — you shall enjoy as much benefit from the arrangement as myself. Hark! somebody knocks — it must be the Captain.'

And so it was; he had come to inquire if the ladies were comfortable, and on receiving an affirmative answer, was about to bid them good night and depart, when Josephine invited him to sit down and have a glass of wine with them. It was not in the nature of the good Captain to decline an invitation when extended by a pretty woman. The mother and daughter, tastefully attired in superb evening dresses, looked irresistibly charming — the more so, perhaps, because their cheeks were suffused with the rosy hues of wine and passion.

'I have been thinking, Captain,' said Josephine, casting her brilliant eyes upon the carpet — 'that it is unjust for us to drive you from your cabin, and make you pass the night in some less comfortable place. Mother and I have been talking about it, and we both think you had better sleep in here, as usual.'

'What — and drive you ladies out?' cried the Captain — 'couldn't think of it, upon my honor.'

'Oh, it doesn't necessarily follow that we must be driven out,' said Josephine, raising her eyes to his face, and smiling archly — 'you silly man, don't you see that we want to be very kind to you?'

'Is it possible?' exclaimed the Captain, almost beside himself with joy — 'dear ladies, you cannot be jesting, and I accept your offer with gratitude and delight. Good heavens, what a lucky fellow I am!'

And clasping both ladies around the waists, he kissed them alternately, again and again. That night was one of guilty rapture to all the parties; but the particulars must be supplied by the reader's own imagination.

***

And now, behold Mrs. Lucretia Franklin and her daughter Josephine, in the great city of Boston! The same day of their arrival they hired a handsome house, already furnished in Washington street: and the next day they made their *debut* in that fashionable thoroughfare, by promenading, in dresses of such magnificence and costliness, that they created a tremendous excitement among the bucks and belles who throng there every fine afternoon.

'Who can they be?' was asked by every one, and answered by no one. The dandy clerks, in high dickies and incipient whiskers, rushed to the doors and windows of their stores, to have a glimpse of the two beautiful *unknowns*; the mustachioed exquisites raised their eye-glasses in admiration, and murmured, 'dem foine,' the charming Countess, the graceful Cad, and the bewitching Jane B — — t, were all on the *qui vive* to ascertain the names, quality and residence of the two fair strangers, who were likely to prove such formidable rivals in the hearts and purses of the lady-loving beaux of the city.

That evening they went to the opera, and while listening to the divine strains of Biscaccianti, became the cynosure of a thousand admiring glances. And that night, beneath the windows of their residence, a party of gallant amateurs, with voice and instrument, awoke sounds of such celestial harmony, that the winged spirits of the air paused in their aerial flight to catch the choral symphony that floated on the soft breezes of the moon-lit night!

FOOTNOTES:

[4] A fact, derived by the Author from the private history of a fashionable courtezan.

CHAPTER XXII

Showing the Desperate and Bloody Combat which took place in the Dark Vaults.

'You will pray for death in vain; death shall not come to your relief for years,' were the words of the miscreant who had shut up poor Frank in that loathsome dungeon; — and like a weight of lead, that awful doom oppressed and crushed the heart of our hero, as he lay stretched upon the stone floor of the cell, with the maniac Dwarf gibbering beside him, and staring at him with its serpent-like and malignant eyes.

While lying there, weak with hunger, and his soul filled with despair, a wild delirium took possession of his senses, and in his diseased mind horror succeeded horror. First, the misshaped Dwarf seemed transformed into a huge vulture, about to tear him to pieces with its strong talons; then it became a gigantic reptile, about to discharge upon him a deluge of poisonous slime; then it changed to the Evil One, come to bear him to perdition. Finally, as the wildest paroxysms of his delirium subsided, the creature stood before him as the Image and spirit of the Dead Man, appointed to torture and to drive him mad.

'Die, thou fiend incarnate!' he exclaimed, in a phrenzy of rage and despair; and starting from the ground, he rushed upon the creature and attempted to strangle it. But with an appalling yell, it struggled from his grasp, and leaping upon his shoulders bore him to the earth with a force that stunned him; and then it fastened its teeth in his flesh and began to drink his blood.

But the fates willed that Sydney was not thus to die; for at that moment the iron door was suddenly thrown open, and the glare of a lantern shone into the dungeon; then there entered a person whose features were concealed by a hideous mask, and the dwarf quitted its hold of the victim, and flew screaming into a corner.

'He must be revived ere he is brought to judgement,' said the Mask; and he raised Sydney in his arms, carried him out of the dungeon, and fastened the door.

Then the Mask stepped upon the platform with his burden, and descended into the dark abyss. When Frank recovered his senses, he found himself in a sort of cavern which was lighted by a lamp suspended from the ceiling. He was lying upon a rude bed; and near him, silent and motionless, sat a masked figure.

'Where am I — and who art thou?' demanded our hero, in a feeble tone, as a vague terror stole over him.

The Mask replied not, but rising, brought him a cup of wine and some food, of which he partook with eagerness. Much refreshed, he sank back upon his pillow, and fell into a long, deep slumber. When he awoke, he found himself in the same cavern, on the same bed, and guarded as before by the mysterious Mask, who now spoke for the first time.

'Arise and follow me,' said he. — Sydney obeyed, and followed the Unknown through a long passage, and into a vast hall or cavern, brilliantly lighted. Glancing around him, he saw at once that he was in the Dark Vaults, in that part called the 'Infernal Regions,' the rendezvous of the band of miscreants known as the 'Jolly Knights of the Round Table.'

Seated around that table was a company of men, to the number of about fifty, all so hideously masked, that they seemed like a band of demons just released from the bottomless pit. They sat in profound silence, and were all so perfectly motionless that they might have been taken for statues rudely chiseled from the solid rock.

In the centre of the table, upon a coffin, sat the Judge of that awful tribunal, arrayed from head to foot in a blood-red robe: he wore no mask — why need he? What mask could exceed in hideousness the countenance of the Dead Man?

Sydney was compelled to mount the table, and seat himself before his Judge, who thus addressed him: —

'Prisoner, you are now in the presence of our august and powerful band, — the Knights of the Round Table, of which I have honor to be the Captain. I am also Judge and Executioner. — The charges I have against you are already known to every

Knight present. It but remains for them to pronounce you guilty, and for me to pass and execute sentence upon you. Attention, Knights! those of you who believe the prisoner to be guilty, and worthy of such punishment as I shall choose to inflict upon him, will *stand up!*'

Every masked figure arose, excepting *one*! and that one remained silent and motionless. To him the judge turned with a savage scowl.

'How now, Doctor!' he cried in a voice of thunder — 'do you dare dissent from the decision of your comrades? Stand upon your feet, or by G — — I'll spring upon you and tear you limb from limb!'

But the Doctor stirred not.

'By hell!' roared the Dead Man, foaming with rage — 'dare you disobey the orders of your Captain? Villain, do you seek your own death?'

'*Dare?*' exclaimed the Doctor, tearing off his mask, and confronting his ruffian leader with an unquailing eye — '*dare!* Why, thou white-livered hound, I dare spit upon and spurn ye! And forsooth, ye call me a villain — you coward cut-throat, traitor, monster, murderer of weak women and helpless babes! I tell you, Dead Man, your Power is at an end in these Vaults. There are robbers, there may be murderers here — although thank God, *I* never shed human blood — but bad as we are, your damnable villainy, your cruelty and your tyranny have disgusted us. I for one submit to your yoke no longer; so may the devil take you, and welcome!'

Sydney now for the first time recognized in the speaker, the same individual who sought to rob him one night in the Park, and whose gratitude he had won by presenting him with a fifty dollar bill.

The Dead Man glared from some moments in silence upon the bold fellow who thus defied him. At length he spoke —

'Fool! you have presumed to dispute my authority as Captain of this band, and your life is forfeit to our laws. But, by Satan! I admire your courage, and you shall not die without having a chance for your life. You shall fight me, hand to hand — here to-night, at once; the Knights shall form a ring, and we will arm ourselves with Bowie knives; *cut and slash* shall be the order of the combat; no quarters shall be shown; and he who cuts out his adversary's heart, and presents it to the band on the point of his knife, shall be Captain of the Round Table. Say do you agree to this?'

'Yes!' replied the Doctor, much to the disappointment of his challenger, who would have been glad had the offer been rejected. However, there was no retracting, and instant preparations were made for the combat. Sydney was placed in charge of two men, in order to prevent his escape; and the Knights formed themselves into a large ring, while the combatants prepared for the encounter. Both men stripped to the skin; around their left arms they wrapped blankets to serve as shields; and in their right hands, they grasped long, sharp Bowie knives, whose blades glittered in the brilliant light of the many candles. All was soon ready, and the adversaries entered the ring, amid profound silence. — Poor Sydney contemplated the scene with painful interest; how sincerely he prayed that the Doctor might prove victorious in the combat!

Gaunt and bony, the Dead Man looked like a skeleton; yet the immense muscles upon his fleshless arms, indicated prodigious strength. He looked terribly formidable, with his livid face, deadly eye and jaws firmly set — his long fingers clutching his knife with an iron grasp, and his left arm raised to protect himself. — The Doctor was a large, dark-complexioned, handsome man — an Apollo in beauty and a Hercules in strength, presenting a singular contrast to the hideous, misshapen being with whom he was about to engage in deadly conflict.

Cautiously they advanced towards each other, with knives upraised. Standing scarce five feet apart, they eyed each other for two minutes; not a muscle moved; with a howl like that of a hyena, the Dead Man sprang upon his enemy, and gave him a severe gash upon his shoulder; but the Doctor, who was an accomplished pugilist, knocked his assailant down, and favored him with a kick in the jaw that left its mark for many a day, and did not enhance his beauty.

The Dead Man arose, grinding his teeth with passion, but advancing with extreme caution. By a rapid and dexterous movement of his foot, he tripped the Doctor down, and having him at that disadvantage, was about to bury his knife in his heart, when several of the band rushed forward and prevented him, exclaiming —

'When you were down, the Doctor suffered you to regain your feet, and you shall allow him the same privilege. Begin again on equal terms, and he who gets the first advantage, shall improve it.'

'Curses on you for this interference,' growled the ruffian, as he reluctantly suffered the Doctor to arise. The combat was then renewed with increased vigor on both sides. Severe cuts were given and received; two of the Doctor's fingers were cut off, and Sydney began to fear that he would be vanquished, when, rallying desperately, he closed with the Dead Man, and with one tremendous stroke, severed the miscreant's right hand from his wrist! Thus disabled, he fell to the ground, bathed in blood.

'I'll not take your life, miserable dog,' cried the Doctor, as he surveyed his fallen adversary with a look of contempt — 'as I have deprived you of that murderous hand, you shall live. You are now comparatively harmless — an object of pity rather than of fear. I am a surgeon, and will exert my skill to stop the effusion of blood.'

The Dead Man had fainted. He was laid upon the Round Table, and the Doctor dressed the wound. Then he turned to his comrades, and said, 'Gentlemen of the Round Table, you will admit that I have fairly conquered our leader; I have spared his life not in the hope that he will ever become a better man, for that is impossible — but that he may be reserved for a worse fate than death by my knife. He shall live to die a death of horror.'

The band crowded around the Doctor, clapping their hands,

and exclaiming — 'Hail to our new Captain!'

'Not so,' cried the Doctor — 'to-night I leave this band forever. Nay, hear me, comrades — you know that I am not a bad man by nature — you are aware that I have been driven to this life by circumstances which I could not control. You are satisfied that I never will betray you; let that suffice. Should any of you meet me hereafter, you will find in me a friend, provided you are inclined to be honest. — I have a word to say in regard to this prisoner; he is my benefactor, having once supplied my wants when I was in a condition of deep distress. I am grateful to him, and wish to do him a service. He has been brought before you by the Captain, for some private wrongs, which have not affected you as a band. Say, comrades, will you set him free?'

Many of the band seemed inclined to grant this favor; but one, who possessed much influence, turned the current of feeling against Sydney, by saying —

'Comrades, listen to me. Though our Captain is conquered, we will not do him injustice. This man is his prisoner, captured by his hand, and *he* alone can justly release him. Let the Doctor depart, since he wishes it; but let the prisoner be kept in custody; to be disposed of as our Captain may see proper.'

This speech was received with applause by the others. The Doctor knew it would be useless to remonstrate; approaching Sydney, he whispered —

'Have courage, sir — in me you have a friend who will never desert you. I shall be constantly near you to aid you at the first opportunity. Farewell.'

He pressed Sydney's hand, bade adieu to his comrades, and left the Vaults.

The Dead Man slowly revived; on opening his eyes, his first glance rested upon his prisoner, and a gleam of satisfaction passed over his ghastly visage. At his request, two of the band raised him from the table, and placed him in a chair; then, in a feeble voice, he said —

'Eternal curses on you all, why have you suffered the Doctor to escape? Hell and fury — my right hand cut off! — But no matter; I shall learn to murder with the other. Ha, Sydney! you are there, I see; the Doctor may go, in welcome, since *you* are left to feel my vengeance. I am too weak at present to enjoy the sight of your torture, and the music of your groans. Back to your dungeon, dog; yet stay — the dwarf may kill you, and thus cheat me of my revenge; it is not safe to confine you with him any longer. Maggot and Bloodhound, take Sydney and shut him up in the *Chamber of Death.*'

Two of the worst villains of the gang, who answered to the singular names of Maggot and Bloodhound, seized Sydney by his arms, and dragged him along one of the dark passages which branched off from the Vault. The Dead Man himself followed, bearing a lantern in his only remaining hand.

They arrived at a low iron door, in which was a grating formed of thick bars of the same metal. This door being opened, the party descended a flight of stone steps, and entered an apartment of great extent where the damp, chill air was so charged with noxious vapours, that the light of the lantern was almost extinguished. The stone walls and floor of this dungeon were covered with green damp; and from the ceiling in many places dripped a foul moisture. The further extremity of the place was involved in a profound darkness which could not be dissipated by feeble rays of the lamp.

'Here,' said the Dead Man, addressing his prisoner — 'you will be kept in confinement for the rest of your life — a confinement varied only by different modes of torture which I shall apply to you, from time to time. This dungeon is called the Chamber of Death — for what reason you will ere long find out. It is built directly under the sewers of the city, which accounts for the liquid filth that oozes through the ceiling. Many persons have been shut up in this place, for offences against our band and against me; and not one of them has ever got out, either alive or dead! To-morrow I shall visit you, and bring you food — for I do not wish you to die of hunger; I will endeavor to protract, not shorten your life, so that I may longer enjoy the pleasure of torturing you. To-morrow, perhaps, you shall receive your first lesson in my methods of torture. Adieu — come, comrades, let's leave him the lamp, that he may contemplate the horrors of the place — for darkness here is bliss.'

The three villains ascended the steps and left the dungeon, having first carefully locked the door.

Poor Sydney fell upon his knees on the cold, damp floor, and prayed earnestly for either a safe deliverance from that awful place, or a speedy death. Somewhat comforted by the appeal to a Supreme Being, whose existence all men acknowledge in times of peril, he arose, and taking the lamp resolved to explore the dungeon. He had not proceeded far before a spectacle met his gaze which caused him to pause in horror and affright.

Seated around a vast table, was a row of figures fantastically dressed and in every extravagant attitude. At first, Frank thought that they were living creatures; but observing that they did not move, he approached nearer, and discovered that they were skeletons. Some were dressed as males, others as females; and many of them, in fearful mockery of death, had been placed in attitudes the most obscene and indecent. Presiding over this ghastly revel, was a gigantic skeleton, arrayed in what had once been a splendid theatrical dress, and grasping in its fleshless hand a large gilt goblet; this figure was seated on a sort of throne, made of rough boards.

These were the skeletons of those who had died in the Vaults, as well as of those persons who, having fallen into the power of the band of villains, had been murdered in that dungeon, by starvation or torture. With infernal ingenuity, the Dead Man had arrayed the skeletons in fanciful costumes, which had been plundered from the wardrobe of a theatre; and placed them in the most absurd and indecent positions his hellish fancy could devise. The large skeleton, which seemed to preside over the others, was the remains of a former Captain of the band, celebrated for his many villainies and gigantic stature.

While gazing upon this figure, Sydney distinctly saw the head, or skull, nod at him. Astonished at this, yet doubting the evidence of his own eyesight, he approached nearer, and held the lamp close up to it; again it moved, so plainly as to admit of no further doubt. Our hero was not superstitious, but the strangeness of this incident almost terrified him, and he was about to make a rapid retreat to the other side of the dungeon, when the mystery was explained in a manner that would have been ludicrous under any other circumstances: a large cat leaped from the skull, where it had taken up an abode, and scampered off, to the great relief of Sydney, who was glad to find that the nod of the skeleton proceeded from such a trifling cause.

On the back of each chair whereon was seated a member of the ghostly company was written the name which he or she had borne during life. Judges, magistrates and police officers were there, who had rendered themselves obnoxious to the gang, in years past, by vigilance in detecting, or severity in passing sentences upon many of its members. These individuals had been waylaid by their ruffian enemies, and made to die a lingering death in that dungeon; their fate was never known to their friends, and their sudden and unaccountable removal from the world, was chronicled in the newspapers, at the time, under the head of *mysterious disappearance.* Ladies, whose testimony had tended to the conviction of the band, were there; but their fate had been doubly horrible, for previous to their imprisonment in the dungeon, they had been dishonored by the vile embraces of almost every ruffian in the Vaults; and even after death, they had been placed in attitudes unseemly and shameful. But the horror of Sydney, while beholding these things, was soon absorbed in a discovery which to him was ten times more horrible than all the rest; for written on the chair of a female figure, was the name of his aunt Mrs. Stevens!

It will be remembered that this lady was murdered by the Dead Man, at her residence in Grand Street; on the night of the masquerade ball, in order to prevent her giving favorable testimony at the trial of Sydney. Having been found, suspended by the neck, it was at first supposed that she committed suicide; but that belief was removed from the public mind, when it was found that a robbery had been committed in the house. It was then apparent that she had been inhumanely murdered. Her servant testified that a strange man had called on her mistress that evening whom she would not be able to recognize, his face having been concealed in the folds of his cloak. After admitting him into the house, and calling Mrs. Stevens, the girl had gone out on a short errand, and on her return, found her mistress in the situation described, and quite dead. The old lady was buried; but her murderer broke open the tomb, and carried the corpse to the dungeon of the Vaults, where he had placed her with the other victims, in the position in which Sydney, her nephew, now found her.

'It is as I suspected,' thought our hero, as he sadly viewed the remains of his poor aunt — 'that villain murdered her, and now it is forever out of my power to avenge her blood. Ha! what's this? — *my name*, upon an empty chair.'

And so it was; the name, Francis Sydney, was written out on the back of an unoccupied chair; he comprehended that this was designated to be *his* seat when he should form one of that awful crew, in the chamber of Death.

Suddenly, the damp, foul air of the place extinguished the light of his lamp, and he found himself in total darkness.

CHAPTER XXIII

*Showing how Sydney was tortured in the Chamber of Death, and
how he made his escape through the City Sewers.*

Groping his way to the extremity of the dungeon, Frank sat
down upon the stone steps, his mind a prey to feelings of keenest
horror and despair. His soul recoiled from the idea of suicide, as a
heinous crime in the sight of Heaven, or he would have dashed
his brains out against the walls of his prison, and thus put an end
to his misery. Vainly he tried to forget his sorrows in sleep; no
sooner would he close his eye-lids, than the band of skeletons
would seem to rush towards him, and with fleshless arms beckon
him to join their awful company.

Slowly, slowly passed the hours away. Numbed with cold,
and paralyzed with the terrors of his situation, Sydney was at last
sinking into a state of insensibility, when he was aroused by the
loud noise caused by the opening of the dungeon door, and the
gleam of a lantern flashed upon him. He staggered to his feet, and
saw that his visitors were the two villains, Maggot and Bloodhound. One of them came down the steps and deposited upon
the floor a small basket and a lamp.

'Here,' said he — 'is some *grub* for you, and a light to scare
away the ghosts. Eat your fill — you will need it; for in an hour
from this time, our captain will visit you to commence his tortures, in which I and my comrade will be obliged to help him.'

'Why will you aid that wretch in his cruelties?' asked Sydney
— 'I never injured you; pray act like a man of heart and feeling,
and release me from this dreadful place.'

'*Release you!*' cried the man — 'I dare not. True, I have no
animosity against you, young man; but our Captain has, and
were I to let you go, life would not be worth a minute's purchase.
I'd not incur that man's wrath for a million of money. No, no,
make up your mind to the worst — you can never go out of this
dungeon.'

With this consoling assurance, the man and his comrade

took their departure. On examining the contents of the basket, our hero found an ample supply of good, wholesome food, and a jug of water; and while heartily partaking of these necessities, (of which he stood in great need,) he could not help comparing his situation with that of an animal being fattened for slaughter!

An hour elapsed; the dungeon was again opened, and the Dead Man entered, followed by Maggot and Bloodhound. The two latter worthies carried between them an apparatus of singular appearance and construction.

'Well, dog,' cried the Dead Man, 'how do you like your new kennel? Not so comfortable, I'll swear, as your fine house on Broadway! Faith, a fine prayer you made last night, after we left you; you called on God to help you — ha, ha! Fool — *he* cannot help you! — *I* alone can do it. Down, then, on your marrow bones and worship me!'

And saying this, he raised his right arm, and with it struck his victim heavily on his head; the extremity of the arm, where the hand had been cut off, had been furnished with a piece of iron like a sledge-hammer, to enable the ruffian to possess the means of attack and defence. Fortunate it was that the blow did not fracture Sydney's skull.

Meanwhile Maggot and Bloodhound had placed the machine which they had brought with them upon the floor and began to prepare it for use. The vaults of the Spanish Inquisition never contained a more horrible instrument of torture. It was a box made of iron and shaped like a coffin; the sides and bottom were covered with sharp nails, firmly fixed with their points outwards; beneath the box was a sort of furnace, filled with shavings and charcoal. This apparatus was called by the ruffians — *The Bed of Ease.*

Sydney was made to strip himself entirely naked, and lie down in the box; then the cover was fastened on. The points of the nails penetrated his flesh, causing him the most excruciating torture; blood started profusely from all parts of his body, and he could scarce repress groans of the most heart-felt anguish. But this was nothing to what he was doomed to endure; for the demons in human shape kindled a fire beneath him, and when nature could hold out no longer, and he screamed with agony, his tormentors roared with laughter.

They released him when a cessation of his cries warned them that he could hold out no longer without endangering his life — for they wished him to live to endure future torments. He was truly a pitiable object when taken from the box — his flesh torn and bleeding, and horribly burnt. They rubbed him with oil, assisted him to dress and laid him upon a heap of straw which one of them brought. They then left him, after assuring him that, as soon as he was healed, they had tortures in store for him much more severe than the one just inflicted. The iron box they left behind them in the dungeon, probably intending to use it again on some future occasion.

In what a deplorable situation did poor Sydney now find himself placed! Nearly dead with the torments which he had just undergone, his mind was harassed by the dread of other and more severe tortures yet in store for him. How gladly would he have bared his bosom to the deadly stroke of the knife, or the fatal discharge of the pistol!

But exhausted nature could hold out no longer, and he fell into a deep sleep, from which he was awakened by the entrance of some person into the dungeon. Starting up, he was confronted by the dark and menacing visage of the Dead Man. The villain was alone and held in his left hand a large knife; Sydney perceived, by his unsteady gait, his wildly rolling eyes, and his thick, indistinct utterance, that he was much intoxicated.

'I am come, dog,' said he, with a look that a demon might have envied — 'to feast upon your heart, and drink your blood. My soul is hungry. I wish you had a thousand lives for me to take. Sit up, and let me dig out your eyes, and cut off your nose, ears and fingers — for you must die by inches! Get up, I say!'

'The monster is drunk,' thought Sydney; 'had I a weapon and sufficient strength, I might perhaps overcome him; but alas! I am weak and sore — '

'Get up!' again roared the ruffian,'that I may sacrifice ye upon the flaming altar of Satan, my deity. My heart is a coal of fire; it burns me, and blood alone can quench it!'

With the howl of a wild beast, he threw himself upon his victim.

But ere he could strike the deadly blow, he was writhing and struggling in the powerful grasp of a tall, stout man, who at that crisis rushed into the dungeon.

'Now, reptile, I have thee!' muttered the Doctor, (for it was he) as with mighty and resistless strength he dashed the miscreant to the floor and deprived him of his knife.

But the Dead Man struggled with all the fury of desperation; with his *iron hand* he made rapid and savage passes at the head of his assailant, knowing that a single well-directed blow would stun him. But the Doctor's science in pugilism enabled him to keep off the blows with ease, while he punished his antagonist in the most thorough and satisfactory manner. Finding himself likely to be overcome, the villain yelled at the top of his voice — 'Treason! murder! help!'

'Your handkerchief, Mr. Sydney — quick!' cried the Doctor. Frank, who had already arisen from his bed of straw, handed his gallant protector the article he had called for — and, though very weak, assisted in gagging the vanquished ruffian, who, breathless and exhausted, could now offer but a slight resistance.

'Into the box with him!' exclaimed the Doctor, and the next minute the Dead Man was stretched upon the points of the sharp nails; the lid was closed upon him, the fire was lighted beneath, and he writhed in all the torture he had inflicted upon poor Sydney.

Suddenly, the Doctor assumed a listening attitude, and whispered to his companion —

'By heavens, the band is aroused, and the Knights are coming to the rescue. If they capture us, we are lost! There is but one way for us to escape — and that is *through the sewers*, a dreadful avenue! Will you dare it?'

'I will dare anything, to escape from this earthly hell!' cried our hero, vigor returning to his frame as he thought of liberty.

'Follow me, then,' said the Doctor, taking up the lamp, and hurrying up the dungeon steps; he led the way, at a rapid pace, up another high flight of steps, to a point which overlooked the city sewers. By the dim light of the lamp, Frank saw, twenty feet below, the dark, sluggish and nauseous stream of the filthy drainings of the vast city overhead, which, running thro' holes under the edges of the sidewalk, collect in these immense subterranean reservoirs, and are slowly discharged into the river.

'Leap boldly after me — you will land in the mud, and break no bones,' said the Doctor — 'our enemies are at our heels!' A fact that was demonstrated by the sound of many footsteps hurrying rapidly towards them.

The Doctor leaped into the dark and terrible abyss. Sydney heard the splash of his fall into the muddy water, and nerving himself for the deed, jumped in after him; he sank up to his chin in the loathsome pool. His friend grasped his hand, and whispered — 'We are now safe from our pursuers, unless they follow us, which is hardly probable; for I confess these sewers are so full of horrors, that even those villains would hesitate to pass through them, unless under circumstances as desperate as ours.' Frank shuddered. 'Will they not fire upon us?' he asked. The Doctor answered: —

'No, they dare not; for the noise of fire-arms would be heard in the streets above, and people might be led to inquire into the cause of such a phenomena. Fortunately my lamp is not extinguished, and as the mud is not over our heads, we may make our way out of this infernal trap, provided we are not devoured by rats and reptiles, which swarm here. Ah, by Jupiter, there are our pursuers!'

And as he spoke, some fifteen or twenty men appeared above them, on the point from which they had jumped. On seeing the fugitives, they setup a shout of surprise and anger.

'A pretty trick you've served us, Doctor,' called out the fellow known as Bloodhound — 'you've nearly roasted the Dead

Man, and carried off his prisoner; however, we rescued our Captain just in time to save his life. You had better come back, or we'll blow your brains out!' — and he levelled a pistol.

'Blow and be d — — d,' coolly remarked the Doctor, who knew very well that he dare not fire — 'come, Mr. Sydney, follow me, and leave these fellows to talk to the empty air.'

With much difficulty the two fugitives began to move off through the mud and water.

'What, cowards, will you let them escape before your eyes?' roared the Dead Man, as he rushed up to the brink of the chasm, and glared after Sydney and his friend with flaming eyes. 'Plunge in after them, and bring them back, or by G — — every man of you shall die the death of a dog!'

Not a man stirred to obey the order; and the miscreant would have leaped into the sewers himself, had they not forcibly held him back.

'No, no, Captain,' cried Maggot — 'the Doctor's too much for you; you've only got one hand now, and you'd be no match for him, for he's the devil's pup at a tussle. Let them both slide this time; you may catch them napping before long. As it is, they've got but a devilish small chance of escape, for it rains terribly overhead, which will fill up the sewers, and drown them like kittens.'

Meanwhile, Frank and his brave deliverer struggled manfully through the foul waters which encompassed them. Soon an angle in the wall concealed them from their enemies; and they entered a passage of vast extent, arched overhead with immense blocks of stone. This section of the sewers was directly under Canal street, and pursued a course parallel with that great avenue, until its contents were emptied into the North river. Our subterranean travellers could distinctly hear the rumbling of the carts and carriages in the street above them, like the rolling of thunder.

It was an awful journey, through that dark and loathsome place. At every few steps they encountered the putrid carcase of some animal, floating on the surface of the sickening stream. As they advanced, hundreds of gigantic rats leaped from crevices in the wall, and plunged into the water. Their lamp cast its dim rays upon the green, slimy stone-work on either side of them; and their blood curdled with horror as they saw, clinging there, hideous reptiles, of prodigious size, engendered and nourished there. They imagined that at every step they took, they could feel those monsters crawl and squirm beneath their feet — and they trembled lest the reptiles should twine around their limbs, and strike deadly venom to their blood. But a new terror came to increase their fears; the water was growing deeper every instant, and threatened to overwhelm them. Sydney overcome by the awful effluvia, grew too sick and faint to proceed further; he requested the Doctor to leave him to his fate — but the gallant man raised his sinking form in his powerful arms, and struggled bravely on. 'Courage, my friend,' cried the Doctor — 'we are near the river, for I see a light ahead, glimmering like a star of hope!' In ten minutes more they emerged from the sewers, and plunged into the clear waters of the North river.

Without much difficulty they got on board of a sloop which lay moored at the wharf; and as Sydney had money, he easily procured a change of raiment for himself and friend, from the skipper, who was too lazy to ask any questions, and who was very well satisfied to sell them two suits of clothes at five times their value. Frank took the Doctor to his home, resolved never to part with so faithful and gallant a friend, whose faults had been the faults of unfortunate circumstances, but whose heart, he felt assured, was 'in the right place.'

Poor Clinton, the dumb boy, welcomed his master and his old acquaintance the Doctor, with mute eloquence. Dennis, the Irish footman, was almost crazy with delight at Mr. Sydney's safe return, swearing that he thought him 'murthered and kilt intirely.'

That awful night was so indelibly stamped upon the memory of our hero, that often, in after times, it haunted him in his dreams.

CHAPTER XXIV

*The Marriage — The Intoxicated Rector — Miseries of an aged
Bridegroom on his Wedding Night.*

Mrs. Belmont was seated in the elegant parlor of her residence in Reade street. It was the evening appointed for her marriage with Mr. Hedge, and she was dressed in bridal attire — a spotless robe of virgin white well set off her fine form and rich complexion, while a chaplet of white roses made a beautiful contrast with the dark, luxuriant hair on which it rested.

A superb French clock on the marble mantel piece proclaimed in silvery tones, the hour of seven.

'He will soon be here,' she murmured — 'to carry me to the house of the clergyman, there to be made his wife. How little the fond, foolish old man suspects the snare in which he is about to fall! How admirably have my artifices deceived him! And the other evening when in the heat of passion, he pressed me to grant him a certain favor in advance of our marriage, how well I affected indignation, and made him beg for forgiveness! Oh, he thinks me the most virtuous of my sex — but there is his carriage; now for the consummation of my hopes!'

Mr. Hedge entered the room, and raising her jewelled hand to his lips, kissed it with rapture. The old gentleman was dressed in a style quite juvenile; — his coat was of the most modern cut, his vest and gloves white, and his cambric handkerchief fragrant with *eau de cologne*. To make himself look as young as possible, he had dyed his gray hair to a jet black, and his withered cheeks had been slightly tinged with *rouge*, to conceal the wrinkles, and give him a youthful, fresh appearance. He certainly looked twenty years younger than ever, but he could not disguise his infirm gait and the paralytic motions of his body.

But let not the reader suppose that he was either a superannuated coxcomb or a driveling dotard. He was a man of sense and feeling, but his passion for Julia had, for the time, changed all his manner and habits. — He saw that she was a young and lovely woman, about to give herself to the arms of a man thrice her age; and he wished to render the union less repugnant to her, by appearing to be as youthful as possible himself. Therefore, he had made up his toilet as we have described, not from personal vanity, but from a desire to please his intended bride.

We wish not to disguise the fact that Mr. Hedge was an exceedingly amorous old gentleman; and that in taking Julia to his matrimonial embrace, he was partially actuated by the promptings of the flesh. But in justice to him we will state that these were not the only considerations which had induced him to marry her; he wanted a companion and friend — one whose accomplishments and buoyancy of spirits would serve to dispel the loneliness and *ennui* of his solitary old age. Such a person he fancied he had found in the young, beautiful 'widow,' Mrs. Belmont.

'Sweetest Julia,' said the aged bridegroom, enclosing her taper waist with her arm — 'the carriage is at the door, and all is in readiness to complete our felicity. To-night we will revel in the first joys of our union in my own house — to-morrow, as you have requested, we depart for Boston.'

'Ah, dearest,' murmured Julia, as her ripe lips were pressed to his — 'you make me so happy! How young you look tonight! What raptures I anticipate in your arms! Feel how my heart beats with the wildness of passion!'

She placed his hand into her fair, soft bosom, and he felt that her heart was indeed throbbing violently; yet 'twas not with amorous passion, as she had said; no, 'twas with fierce triumph at the success of her schemes.

The contact of his hand with her voluptuous charms, inflamed him with impatient desire.

'Come,' cried he, — 'let us no longer defer the blissful hour that gives you to my arms.'

In a few minutes Julia was ready; and the happy pair, seating themselves in the carriage, were driven to the abode of Dr. Sinclair, who was to perform the marriage ceremony.

We said *happy* pair — yes, they were indeed so; the old gen-

tleman was happy in the prospect of having such a beautiful creature to share his fortune and bed; and the young lady was happy
in the certainty of having secured a husband whose wealth would
enable her to live in luxury and splendor.

They arrive at the rector's residence, and are ushered into a
spacious apartment. Everything is handsome and costly, yet everything is in disorder; judging from appearances one would suppose that the place was occupied by a gentleman of intemperate
habits — not by a minister of the gospel. The rich carpet is disfigured with many stains, which look marvelously like the stains
produced by the spilling of port wine. The mirror is cracked; the
sofa is daubed with mud; a new hat lies crushed beneath an overturned chair. An open Bible is upon the table, but on it stand a
decanter and a wine-glass; and the sacred page is stained with the
blood-red juice of the grape. On the mantle-piece are books,
thrown in a confused pile; the collection embraces all sorts —
Watts' hymn book reposes at the side of the 'Frisky Songsters,' the
Pilgrim's Progress plays hide-and-seek with the last novel of Paul
de Kock; while 'Women of Noted Piety' are in close companionship with the 'Voluptuous Turk.'

Soon the rector enters, and there is something in his appearance peculiar, if not suspicious. His disordered dress corresponds
with his disordered room. His coat is soiled and torn, his cravat is
put on awry, and his linen is none of the cleanest. He salutes
Brother Hedge and his fair intended, in an unsteady voice, while
his eyes wander vacantly around the apartment, and he leans
against a chair for support.

'How very strangely he looks and acts,' whispered Julia to
her frosty bridegroom — 'surely he can't be *tipsy*?'

'Of course not,' replied Mr. Hedge — 'such a supposition
with reference to our beloved pastor would be sacrilege. He is
only somewhat agitated; he is extremely sensitive, and deep
study has doubtless operated to the injury of his nervous system.
My dear Brother Sinclair, we are waiting for you to perform the
ceremony,' he added, in a louder tone.

'Waiting — ceremony — ' said the rector, abstractedly, gazing upward at the ceiling — 'Oh, marriage ceremony, you mean? Ah, yes, I had forgotten. Certainly. Quite right, Brother Hedge, or Ditch — ha, ha! Excuse me. All ready.'

We shall not attempt to imitate the rector, in his manner of performing the ceremony, as we deem the matter to be too serious for jest; but we will say, never before was ceremony performed in so strange a manner. However, to all intents and purposes, they were married; and at the conclusion of the service, the bridegroom slipped a fifty-dollar note into the rector's hand, and then conducted his lovely bride to the carriage, in which they were soon driven to Mr. Hedge's residence in Hudson street.

In explanation of the singular conduct of Dr. Sinclair, we will state that he became a wine-bibber and a drunkard. Remorse for his amorous follies with Josephine, and horror at her crimes, had driven him to drown such painful remembrances in the bottle. The very next day after he had accused the mother and daughter of the murder, he drank himself into a state of intoxication, and each subsequent day witnessed a renewal of the folly. On the Sabbath, he managed to preserve a tolerably decent degree of sobriety, but his appearance plainly indicated a recent debauch, and his style of preaching was tame and irregular. His congregation viewed him with suspicion and distrust privately; but as yet, no public charge had been made against him. He knew very well that he could not long continue in his own unworthy course, and be a minister of the gospel; he plainly saw the precipice over which he hung — but with mad infatuation he heeded not the danger, and rushed onwards to his ruin. His house became the scene of disorder and revelry. His servants neglected their duties when he so far forgot himself as to make them familiar associates of his orgies. The voice of prayer was no longer heard in his dwelling: the Bible was cast aside. Blasphemy had supplanted the one and obscene books had taken the place of the other. We shall see how rapid was his downfall, and to what a state of degradation he sunk at last.

But we return for the present to Mr. Hedge and his newly-made wife. They alighted at the old gentleman's princely mansion in Hudson street and entered a magnificent apartment in which a bridal supper had been prepared for them. Julia, as the mistress of the house, was received with the most profound respect by half a score of domestics, clad in plain but costly livery. Everything betokened unbounded wealth, and the repast was served on a scale of splendid luxury — every article of plate being of massive silver. Viands the most *recherche* graced the board, and wines the most rare added zest to the feast. There, sparkling like the bright waters of the Castalian fountain, flowed the rich Greek wine — a classic beverage, fit for the gods; there, too, was the delicate wine of Persia, fragrant with the spices of the East; and the diamond-crested champagne, inspiring divinities of poesy and Love.

'Drink, my Julia,' cried the happy bridegroom — 'one cup to Hymen, and then let us seek his joys in each other's arms. I have a chamber prepared for us, which I have dedicated to Venus and to Cupid; there hath Love spread his wing, and beneath it shall we enjoy extatic repose. Come, dearest.'

He took her hand, and preceded by a female domestic bearing candles, conducted her up a broad marble staircase; they entered an apartment sumptuously furnished — it was the bridal chamber. The footstep fell noiseless upon the thick and yielding carpet; each chair was a gilded throne, and each sofa a luxurious divan, cushioned with purple velvet. Vast paintings, on subjects chiefly mythological, were reflected in immense mirrors, reaching from floor to ceiling. The bed was curtained with white satin, spangled with silver stars; and a wilderness of flowers, in exquisite vases, enriched the atmosphere with their perfume.

The old gentleman kissed his bride, whispered a few words in her ear, and left the chamber, followed by the domestic. Then Julia was waited upon by two young ladies, dressed in white, who saluted her respectfully, and signified their desire to assist her in disrobing.

'We are only servants, madam,' said they, modestly, — 'we perform the duties of housekeepers for Mr. Hedge, and are highly honored if we can be of service to his lady.'

But the truth is, these young ladies were the illegitimate daughters of the old gentleman. Tho' Julia was his first wife, in his young days he had formed an attachment for a poor but lovely young woman; circumstances would not admit of his marrying her, and as she loved him in return, they tasted the joys of Venus without lighting the torch of Hymen. The young woman became *enciente,* and died in giving birth to twins — both daughters. Mr. Hedge brought these children up under his own roof, and educated them liberally; yet while he treated them with the most indulgent kindness, he never acknowledged himself to be their father, fearing that if the fact became known, it would injure his reputation as a man and a Christian, he being a zealous church member. The girls themselves were ignorant of their parentage, and only regarded Mr. Hedge as their generous benefactor. They had been taught to believe that they had been abandoned by their parents in their infancy, and that the old gentleman had taken them under his protection from motives of charity. They were of a gentle disposition, beloved by all who knew them, and by none more so than by Mr. Hedge, who maintained them as ladies although he suffered them to superintend the affairs of his extensive bachelor establishment. Their names were Emma and Lucy.

While these young ladies are engaged in disrobing the fair (but *not* blushing) bride, let us seek the newly-elected husband, in the privacy of his library.

A library — How we love to linger in such a place, amid the thousands of volumes grown dingy with the accumulated dust of years! — We care not for one of your modern libraries, with its spruce shelves, filled with the sickly effusions of romantic triflers — the solemn, philosophical nonsense of Arthur, the dandified affectation of Willis, and the clever but wearisome twittle-twattle of Dickens — once great in himself, now living on the fading reputation of past greatness; we care not to enter a library made up of such works, all faultlessly done up in the best style of binder. No — we love to pass long solitary hours in one of those old depositories of choice literature made venerable by the rich mellowing of time, and the sombre tapestry of cobwebs which are undisturbed by the intrusive visitation of prim housemaids. There, amid antique volumes, caskets of thought more precious than gems, how delightful to commune with the bright spirit of dead authors, whose inspired pens have left behind them the glorious scintillations of immortal genius, which sparkle on every page! When the soft light of declining day steals gently into the dusky room, and dim shadows hover in every nook, the truly contemplative mind pores with a quiet rapture over the sublime creations of Shakespeare, the massive grandeur of Scott, and the glowing beauties of Byron. Then are the dull realities of life forgotten, and the soul revels in a new and almost celestial existence.

In such a place do we now find Mr. Hedge, but he is not feasting on the delicacies of an elevated literature. Far differently is he engaged: he is entirely undressed, and reclining at full length in a portable bath, which is one-third full of *wine*. Such luxurious bathing is often resorted to by wealthy and superannuated gentlemen, who desire to infuse into their feeble limbs a degree of youthful activity and strength, which temporarily enables them to accomplish gallantries under the banner of Venus, of which they are ordinarily incapable.

'Oh that I were young!' ejaculated the bridegroom, as with a melancholy air he contemplated his own wasted frame. 'Would that thro' my veins, as in days of yore, there leaped the fiery current of vigorous youth! Alas seventy winters have chilled my blood and while my wishes are as ardent as ever, my physical organization is old, and weak, and shattered — and I fear me, cannot carry out the warm promptings of my enamored soul. How gladly would I give all my wealth, for a new lease of life, that I might revel in the joys of youth again!'

He rang a small bell, and a valet entered, bearing a dish containing a highly nutritious broth, which he had caused to be prepared on account of its invigorating properties. After partaking of this rich and savory mess, and having drank a glass of a certain cordial celebrated for its renovating influence, he arose, and his valet rubbed him vigorously with a coarse towel, then slipping on a few garments and a dressing-gown, he repaired to the bridal chamber with a beating heart.

The two young ladies, having performed their task, had retired, and Julia was on the couch awaiting her husband's coming. As he entered, she partly rose from her recumbent posture, with a smile of tender invitation lighting up her charming face; and rushing forward, he strained her passionately to his breast.

Then came a torrent of eager kisses, and a thousand whispered words of tenderness and love — sincere on the part of the old gentleman, but altogether affected on the part of Julia, who felt not the slightest degree of amorous inclination towards him. Yet he imagined her to be, like himself, fired with passion, and full of desire. His eyes feasted upon the beauties of her glorious form, which, so seductively voluptuous, was liberally exposed to his gaze; and his trembling hand wandered amid the treasures of her swelling bosom, so luxuriant in its ripened fullness.

Soon the withered form of the aged bridegroom is encircled by the plump, soft arms of his beautiful young bride. There are kisses, and murmurings, and sighs — but there is a heavy load of disappointment on the heart of the husband, who curses the three score and ten years that bind his warm wishes with a chain of ice; and he prays in vain for the return — even the temporary return — of glad youth, with its vigor, and its joys.

Julia comprehends all, and secretly congratulates herself on his imbecility which releases her from embraces that are repugnant to her, though she assumes an air of tender concern at his distress. Maddened at a failure so mortifying, Mr. Hedge half regrets his marriage.

Oh, why does weak tottering age seek to unite itself with warm, impetuous youth! The ice of winter is no congenial mate for the fresh, early flower of spring. How often do we see old, decrepit men wooing and wedding young girls, purchased by wealth from mercenary parents! Well have such sacrifices to Lust and Mammon, been termed *legalized prostitution*. And does not such a system excuse, if not justify, infidelity on the part of the wife? An old, drivelling dotard takes to his home and bed a virgin in her teens, whom he has purchased, but as he has gone through a formal ceremony, law and the world pronounce her wife. His miserable physical incapacity provokes without satisfying the passions of his victim; and in the arms of a lover she secretly enjoys the solace which she cannot derive from her legal owner. Then, if she is detected, how the world holds up its ten thousand hands in pious horror! — Wives who have *young* husbands are eloquent in their censure; old women who have long passed the rubicon of love and feeling, denounce her a *shameless hussey*; while the old reprobate who calls himself her husband, says to his indignant and sympathizing friends — 'I took her from a low station in life; I raised her to a position of wealth and rank, and see how ungrateful she is.'

Irritated by the disappointment, he arose, threw on his garments, and muttering a confused apology, left the chamber, taking with him a light. As he closed the door behind him, Julia burst into a gay silvery laugh.

'Poor old man!' she said to herself, — 'how disconcerted he is!' I could scarce keep myself from laughing. Well, he is not likely to prove very troublesome to me as a husband, and I'm glad of it, for really, the pawings, and kisses, and soft nonsense of such an old man are disgusting to me. Heigho! when we get to Boston, I must look out for a lover or two, to atone for the lamentable deficiencies of that withered cypher.'

When Mr. Hedge quitted the chamber, he went directly to his library, and rang the bell violently. In a few minutes the summons was answered by his valet. This man was of middle age, and rather good-looking, but possessed what is generally called a wicked eye.

'Brown,' said his master — 'make a fire in this room, and bring up some wine and refreshments. I shall pass the night here.'

'The devil!' thought Brown, as he sat about obeying these orders — 'master going to pass the night in his library, and just married to a woman so handsome that one's mouth waters to look at her! They've either had a quarrel, or else the old man has found himself mistaken in some of his calculations. I'm a fool if I don't turn things to my advantage. I see it all; she has cheated old Hedge into marrying her, although she has a husband already. She did not know me, in this livery; but she soon shall know me.

Why, she's in my power completely, and if she don't do just as I want her to, d — — n me if I don't *blow* on her, and spoil all her fun!'

We may as well enter into an explanation at once. This valet, called Brown, was no other than Davis — Frank Sydney's former butler — who had been sent to the State Prison for the term of five years, for his participation in the attempt to rob his master's house. In less than a month after his removal to Sing Sing, he was pardoned out by the Governor, who, being a good-natured man, could not refuse to grant the request of the prisoner's friends. On being set at liberty, Davis assumed the name of Brown, and entered the service of Mr. Hedge as valet. He had instantly recognized in the newly-made wife of his master, his former mistress, Mrs. Sydney; — but she knew him not, as his appearance was greatly changed. Being a shrewd fellow, he saw through the whole affair, and understanding her exact position, was resolved to take advantage of it, as soon as a proper opportunity should present itself.

The fire was made, the refreshments were brought, and the valet stood as if awaiting further orders.

'Sit down, Brown,' said his master, 'and take a glass of wine. You know that I was married to-night to a young lady — you saw her. Ah, she's a beautiful creature; and yet she might as well be a stick or a stone, for I am too old and worn-out to enjoy her charms. I did wrong to marry her; she's an estimable lady, and deserves a husband capable of affording her the satisfaction which I cannot — Yet I'll do my utmost to make her happy; I know that she will be faithful to me. Hereafter we will occupy separate chambers; and as I cannot discharge the duties of a husband, I will become a father to her. To-morrow we depart for Boston; and as I still need the services of a valet, you can go with me if you choose.'

'Thank'ee, sir; I shall be glad to go with you,' said Brown.

'Then that matter is settled,' rejoined Mr. Hedge — 'you can leave me now; I shall not want you again to-night. I will stretch myself upon this sofa, and try to sleep.'

The valet bade his master good night, and left the library; but instead of going to his own room, he crept stealthily towards the chamber of Julia, now Mrs. Hedge. At the door he paused and listened; but hearing nothing, he softly opened the door, and glided in with noiseless steps, but with a palpitating heart, for it was a bold step he was taking — he, a low menial, to venture at midnight into the bed-chamber of his master's wife! Yet he was a daring fellow, lustful and reckless; and he fancied that his knowledge of the lady's true history, and her fear of exposure, would render her willing to yield her person to his wishes.

He approached the bed, and found that she was sleeping. The atmosphere of the room was warm and heavy with voluptuous perfumes; and the dying light of the wax candles shed but a dim and uncertain ray upon the gorgeous furniture, the showy drapery of the bed, and the denuded form of the fair sleeper; denuded of everything but one slight garment, whose transparent texture imperfectly concealed charms we dare not describe. How gently rose and fell that distracting bosom, with its prominent pair of luscious *twin sisters*, like two polished globes of finest alabaster! A soft smile parted her rosy lips, disclosing the pearly teeth; and her clustering hair lay in rich masses upon the pillow. So angelic was her appearance, and so soft her slumbers that a painter would have taken her as a model for a picture of Sleeping Innocence. Yet, within that beautiful exterior, dwelt a soul tarnished with guilty passion, and void of the exalted purity which so ennobles the exquisite nature of woman.

Long gazed the bold intruder upon that magnificent woman; and the sight of her ravishing charms made his breath come fast and thick, and his blood rushed madly through his veins. Trembling with eager wishes and a thousand fears, he bent over her and, almost touching his lips to hers, inhaled the fragrance of her breath, which came soft as a zephyr stirring the leaves of a rose. Then he laid his hand upon her bosom, and passed it daringly over the swelling and luxuriant outlines. Julia partially awoke, and mistaking the disturber of her slumbers for Mr. Hedge, languidly opened her eyes, and murmured — 'Ah, dearest, have you returned?'

The valet replied by imprinting a hot kiss upon her moist, red lips; but at that moment the lady saw that it was not her husband who had ravished the kiss. Starting up in bed she exclaimed, in mingled surprise and alarm —

'Good heavens, who is this? — Fellow, what do you want, how dare you enter this chamber?'

'Why, ma'am,' said Brown, doggedly — 'I knew that master is old, and no fit companion for such a lively young woman as you be, and I thought — '

'No more words, sir!' cried Julia, indignantly — 'leave this room instantly — go at once, and I am willing to attribute your insolence to intoxication — but linger a moment, and I will alarm the house, and give you up to the anger of your master!'

'Oh, no missus,' said the fellow, coolly — 'If *that* be your game, I can play one worth two of it. Give the alarm — rouse up the servants — bring your husband here — and I'll expose you before them all as the wife of Mr. Sydney, turned out by him, for a nasty scrape with a negro footman! Missus you don't remember me, but I've lived in your house once, and know *you* well enough. I am Davis, the butler, very much at your service.'

'I recollect you now,' rejoined Julia, scornfully — 'You are the scoundrel who treacherously admitted burglars into the house, and who was captured and sent to the State Prison, from which you were pardoned, as I saw stated in the newspapers. You are mistaken if you think that a dread of exposure will induce me to submit to be outraged by you. Heavens, I will not yield my person to every ruffian who comes to me with threats of exposure! Vile menial, I will dare ruin and death sooner than become the slave of your lust!'

As she uttered these words with a tone and air of indignant scorn, she looked more superbly beautiful than ever — her dark eyes sparkled, her cheeks glowed, and her uncovered bosom heaved with excitement and anger.

But Brown was a determined ruffian, and resolved to accomplish his purpose even if obliged to resort to force. Grasping the lady by both arms, he said, in a stern whisper —

'Missus, I am stronger than you be — keep quiet, and let me have my way and you shan't be hurt; but if you go to kicking up a rumpus, why d — — n me if I won't use you rather roughly.'

He forced her back upon the bed, and placed his heavy hand over her mouth, to prevent her from screaming. Holding her in such a position that she could not move, he covered her face, neck and breasts with lecherous kisses; and was preparing to complete the outrage, when the report of a pistol thundered through the chamber, and the ruffian fell upon the carpet, weltering in his blood. His body had been perforated by a ball from a revolver, in the hands of Mr. Hedge.

'Die, you d — — d treacherous villain,' cried the old gentleman, swearing for the first time in his life.

The dying wretch turned his malignant eyes upon Julia, and gasped, faintly —

'Mr. Hedge — your wife — false — negro — Sydney — '

He could say no more, for the hand of death was upon him; and gnashing his teeth with rage and despair, he expired.

Mr. Hedge had paid no attention to the ruffian's dying words; for he had caught Julia in his arms, and was inquiring anxiously if she were hurt.

'No, dearest,' she replied — 'only frightened. But how came you to arrive so opportunely to my rescue?'

'I was endeavoring to get some sleep on the sofa in my library,' answered the old gentleman — 'when suddenly I fancied I heard a noise in your chamber. Thinking that robbers might have got into the house, I grasped a pistol, and cautiously approached the door of this room. Pausing a moment to listen, I heard the villain threaten you with violence in case you resisted; the door being open a little, I stepped into the room without making any noise, and saw him preparing to accomplish the outrage. Then I raised my pistol with unerring aim, and put a ball through his infernal carcass. Thank heaven, I have reserved my Julia from a fate worse than death.'

Fortunately for Julia, he had not heard what had passed between her and the valet, in reference to her exposure. He believed her to be the most virtuous of her sex; while she was beyond measure rejoiced that Davis, who might have ruined her, was now dead.

The next day the newly-married pair left New York for the city of Boston, according to previous arrangement. Arrived in that great metropolis, they took up their quarters at the most fashionable hotel, there to remain until Mr. Hedge should purchase a suitable house in which to take up their permanent residence.

Julia had not neglected to bring her maid Susan with her, as that discreet abigail might be of service to her in any little matter of intrigue she might engage in. Nero, the black, she had discharged from her service.

Her greatest happiness now arose from the belief that she had now escaped from the persecutions of the Dead Man.

CHAPTER XXV

*Servants' Frolics — a Footman in Luck — a Spectre — a Footman
out of Luck — the Torture — the Murder, and Destruction of
Franklin House.*

We left Franklin House in charge of Simon, the favorite footman of Mrs. Franklin, who was to take care of the house until it should be sold, and then join his mistress in Boston.

Now, although Simon was an honorable, faithful fellow enough, he soon grew intolerably lonesome, and heartily tired of being all alone in that great mansion. To beguile his time, he often invited other servants of his acquaintance to come and sup with him; and regardless of the orders of his mistress, several of his visitors were females. These guests he would entertain in the most sumptuous manner; and Franklin House became the scene of reckless dissipation and noisy revels, such as it had seldom witnessed before.

One evening Simon invited a goodly number of his friends to a 'grand banquet,' as he pompously termed it; and there assembled in the spacious parlor about twenty male and female domestics from various houses in the neighborhood. The males included fat butlers, gouty coachman, lean footmen and sturdy grooms; and among the females were buxom cooks, portly laundresses and pretty ladies' maids. Simon had well nigh emptied the cellar of its choice contents, in order to supply wine to his guests; and towards midnight the party became uproarious in the extreme.

We shall not attempt to sketch the toasts that were offered, nor the speeches that were made; neither shall we enter too minutely into the particulars of the game of 'hide-and-seek,' in which they indulged — or tell how our handsome footman chased some black-eyed damsel into a dark and distant chamber, and there tussled her upon the carpet, or tumbled her upon the bed, or perpetrated other little pleasantries of a similar nature. Suffice it to say, all these amusements were gone through with by the company, until tired of the sport, they reassembled in the parlor, and gathering around the fire, began to converse on ghosts.

Reader, have you ever, at the solemn hour of midnight, while listening to the recital of some fearful visitation from the land of spirits, felt your hair to bristle, and your flesh to creep, and your blood to chill with horror, as you imagined that some terrible being was at that moment standing outside the door, ready to glide into the room and stand beside your chair? Did you not then dread to look behind you as you drew close to your companions, and became almost breathless with painful interest in the story?

Solemn feeling prevailed among Simon's guests, as Toby Tunk, the fat coachman, who had been relating his experience in ghosts uttered the following words: —

'Well, I was sitting by the coffin, looking at the corpse, when the door slowly opened, and — '

Toby was fearfully interrupted, for the door of that room DID slowly open and there entered a being of so terrible an aspect, that all the assembled guests recoiled from its presence with horror and affright. It advanced towards the fireplace, seated itself in an unoccupied chair, and surveyed the company with menacing eyes.

The form of the spectre was tall, and its countenance was ghastly and awful to behold; it was enveloped in a cloak, and where its right hand should have been, was a massive piece of iron which joined the wrist.

At length, after an interval, during which all the guests came near dying with fear, it spoke in a harsh and threatening tone: —

'Those of ye that belong not in this house, depart instantly, on peril of your lives; and if any there be who *do* belong here, let them remain, and stir not!'

All, with the exception of poor Simon, tremblingly left the room and the house, resolved never again to cross the threshold of a place visited by such fearful beings. The spectre then turned to the affrighted footman, and said, with a hideous frown —

'Now, rascal, tell me what has become of your mistress and her daughter — where have they gone — speak!'

But Simon, imagining that he had to do with a being from the other world, fell upon his knees and began to mutter a prayer.

'Accursed fool!' cried the supposed spectre, striking him with his iron hand — 'does *that* feel like the touch of a shadowy ghost? Get up, and answer me; I am no ghost, but a living man — living, though known as the Dead Man. Where have the two Franklin ladies gone?'

Now Simon, convinced that his visitor was indeed no ghost, was beginning to regain his natural shrewdness: and remembering the injunctions of his mistress, not to reveal where she had gone, with her daughter, he replied, in accordance with the instructions which he had received —

'The ladies have gone to Philadelphia.'

'Liar!' cried the Dead Man — 'you betray yourself; had you answered with more hesitation, I might have believed you — the readiness of your reply proves its falsehood. Now, by hell! tell me correctly where the ladies have gone, or I'll murder you!'

'Not so fast, old dead face,' cried Simon, who was a brave fellow, and had by this time recovered all his courage — 'perhaps you mightn't find it so easy to murder me, as you imagine. Once for all, I'll see you d — — d before I will tell you where the ladies have gone.'

The Dead Man smiled grimly as he surveyed the slight form of the footman; then, in a fierce tone, he demanded —

'Are you mad? — Do you want to rush on headlong to ruin and death? Do you know me? I am one whose awful presence inspires fear in my friends, consternation in my foes. Puny wretch, will you give me the required information, ere I crush you as a worm?'

'No!' replied Simon, decidedly.

'Bah! I shall have work here,' said the other, calmly: then he sprung upon the footman, who, altogether unprepared for so sudden an attack, could make but a feeble resistance, especially in the grasp of a man who possessed more than twice his strength.

The struggle was brief, for the Dead Man handled him as easily as if he were a child. Soon he was gagged and bound fast to a chair; — then the miscreant, with a diabolical grin, thrust the poker into the fire, and when it became red-hot, he drew it forth, saying —

'I have found a way to loosen your tongue, d — — n you! When you get ready to answer my question, nod your head, and the torture shall cease.'

The monster applied the iron to various parts of his victim's body, burning through the clothes, and deep into the flesh. Simon winced with intense torture, yet he did not give the designated sign in token of submission until the skin was entirely burnt from his face, by the fiery ordeal.

Then the Dead Man removed the gag from his mouth, and asked —

'Where have the Franklin ladies gone, you infernal, obstinate fool?'

'To Boston,' gasped the miserable young man, and fainted. Ah! Simon, thy faithfulness to thy worthless mistress was worthy of a better cause!

'Boston, hey?' growled the villain — 'then, by G — — , I must go to Boston, too. Ah, I'm not at all surprised at their selecting that city for their place of refuge — for it is the abode of hypocrisy and lust; and they no doubt anticipate reaping a rich harvest there. But ere I depart for that virtuous and Christian city, I must finish my business here. And first to silence this fool's tongue forever!'

He drew forth his deadly knife, and plunged it up to the hilt in his victim's throat. With scarce a groan or struggle, poor Simon yielded his spirit into the hands of his Maker.

The murderer viewed his appalling work with satisfaction. His eyes seemed to feast upon the purple stream that gushed from the wound, and stained the carpet. It seemed as if, in the ferocity of his soul, he could have *drank* the gory flood!

'Would that the human race had but one single throat, and I could cut it at a stroke,' he cried, adopting the sentiment of another: then, taking a lamp, he left the room, with the intention of exploring the house.

One apartment he found carefully locked; and he was obliged to exert all his strength to break in the door. This room was furnished in a style of extravagant luxury; it was of great extent, and adorned with a multitude of paintings and statues, all the size of life.

A silken curtain, suspended across the further end of the room, bore in large gilt letters, the words 'Sanctuary of the Graces.' And behind the curtain were collected a large number of figures, exquisitely made of wax, representing males and females, large as life, and completely nude, in every imaginable variety of posture, a few classical, others voluptuous, and many positively obscene.

In this curious apartment — a perfect gallery of amorous conceptions — Josephine and her mother were in the habit of consummating those intrigues which they wished to invest with extraordinary *eclat* and voluptuousness. Here they loved to feed their impure tastes by contemplating every phase of licentious dalliance; and here they indulged in extravagant orgies which will admit of no description.

The intruder into this singular scene noticed a small iron apparatus attached to the wall; a sudden idea struck him — advancing, he touched a spring, and instantly every wax figure was in motion, imitating the movements of real life with wonderful fidelity! A closet in one corner contained the machinery of these automatons; and the whole affair was the invention of an ingenious German, whose talents had been misapplied to its creation. It had formerly constituted a private exhibition; but, after the murder of her husband, Mrs. Franklin had purchased it at a large cost.

'By Satan!' cried the Dead Man — 'those Franklins are ladies after my own heart; lecherous, murderous and abandoned, they are meet companions for me. What a splendid contrivance! It needs but the additions of myself and the superb Josephine, to render it complete!'

He left the room, and entered an elegant bed-chamber which adjoined it. It was the chamber of Josephine; and her full-length portrait hung upon the wall; there was her proud brow, her wanton eyes, her magnificent bust, uncovered, and seeming to swell with lascivious emotions. Everything was sumptuous, yet everything lacked that beautiful propriety which is so charming a characteristic of the arrangements of a virtuous woman — one whose purity of soul is mirrored in all that surrounds her. The bed, gorgeous though it was, seemed, in its shameless disorder, to have been a nest of riotous harlotry. Costly garments lay trampled under foot; a bird in a golden-wired prison, was gasping and dying for want of nourishment; splendidly-bound books, with obscene contents, were scattered here and there, and a delicate white slipper, which Cinderella might have envied, was stuffed full with letters. The Dead Man examined the documents; and among them was a paper, in the handwriting of Josephine, which we shall take the liberty of transcribing: —

'PRIVATE JOURNAL. — 'Monday. Passed last evening with Signor Pacci, the handsome Italian Opera singer. Was rather disappointed in my expectations; he is impetuous, but * * * *.'

'Tuesday. Have just made an appointment with — — the actor; he came to my box last night, between the acts, and made a thousand tender pretensions. *Mem.* — must try and get rid of Tom the coachman — am tired of him; besides it is *outre* to permit liberties to a menial.'

'Thursday. Am bored to death with the persecutions of Rev. Mr. — — . I cannot endure him, he is so ugly. *Mem.* — His son is a charming youth of sixteen; must try and get him.'

'Saturday. Dreadfully provoked with mother for her disgraceful *liaison* with her new coachman. She promised to discharge the fellow — did not perceive my drift. *Mem.* — Am to admit him to-night to my chamber.'

'Sunday. Heard Mr. — — preach; he visits me to-night.'

Having perused this precious *morceau*, the Dead Man thrust it into his pocket, and then, after a moment's reflection, deliberately applied the flame of the lamp to the curtains of the bed; and having waited to see the fire fairly started, he ran rapidly down stairs, and escaped from the house.

Within a quarter of an hour afterwards, Franklin House was entirely enveloped in flames; and notwithstanding every effort was made to save the building, it was completely destroyed. In one short hour that magnificent and stately pile was reduced to a heap of smoking ruins.

The destruction of this house and the property contained in it, brought Mrs. Franklin and her daughter to absolute poverty. When the news of the event reached them in Boston they were far from supposing that it was caused by the hideous ruffian whom they had so much reason to fear; they attributed the conflagration to the carelessness of Simon, and knew nothing of his having been murdered, but thought that, being intoxicated, he had perished in the flames.

The mother and daughter held a long consultation as to the best means of retrieving their ruined fortunes; and the result was, they determined to send for Sophia, in order to make use of her in a damnable plot, which, while it would supply them abundantly with cash, would forever ruin the peace and happiness of that innocent and pure-minded girl.

In answer to the summons, Sophia left the home of her relative in New Jersey, and joined her mother and sister in Boston. They received her with every demonstration of affection; and little did she suspect that an infamous scheme had been concocted between them, to sacrifice her upon the altars of avarice and lust.

CHAPTER XXVI

*Scene on Boston Common — George Radcliff — the Rescue —
Two Model Policemen — Innocence protected — the Duel, and
the Death — the Unknown.*

After Frank Sydney's escape from the Dark Vaults, through
the City Sewers, he did not deem it prudent to remain longer in
New York. Accordingly, accompanied by the Doctor, the dumb
boy Clinton, and his faithful servant Dennis, he left the city, to
take up his abode elsewhere. None of his friends knew the place
of his destination; some supposed that he had gone to Europe;
others thought that he had emigrated to the 'far West'; while
many persons imagined that he had exhausted his fortune, and
been obliged to leave by the persecutions of creditors. Those who
had been accustomed to borrow money from him, regretted his
departure; but those who had been afflicted with jealousy at his
good looks and popularity with *la belle sex*, expressed themselves
as 'devilish glad he'd gone.'

But, in truth, Frank had neither gone to Europe, nor to the
far West, neither had he been driven away by creditors; his fortune was still ample, and adequate to all his wants, present and to
come. Where, then, was our hero flown? impatiently demands the
reader. Softly, and you shall know in good time.

It was a beautiful afternoon, in spring, and Boston Common
was thronged with promenaders of both sexes and all conditions.
Here was the portly speculator of State street, exulting over the
success of his last *shave*; here was the humble laborer, emanci-
pated for a brief season from the drudgery of his daily toil; here
was the blackleg, meditating on future gains; and here the pickpocket, on the alert for a victim. Then there were ladies of every
degree, from the poor, decent wife of the respectable mechanic,
with her troop of rosy children, down to the languishing lady of
fashion, with her silks, her simperings, and her look of *hauteur.*
Nor was there wanting, to complete the variety, the brazen-faced
courtezan, with her 'nods,' and becks, and wreathed smiles, tho'
to class *her* with ladies of any grade, would be sacrilege.

The weather was delicious; a soft breeze gently stirred the trees, which were beginning to assume the fair livery of spring, and the mild rays of the declining sun shone cheerily over the noble enclosure. In the principal mall a young lady was slowly walking with an air pensive and thoughtful.

She could scarce have been over sixteen years of age — a beautiful blonde, with golden hair and eyes of that deep blue wherein dwells a world of expression. In complexion she was divinely fair; her cheeks were suffused with just enough of a rich carnation to redeem her angelic countenance from an unbecoming paleness. Her figure, *petite* and surpassingly graceful, had scarce yet attained the matured fullness of womanhood; yet it was of exquisite symmetry. — Her dress was elegant without being gaudy, and tasteful without being ostentatious.

Have you noticed, reader, while perusing this narrative, that nearly all the characters introduced have been more or less tainted with crime? — Even Sydney, good, generous and noble as he was, had his faults and weaknesses. Alas! human excellence is so very scarce, that had we taken it as the principal ingredient of our book, we should have made a slim affair of it, indeed.

But you may remember, that in the former portions of our story, we made a slight allusion to one Sophia Franklin. *She*, excellent young lady! shall redeem us from the imputation of total depravity. Her virtue and goodness shall illumine our dark pages with a celestial light — even though her mother and sister were *murderesses*!

Sophia Franklin it was, then, whom we have introduced as walking on the Common, with thoughtful and pensive air, on that fine afternoon in early spring.

But *why* thoughtful, and *why* pensive? Surely she must be happy. — There certainly cannot exist a creature made in God's glorious image, who would plant the thorn of unhappiness in the pure breast of that gentle girl?

There is. Her worst enemies are her nearest relatives. Her mother and sister are plotting to sacrifice her to the lust of a rich villain, for gold.

Oh, GOLD! — Great dragon that doth feed on human tears, and human honor, and human blood! Thou art the poor man's phantom — the rich man's curse. Magic is thy power, thou yellow talisman; thou canst cause men and women to forget themselves, their neighbors, their God! See yon grey-headed fool, who hugs gold to his breast as a mother hugs her first born; he builds houses — he accumulates money — he dabbles in railroads. A great man, forsooth, is that miserly old wretch, who stoops from manhood to indulge the dirty promptings of a petty avarice. But is he happy? NO; how can such a thing be happy, even tho' he possess thousands accumulated by his detestable meanness — when men spit on him with contempt; decency kicks him, dishonorable care will kill him, infamy will rear his monument, and the devil will roast him on the hottest gridiron in hell — *and he knows it!*

But to resume. Slowly did Sophia pursue her walk to the end of the mall, and as slowly did she retrace her steps; then, crossing a narrow path, she approached the venerable old elm, whose antique trunk is a monument of time. She had scarcely made two circuits around this ancient tree, when a gentleman who had espied her from a distance, advanced and greeted her with a familiar air. On seeing him, she became much agitated, and would have walked rapidly away, had he not caught her by the arm and forcibly detained her.

This gentleman was a person of distinguished appearance, tall, graceful figure, and fashionably dressed. — His countenance though eminently handsome, was darkly tinged with Southern blood, and deeply marked with the lines of dissipation and care. He wore a jet-black mustache and imperial and his air was at once noble and commanding. 'My pretty Sophia,' said the stranger, in a passionate tone — 'why do you fly from me thus? By heavens, I love you to distraction, and have sworn a solemn oath that you shall be mine, though a legion of fiends oppose me!'

'Pray let me go, Mr. Radcliff,' said the young girl entreatingly — 'you wish me to do wrong, and I cannot consent to it, indeed I cannot. As you are a gentleman, do not persecute me any more.'

'Persecute you — *never!*' exclaimed the libertine; 'become mine, and you shall have the devotion of my life-time to repay you for the sacrifice. Consent, sweet girl.'

'Never!' said Sophia, firmly; 'had you honorably solicited me to become your wife, I might have loved you; but you seek my ruin, and I despise, detest you. Let me go, sir, I implore — I command you!'

'Command *me!*' exclaimed the libertine, his eyes sparkling with rage — 'silly child, it is George Radcliff who stands before you; a man whom none dare presume to command, but whom all are accustomed to *obey!* I am a monarch among women, and they bow submissive to my wishes. Listen, Sophia; I have for years plucked the fairest flowers in the gardens of female beauty, but I am sated with their intoxicating perfume, and sick of their gaudy hues. Your luxurious mother and fiery sister were acceptable to me for a time, and I enjoyed their voluptuous caresses with delight; but the devil! the conquest was too easily achieved. I soon grew tired of them and was about to withdraw my patronage, when to retain it, they mentioned *you*, describing you to be a creature of angelic loveliness; my passions were fired by the description, and I longed to add so fair and sweet a lily to the brilliant bouquet of my conquests. They sent for you to New Jersey; you came, and surpassed my highest anticipations. I paid your mother and sister a large sum for you, promising to double the amount as soon as you should become mine. I have so far failed in my efforts; unwilling to use violence, I have tried to accomplish my object by entreaty. — Now, since you will not listen to my entreaties, I shall resort to force. — This very night I have arranged to visit you, and then — and *then*, sweet one — '

He drew the shrinking girl towards him, and in spite of her resistance, profaned her pure lips with unholy kisses. During the conversation just related, day had softly melted into dim twilight, and the loungers on the Common had mostly taken their departure; very few were in the vicinity of Radcliff and Sophia — and there was but one person who saw the scene of kissing and struggling that we have described. That person was a young and handsome man, well-dressed, and possessing an open, generous and manly countenance. Observing what was going on between the pair, and seeing that the young lady was suffering violence from her companion, he silently approached, nobly resolved to protect the weaker party, at all hazards.

Sophia had partially escaped from the grasp of Radcliff, and he was about to seize her again, when the young man just mentioned stepped forward, and said, calmly —

'Come, sir, you have abused that young lady enough; molest her no further.'

'And who the devil may you be, who presumes thus to interfere with a gentleman's private amusements?' demanded the libertine, with savage irony: but the bold eyes of the other quailed not before his fierce glance.

'It matters not particularly who I am,' replied the young man, sternly — 'suffice it for you to know that I am one who is bound to protect a lady against the assaults of a ruffian, even if that ruffian is clad in the garb of a gentleman.'

'Oh, sir,' said Sophia, bursting into tears — 'God will reward you for rescuing me from the power of that bad man.'

Radcliff's eyes literally blazed with fury as he strode towards the young lady's protector.

'You called me a ruffian,' said he, 'take *that* for your impudence,' and he attempted to strike the young man — but the blow was skillfully warded off, and he found himself extended on the grass in a twinkling.

Two policeman now ran up and demanded the cause of the fracas. The young man related everything that had occurred, whereupon the officers took Radcliff into custody.

'Fellow,' said the individual, haughtily addressing his antagonist, — 'you are, I presume, nothing more than a shopman or common mechanic, beneath my notice; you therefore may hope to escape the just punishment of your insolence to-night.'

'You are a liar,' calmly responded the other — 'I am neither a shopman nor a mechanic, and if I were, I should be far superior to such a scoundrel as you. I am a gentleman; your equal in birth and fortune — your superior in manhood and in honor. If you desire satisfaction for my conduct to-night, you will find me at the Tremont House, at any time. My name is Francis Sydney. I shall see this lady in safety to her residence.'

Radcliff was led away by the two officers. They had proceeded but a short distance, when he thus addressed them —

'My good fellow, it is scarcely worth while to trouble yourselves to detain me on account of this trifling affair. Here's five dollars a piece for you — will that do?'

'Why, sir,' said one of the fellows, pocketing his V, and giving the other to his companion — 'we can't exactly let you go, but if you tip us over and run for it, perhaps we shan't be able to overtake you.'

'I understand you,' said Radcliff, and he gave each of those *faithful* officers a slight push, scarce sufficient to disturb the equilibrium of a feather, whereupon one of them reeled out into the street to a distance of twenty feet, while the other fell down flat on the sidewalk in an apparently helpless condition, and the prisoner walked away at a leisurely pace, without the slightest molestation.

Meanwhile, Frank Sydney escorted Sophia to the door of her residence in Washington street. The young lady warmly thanked her deliverer, as she termed him.

'No thanks are due me, miss,' said Frank — 'I have but done my duty, in protecting you from the insults of a villain. I now leave you in safety with your friends.'

'Friends!' said the fair girl, with a deep sigh — 'alas, I have no friends on earth.'

The tone and manner of these words went to the heart of our hero; he turned for a moment to conceal a tear — then raised her hand respectfully to his lips, bade her farewell, and departed.

Sophia entered the house, and found her mother and sister in the parlor. They greeted her with smiles.

'My darling Soph,' said Mrs. Franklin — 'that charming fellow was much disappointed to find that you had gone out. We told him that you had probably gone to walk on the Common, and he went in search of you.'

Sophia related all that had occurred to her during her absence. She complained of the libertine's treatment of her with mingled indignation and grief.

'Pooh! sis,' exclaimed Josephine, — 'you mustn't think so hard of Mr. Radcliff's attentions. You must encourage him, for he is very rich, and *we need money.*'

'Must you have money at the expense of my honor?' demanded Sophia, with unwonted spirit.

'And why not?' asked her mother in a severe tone. 'Must we starve on account of your silly notions about virtue, and such humbug? Your sister and I have long since learned to dispose of our persons for pecuniary benefit, as well as for our sensual gratification — for it is as pleasurable as profitable; and you must do the same, now that you are old enough.'

'Never — never!' solemnly exclaimed Sophia — 'my poor, dead father — '

'What of him?' eagerly demanded both mother and daughter, in the same breath.

'He seems to look down on me from Heaven, and tell me to commit no sin,' replied the young girl.

'Nonsense,' cried the mother — 'but go now to your chamber, and retire to bed; to-night at least, you shall rest undisturbed.'

Sophia bade them a mournful good night, and left the room. When the door closed upon her, Josephine glanced at her mother with a look of satisfaction.

'Radcliff will be here to-night at twelve,' said she — 'according to his appointment, for he will find no difficulty in procuring his discharge from custody. Once introduced into Sophia's chamber, he will gain his object with little trouble; then he will pay us the remaining thousand, as agreed upon.'

'And which we need most desperately,' rejoined her mother — 'how unfortunate about the burning of our house! It has reduced us almost to our last penny.'

'The loss is irreparable,' sighed Josephine — 'what divine raptures we used to enjoy in the 'Sanctuary of the Graces!' And there, too, was my elegant wardrobe and that heavenly French bed!'

These two abandoned women then retired to their respective chambers, to await the coming of Radcliff. At midnight he came. He was admitted into the house by Mrs. Franklin, and conducted to the chamber of Sophia, which he entered by means of a duplicate key furnished him by the perfidious mother.

The libertine had not observed, on entering the house, that he was followed by a man at a short distance. He was too intent upon the accomplishment of his vile desire, to notice the close proximity of one who was determined to oppose him in its execution. Sydney had expected that Radcliff would be liberated, and felt assured that he would seek his victim again that night. He comprehended that the poor girl resided with those who would not protect her, and he nobly resolved to constitute himself her friend. He had lingered around the house for hours, and when he saw the libertine approaching, followed him to the very door, at which he stationed himself, and listened.

Soon a piercing shriek proceeding from an upper chamber, told him that the moment for his aid had arrived. The street door was fortunately not locked, and was only secured by a night latch; this he broke by one vigorous push, and rushing through the hall, mounted the stairs, and entered the chamber from which he judged the cry of distress had issued.

Then what a sight presented itself! Sophia, in her night dress, her hair in wild disorder, struggling in the arms of the villain

Radcliff, whose fine countenance was rendered hideous by rage and passion.

'What!' he exclaimed — '*you* here? By G — — , you shall rue your interference with my schemes. How is it that you start up before me just at the very moment when my wishes are about to be crowned with success?'

'I will not parley with you,' replied Frank — 'the chamber of this young lady is no fitting place for a dispute between us. As you claim to be a gentleman, follow me hence.'

'Lead on, then,' cried the libertine, foaming with rage. 'I desire nothing better than an opportunity to punish your presumption.'

As they descended the stairs, Josephine and her mother, alarmed by the noise of the dispute, issued from their rooms, and when Frank had given them a hasty explanation, the latter angrily demanded how he dared intrude into that house, and interfere in a matter with which he had no business.

'Madam,' replied our hero — 'you are, I presume, the mother of that much abused young lady up stairs. I see that you countenance the ruin of your daughter. I tell you to beware — for I shall take proper measures to expose your vileness, and have *her* placed beyond the reach of your infernal schemes.'

He then left the house followed by Radcliff. After proceeding a short distance, the latter paused, and said —

'We can do nothing to-night, for we have no weapons, and to fight otherwise would scarce comport with the dignity of gentlemen. Meet me to-morrow morning, at the hour of six, upon this spot; bring with you a friend, and pistols; we will then repair to some secluded place, and settle our difficulty in honorable combat.'

'But what assurance have I that you will keep the appointment?' demanded Sydney; 'how do I know that this is not a mere subterfuge to escape me?'

'Young man, you do not know me,' rejoined Radcliff, and his

breast swelled proudly. 'Do you think I'd resort to a base lie? Do you think that I *fear* you? I confess I am a libertine, but I am a man of honor — and that honor I now pledge you that I will keep the appointment; for, let me tell you, that I desire this meeting as much as you do.'

Strange inconsistency of terms! — 'A libertine — but a man of *honor*!' This creed is preached by thousands of honorable adulterers. A seducer is of necessity a liar and a scoundrel — yet, forsooth, he is a man of *honor*!

'Very well, sir,' said Sydney — 'I have no doubt you will come.' And with a cool 'good night,' they separated.

The next morning early, at a secluded spot in Roxbury neck, four men might have been seen, whose operations were peculiar. Two of them were evidently preparing to settle a dispute by the 'code of honor.' The other two (the seconds) were engaged in measuring off the distance — ten paces.

The morning was dark and cloudy, and a drizzling rain was falling. It was a most unpleasant season to be abroad, especially to execute such business as those four men had in hand.

Sydney had chosen for his second 'the Doctor'; while Radcliff had brought with him a tall individual, whose countenance was mostly concealed by an enormous coat collar and muffler, and a slouched hat. Two cases of pistols had been brought, and as 'the Doctor' was an accomplished surgeon, it was deemed unnecessary to have the attendance of another.

At length all was ready, and the antagonists took their places, with their deadly weapons in their hands. Both men were cool and collected; Radcliff was a most accomplished duelist, having been engaged in many similar encounters; and his countenance was expressive of confidence and unconcern. Sydney had never before fought a duel, yet, feeling assured of the justice of his cause, he had no apprehension as to the result. It may be asked why he so interested himself in a young lady he had never before seen, as to engage in a bloody encounter for her sake. We answer, he was prompted so to do by the chivalry of his disposition, and by a desire to vindicate the purity of his motives, and the sincerity of his conduct. He wished to let that unprincipled libertine see that he was no coward, and that he was prepared to defend the rights of a helpless woman with his life.

The word was given to fire, and both pistols were discharged at once. Sydney was wounded slightly in the arm; but Radcliff fell, mortally wounded — his antagonist's ball had pierced his breast.

Sydney bent over the dying man with deep concern; his intention had been merely to wound him — he had no desire to kill him; and when he saw that his shot had taken a fatal effect, he was sincerely grieved. He could not deny to himself that he felt a deep interest in the splendid libertine, whose princely wealth, prodigal generosity, magnificent person, and many amours, and rendered him the hero of romance, and the most celebrated man of the day. He knew that Radcliff's many vices were in a slight degree palliated by not a few excellent qualities which he possessed; and he sighed as he thought that such a brilliant intellect and such a happy combination of rare personal advantages should cease to exist, ere the possessor could repent of the sins of his past life.

Radcliff's second, the tall man with the shrouded countenance, walked to a short distance from the melancholy group, with a gloomy and abstracted air. While the Doctor made vain efforts to alleviate the sufferings of Radcliff, that unhappy man raised his dying eyes to Sydney's face, and said, faintly: —

'Young man, my doom is just. — Continue to be kind to Sophia Franklin, whom I would have wronged but for your timely interference; but beware of her mother and sister — they are devils in the shape of women. They would have sold her to me for gold — wretches that they were, and villain that I was!'

'Can I do anything for you?' asked Frank, gently.

'Nothing — but listen to me; the pains of death are upon me, and my time is short. You see my second — that tall, mysterious-looking person? I have known him, for many years — he is a villain of the deepest dye — one whom I formerly employed to kidnap young girls for my base uses. Last night I met him for the first time for a long period; I told him that I was to fight a person named Sydney this morning; he started at the mention of your name, and eagerly desired to act as my second. I consented. He is your most inveterate enemy, and thirsts for your blood. He seeks but an opportunity to kill you. *He fears your second*, and that prevents him from attacking you at once. Beware of him, for he is — is — is — the — '

Radcliff could not finish the sentence, for the agonies of death were upon him. His eyes glazed, his breath grew fainter and fainter; and in a few moments he expired.

Thus perished George Radcliff — the elegant *roue* — the heartless libertine — the man of pleasure — brilliant in intellect, beautiful in person, generous in heart — but how debased in soul!

They laid the corpse down upon the smooth, green sward, and spread a handkerchief over the pale, ghastly features. Then they turned to look for the mysterious second; he was seated, at some distance, upon a large rock, and they beckoned him to approach. He complied, with some hesitation; and the Doctor said to him —

'Sir, you seem to manifest very little interest in the fate of your friend; you see he is dead.'

'I care not,' was the reply — 'his death causes me no grief, nor pleasure; he was no enemy of mine, and as for friends, I have none. Grief and friendship are sentiments which have long since died in my breast.'

'By heavens!' exclaimed the Doctor — 'I know that voice! The right hand jealously thrust into your breast — your face so carefully concealed — the dying words of Radcliff — tell me that you are — '

'The Dead Man!' cried the stranger, uncovering his face — 'you are right — I am he! Doctor, I did not expect to find you with Sydney, or I should not have ventured. I came to execute vengeance — but your presence restrains me; crippled as I am, I fear you. No matter; other chances will offer, when you are absent. That escape of yours through the sewers was done in masterly style. Doctor, you are a brave fellow, and your courage inspires me with admiration; you are worthy to follow my reckless fortunes. Let the past be forgotten; abandon this whining, preaching Sydney, and join me in my desperate career. Give me your hand, and let us be friends.'

The Doctor hesitated a moment, and, to Sydney's unutterable amazement, grasped the Dead Man's hand, and said —

'Oh, Captain, I will re-enlist under your banner; I am tired of a life of inactivity, and long for the excitement and dangers of an outlaw's career! We are friends, henceforth and forever.'

The Dead Man grinned with delight; but poor Sydney was thunderstruck.

'Good God!' he exclaimed — 'is it possible that you, Doctor, will desert me, after swearing to me an eternal friendship? You, whom I once benefitted — you, who have since benefitted me — you, whom I thought to be one of the best, bravest, and most faithful men under the sun — notwithstanding your former faults — to prove traitor to me now, and league yourself with my worst enemy? Oh, is there such a thing as honesty or truth on earth?'

The Doctor was silent; the Dead Man whispered to him —

'Let us kill Sydney — he is no friend to either of us, and why should he live?'

'No,' said the Doctor, decidedly — 'we will harm him not, at least for the present. At some future time you may do with him as you will. Let us go.'

And they went, leaving our hero in a frame of mind almost distracted with remorse and sorrow — remorse, that he had killed a fellow creature — sorrow, that a man whom he had regarded as a friend, should prove so perfidious.

He retraced his way to the city, and returned to his hotel. The body of poor Radcliff was shortly afterwards found by several laborers, who conveyed it to the city, where an inquest was held over it. A verdict of *suicide* was rendered by the jury, who, short-sighted souls, comprehended not the mysteries of duelling; and the 'rash act' was attributed by the erudite city newspapers to 'temporary insanity'!

For three or four days after these events, Sydney was confined to his bed by illness. His wounded arm pained him much, and he had caught a severe cold upon the wet, drizzly morning of the duel. Clinton, the dumb boy, attended him with the most assiduous care. This poor youth had learned the 'dumb alphabet,' or language of signs, to perfection; and as his master had also learned it, they could converse together with considerable facility. Sydney was beginning to recover from his indisposition, when one evening Clinton came into his room, and communicated to him a piece of information that astounded him. It was, that Julia, his wife, was then stopping at that very same hotel, as the wife of an old gentleman named Mr. Hedge — that she was dressed superbly, glittering with diamonds, appeared to be in the most buoyant spirits, and looked as beautiful as ever.

CHAPTER XXVII

*The Ruined Rector — Misery and Destitution — the All Night
House — A Painful Scene — Inhospitality — the Denouement.*

We now return to Dr. Sinclair, whom we left on the downward path to ruin. The unfortunate man was now no longer the rector of St. Paul's; a committee of the congregation had paid him an official visit, at which he had been dismissed from all connection with the church. His place was supplied by a clergyman of far less talent, but much greater integrity.

Mr. Sinclair (for such we shall hereafter call him,) was not possessed of wealth — for though he had lived in luxury, he had depended entirely upon his salary for subsistence; and now that he was turned from his sacred occupation, dishonored and disgraced, he found himself almost penniless. He had no friends to whom he could apply for assistance, for his conduct had been noised abroad, and those who formerly had loved and reverenced him, now turned their backs upon him with cold contempt.

Instead of endeavouring to retrieve his fallen reputation by repentance and good conduct, he no sooner found himself shorn of his clerical honors, than he abandoned himself to every species of degraded dissipation. In two weeks after his removal from the church he was without a home; then he became the associate of the most vile. Occasionally he would venture to the house of some one of his former congregation, and in abject tones implore the gift of some trifling sum; moved by his miserable appearance, though disgusted by his follies, the gentleman would perhaps hand him a dollar or two, and sternly bid him come there no more. Sinclair would then hasten to the low pot house in Water Street which he made his resort, and amid his vagabond companions expend the money in the lowest debauchery.

Perhaps the reader may say the thing is impossible — no man could fall so rapidly from a high and honorable position, as to become in a few short weeks the degraded creature Sinclair is now represented to be. But we maintain that there is nothing exaggerated in the picture we have drawn. Here is a church congregation eminently aristocratic, wealthy, and rigidly particular in the nicest points of propriety. The pastor proves himself unworthy of his sacred trust; he disgraces himself and them by indulgence in vice, which is betrayed by his looks and actions. Too haughty and too impatient to take the erring brother by the hand, and endeavor to reclaim him, they at once cast him off with disgust, and fill his place with a more faithful pastor. Humbled and degraded, rendered desperate by his unhappy situation, the miserable man abandons himself yet more recklessly to the vice; his self-respect is gone, the finger of scorn is pointed at him, and to drown all consciousness of his downfall, he becomes a constant tipple and an irreclaimable sot.

The low groggery in Water street where poor Sinclair made his temporary home, was extensively known as the 'All Night House,' from the fact of its being kept open night and day. As this establishment was quite a feature in itself, we shall devote a brief space to a description of it.

It was situated on the corner of Catherine street, opposite the Catherine Market — a region remarkable for a very 'ancient and fish-like smell.' This Market was a large, rotten old shanty, devoted to the sale of stale fish, bad beef, dubious sausages, suspicious oysters, and dog's meat. Beneath its stalls at night, many a 'lodger' often slumbered; and every Sunday morning it was the theatre of a lively and amusing scene, wherein was performed the renowned pastime of 'niggers dancing for eels.' All the unsavory fish that had been accumulated during the week, was thus disposed of, being given to such darkies as won the most applause in the science of the 'heel and toe.' The sport used to attract hundreds of spectators, and the rum shops in the vicinity did a good business.

Suppose it to be midnight; let us enter the All Night House, and take a view. We find the place crowded with about forty men and boys, of all ages, conditions and complexions. Here is the veteran loafer, who had not slept in a bed for years — his clothes smelling of the grease and filth of the market stalls; here is the runaway apprentice, and here the dissipated young man who has been 'locked out,' and has come here to take lodgings. The company are all seated upon low stools; some are bending forward in painful attitudes of slumber; others are vainly trying to sit upright, but, overcome by sleep, they pitch forward, and recover themselves just in time to avoid falling on the floor.

Notice in particular this young man who is seated like the rest, and is nodding in an uneasy slumber. His clothes are of broadcloth, and were once fashionable and good, but now they are torn to rags, and soiled with filth. His hands are small and white; his hair, luxurious and curling naturally, is uncombed; his features are handsome, but bruised and unwashed. This is Sinclair!

The bar-keeper of this place is quite a character in his way. He rejoices in the title of 'Liverpool Jack,' and is the *bully of Water street* — that is, he is considered able to thrash any man that travels in that region. He is a blustering, ruffianly fellow, full of 'strange oaths.' He wears a red flannel shirt and tarpaulin hat; and possesses a bull-dog countenance expressive of the utmost ferocity.

'Hello, you fellers,' cries Liverpool Jack, savagely surveying the slumbering crowd — 'yer goin' to set there all night and not paternize de *bar* — say? Vake up, or by de big Jerusalem cricket I'm bound to dump yer all off de stools!'

Some of the poor devils arouse themselves, and rub their eyes; but the majority slumbered on. Liverpool Jack becomes exasperated, and rushing among them, seizes the legs of the stools, and dumps every sleeper upon the floor. Having accomplished this feat, he resumes his place behind the bar.

The door opens, and a party of young bloods enter, who are evidently 'bound on a time.' — They are all fashionably dressed; and one of them, drawing a well-filled purse from his pocket, invites all hands up to drink — which invitation, it is needless to say, was eagerly accepted. Sinclair crowded up to the bar, with the others and one of the new comers, observing him, cries out —

'By jingo, here's parson Sinclair! Give us a sermon, parson, and you shall have a pint of red-eye!'

'A sermon — a sermon!' exclaimed the others. Sinclair is placed upon a stool, and begins a wild, incoherent harangue, made up of eloquence, blasphemy and obscenity. His hearers respond in loud 'amens,' and one of the young bloods, being facetiously inclined, procures a rotten egg, and throws it at the unhappy man, deviling his face with the nauseous missile. This piece of ruffianism is immediately followed by another; the stool on which he stands is suddenly jerked from beneath him, and he falls violently to the floor, bruising his face and head shockingly.

Roars of laughter follow this deed of cruelty; poor Sinclair is raised from the floor by Liverpool Jack, who thrusts him forth into the street with a curse, telling him to come there no more.

It is raining — a cold, drizzly rain, which penetrates through the garments and strikes chill to the bones. On such a night as this, Sinclair was wont to be seated in his comfortable study, before a blazing fire, enveloped in a luxurious dressing gown, as he perused some interesting volume, or prepared his Sabbath sermon; then, he had but to ring a silver bell, and a well-dressed servant brought in a tray containing his late supper — the smoking tea urn, the hot rolls, the fresh eggs, the delicious bacon, the delicate custard, and the exquisite preserves. Then, he had but to pass through a warm and well — lighted passage, to reach his own chamber; the comfortable bed, with its snowy drapery and warm, thick coverlid, invited to repose; and his dreams were disturbed by no visions of horror or remorse. All was purity, and happiness, and peace.

Now, how different! Houseless, homeless, shelterless — ragged, dirty, starving — diseased, degraded, desperate! Unhappy Sinclair, that was a fatal moment when thou did'st yield to the fascinations of that beautiful Josephine Franklin!

It was near one o'clock, and the storm had increased to a perfect hurricane. The miserable man had eaten nothing that day; he tottered off with weakness, and was numbed with the cold. By an irresistible impulse he wandered in the direction of his former home in Broadway. He found the house brilliantly illuminated — strains of heavenly music issued from it — lovely forms flitted past the windows, and peals of silvery laughter mingled with the howling of the tempest. A grand party was given there that night; the occupant of the house was a man of fashion and pleasure, and he was celebrating the eighteenth birth-day of his beautiful daughter.

Sinclair lingered long around the house — it seemed as if some invisible power attracted him there. From the basement there arose the grateful, savory odor of extensive cooking.

'I am starving,' said he to himself — 'and they have plenty here. I will go to the door, like a beggar, and implore a morsel of food.'

With feeble steps he descended to the basement, and with a trembling hand he knocked at the door. It was opened by a fat, well-fed servant, in livery, who demanded, in a surly tone, what he wanted?

'In heaven's name, give me food, for I am starving.'

'Ugh — a beggar!' said the servant, with disgust — 'get you gone, we've nothing for you; master never encourages vagrants.'

The door was shut in Sinclair's face; with an aching heart he crawled up the steps, and then, as if suddenly nerved with a desperate resolve, he approached the front door, and rang the bell. The door was opened by a footman, who stared at the intruder with surprise and suspicion.

'Tell your master,' said Sinclair, faintly, 'that a person is here who must speak with him. It is a matter of life and death.'

The servant did as requested; in a few minutes he returned and said:

'Master says that if your business is particular you must come into the drawing room; he's not coming out here in the cold.'

He followed the servant thro' the hall; and in a moment more found himself standing in the brilliantly lighted drawing-room, in the presence of a numerous party of ladies and gentlemen. His miserable appearance created quite a sensation in that fashionable circle.

'Aw, 'pon my honor,' lisped a dandy, raising his eye-glass and taking a deliberate survey of the intruder, 'what have we heah? quite a natural curiosity, dem me!'

'Oh, what an odious creature;' exclaimed a young lady with bare arms, naked shoulders, and the reddest possible hair.

'Quite shocking!' responded her admirer, a bottle-nosed specimen of monkeyism.

'I shall positively faint,' cried an old tabby, in a large turban; but as nobody noticed her, she didn't faint.

The host himself now advanced, and said, sternly,

'Well, fellow, what d'ye want? — Speak quickly and begone, for this is no place for you. You d — — d stupid scoundrel,' (to the servant,) 'how dare you bring such a scare-crow here?'

'I wish to speak with you alone, sir,' said Sinclair, humbly.

The host motioned him to step out into the hall, followed him there, and commanded him to be as brief as possible.

Sinclair told him who he was, and the circumstances of misery and destitution in which he was placed. His listener shook his head incredulously, saying,

'It is a good game, my fine fellow, that you are trying to play off; you are an excellent talker, but you will find it hard to make people believe that you are Dr. Sinclair. In one word, you're an impostor. What, *you* a clergyman! Pooh, nonsense! — There, not another word, but clear out instantly. John, show this fellow the door, and never admit him again!'

As poor Sinclair passed out of the door, he heard the company laugh long and loud at the supposed imposition he had attempted to practise upon Mr. Grump, the 'worthy host.' Now be it known that this Mr. Grump was one of the most arrant scoundrels that ever went unhung. Low-bred and vulgar, he had made a fortune by petty knavery and small rascalities. He was a master printer; one of those miserable whelps who fatten on the unpaid labor of those in their employ. An indignant 'jour' once told him, with as much truth as sarcasm, that 'every hair on his head was a fifty-six pound weight of sin and iniquity!' He well knew that the poor wretch who had applied to him for relief, was no imposter; for he had heard Dr. Sinclair preach a hundred times, and he had recognized him instantly, notwithstanding his altered aspect. But he had pretended to believe him an impostor, in order that he might have a good excuse for withholding assistance from the unfortunate man.

Rudely did the servant thrust forth poor Sinclair into the in-hospitable street and the fearful storm. The rain now fell in torrents; and the darkness was so intense, that the hapless wanderer cou'd only grope his way along, slowly and painfully. — Upon one corner of the street the foundation for a house had recently been dug, forming a deep and dangerous pit, lying directly in Sinclair's path: no friendly lantern warned him of the peril — no enclosure was there to protect him from falling. Unconscious of the danger, he slowly approached the brink of the pit; now he stood upon the extreme edge, and the next instant *he fell*! There was a dull, dead sound — then a stifled groan — and all was still!

Morning dawned, bright and clear, the storm had subsided during the night, and the glorious sun arose in a cloudless sky. A crowd was collected on the corner of Broadway and one of the narrow streets which cross its lower section. They were gazing at a terrible spectacle: the body of a man lay in a deep pit below them, shockingly mangled; he had fallen upon a heap of stones — his brains were dashed out, and his blood scattered all around. Among the spectators was a portly, well-dressed man, who looked at the body steadfastly for some time, and then muttered to himself —

'By G — — , it is Dr. Sinclair, and no mistake! Too bad — too bad! — When he came to my house last night, I little thought to see him dead this morning! Plague on it, I ought to have given the poor devil sixpence or a shilling. No matter — he's better off now. He was a talented fellow — great pity, but can't be helped.'

Yes, it *could* have been helped, Mr. Grump; had you kindly taken that poor unfortunate by the hand, and afforded him food and shelter for a brief season, he never would have met that tragical end, but might have lived to reform, and lead a life of usefulness and honor; yes, he might have lived to bless you for that timely aid.

Reader, 'speak gently to the erring.' Do not too hastily or too harshly condemn the follies or faults of others. A gentle word, spoken in kindness to an erring brother, may do much towards winning him back to the path of rectitude and right. Harsh words and stern reproofs may drive him on to ruin.

But let us return to the crowd collected around the mangled body of Sinclair.

'It's a sin and a shame,' said a stout man, in working clothes, 'that there wasn't some kind of a fence put around this infernal trap. Where was the Alderman of this ward, that *he* didn't attend to it?'

'Be careful what you say, fellow,' said Mr. Grump, turning very red in the face, 'I'd have you to know that *I* am the Alderman of this ward!'

'Are you? — then let me tell you,' said the man, contemptuously, 'that you bear the name of being a mean, dirty old scamp; and if it was not for fear of the law, I'd give you a d — — d good thrashing!'

Alderman Grump beat a hasty retreat while the crowd set up a loud shout of derision — for he was universally hated and despised.

The Coroner arrived — the inquest was held; and a 'verdict rendered in accordance with the facts.' The body was taken to the 'Dead House;' and as no friend or relative appeared to claim it, it was the next day conveyed to Potter's Field, and there interred among city paupers, felons and nameless vagrants.

CHAPTER XXVIII

*The Disguised Husband — the False Wife — the Murder — the
Disclosure, and Suicide.*

Reader, let thy fancy again wing its flight from New York to our own city of Boston.

It was a strange coincidence that Frank Sydney and his wife Julia should tarry again beneath the same roof; yet they were not destined to meet under that roof — for the next day after Frank made the discovery, Mr. Hedge and the young lady removed from the Hotel to a splendid house which had been fitted up for them in the most aristocratic quarter of the city.

'I must see Julia once again,' said Frank to himself, when informed of her departure; — 'I must see and converse with her again, for I am anxious to see if she has really reformed, since her marriage with this Mr. Hedge, whom I have heard spoken of as a very respectable old man. Of course, he can know nothing of her former character; and if I find her disposed to be faithful to her present husband, Heaven forbid that I should ruin her by exposure! But I must so disguise myself that she shall not recognise me; this I can easily do, for I am well acquainted with the art of disguise. I shall have no difficulty in meeting her on some of the fashionable promenades of the city, then my ingenuity will aid me in forming her acquaintance. My plan shall be put into immediate execution.'

Our hero felt considerable uneasiness in the knowledge that the Dead Man was then in the city; and when he reflected that the Doctor had joined that arch miscreant, he knew not what infernal plot might be concocted against his liberty or life. He puzzled his brain in vain to account for the Doctor's singular conduct in deserting him for the friendship of a villain; and he was forced to arrive at the unwelcome conclusion, that the Doctor was a man whose natural depravity led him to prefer the companionship of crime to the society of honesty and honor.

Sydney never ventured abroad without being thoroughly armed; and he was determined, if attacked by his enemies, to sell his life as dearly as possible.

He had called once upon Miss Sophia Franklin, since the night he had rescued her from the designs of the libertine Radcliff; Josephine and her mother plainly evinced by their looks that they did not relish his visit; but the fair Sophia received him with every demonstration of gratitude and pleasure. She could not deny to herself that she felt a deep and growing interest in the handsome young stranger, who had so gallantly defended her honor: while on his part, he sympathized with her unfortunate situation, on account of her unprincipled relatives, and admired her for her beauty and goodness. He sighed as he thought that his abandoned wife was a barrier to any hopes which he might entertain in reference to Sophia; for he felt that he could joyfully make the young lady his bride, and thus preserve her from her mother and sister, were there no obstacle in the way. When he contrasted her purity and virtue with the vices of Julia, he cursed his destiny that had placed so great a prize beyond his grasp.

Sophia, as yet, knew nothing of Frank's history, and was of course ignorant that he had a wife. Sweet hopes swelled the maiden's bosom, when the thought arose in her pure heart that she might be beloved by one whom she knew was worthy of her tenderest regard.

It was with a high degree of satisfaction that Julia now found herself, by the liberality of Mr. Hedge, mistress of a splendid establishment. — Her dresses, her jewelry, her furniture were of the most magnificent kind; her husband placed no restraint upon her whatever, he slept in a separate chamber, and never annoyed her with his impotent embraces; each morning he was accustomed to meet her in the breakfast parlor, and partake with her the only meal they took together during the day; after the repast, he would usually present her with money sufficient to do her fashionable 'shopping;' then he would kiss her rosy cheek, bid her adieu, and leave her to pass the day as her fancy or caprice might dictate.

Enjoying such a life of luxurious ease, Julia was almost perfectly happy. Yet her cup was not quite full; there was one thing wanting to complete the list of her pleasures — and this deficiency occupied her thoughts by day, and her dreams by night. Not to keep the reader in suspense, she longed for a handsome and agreeable lover — yet none could she find suited to her taste or wishes. True, she might have selected one from among the many gentlemen of leisure 'about town,' who are always ready to dangle at the heels of any woman who will clothe and feed them for their 'services.' — But she preferred a lover of a more exalted grade; one whose personal beauty was set off by mental graces, and superior manners. And he must be poor; for then he would be more dependent upon her, and consequently, more devoted and more constant.

Time passed, and still Julia had no lover. — Mr. Hedge mentally gave her credit for the most virtuous fidelity; yet the amorous fair one was constantly on the *qui vive* to catch in her silken meshes some desirable man with whom she might in secret pass the hours of her voluptuous leisure.

One day, while promenading Tremont street, her eyes rested upon a gentleman whose appearance sent a thrill of admiration and desire through every fibre of her frame. His figure, of medium height, was erect and well-built; his gait was dignified and graceful; his dress, in exact accordance with the *mode*, was singularly elegant and rich — but a superb waistcoat, a gorgeous cravat in which glittered a diamond pin, and salmon-colored gloves, were the least attractive points in his appearance; for his countenance was eminently handsome and striking. His hair fell in rich masses over a fine, thoughtful brow; his eyes were dark, piercing, and full of expression and fire; and the lower part of his face was almost completely hidden by a luxuriant growth of whiskers, imperial and moustache. Whatever of foppishness there might be in his dress, was qualified by the dignified grace of his manner.

'He is a charming creature, and I must catch him,' thought Julia. So, on the next day when she met him again, and at the moment when his eyes were fixed admiringly upon her countenance, she smiled, then blushed in the most engaging manner, and passed on in sweet confusion. The gallant gentleman, encouraged by the smile and blush, turned and followed her. She walked on as far as the Common, entered, and regardless of her satin dress, seated herself upon one of the sheet-iron covered benches. The gentleman (bold fellow!) seated himself upon the same bench, though at a respectful distance. Julia blushed again, and cast down her beautiful eyes.

You know very well, reader, how two persons, who are not acquainted, always begin a conversation. The weather is the topic first touched upon; — and that hackneyed subject merges easily and naturally into more agreeable discourse. So it was with Julia and her gallant; in less than half an hour after seating themselves on that bench, they were sociably and unrestrainedly conversing on the theatres, the opera, the last novel, and other matters and things pertaining to the world of fashion and amusement. The lady judged her companion, by a slight peculiarity in his accent, to be a foreigner — a circumstance that raised him still more in her estimation, for our amorous American ladies adore foreigners. He was also a man of wit, education and talent; and Julia became completely fascinated with him. He proposed an exchange of cards; she assented, and found her new friend to be the 'Signor Montoni'; and he subsequently informed her that he was an Italian teacher of languages — a piece of information that gave her pleasure, as his following a profession was a pretty certain indication that he was poor.

When Julia returned home, the Italian accompanied her to the door. The next day they met again, and the next; and the intimacy between them increased so rapidly, that within a week after their confidential chat on the Common, Montoni called on Julia at her residence. But the lady noticed that he had suddenly grown reserved and bashful; and he made this and their other interviews provokingly short. She had hoped to have found in him an impetuous and impassioned lover — one who needed but the opportunity to pluck the ripe fruit so temptingly held out to him; but she found him, instead, an apparently cold and passionless man, taking no advantage of his intimacy with her, and treating her with a distant respect that precluded all hope in her bosom of a successful amour.

In vain did the beautiful wanton assail him with inviting glances and seductive smiles; in vain did she, while in his presence, recline upon the sofa in attitudes of the most voluptuous abandonment; in vain did she, as if unconsciously, display to his gaze charms which might have moved an anchorite — a neck and shoulders of exquisite proportions, and a bosom glowing and swelling with a thousand suppressed fires. He withstood all these attacks, and remained calm and unmoved. When she gave him her hand to kiss at parting, he would merely raise it to his lips, and leave her with a cold 'adieu.'

'He is cold — senseless — unworthy of my regard; I will see him no more,' said Julia to herself. Yet when the image of the handsome Italian arose before her, so calmly noble, so proudly composed, her resolution forsook her, and she felt that he held her, heart and soul, under some strange and magical fascination.

'Yes, I love him,' she cried, bursting into a passionate flood of tears — 'devotedly, madly love him. Oh, why am I the suppliant slave of this cold stranger? why cannot I entice him to my arms? Distraction: my most consummate art fails to kindle in his icy breast a single spark of the raging fire that is consuming me!'

It may be proper to mention that Mr. Hedge knew nothing of the Italian's visits to his wife; for Julia received him in a private parlor of her own, and there was no danger of interruption. The old gentleman passed most of his evenings in his library; and having implicit faith in the integrity of his wife, he allowed her to spend her evenings as she chose.

One evening Signor Montoni visited Julia rather earlier than usual; and she resolved that evening to make a desperate effort to conquer him, even if obliged to make known her wishes in words.

During the evening she exerted herself, as usual, to captivate him, and bring him to her feet. She sang — she played — she liberally displayed the graces of her person, and the charms of her accomplished mind, but still in vain. — There he sat, with folded arms, in deep abstraction, gazing at the elaborate figures on the gorgeous carpet.

At nine o'clock, Montoni arose, and took the lady's hand to

bid her adieu. She gently detained him, and drew him towards
her upon the sofa.

'Listen to me, Montoni;' said she, gazing into his eyes with an
expression of deep fondness — 'listen to me, and I will speak
calmly if I can, though my heart is beating in wild tumult. Call
me unwomanly, bold, wanton if you will, for making this declaration — *but I love you!* — God only knows how ardently, how
passionately. The first moment I saw you, your image impressed
itself indelibly upon my heart; in person, you were my *beau ideal*
of manhood — and in mind I found you all that I could wish. I
have sought to make you my lover — for my husband is old and
impotent, and my passions are strong. Look at me, Montoni; am I
ugly or repulsive? Nay, the world calls me beautiful, yet I seek to
be beautiful only in your eyes, my beloved. Why, then, have you
despised my advances, disregarded my mute invitations, and left
me to pine with disappointment and with hope deferred? Why
will you not take me in your arms, cover me with kisses, and
breathe into my ear the melody of your whispered love?'

The lady paused, and the Italian gazed at her with admiration. Ah, how beautiful she looked! and yet how like a fiend in
the shape of a lovely woman, tempting a man to ruin!

'Lady,' said Montoni, as a shade of sadness passed over his
fine features — 'you have mentioned your husband, and the recollection that you *have* a husband forbids that I should take advantage of your preference for me. God forbid that I should be
the cause of a wife's infidelity! Pardon me, lady — you are very
beautiful; the Almighty never created so fair a sanctuary to become the dwelling place of sin; be advised, therefore, to suppress
this guilty passion, and remain faithful to your husband, who, old
though he be, has claims upon your constancy.'

'I long for the declarations of a lover, not the reasonings of a
philosopher,' cried Julia passionately. — 'Thou man of ice, nothing can melt you?'

'Remember your duty to your husband,' said Montoni,
gravely, as he arose to depart. 'I will see you to-morrow evening
— adieu.'

He left her to her reflections. — Wild, tumultuous thoughts arose in her mind; and from the chaos of her bewildered brain, came a Hideous Whisper, prompting her to a bloody crime.

She thought of her husband as an obstacle to her happiness with Montoni; and she began to hate the old man with the malignity of a fiend.

'Curses on the old dotard!' she cried, in a paroxysm of rage — 'were it not for *him*, I might revel in the arms of my handsome Italian, whose unaccountable scruples will not permit him to enjoy the bliss of love with me, while I have a husband. — Were that husband DEAD — '

Then, like a Mighty Shadow, came that dark thought over her soul. Myriads of beautiful demons, all bearing the semblance of Montoni, seemed to gather around her, and urge her to perpetrate a deed of — *murder*!

But then a fair vision spread itself before her wandering fancy. There was her girlhood's home — far, far away in a green, flowery spot, where she had dwelt ere her life had been cast amid the follies and vices of cities. Then she thought of her mother — that gentle mother, whose heart she had broken, and who was sleeping in the old church-yard of her native village. — A tear dim'd her brilliant eye as these better feelings of her nature gained a temporary ascendancy: but she dashed her tear away, and suppressed the emotions of her heart, when the image of the fascinating Italian arose before her.

'He must be mine! I swear it by everything in heaven, earth or hell — he must be mine! Yes, though I stain my soul with the blackest crime — though remorse and misery be my lot on earth — though eternal torment be my portion in the world to come — he must and shall be mine! Aid me, ye powers of hell, in this my scheme — make my heart bold, my hand firm, my brain calm; for the deed is full of horror, and the thought of it chills my blood; I shudder and turn sick and dizzy — yet, for thy sake, Montoni, I WILL DO IT!'

That night the wretched woman slept not; but in the solitude of her chamber employed her mind in endeavoring to form some plan by which to accomplish her fell purpose with secrecy and safety. Ere morning dawned, she had arranged the *programme* of the awful drama in which she was to play the part of a murderess.

When Mr. Hedge met her at breakfast, he noticed that she appeared feverish and unwell; and with almost parental solicitude, he gently chided her for neglecting to take proper care of her health.

'My dear Julia,' said he — 'you must not pour out the golden sands of youth too fast. If you will suffer me to offer you advice, you will go less abroad, and endeavor to seek recreation at home. You know my ardent affection for you alone prompts me to make this suggestion.'

Julia slightly curled her lip, but said nothing. The kindness of her husband's manner did not in the least affect her, or alter the abominable purpose of her heart. Mr. Hedge did not notice her contemptuous look; he gave her a sum of money, as usual, kissed her and bade her adieu.

When he had gone, she dressed herself in her plainest attire, and going into an obscure part of the city, entered an apothecary's shop and purchased some arsenic. She then retraced her steps to her residence, and found that Mr. Hedge, contrary to his usual custom, had returned, and would dine at home. This arrangement afforded her much satisfaction.

'The fates are propitious,' said she — 'to-night Montoni shall find me without a husband.'

Mr. Hedge and Julia dined alone; dispensing with the attendance of a servant, they never were more sociable or more affectionate together.

The old gentleman was in high spirits. 'My dear,' said he, 'your presence to-day inspires me with an unusual degree of happiness — and egad, I feel younger than ever. Pledge me in a bumper of good old port.'

'I cannot endure port,' said Julia — 'sparkling champagne for me. I will ring for some.'

'By your leave, madam,' said her husband, with an air of gallantry; and rising, he walked across the room, and rang the bell.

Quick as lightning, Julia took a small paper parcel from her bosom, and breaking it open, poured a white powder into her husband's glass, which was nearly full of port wine.

Mr. Hedge resumed his seat, and raising the fatal glass to his lips, slowly drained it to the dregs. Just then the butler entered, in answer to the summons; and in obedience to Julia's order, he brought in a bottle of champagne, and withdrew.

'I am very unwell,' said the old gentleman — 'my love, will you assist me to my chamber?' He arose with difficulty, and with her aid reached his chamber, and lay down upon the bed. Instantly he closed his eyes, and seemed to fall into a deep slumber.

'He will wake in another world,' murmured the guilty woman, as she saw the hue of death beginning to overspread his features. No repentance, no remorse, touched her vile heart; calmly she surveyed her victim for a few moments — then, not wishing to witness his dying agonies, she left the chamber, having carefully locked the door.

That afternoon she went out and purchased a new and magnificent set of jewels. If for a moment the recollection of her horrible crime obtruded itself upon her mind, she banished it by thinking of her adored Montoni. Hers was a kind of mental intoxication, under the influence of which she could have perpetrated the most enormous crimes, blindly and almost unconsciously.

Returning home she prepared her toilet with the most elaborate care. A French 'artist,' (all barbers are *artists*, by the way,) was sent for, who arranged her beautiful hair in the latest *mode*; and when arrayed in her superb evening dress of white satin with her fair neck, her wrist and her lovely brow blazing with jewels, she looked like some queen of Oriental romance, waiting to receive the homage of her vassals.

And when, as the clock struck eight, the Signor Montoni entered, who can wonder that he thought her divinely lovely, as he glanced at her face radiant with smiles, her cheek suffused with the rich hues of health and happiness, and her eyes sparking with delight at seeing him?

We said *happiness* — 'twas not the deep, quiet happiness of the heart, but the wild, delirious joy of the intoxicated brain.

'Dear Montoni,' she cried, embracing and kissing him — 'your presence never gave more pleasure. I have waited for your coming with impatience. You are mine now, you cannot deny me — the obstacle is removed. — Oh, my God, what happiness!'

'Lady,' replied the Italian, in his usual cold and respectful tone, as he disengaged himself from her embrace, 'what means this agitation? You speak of an *obstacle* as being removed; pray explain the enigma.'

'Signor Montoni,' cried Julia, her eyes flashing almost fearfully — 'when I spoke to you of love last night, you preached to me of my husband, and my duty to him. The recollection that I *had* a husband, you said, forbade that you should take advantage of my preference for you. Rejoice with me, Montoni — come to my arms — my husband is no more!'

'How — what mean you?' demanded the Italian, in breathless astonishment.

'Follow me,' she said; and taking a lamp, she led the way to the chamber of Mr. Hedge. She unlocked the door, they entered, and she beckoned her companion to approach the bed.

Montoni advanced, and gazed upon the swollen, disfigured face of a corpse!

'Your husband — dead!' cried the Italian. 'By heaven there has been foul play here. Woman, can it be possible — '

'Yes, all things are possible to Love!' exclaimed Julia, laughing hysterically; — "twas I did the deed, Montoni; for *your* dear sake I killed him!'

'Murderess!' cried Montoni, recoiling from her with horror, 'has it come to this? — Then indeed it is time that this wretched farce should end!'

He tore off the wig, the false whiskers, imperial and moustache — and Frank Sydney stood before her! With a wild shriek she fell senseless upon the carpet.

'God of heaven!' exclaimed Frank — 'what infernal crimes blot thy fair creation! Let me escape from this house, for the atmosphere is thick with guilt, and will suffocate me if I remain longer!'

And without casting one look at the ghastly corpse, or the swooning murderess upon the floor, he rushed from the house, and fled rapidly from it, as though it were the abode of the pestilence.

Miserable Julia! She awoke to a full consciousness of her guilt and wretchedness. The intoxication of her senses was over; her delirium was past, and horrible remorse usurped the place of passion in her breast. — She arose, and gazed fearfully around her; there lay the body of her murdered victim, its stony eyes turned towards her, and seeming to reproach her for the deed. She could not remain in that awful chamber, in the presence of that accusing corpse, whose blood seemed to cry out for vengeance; she ran from it, and at every step imagined that her dead husband was pursuing her, to bring her back.

Not for worlds would she have remained that night in the house; hastily throwing on a bonnet and shawl, she issued forth into the street. She cared not where she went, so long as she escaped from the vicinity of that scene of murder. In a state of mind bordering on distraction, the wretched woman wandered about the streets until a late hour; the disorder of her dress, the wildness of her appearance, induced many whom she met to suppose her to be intoxicated; and several riotous young men, returning from a theatre, believing her to be a courtezan, treated her with the utmost rudeness, at the same time calling her by the most opprobrious names, until a gentleman who was passing rescued her from their brutality.

Midnight came, and still was the unhappy Julia a wanderer through the streets. At length she found herself upon Charlestown bridge; and being much fatigued, she paused and leaned against the railing, uncertain what to do or where to go. That hour was the most wretched of her life; her brain was dizzy with excitement — her heart racked with remorse — her limbs weak with fatigue, and numbed with cold. The spirit of Mr. Hedge seemed to emerge from the water, and invite her with outstretched arms to make the fatal plunge; and when she thought of his unvaried kindness to her, his unbounded generosity, and implicit faith in her honor, how bitterly she reproached herself for her base ingratitude and abominable crime! Oh, how gladly would she have given up her miserable life, could she but have undone that fearful deed! And even in that wretched hour she cursed Frank Sydney, as being the cause of her crime and its attendant misery.

'May the lightning of heaven's wrath sere his brain and scorch his heart!' she said — 'had he not, disguised as the Italian, won my love and driven me to desperation, I now should be happy and comparatively guiltless. But, by his infernal means, I have become a murderess and an outcast — perhaps doomed to swing upon the scaffold! But no, no; — sooner than die *that* death, I would end my misery in the dark waters of this river, which flows so calmly beneath my feet!'

She heard the sound of approaching footsteps, and saw two men advancing on the opposite foot-path of the bridge. She crouched down to avoid observation; and as they passed, she distinctly heard their conversation.

'Have you heard,' said one, 'of the case of murder in — — street?'

'No; how was it?' demanded the other.

'Why, a rich old fellow named Hedge was found this evening in his chamber, stone dead, having been poisoned by his wife, who they say is a young and handsome woman. It is supposed she did it on account of a lover, or some such thing; and since the murder, she has disappeared — but the police are on her track, and they won't be long in finding her. 'Twill be a bad job for her.'

The men passed on out of sight and hearing; but the words struck terror to the heart of Julia. She started up and gazed wildly around her, expecting every moment to see the myrmidons of the law approaching, to drag her away to prison. Then she looked down upon the calm river, on whose placid breast reposed the soft moonlight.

'Why should I live?' she murmured, sadly — 'earth has no longer any charms for me; the past brings remorse, the present is most wretched, the future full of impending horror! Death is my only refuge; the only cure for all my sorrows. Take me to thy embrace, thou peaceful river; thou canst end my earthly woes, but thou canst not wash off the stains of guilt from my soul! There may be a hell, but its torments cannot exceed those of this world — '

She mounted upon the topmost rail of the bridge, clasped her hands, muttered a brief prayer, and leaped into the river. There was a splash — a gurgling sound — and then profound and solemn silence resumed its reign.

> One more unfortunate,
> Weary of breath,
> Rashly importunate,
> Gone to her death!

> The bleak wind of March
> Made her tremble and shiver;
> But not the dark arch
> Of the black flowing river;
> Mad from life's history,
> Glad to death's mystery,
> Swift to be hurl'd —
> Any where, any where
> Out of the world!

> In she plunged boldly,
> No matter how coldly

The rough river ran —
Over the brink of it,
Picture it — think of it, Dissolute Man!

Owning her weakness,
Her evil behaviour!
And leaving, with meekness,
Her sins to her Saviour!

CHAPTER XXIX

Wherein one of the Characters in this Drama maketh a sudden and rapid exit from the stage.

In an upper apartment of an old, rickety wooden building in Ann street, two men were seated at a rough deal table, engaged in smoking long pipes and discussing the contents of a black bottle. Not to keep the reader in suspense, we may as well state at once that these two individuals were no other than our old acquaintances, the Dead Man and the Doctor.

The room was dusky, gloomy, and dirty, with a multitude of cob-webs hanging from the ceiling, and the broken panes in the windows stuffed full of rags. The smoke-dried walls were covered with rude inscriptions and drawings, representing deeds of robbery and murder; and a hanging scene was not the least prominent of these interesting specimens of the 'fine arts.' The house was a noted resort for thieves, and the old harridan who kept it was known to the police as a 'fence,' or one who purchased stolen goods.

'Yes, Doctor,' cried the Dead Man, with an oath, as he slowly removed the pipe from his lips, and blew a cloud which curled in fantastic wreaths to the ceiling — 'this state of affairs won't answer: we must have money. And money we *will* have, this very night, if our spy, Stuttering Tom, succeeds in finding out where those Franklin ladies live. The bottle's out — knock for another pint of *lush.*'

The Doctor obeyed, and in answer to the summons an old, wrinkled, blear-eyed hag made her appearance with the liquor. This old wretch was the 'landlady' of the house; she had been a celebrated and beautiful courtezan in her day, but age and vice had done their work, and she was now an object hideous to look upon. Though tottering upon the verge of the grave (she was over eighty,) an inordinate love of money, and an equal partiality for 'the ardent,' were her characteristics; but stranger than all, the miserable old creature affected still to retain, undiminished, those amorous propensities which had distinguished her in her youth!

This horrible absurdity made her act in a manner at once ludicrous and disgusting; and the Dead Man, being facetiously inclined, resolved to humor her weakness, and enjoy a laugh at her expense by pretending to have fallen in love with her.

'By Satan!' he cried, clasping the old crone around the waist — 'you look irresistible to-night, mother: I've half a mind to ravish a kiss from ye — ha, ha, ha!'

'Have done, now!' exclaimed the hag, in a cracked tone, at the same time vainly endeavoring to contort her toothless jaws into an engaging simper, while the Doctor nearly burst with laughter — 'have done now, or I'll slap ye for your impudence. But, faith, ye are such a pleasant gentleman, that I don't mind bestowing a kiss or two upon ye!'

'You're a gay old lass,' said the Dead Man, without availing himself of the old lady's kind permission — 'you have been a 'high one' in your time, but your day is nearly over.'

'No, no!' shrieked the old wretch, while her head and limbs quivered with palsy — 'don't say that — I'm young as ever, only a little *shakey,* or so — I'm not going to die for many, many years to come — ha, ha, ha! a kiss, love, a kiss — '

The old woman fell to the floor in a paralytic fit, and when they raised her up, they found that she was dead!

'Devil take the old fool!' cried the Dead Man, throwing the corpse contemptuously to the floor — 'I meant to have strangled her some day, but I now am cheated of the sport. No matter; drink, Doctor!'

The dead body was removed by several of the wretched inmates of the house, just as Stuttering Tom entered to announce the result of his search for the Franklin ladies.

Tom was a short, dumpy specimen of humanity, with red hair, freckled face, nose of the pug order, and goggle eyes. His dress was picturesque, if not ragged: his coat and pants were so widely apart, at the waist, as to reveal a large track of very incorrect linen; and the said coat had been deprived of one of its tails, an unfortunate occurrence, as the loss exposed a large compound fracture in the rear of the young gentleman's trowsers, whereby he was subjected to the remark that he had 'a letter in the post office.' His name was derived from an inveterate habit of stuttering with which he was afflicted; and he related the issue of his search somewhat in the following manner:

'You see, I ha-ha-happened to be l-loafing down Wa-Wa-Washington street, this evening, quite pro-miscus like, ven I seed two vim-vimmen, as vos gallus ha-handsum, and dr-dressed to kill, a valking along, vich puts me in m-m-mind of the F-F-Franklin vimmen, as you hired me to f-f-find out. So I up and f-follers 'em, and by-and-by a f-fellers meets 'em and says, says he, 'Good evening, Missus and Miss F-F-Franklin.' These is the werry victims, says I to myself; and I f-f-foller them till they goes into a house in Wa-Washington street — and here I am.'

'You have done well, Tom,' said the Dead Man, approvingly — 'you must now conduct us to the house in Washington street which the ladies entered: it is nine o'clock, and time that we should be up and doing.'

Stuttering Tom led the way, and the three issued from the house. Ann street was 'all alive' at that hour; from every cellar came forth the sound of a fiddle, and the side-walks were crowded with a motley throng of Hibernians, Ethiopians, and Cyprians of an inferior order. Talk of Boston being a moral city! There is villainy, misery and vice enough in Ann street alone, to deserve for the whole place the fate of Sodom and Gomorrah.

The Dead Man and the Doctor, under the guidance of Stuttering Tom, soon reached the house in Washington street where Josephine and her mother had taken up their residence. The guide was then rewarded and dismissed; the two adventurers ascended the steps, and one of them rang the door-bell.

A servant girl answered the summons, and in reply to their inquiries informed them that the ladies were both in the parlor.

'Show us up there,' said the Dead Man, in a commanding tone, as he concealed his hideous face behind his upturned coat-collar. The girl obeyed, and having conducted them up a flight of stairs, ushered them into an apartment where Josephine and her mother were seated, engaged there in playing *ecarte*.

Their confusion and terror may easily be imagined, when turning to see who their visitors were, their eyes rested upon the awful lineaments of the DEAD MAN!

'Your humble servant, ladies,' said the villain, with a triumphant laugh — 'you see you cannot hide from me, or escape me. Fair Josephine, you look truly charming — will you oblige me with a private interview?'

'It will be useless,' said Josephine coldly, as she recovered some portion of her composure — 'we have no more money to give you.'

'You can give me something more acceptable than *money*,' rejoined the other, with a horrible leer — 'at our last interview I told you what I should require at our next. Doctor, I leave you with the voluptuous mother, while I make court to the beautiful daughter.'

He grasped Josephine violently by the arm, and dragged her from the room, forced her into an adjoining apartment, and thrust her brutally upon a sofa, saying with a fearful oath —

'Dare to resist me, and I'll spoil your beauty, miss! Why do you act the prude with me — *you*, a shameless hussey, who has numbered more amours than years?'

'Odious ruffian!' exclaimed Josephine, no longer able to control her indignation — 'I view you with contempt and loathing. Sooner than submit to your filthy embraces, I will dare exposure, and death itself! Think not to force me to a compliance with your wishes — I will resist you while life animates my frame. I fear you not, low villain that you are.'

The Dead Man raised his *iron hand* as if to dash out her brains for her temerity. — But he checked himself, and surveyed her with a sort of calm ferocity, as he said — 'Young lady, since you are determined to oppose my wishes, I will not force you.

Neither will I kill you; yet my vengeance shall be more terrible than death. You are beautiful and you pride yourself upon that beauty — but I will deprive you of your loveliness. You call me hideous — I will make you hideous as I am. Your cheeks shall become ghastly, your complexion livid, and your brilliant eyes shall become sightless orbs — for the curse of *blindness* shall be added to your other miseries. Obstinate girl, bid an eternal farewell to eyesight and beauty, for from this moment you are deprived of both, forever!'

He drew from his pocket a small phial, and with the quickness of lightning dashed it in the face of the unfortunate Josephine. It was shattered in a hundred pieces, and the contents — VITRIOL — ran in her eyes and down her face, burning her flesh in the most horrible manner. She shrieked with agony the most intense, and the Doctor rushed into the room, followed by Mrs. Franklin. They both stood aghast when they beheld the awful spectacle.

The Doctor was the first to recover his presence of mind; he rushed to the aid of the burning wretch, and saved her life, though he could not restore her lost eyesight, or remove the horrible disfigurement of her burned and scarred visage. Mrs. Franklin was so overcome at her daughter's misfortune and sufferings that she fell upon the floor insensible.

At that moment the door of the apartment was violently thrown open, and a young gentleman entered. The Dead Man and the Doctor turned, and in the newcomer recognised Frank Sydney!

It will be necessary to explain the mystery of Frank's sudden appearance at that emergency. A day or two after the suicide of Julia, the body of that wretched woman was picked up by some fisherman, and conveyed to the city, where it was immediately recognized as the lady of Mr. Hedge. The circumstance of her death soon came to the knowledge of our hero; and while he could not help shedding a tear as he thought of her melancholy fate (she had once been his wife, and he had once loved her,) he could not deny to himself that he derived a secret joy from the thought, that now his hopes with reference to Sophia Franklin were not without some foundation. Acting upon this impulse, he had taken the earliest opportunity to call upon the young lady; and at that interview, he had with his customary frankness, related to her his entire history, and concluded his narrative by making her an offer of his hand and heart — and, reader, that honorable offer was accepted with the same frankness with which it was made. On the evening in question, Frank was enjoying one of those charming *tete-a-tetes* with his Sophia, which all lovers find so delightful, when the agonizing screams of the suffering Josephine brought him to the room, as we have seen, and he found himself, to his astonishment, standing face to face with the Dead Man and the Doctor.

'Why, blood and fury!' cried the former, a gleam of pleasure passing over his horrid features — 'here is the very man of all men upon earth, whom I most desired to see. Sydney, you are welcome.'

'What damnable villainy have you been at now?' demanded Frank, recovering his courage and presence of mind, altho' he had reason to believe that he had fallen into the power of his worst enemy in the world.

'What business is that of yours?' growled the Dead Man — 'Suffice it for you to know that my *next* act of villainy will be your assassination.'

Our hero drew a revolver from his pocket, and levelled it at the villain's head, saying —

'Advance but a step towards me, and you are a *dead man* indeed — Scoundrel! I am no longer a prisoner in your dungeon vaults, but free, and able to protect myself against your brutal cruelty. Though you are aided by the Doctor, whom I once thought my friend, I fear you not, but dare you to do your worst.'

'You are brave, Sydney,' said the Dead Man, with something like a grim of admiration — 'but I hate you, and you must die. From the first moment when I met you in the Dark Vaults, to the present time, I have observed something in you that inspires me with a kind of *fear* — a moral superiority over my malice and hatred that inflames me with jealous rage. Even when you were in my power, undergoing my trials and tortures, I have observed contempt upon your lip and scorn in your eye. I once called you coward — but you are a man of doubtless courage, and by Satan! I have half a mind to shake hands with you and call you friend.'

During this harangue, Frank had unconsciously lowered his pistol, not suspecting that the long speech was merely a ruse of the Dead Man to spring upon him unawares. While he stood in an attitude poorly calculated for defence, the miscreant suddenly, with the quickness of lightning, sprang upon him, and with irresistible force hurled him to the floor.

But our hero received an aid which was as unexpected as it was welcome; for the Doctor threw himself upon the Dead Man, grappled him by the throat, and nearly strangled him. In vain the ruffian struggled — he was in the grasp of an adversary too powerful and too intrepid to be successfully resisted by him. Panting and breathless, he was soon vanquished by his ancient enemy, who, having tied his arms behind him with a strong cord, regarded him with a look of hatred and contempt.

'Why, Doctor, what means this?' demanded the villain, in astonishment at having been so desperately attacked by one whom he had lately regarded as a friend.

'It means, d — — n you,' coolly replied the other — 'you have been deceived and foiled. In deserting Mr. Sydney to join *your* bloody standard, I acted in accordance with a plan which I had formed to entrap and conquer you. I know that as long as I remained the professed friend of Mr. Sydney, you would view me with distrust and fear, and consequently, that you would be always on the alert to guard against any attempt of mine to wreak my vengeance on you. So I professed to become your friend, and pretended to attach myself to your interest, knowing that a good opportunity would thereby be afforded me to frustrate any scheme you might form against the life or safety of Mr. Sydney. You see how well I have succeeded; you are completely in my power, and by G — — d, this night shall witness the termination of your bloody and infamous career.'

'You surely will not murder me,' said the Dead Man, frightened by the determined tone and manner of a man whose vengeance he had reason to dread.

'To take your accursed life will be no murder,' replied the Doctor — 'you are a thousand times worse than a poisonous reptile or a beast of prey, and to kill you would be but an act of justice. Yet do not flatter yourself with the prospect of an easy and comparatively painless death; I have sworn that you shall die a death of lingering torture, and you will see how well I'll keep my oath. My knowledge as a physician, and natural ingenuity, have furnished me with a glorious method of tormenting you; and although you are a master in the art of torture, you will see how far I have surpassed you.'

'You have, by serving me this trick, proved yourself to be both a liar and a traitor,' remarked the Dead Man, bitterly.

'Any means,' rejoined the Doctor, calmly — 'are justifiable in overthrowing such an infernal villain as you are; but I see the motive of your sneer — you wish to enrage me, that I may stab you to the heart at once, and place you beyond the reach of protracted torment. You shall fail in this, for I am cool as ice. Before commencing operations upon you, I must attend professionally to those ladies.'

Mrs. Franklin was easily recovered from her fainting fit; — and the suffering Josephine received at the skillful hands of the Doctor every care and attention which her lamentable case demanded. He pronounced her life in no danger; but alas! her glorious beauty was gone forever — her face was horribly burnt and disfigured, and her brilliant eyes were destroyed; she was stone blind!

Thus it is that the wicked are often the instruments of each other's punishment in this world, as devils are said to torment each other in the next.

The mother and daughter having been properly looked after, Frank Sydney took the Doctor aside, and warmly thanked him for his timely and acceptable aid.

'You have proved yourself to be a true and faithful man,' said he grasping his friend's hand — 'and my unjust opinions in regard to you have given place to the highest confidence in your integrity and honor. You have saved my life tonight, and not for the first time. I owe you a debt of gratitude; and from this moment we are sworn friends. You shall share my fortune, and move in a sphere of respectability and worth.'

'Mr. Sydney,' said the Doctor, much affected — 'do you remember that night I met you in the Park, and would have robbed you? I was then moneyless and starving. I will not now stop to relate how I became reduced to such abject wretchedness, but I must do myself the justice to say that my downfall was produced by the rascalities of others. Your liberality to me upon that night was an evidence to my mind that the world was not entirely heartless and unjust; and tho' I did not immediately forsake the evil of my ways, yet your kindness softened me, and laid the foundation of my present reformation. — Noble young man, I accept the offer of your friendship with gratitude, but I will not share your fortune. No — my ambition is, to build up a fortune of my own, by laboring in my profession, in which I am skilled. By following a course of strict honor and integrity, I may partially retrieve the errors of my past life.'

'I cannot but commend your resolution,' remarked Frank — 'but you must not refuse to accept from me such pecuniary aid as will be necessary to establish you in a respectable and creditable manner. — But in regard to this miscreant here; you actually intend to kill him by slow torture?'

'I do,' replied the Doctor, in a determined manner — 'and my only regret is that I cannot protract his sufferings a year. Do not think me cold-blooded or cruel, my dear friend; that villain merits the worst death that man can inflict upon him. If we were to hand him over to the grasp of the law, for his numerous crimes, his infernal ingenuity might enable him to escape. Our only security lies in crushing the reptile while we have him in our trap.'

'I shall not interfere with you in your just punishment of the villain,' said our hero — 'but I must decline being present. The enormous crimes he had committed, and the wrongs which I have sustained at his hands, will not allow me to say a single word in his behalf — yet I will not witness his torments.'

'I understand and respect your scruples; I being a physician, such a spectacle cannot affect my nerves. — You will please assist me to place the *subject* upon this table, and then you can retire.'

They raised the Dead Man from the floor, and placed him on a large table which stood in the centre of the room. Frank then bade the Doctor a temporary farewell, and passing through the hall was about to leave the house, when a servant informed him that Miss Sophia Franklin wished to see him. He joyfully obeyed the summons, and found the young lady in deep distress at the condition of her sister Josephine, and very anxious for an explanation of the terrible cause. Frank stated all he knew of the matter, and we leave him to the task of consoling her, while we witness the operations of the Doctor upon his living *subject*.

In the first place, he tied the Dead Man down upon the table so firmly, that he could not move a hair's breadth. During this process, the miserable victim, losing all his customary bravado and savage insolence, begged hard to be killed at once, rather than undergo the torments which he dreaded. But the Doctor only laughed, and drew from his pocket a case of surgical instruments; he then produced a small phial, which he held close to his victim's eyes, and bade him examine it narrowly.

'You see,' said he, 'this little phial? — it contains a slow poison of peculiar and fearful power. You shall judge of its effects yourself presently. I will infuse it into your blood, and it will cause you greater agony than melted lead poured upon your heart.'

'For God's sake, Doctor,' cried the wretch, — 'spare me *that*! I have heard you tell of it before. Will nothing move you? Show me mercy, and I will reveal to you many valuable and astounding secrets, known only to me. I will tell you where, within twenty miles of Boston, I have buried over twenty thousand dollars in gold and silver; I will myself lead you to the spot and you shall have it all — all! I will furnish you with a list of fashionable drinking houses in the city, where is sold liquor impregnated with a slow but deadly poison, which in two years will bring on a lingering disease, generally thought to be consumption; this disease always terminates in death, and the whole matter is arranged by physicians, who thus get a constant and extensive practice. I will take you to rooms where persons, under the name of 'secret societies,' privately meet to indulge in the most unnatural and beastly licentiousness. I will prove to you, by ocular demonstration, that in *certain cities* of the Union, not a letter passes through the post offices, that is not broken open and read, and then re-sealed by a peculiar process — by which means much private information is gained by the police, and the most tremendous secrets often leak out, to the astonishment of the parties concerned. I will communicate to you a method by which the most virtuous and chaste woman can be made wild with desire, and easily overcome. I will show you how to make a man drop dead in the street, without touching him, or using knife or pistol — and not a mark will be found on his person. I will — '

'That'll do,' said the Doctor, dryly — 'the matters you have mentioned are mostly no secrets to me; and if your object was to gain time and dissuade me from my purpose, you have signally failed. Villain! your long career of crime is now about to receive its reward. Prayers and entreaties shall not avail you; and to put an end to them, as well as to prevent you from yelling out in your agony — by which people would be attracted hither — I will take the liberty to *gag* you.'

In forcing the jaws of the Dead Man widely apart, in order to accomplish that purpose, the victim contrived to get one of his tormentor's fingers between his teeth, and it was nearly bitten off ere it could be disengaged. This enraged the Doctor so that he was about to kill his enemy instantly, but he checked himself; and having effectually gagged him, he prepared to commence the terrible ordeal.

Taking a lancet from the case, he made an incision in the subject's right arm; then, in the wound, he poured a few drops of the contents of the phial. The effects were instantaneous and terrible; the poison became infused in every vein of the sufferer's body, and his blood seemed changed to liquid fire; he writhed in mighty agony — his heart leaped madly in his breast, in the intensity of his torment — his brain swam in a sea of fire — his eyes started from their sockets, and blood oozed from every pore of his body.

These awful results were produced by a wonderful chemical preparation, known to but few, and first discovered in the days of the Spanish Inquisition. It was then termed the 'Ordeal of Fire;' and the infernal vengeance of hell itself could not have produced torment more intense or protracted; for though it racked every nerve and sinew in the body, filling the veins with a flood like molten lead, it was comparatively slow in producing death, and kept the sufferer for several hours writhing in all the tortures of the damned.

For two mortal hours the miserable wretch endured the torment; while the Doctor stood over him, viewing him with a fixed gaze and an unmoved heart. Then he removed the gag from the sufferer's mouth, and poured a glass of water down his throat, which temporarily assuaged his agony.

'Doctor,' gasped the dying wretch — 'for God's sake stab me to the heart, and end my misery! I am in hell — I am floating in an ocean of fire — my murdered victims are pouring rivers of blazing blood upon me — my soul is in flames — my *heart* is RED HOT! Ah, kill me — kill me!'

The Doctor, after a moment's deliberation, again took an instrument from his case, and skillfully divided the flesh in the region of the abdomen, making an incision of considerable extent. He then produced a small flask of gunpowder, in the neck of which he inserted a straw filled with the same combustible; and in the end of the straw he fastened a small slip of paper which he had previously prepared with saltpetre. Having made these arrangements, he placed the powder flask completely in the victim's abdomen, leaving the slow match to project slightly from the wound. The Dead Man was perfectly conscious during this horrible process, notwithstanding he suffered the most excruciating pain.

'You are going to blow me to atoms, Doctor,' he with difficulty articulated, as a ghastly smile spread over his hideous features — 'I thank you for it; although I hate and curse you in this
my dying hour. Grant me a moment longer; if the spirits of the
dead are allowed to re-visit the earth, *my* spirit shall visit you! Ha,
ha, ha! In a few seconds, I shall be free from the power of your
torture — free to follow you like a shadow through life, free to
preside in ghastly horror over your midnight slumbers and to
breathe constantly in your ear, curses — curses — curses!'

'Miserable devil, your blood-polluted spirit will be too
strongly bound to hell, to wander on earth,' said the Doctor, with
a contempt not unmingled with pity. 'Farewell, thou man of
many crimes; for the wrongs you have done me, I forgive you,
but human and divine justice have demanded this sacrifice.'

He ignited a match, touched it to the paper at the end of the
straw, and hastily retreated to the further extremities of the room.

It was an awful moment; slowly the paper burnt towards the
straw — so slowly, that the victim of this awful sacrifice had time
to vent his dying rage in malignant curses, on himself, his tormentor, and his Maker! The straw is reached — the fire runs
down to the powder flask with a low hiss — and then —

Awful was the explosion that followed; the wretch was torn
into a hundred pieces; his limbs, his brains, his blood were scattered all about. A portion of the mangled carcass struck the Doctor; the lamp was broken by the shock and darkness prevailed in
the room.

The inmates of the house, frightened at the noise, rushed to
the scene of the catastrophe with lights. Frank Sydney, Sophia
and Mrs. Franklin, as well as several other male and female domestics, entering the apartment, stood aghast at the shocking
spectacle presented to their gaze. There stood the Doctor, with
folded arms and his face stained with blood; here an arm, here, a
blackened mass of flesh; and here, the most horrible object of all,
the mutilated and ghastly head, with the same expression of ma-

lignant hate upon its hideous features as when those livid lips had last uttered curses!

'The deed is done,' said the Doctor, addressing Sydney, with a grim smile — 'justice has its due at last, and the diabolical villain has gone to his final account. Summon some scavenger to collect the vile remains, and bury them in a dung-hill. To give them Christian, decent burial would be treason to man, sacrilege to the Church, and impiety to God!'

Thus perished the 'Dead Man,' a villain so stupendous, so bloodthirsty and so desperate that it may well be doubted whether such a monster ever could have existed. But this diabolical character is not entirely drawn from the author's imagination; neither is it highly exaggerated; — for the annals of crime will afford instances of villainy as deep and as monstrous as any that characterized the career of the 'Dead Man' of our tale. What, for example, can be more awful or incredible than the hideous deed of a noted criminal in France, who, having ensnared a peasant girl in a wood, brutally murdered her, then outraged the corpse, and afterwards *ate a part of it*? Yet no one will presume to doubt the fact, as it forms a portion of the French criminal records. Humanity shudders at such instances of worse than devilish depravity.

Moreover, to show that we have indulged in no improbabilities in portraying the chief villain of our tale, we assert that a person bearing that name and the same disfigurement of countenance, *really existed* not two years ago. He was renowned for his many crimes, and was murdered by a former accomplice, in a manner not dissimilar to the death we have assigned to him in the story.

But we turn from a contemplation of such villains, to pursue a different and somewhat more agreeable channel.

CHAPTER XXX

*Showing that a man should never marry a woman before he sees
her face — The Disappointed Bridegroom — Final Catastrophe.*

Two months passed away. Two months! — how short a
space of time, and yet, perchance, how pregnant with events affecting the happiness and the destiny of millions! Within that
brief span — the millionth fraction of a single sand in Time's great
hour-glass — thousands have begun their existence, to pursue
through life a career of honor, of profit, of ambition, or of crime!
— and thousands, too, have ceased their existence, and their
places are filled by others in the great race of human life.

But a truce to moralizing. — Two months passed away, and
it was now the season of summer — that delicious season, fraught
with more voluptuous pleasures than virgin spring, gloomy au-
tumn or hoary winter. It was in rather an obscure street of Boston
— in a modest two-story wooden house — and in an apartment
plainly, even humbly furnished, that two ladies were seated, engaged in an earnest conversation.

One of these ladies was probably near forty years of age, and
had evidently once been extremely handsome; her countenance
still retained traces of great beauty — but time, and care, and
perhaps poverty, were beginning to mar it. Her figure was good,
though perhaps rather too full for grace; and her dress was very
plain yet neat, and not without some claims to taste.

Her companion was probably much younger, and was attired with considerable elegance; yet a strange peculiarity in her
costume would have instantly excited the surprise of an observer
— for although the day was excessively warm, she wore a thick
veil, which reached to her waist, and effectually concealed her
face. She conversed in a voice of extraordinary melody; and the
refined language of both ladies evinced that they had been accustomed to move in a higher sphere of society than that in which
we now find them.

'At what time do you expect him here?' asked the oldest
lady, in continuation of the discourse in which they had previ-

ously been engaged.

'At eight o'clock this evening,' replied the other. 'He is completely fascinated with me; and notwithstanding I have assured him, over and over again, that my countenance is horribly disfigured, and that I am entirely blind, he persists in believing that I am beautiful, and that I have perfect eye-sight, attributing my concealment of face to a whim.'

'Which opinion you have artfully encouraged, Josephine,' said Mrs. Franklin. — The reader has probably already guessed the identity of the two ladies; this was the mother and her once beautiful, but now hideous and blind daughter. They were reduced to the most abject poverty, and had been forced to leave their handsome residence in Washington street, and take up their abode in an humble and cheap tenement. Entirely destitute of means, they were obliged to struggle hard to keep themselves above absolute want. Josephine, being a superb singer, had obtained an engagement to sing in one of the fashionable churches; but as she always appeared closely veiled, the fact of her being so terribly disfigured was unsuspected. The beauty of her voice and the graceful symmetry of her figure had attracted the attention and won the admiration of a wealthy member of the church, who was also attached to the choir; and as she was always carefully conducted in and out of the church by her mother this gentleman never suspected that she was blind. He had framed an excuse to call upon her at her residence; and, tho' astonished to find her veiled, at home — and tho' he had never seen her face — he was charmed with her brilliant conversation, and resolved to win her, if possible. The very mystery of her conduct added to the intensity of his passion.

Mr. Thurston, (the church member), continued his visits to Josephine, but never saw her face. When he grew more familiar, he ventured upon one occasion to inquire why she kept herself so constantly veiled; whereupon she informed him that her face had been disfigured by being scalded during her infancy, which accident had also deprived her of sight. But when he requested her to raise her veil, and allow him to look at her face, she refused with so much good-humored animation, that he began to suspect the young lady of having playfully deceived him.

'This interesting creature,' thought he, 'is trying to play me a trick. — She hides her face and pretends to be a fright, while the coquetry of her manners and the perfect ease of her conversation convince me that she cannot be otherwise than beautiful. — What, the owner of that superb voice and that elegant form, *ugly*? Impossible! Now I can easily guess her object in trying to play off this little piece of deception upon me; I have read somewhere of a lady who kept her face constantly veiled, and proclaimed herself to be hideously ugly, which was universally believed, notwithstanding which she secured an admirer, who loved her for her graces of mind; he offered her his hand, and she agreed to marry him, provided that he would not seek to behold her face until after the performance of the ceremony — adding, that if he saw how ugly she was, he would certainly never marry her. 'I love you for your mind, and care not for the absence of beauty,' cried the lover. They were married; they retired to their chamber. 'Now prepare yourself for an awful sight,' — said the bride, slowly raising her veil. The husband could not repress a shudder — he gazed for the first time upon the face of his wife — when lo and behold! instead of an ugly and disfigured face, he saw before him a countenance radiant with celestial beauty! 'Dear husband,' said the lovely wife, casting her arms around her astonished and happy lord, 'you loved me truly, although you thought me ugly; such devotion and such disinterested love well merit the prize of beauty.'

'Now, I feel assured,' said Mr. Thurston to himself, pursuing the current of his thoughts — 'that this young lady, Miss Franklin, is trying to deceive me in a similar manner, in order to test the sincerity of my affection; and should I marry her, I would find her to be a paragon of beauty. Egad, she is so accomplished and bewitching, that I've more than half a mind to propose, and make her Mrs. T.'

The worthy deacon (for such he was,) being a middle-aged man of very good looks, and moreover very rich, Josephine was determined to 'catch him' if she could; she therefore took advantage of his disbelief in her deformity, and, while she persisted in

her assurances that she was hideously ugly, she made those assurances in a manner so light and playful, that Mr. T. would have
taken his oath that she was beautiful, and he became more and
more smitten with the mysterious veiled lady, whose face he had
never seen.

Josephine, with consummate art, was resolved, if possible, to
entice him into matrimony; and once his wife, she knew that in
case he refused to live with her on discovering her awful deformity, he would liberally provide for her support, and thus her
mother and herself would be enabled again to live in luxury. As
for Sophia, she no longer lived with them — the fair, innocent girl
had gone to occupy a position to be stated hereafter.

We now resume the conversation between Mrs. Franklin and
her daughter, which we interrupted by the above necessary explanation. — 'Which opinion you have artfully encouraged, Josephine,' said Mrs. Franklin — 'and you will of course suffer him to
enjoy that opinion, until after your marriage with him, which
event is, I think, certain; then you can reveal your true condition
to him, and if he casts you off, he will be obliged to afford you a
sufficient income, which we both so much need; for he cannot
charge you with having deceived him, as you represent to him
your real condition, and if he chooses to disbelieve you, that is his
own affair, not yours.'

'True, mother; and the marriage must be speedily accomplished, for we are sadly in need of funds, and all my best dresses
are at the pawnbroker's. Alas, that my beauty should be destroyed — that beauty which would have captured the hearts and
purses of so many rich admirers! I am almost inclined to rejoice
that my eyesight is gone, for I cannot see my deformity. Am I
very hideous, mother?'

'My poor, afflicted child,' said Mrs. Franklin, shedding tears
— 'do not question me on that subject. Oh, Josephine, had I, your
mother, set you an example of purity and virtue, and trained you
up in the path of rectitude, we never should have experienced
our past and present misery, and you, my once beautiful child,
would not now be deformed and blind. Alas, I have much to re-

proach myself for.'

'Tut, mother; you have grown puritanical of late. Let us try to forget the past, and cherish hope for the future. — How very warm it is!'

She retired from the window to avoid the observation of the passers-by, and removed her veil. Good God! — Can she be the once lovely Josephine! Ah, terrible punishment of sin!

Her once radiant countenance was of a ghastly yellow hue, save where deep purple streaks gave it the appearance of a putrefying corpse. Her once splendid eyes, that had so oft flashed with indignant scorn, glowed with the pride of her imperial beauty, or sparkled with the fires of amorous passion, had been literally burned out of her head! That once lofty and peerless brow was disfigured by hideous scars, and a wig supplied the place of her once clustering and luxuriant hair. — She was as loathsome to look upon as had been her destroyer, the Dead Man. Oh, it was a pitiful sight to see that talented and accomplished young lady thus stricken with the curses of deformity and blindness, through her own wickedness — to see that temple which God had made so beautiful and fair to look upon, thus shattered and defiled by the ravages of sin!

Evening came, and with it brought Mr. Thurston. Josephine, seated on a sofa and impenetrably veiled, received him with a courteous welcome; — and comported herself so admirably and artfully, that the most critical observer would not have imagined her to be blind, but would have supposed her to be wearing a veil merely out of caprice, or from some trifling cause. — When she spoke to her lover, or was addressed by him, she invariably turned her face towards him, as if unconsciously; and the gentleman chuckled inwardly, as he thought he saw in that simple act an evidence of her being possessed of the faculty of sight.

But one incident occurred which doubly confirmed him in his belief; it was an artful contrivance of Josephine and her mother. Previous to Mr. Thurston's arrival, a rose had been placed upon the carpet, close to Josephine's feet; and during a pause in the conversation, while apparently in an abstracted mood, she leaned forward, took it up by the stem, and began slowly to pick it to pieces, scattering the leaves all about her.

'By Jupiter, I have her now!' said the lover to himself, triumphantly — and then he abruptly said —

'How now, Josephine! If you are blind, how saw you that rose upon the carpet?'

Josephine, affecting to be much confused, stammered out something about her having discovered the rose to be near her by its fragrance; but Mr. Thurston laughed and said —

'It won't do, my dear Miss Franklin; it is evident that you can see as well as I can. Come, end this farce at once, and let me see your face.'

'No, you shall not, for I have vowed that the first man who beholds my face shall be my husband.'

'Then hear me, Josephine,' cried her lover, raising her fair hand to his lips — 'I know not what singular whim has prompted you in your endeavors to make me think you ugly and blind, but this I know, you have inspired me with ardent love. I *know* you to be beautiful and free from imperfection of sight — nay, do not speak — but I will not again allude to the subject, nor press you to raise your veil, until after our marriage — that is, if you will accept me. Speak, Josephine.'

'Mr. Thurston, if, after my many solemn assurances to you that I am afflicted in the manner I have so often described, you ask me to become your wife — here is my hand.'

'A thousand thanks, my beautiful, mysterious, veiled lady!' exclaimed the enraptured lover — 'as to your being afflicted — ha, ha! — I'll risk it, I'll risk it! Naughty Josephine, I'll punish you hereafter for your attempt to deceive me!'

The poor man little suspected how egregiously she *was* deceiving him! — He was a person of no natural penetration, and could no more see thro' her designs, than through the veil which covered her face.

Midnight came, and found Josephine and her victim still seated upon the sofa in the little parlor, her head reposing upon his shoulder, and his arm encircling her waist. He felt as happy as any man can feel, who imagines he has won the love of a beautiful woman; but had he known the blackness of her heart, and seen the awful hideousness of her face, how he would have cast her from him with contempt and loathing!

When about to take his leave, he lingered in the entry and begged her to grant him a kiss; she consented, on condition that it should be a 'kiss in the dark.' The candle was extinguished, she raised her veil, and he pressed his lips to hers. Could he have seen her ghastly cheek, her eyeless sockets, and the livid lips which he so rapturously kissed, his soul would have grown sick with horror. But he departed, in blissful ignorance of her deformity of body and impurity of soul.

We hasten to the final catastrophe. They were married. The eager bridegroom conducted his veiled and trembling bride to the nuptial chamber. — Josephine was much agitated; for the grand crisis had arrived, which would either raise her to a comfortable independence, or hurl her into the dark abyss of despair.

'Is it very light here?' she asked. 'Yes, dearest,' replied the husband — 'I have caused this our bridal chamber to be illuminated, in order that I may the better be enabled to feast my eyes upon your beauty, so long concealed from my gaze.'

'Prepare yourself,' murmured Josephine, 'for a terrible disappointment. I have not deceived you. — Behold your bride!'

She threw up her veil.

LETTER FROM MRS. SOPHIA SYDNEY TO A LADY.

You cannot imagine, my dearest Alice, what a life of calm felicity I enjoy with my beloved Francis, in our new home among the majestic mountains of Vermont. Had you the faintest conception of the glorious scenery which surrounds the little rustic cottage which we inhabit, (our ark of safety — poor, wearied doves that we are!) you would willingly abandon your abode in the noisy, crowded metropolis, to join us in our beautiful and secluded retreat.

Our dwelling is situated on the margin of a clear and quiet lake, whose glassy surface mirrors each passing cloud, and at night reflects a myriad of bright stars. We have procured a small but elegant pleasure barge, in which we often gently glide over those placid waters, when Evening darkens our mountain home with the shadow of her wing, and when the moon gilds our liquid path with soft radiance. Then, while my Francis guides the little vessel, I touch my guitar and sing some simple melody; and as we approach the dark, mysterious shore, my imagination oft conjures up a troop of fairy beings with bright wings, stealing away into the dim recesses of the shadowy forest. And often, when the noon-day sun renders the air oppressive with his heat, I wander into the depths of that forest, where the giant trees, forming a vast arch overhead, exclude the glare of summer, and produce a soft, delicious twilight. My favorite resting place is upon a mossy bank, near which flows a crystal brook whose dancing waters murmur with a melody almost as sweet as the low breathings of an Aeolian harp. — Here, with a volume of philosophic Cowper or fascinating Scott, I sometimes linger until twilight begins to deepen into darkness, and then return to meet with smiles the playful chidings of my husband, for my protracted absence — an offence he can easily forgive, if I present him with a bouquet of wild flowers gathered during my ramble; although he laughingly calls the floral offering a bribe.

We have almost succeeded in banishing the remembrance of our past sorrows, and look forward to the future with trustful hope. I am happy, Alice — very, very happy; and oh! may no care or trouble ever o'ershadow our tranquil home.

CONCLUSION

*'So on your patience evermore attending,
New joy wait on you — here our play has ending.'*

SHAKESPEARE

Reader, our task is done. Thou hast kindly accompanied us through our rambling narrative, until the end; and now it but remains for us to dispose of the *dramatis personae* who have figured in the various scenes, and then bid thee farewell.

Frank Sydney and his beautiful Sophia were united in marriage, and are now residing in one of the most romantic spots to be found in all New England. Sophia has long since ceased all correspondence with her wretched and abandoned mother, who has become the keeper (under an assumed name) of a celebrated and fashionable brothel in West Cedar street.

Josephine Franklin terminated her miserable existence by poison (procured for her by her own mother,) on the day after her marriage with Mr. Thurston, who, when he beheld the hideous deformity of his bride, instead of the beauty which he expected, recoiled with horror — and after bitterly reproaching her, drove her from his presence, bidding her never to let him see her again, and refusing to make the smallest provision for her support. A few days after Josephine's death, Mr. Thurston, overcome with mortification, shot himself through the heart.

The Doctor has become one of the most respectable physicians, in Boston, and enjoys a lucrative and extensive practice. He is married to an amiable lady, and has named his first son after Sydney, his generous benefactor. He has received into his office, as a student of medicine, Clinton Romaine, the dumb boy, who bids fair to become a skilful and useful physician.

Nero, the African, who has played no inconsiderable part in our drama, finally came to Boston, and now follows the respectable occupation of barber, in the vicinity of the Maine Railroad Depot.

In conclusion, if the foregoing pages have in the least degree contributed to the reader's entertainment, or initiated him into any mystery of CITY CRIMES heretofore unknown — and if this tale, founded on fact, has served to illustrate the truth of the ancient proverbs that 'honesty is the best policy' and 'virtue is its own reward' — then is the author amply repaid for his time and toil, and he tenders to the indulgent public his most respectful parting salutations.